THE GAMBLER

Elijah Perry's legs hung over the side of the bed, big as life, as he lay on his pillow with his eyes shut. Joy couldn't stand it a moment longer. With a combination of fury and fear raging inside her, she deposited her tray on the dressing table with a clatter. "Oh, for heaven's sake! I'll help you get back under the covers."

At Joy's exclamation, he opened one eye and had the audacity to grin at her. "Can't take it, huh? Too much man for you, am I?"

Joy felt herself get hot. "Don't be ridiculous, Mr. Perry."

"I'll try."

He truly sounded as though he found it difficult to speak. When she lifted his legs, Joy felt his muscles tense and heard his sharp intake of breath.

After she'd settled him under the covers, she said, "I shall now fetch your shaving gear—if you believe I can be trusted not to cut your throat with the razor."

Elijah Perry's eyes twinkled devilishly. "I think I'll take that chance."

A GAMBLER'S MAGIC

EMMA CRAIG

LOVE SPELL BOOKS   NEW YORK CITY

This one's for Dawn Willis. Thanks Dawn!

LOVE SPELL®

January 2000

Published by

Dorchester Publishing Co., Inc.
276 Fifth Avenue
New York, NY 10001

ISBN 0-505-52358-2

The name "Love Spell" and its logo are trademarks of Dorchester Publishing Co., Inc.

Printed in the United States of America.

Chapter One

Alexander McMurdo first set eyes on Miss Joy Hardesty when the small band of missionaries with whom she was traveling straggled into his wagon yard in Rio Hondo, New Mexico Territory, on the third day of March, 1873. He'd known she was coming—indeed, he had summoned her hither—and he watched curiously from the door of his small home. His house sat right next to his mercantile and dry-goods store at the back of his business establishment's huge yard.

As soon as the group arrived, its leader, the Reverend Mr. Hezekiah P. Thrash, fell to his knees and thanked their blessed heavenly father for having delivered them out of the wilderness. The army unit assigned to protect the missionaries, and the Mescalero scouts riding with them, watched this performance with tolerant fascination. They didn't appear the least surprised by Thrash's behavior.

Alexander McMurdo—Mac to his friends—wasn't surprised, either, and merriment bubbled in him. He had a feeling the reverend would have made a fine actor had not his religious zeal carried him down another road in life. McMurdo held a keen appreciation for enthusiastic people. He smiled at Thrash, nodded to the minister's audience, and decided to add a smallish bit of unearthly zest to everyone's enjoyment.

In this endeavor, he made smoke from his old black briar pipe wreath around his head in a manner he knew to be reminiscent of a halo, and parted the clouds riding high in the sky so that a bright beam of sunlight poured down upon him. He knew he presented an affecting picture for anyone possessed of an ardent nature.

Sure enough, the Reverend Mr. Thrash, seeing Alexander McMurdo bathed in celestial light, lifted his arms unto the heavens and let out with a fevered string of *Hallelujahs, Thanks be to Gods*, and *Praise His holy names*." An eloquent fellow, Thrash. Mac approved.

It looked as if the good reverend's followers, while perhaps not as rapturously moved as he, knew what to do when Thrash carried on in this vein. They got down on their knees, too, and began to add their paeans of thanks to those of their leader.

Mac watched Miss Joy Hardesty with particular interest. It was she among this group in whose welfare and future he had chosen to intervene. She looked around with displeasure, clearly decided there was no help for it, and knelt as well, after first shaking out her handkerchief and settling it on the ground in front of her. In that way, Mac presumed, she hoped to keep dust from dirtying the skirt of her gown. He grinned at so futile a gesture undertaken against such formidable odds.

An interesting female, Joy. Her lips appeared set into a perpetual frown, her eyes peered out at the world guardedly, as if she didn't trust it, and she looked as though she suffered from dyspepsia. Mac took note of her pinched features, mousy bearing, and general air of unhappiness, and decided his errand of mercy had come none too soon.

Never had a female been less aptly named. Poor thing. If there ever had been a joyless specimen sent to languish on the earth, Joy Hardesty was it.

It was a shame, too. McMurdo knew there was a buoyant spirit trapped inside her somewhere, but that it had been beaten down until it barely sparked any longer. She was probably ashamed of that wee remaining spark when it did manage to sputter to life, too. Mac got the feeling she'd been taught to deplore anything even remotely connected with her essential nature; to consider human instincts improper and impure. She'd been driven so far from her original humanity that she believed she needed to quash her individuality whenever it reared what she perceived to be its ugly head.

A sad and pitiful representative of the species, Joy Hardesty. Mac clucked with sympathy—not that she'd appreciate his sympathy. In fact, he was fairly certain she'd resent it like fire.

She was infatuated with Thrash. Mac watched her watch the minister. Her longing was so ill-disguised, Mac could feel it from where he stood. She didn't know it, of course, but what she craved wasn't Thrash himself. What Joy longed for was Thrash's essence, his humanity, his wholehearted, expansive belief in himself and his work.

Although she'd never admit it to anyone, Joy didn't believe in a single thing. She was as expansive as a collapsed bladder. As animated as a dead robin. As happy as a man with a noose around his neck. Mac could see the emptiness in her soul from where he stood. He fancied the desert wind whistling through it as if through a barren cavern.

He heaved a large, sympathetic sigh. She was very like a prickly pear, Joy Hardesty, all thorns and prickles on the outside. A body had to work so hard to discover the soft sweetness hidden with n that few even tried. Not an easy female in any sense of the word. She'd be a tough nut to crack and was likely to fight tooth and nail to hold on to her misery. Gloom was all she'd ever known, after all, and Joy didn't cotton to original thinking. It frightened her. She would most assuredly cause Mac all sorts of trouble. He liked her, though. In fact, he liked her a lot.

It tickled him immensely that she hated him on sight.

Elijah Perry allowed himself only one very small drink from his canteen. The water was brackish, warm, and unpalatable, but Elijah knew he shouldn't feel such a strong sense of indignation about it. It had been his decision to set out into the wild New Mexico Territory; nobody'd forced him. He'd lived in the West long enough to know the water here was full of alkali, the weather harsh, and the landscape bleak and often deadly. He'd headed here on purpose for those very reasons. It was, therefore, unreasonable of him to be peeved at it for possessing all the qualities he'd sought in the first place.

Perverse by nature, he was peeved anyway. His own contradictory emotions tickled his cynical side. Since Elijah's cynical side had grown over the years until it was about all there was left of him, it made him grin now as he hooked the canteen back onto his saddle. "Criminy, Ben, you just can't please some folks."

Ben, Elijah's long-suffering horse, broached no reply. From the way his head drooped, though, Elijah judged he wasn't delighted by their circumstances, either.

After another hour or so, Elijah squinted into the distance, wondering if he'd contracted a brain fever, or if he truly beheld signs of humanity up ahead. His eyes were no longer infallible, as they'd been in his youth. Not for the first time, Elijah considered the prospect of purchasing some spectacles if he ever saw civilization again. He already owned a pair for reading, but he didn't put them on except in private because he still clung to a remnant of his vanity. He shook his head and grinned in a self-mocking manner. "Whoever heard of a gambling man wearing specs, Ben?"

Ben returned no answer to this query either. Undismayed, Elijah shaded his eyes and squinted harder at what might or might not signify a community of man in the distance. He was pretty sure he saw a couple of windmills, although their wooden frameworks were so much the same color as the surrounding countryside, he couldn't be certain.

"Rio Hondo should be around here somewhere, boy," he said kindly, hoping in that way to perk poor Ben up. The horse didn't seem to be impressed, but Elijah felt a little perkier.

Not that Rio Hondo was a hotbed of civilization. In truth, it was a hiccup. A speck. A dot. Or, amended Elijah with his customary dark humor, more likely a blot on the otherwise empty high plains of southeastern New Mexico Territory that the few folks who knew about it had begun calling the Pecos Valley. He'd also heard some people call this region the Seven Rivers country.

He eyed the barren landscape and wondered where those seven rivers were and, if they existed, why there wasn't so much as a speck of greenery to be seen. Strange country, this.

So was Rio Hondo. It was, in fact, a nothing of a place, established as a stopover for cattlemen driving herds to forts in the territory or north to Albuquerque and Santa Fe, or even up into Colorado and on to Kansas and Missouri. It was nothing in the middle of a vaster nothing. It was a place to which nobody ever came and that few knew was there. It was, in short, exactly what Elijah had been seeking.

He didn't know why. All he knew was that during his last night in San Antonio, when he'd won the biggest stake of his gambling life, bedded the most beautiful whore in town, been fawned over by the largest group of the most worthy fellows, and had regaled all of them with the most amusing stories, the emptiness in his soul had finally swallowed up the rest of him. Nothing in the whole of his life mattered, and Elijah felt sick as the enormity of his own nothingness struck him.

That wasn't entirely true. One thing mattered. He patted his vest pocket now, even though he knew his letter to Virginia still resided there. He'd wait until the day before he left Rio Hondo and post it from there, presuming the village had some kind of postal service.

Virginia was the only thing in his life that mattered, however. And, since he was in a brutal truth-telling mood, he reminded himself that he wasn't even sure about her. For all he knew, she'd grown up to be a faithless jade just like all the other females in the world.

And men. Elijah, who knew himself to be as faithless and jaded as any woman, didn't hold Virginia's sex against her. His antipathy was expansive. It included everyone without prejudice.

If she'd changed, he didn't want to know about it. Sometimes he feared that if he discovered Virginia had become like all the rest of the people in the world, the last tiny spark of virtue remaining in him would die, and he'd be left bankrupt—black and shriveled and dried-up. He shivered and told himself to stop thinking about it.

At any rate, the echoing hollowness of his life had ultimately driven Elijah out of San Antonio. He'd felt almost compelled to find an emptiness bigger than himself, as if in that way his own nothingness might be absorbed once and for all, and he might either find peace or disappear altogether.

He snorted—cynically, of course—and grumbled, "Peace. Ha! Damn fool thing for a man to crave."

Hell, the only time he'd ever felt alive had been in the middle of the war, when his life might have been blasted from his body at any second—and by so small a thing as a bullet. The disparity in size between men and bullets and the relative effectiveness of each amused Elijah, if such a black-edged sense of the ridiculous as he possessed could be counted as humor.

Well, it didn't matter now. He was here, and so was Rio Hondo. He was glad for Ben's sake. The poor horse was tired.

Elijah rode Ben down Second Street. He wondered where First Street was and, if such an avenue existed, why it, and not Second, hadn't been accorded the honor of being Rio Hondo's main street. He didn't think hard about it because he didn't care—but he did wonder.

"There's a wagon yard, Ben."

The territory was too new and too raw to have sprouted amenities such as hotels except in the largest of its cities. Elijah figured that this place, McMurdo's Wagon Yard, was where he'd be putting up.

He could probably have found overnight accommodations at the Pecos Saloon. He saw it across the street from the wagon yard, looking shabby and windblown. Around here, everything looked shabby and windblown. But he didn't like trying to sleep in saloons. They were noisy and often violent, and Elijah didn't care to have his sleep, which came to him rarely and never deeply,

13

interrupted by gunfire. Such interruptions had happened before, and they invariably set his heart to racing and him to gasping for breath. He was too old for that sort of nonsense.

No, Elijah thought the wagon yard would suit him down to the ground. He guided Ben through the huge double gates, and prepared himself to smile at the proprietor.

Alexander McMurdo looked up and grinned when a horseman entered his wagon yard.

"Howdy, stranger."

Mac enjoyed speaking the vernacular of the area. It made him feel one with the community. Besides, it irritated Joy Hardesty, and he took satisfaction from that. He shot a glimpse at her now. She'd been sweeping off the front porch of his mercantile establishment and looked as sour as a pickle. It was a familiar expression for her, and it struck Mac as funny.

She'd glanced up from her sweeping when she heard the sound of a horse's hooves and seemed intrigued, in a glum sort of way, by the mounted stranger. When she heard Mac chuckle, she peeked over at him, and her face pinched up even more.

"Ye'll get wrinkles if ye keep scowlin' like that, lass," Mac said kindly. He needled her every now and then because he figured she could use it. Of course she was offended by his levity and renewed her attack on the floor as if it, rather than Mac, had dared mention her gloomy demeanor.

"How-do," said the man in response to Mac's greeting. He grinned, tugged the brim of his dusty black hat politely, drew his horse to a halt, and swung down from the saddle. He let out with a huge groan as soon as his boots hit the earth.

14

Mac grinned back. "Long trip?"

"Very long." The weary traveler put a hand to the small of his back, stretched, and groaned again. "Not as young as I used to be."

"Reckon none of us are."

The man was almost as interesting a specimen as Joy, Mac decided. He was a handsome fellow, although he was right about one thing: he wasn't as young as he used to be.

In spite of the dust covering him, he was as natty as a man could be. He was clad in black trousers, black coat, black boots, and a black vest and hat. The austerity of his garb was offset only by a shirt that would probably be white again if it were laundered, and he wore long gray duster.

The fellow didn't go in for frills, Mac noticed with approval. Nothing as garish as a silver conch gleamed from his belt or hat brim. Even his gun was unobtrusive. A sober accessory, it was set into a black leather holster that rode high on his hip, butt-forward for an easy grab by either hand should such a maneuver prove necessary. The fellow didn't flaunt his skill, but Mac could tell he knew how to use that instrument of death.

Even if Mac didn't already know who the man was, he would have pegged him for a gambler and a wanderer. A bored, slightly dangerous aura hovered about him. He'd probably had women fawning over him all his life because he possessed the world-weary, indifferent attitude of a satyr. Women were always fascinated by difficult men, in Mac's experience.

This fellow had dark hair, silvering around the edges, and a swarthy complexion. He'd lost the washboard belly of his youth, Mac noticed with a silent chuckle, although he sucked his gut in when he spied Joy plying her broom. When he took off his hat to wipe an arm across his sweaty forehead, Mac saw that the hair on his skull was thinning, too. Nope, nowhere near as young as he used to be.

Shoot, the poor fellow'd showed up just in time. Another year or two, and he might have been beyond even Mac's help, and Mac was the most powerful wizard there was. He stuck out a hand. "Alexander McMurdo, young feller. Welcome to Rio Hondo."

The man shook Mac's hand. "Elijah Perry, Mr. McMurdo. Pleased to be here."

"Planning to spend some time with us folks in the territory, are you, Mr. Perry?"

"Thought I'd stay awhile, yes."

"Don't get too many visitors to Rio Hondo."

"Don't expect you do." Elijah Perry smiled slightly, as though the fact appealed to him.

"Well, come on along, and I'll show you where you can take care of your horse and yourself. We don't have us any hotels in Rio Hondo yet, but you can be comfortable here if you don't mind it a little rough."

"I don't mind it rough."

And that was that. Mac led Elijah to a stall, and pointed out the horse feed and curry equipment. Mac indicated the washhouse, and explained that he would gladly provide stew and corn bread and a glass of beer for a nickel, when Mr. Perry was ready to eat. Elijah nodded.

"Of course, Joy over there don't approve of the beer," Mac said with a deliberate twinkle.

Elijah, who hadn't bothered looking in Joy's direction after his first glance, eyed her now. "Yeah. She looks like it."

Mac laughed. "Poor thing. She was with a group of missionaries headed for the Mexican jungles."

"Looks like that, too."

"She took sick, though, and they went on without her. She's workin' for me until she can earn her passage back east again."

Elijah shook his head. "Don't know that I don't feel a little sorry for you, Mr. McMurdo. She doesn't look like an easy sort of female to get on with."

"Joy's only feelin' a little dejected, Mr. Perry. Life's been a disappointment to her, you see."

"Yeah. Life's been a disappointment to a lot of us, Mr. McMurdo."

Mac patted him on the back, and he appeared startled. "Call me Mac, Mr. Perry. Please call me Mac. Everybody does." He winked at Elijah. "Except Joy, of course."

Recovering his composure, Elijah managed a grin and said, "Of course."

Joy listened to the two men talking about her, and wished she were anywhere else on earth but where she was, doing anything else on earth but what she was doing.

It wasn't fair. It wasn't fair that she should have been prevented from fulfilling her God-given destiny by so paltry a thing as influenza.

"It's your own fault," she muttered under her breath. "You know what Mother always told you. You allowed your weakness to prevail. You should have battled the illness, fought it off, vanquished it with your own strength of spirit. And prayer."

She plied the broom more forcefully still as her mother's voice lectured her in her brain. *You're a gutless creature, Joy Hardesty. A leaky vessel.* Joy sniffed disconsolately. "I'm just like my father, in fact. If I don't shape up, even God won't want me."

Already God didn't want her or she'd be in Mexico with Mr. Thrash instead of in Rio Hondo with Alexander McMurdo. Joy knew she was still feeble from her illness when tears sprang up in her eyes. Ruthlessly, because she knew those tears were weak and pitiful and proved her unfit to be her mother's daughter, she swallowed them. "This is a judgment on you, Joy Hardesty. A judgment."

A tear leaked past the armed and fortified barrier she'd erected against it, and Joy heaved a dispirited sigh. Why, oh, why couldn't she do anything but fail in life? Every time she tried to be what her mother wanted her to be, to do what her mother wanted her to do, she failed. Miserably. She'd never been able to do anything else. Which was why she was here, all alone except for the company of a few miserable sinners, in a hostile territory, sweeping a floor for a living.

Knowing she was a failure gnawed at her. Every waking hour of the day, Joy carried the pain of her grief like an open wound in her chest. Every breath hurt her and restricted her breathing. The pain in her chest had been with her since her earliest days on earth, and was now as much a part of her as her skin and hair.

What hurt even more than the knowledge that she was a miserable failure—hurt so much that Joy had been crying herself to sleep every night since she'd overcome her fever and realized what had happened—was knowing that the Reverend Mr. Hezekiah P. Thrash had gone on without her. As if she were of no more significance to him than a mule that, once crippled, had to be abandoned.

According to Mr. McMurdo—and a less worthy example of the human male Joy had yet to meet—Mr. Thrash said he'd send for her if he could. *If* he could. Mr. Thrash hadn't stuck around to tell Joy so himself. Nor had he left her so much as a scribbled note wishing her well and explaining his plans. He'd just consigned her to Mr. McMurdo's care and gone on without her.

"He'll send for me if he can," Joy murmured, sending a spray of dirt off the porch and into the yard. Not that

18

it would stay there. The wind would blow it right back onto the porch again. She didn't know why she bothered, except that she was a Christian woman and Mr. Mc-Murdo, the wicked old scoundrel, was allowing her to work in his mercantile store until she'd made enough money for passage back to Auburn, Massachusetts, where she'd come from.

"I don't want to go back to Auburn," she whispered as she set the broom in the corner. She pressed a hand to the ache in her chest and wondered if everyone in the world hurt like this, or if there was something physically wrong with her. A cancer of the soul, perhaps. "I want to be in the Mexican jungles with Mr. Thrash, preaching to the heathens and saving men's souls."

"There are plenty of heathens around here you can preach to, if you're of a mind to, lass."

Joy jumped and whirled around. She felt her cheeks catch fire. *Jerusalem!* She hated it when Mr. McMurdo sneaked up behind her. He was the most silent fellow Joy had ever met. She considered it merely one more manifestation of his fallen nature, that he should creep about like that. She didn't respond, because she was near tears, and she didn't want to feel any more like a fool than she already did.

"We have us a visitor for a while, Joy, m'dear," the old sinner continued.

Joy saw the tall stranger who had lately ridden in to the wagon yard standing behind Mr. McMurdo. He was a handsome man, but Joy knew better than to expect his insides to match his outsides. She inclined her head slightly, feeling it was only her Christian duty to acknowledge his presence, but unsure how to greet so obviously wicked a man. Joy could tell. He was simply one more example of the revolting, depraved men who wandered around in this part of the world, and he made her want to hug herself to ward off the strange sensations his presence evoked within her.

The visitor tipped his hat.

Although Joy would never, ever, in her wildest fits of discontent, say such a thing aloud, she thought Mr. Mc-Murdo was right about the saving of souls. She'd often wondered, since she'd been abandoned in Rio Hondo, why Mr. Thrash hadn't chosen to spread the word out here, in this wretched territory. The awful, violent men who lived here could benefit from a taste of the Word of God as much as—perhaps more than—any heathen Indian.

"This here's Mr. Elijah Perry, m'dear."

Joy nodded again. She hated it when Mr. McMurdo called her "my dear" in that wretched Scottish accent of his. He sounded so sly and amused. There wasn't a single thing about this place that amused Joy.

Both men stared at her as if waiting for her to do something. Because she was her mother's daughter and would never do anything to which her mother might object—not even be rude to unknown sinners—she gave the stranger one more stiff nod and said, "How do you do?"

The horrid man grinned at her, as if he found her amusing, just as Mr. McMurdo did. "How-do, ma'am?"

Joy hated being the object of others' entertainment.

Twinkling in a most unsuitable manner, Mr. McMurdo then went on to say, "Mr. Perry, please allow me to introduce you to Miss Joy Hardesty."

"Miss Hardesty."

Mr. Elijah Perry's dark eyes seemed to rake her up and down. Joy felt the heat in her cheeks deepen. Why, the man was looking at her as if she were no better than those awful women at the Pecos Saloon! She felt as though she were being stripped naked by his eyes. The lecherous fiend! And Mr. McMurdo, of course, made not the slightest effort to stop him.

Well, she wouldn't let this place or these men get to her. Joy was a proper lady, and a Christian, and she knew this was a tribulation visited upon her by divine Providence to test the nature of her character and moral fiber.

She dropped a curtsy, as stiff as she was. "You have a fine name, Mr. Perry."

"Thank you, Miss Hardesty."

"I'm very pleased to meet you, sir." It wasn't true, but Joy knew that lies in pursuit of graciousness could be forgiven. Her mother had told her so, and her mother had been a saint. Everyone said so.

"Are you really? You astonish me."

Joy popped up from her curtsy as if she'd been goosed. She guessed the bitter twist on Elijah Perry's mouth was supposed to be a smile. Mr. McMurdo's grin was unmistakable. She sniffed to show them both that, while she was willing to be polite, she was above them, by virtue of morality if nothing more.

"Will you please fetch Mr. Perry some stew and corn bread, Joy? I'll be in the back room, gettin' him a glass of beer."

"Certainly." She turned to do Mr. McMurdo's bidding.

Joy wondered if she should say something about the iniquity of drinking. Her mother would have told her this was a golden opportunity, provided by the heavenly father, for her to prove her worth as a crusader and a missionary. She should offer these hardened, dissolute men a brief, kind lecture about the evils of alcoholic spirits. In truth, it was her duty to do so. Joy's mother wouldn't have shirked the task, no matter how unreceptive her audience was certain to be. Joy's mother had been willing to lecture anybody about anything. After all, she'd known best.

Joy's heart was aching, though, and her eyes burned with unshed tears, and her head hurt, and her stomach churned, and the pain in her chest throbbed so hard she could barely walk, much less talk, and she didn't say a word. Some missionary *she* was.

She could feel Mr. McMurdo and Mr. Perry silently mocking her behind her back. *Melancholia.* The word taunted her.

It's melancholia troubling you, Joy. Melancholia is a disease of the spirit fostered by human vanity and fanned by the devil, and you must pray to rid yourself of it.

Yes, Mother.

The ancient conversation followed Joy into the kitchen, and echoed in her brain until she wanted clap her hands over her ears and scream to drown it out.

There was no reason these men's opinions should matter to her. They were sinners. Their view of her shouldn't matter any more than a gentle stirring borne to her upon the breeze—not that there was such a thing in this miserable place. The wind blew a gale every single day, and there wasn't anything gentle within a thousand miles.

Oh, how she missed Auburn! How she missed the lush green of her Massachusetts home. How she missed Mr. Thrash. How she deplored her own weakness of body, mind, and soul. If only she'd remained healthy, she might be with Mr. Thrash now, in the jungles of deepest Mexico, saving the souls of those poor savages who'd never had the opportunity to hear God's message before.

But no. Her melancholia had conquered her best intentions and made her succumb to the influenza.

The road to hell is paved with good intentions, Joy.

Yes, Mother.

Joy shook her head and frowned as she dipped out a hearty portion of the stew. There was the difference in a nutshell, she decided. Unlike the men residing in and

22

around Rio Hondo, those poor South American natives hadn't been given the opportunity to better themselves. Mr. Thrash was going to give it to them.

These men—Alexander McMurdo and Elijah Perry— had heard God's message and chosen to ignore it. *That* was why they seemed so much worse to Joy than those poor benighted savages in the jungle.

Feeling martyred, Joy bore Mr. Perry's stew and corn bread to him on a tray. Mr. McMurdo had a table set up beside the potbellied stove in a corner of his mercantile, where travelers could eat in any weather. The stove was cold today, since the weather had turned unseasonably warm. Elijah Perry lounged in front of it, looking out of place. It was the first time Joy had felt at all akin to him—and she didn't feel much then. Joy was out of place, too, but not for the same reasons.

"Here you are, Mr. Perry." She balanced the tray in one hand and picked up his bowl of stew with the other, preparing to set it down in front of him.

"Allow me, Miss Hardesty."

Joy didn't like it when Mr. Perry took the tray from her and held it politely so she could remove his corn bread, dining utensils, and a napkin. She said, "Thank you," in a stifled voice because she knew she should. She didn't want to thank him for anything.

"You're quite welcome." His own voice was deep and dark and rich, and hinted of Southern evenings and smooth whiskey. Not that Joy would know anything about whiskey, smooth or otherwise.

Because she was uncomfortable, she lifted her chin. She found herself unable to look Mr. Perry in the eye, but directed her glance over his left shoulder. "If you need anything else, please let me know. I shall be working on Mr. McMurdo's books at the counter."

He inclined his head in the manner of a gentleman.

"Thank you, Miss Hardesty. I'll bear it in mind, should I need anything."

Whatever that meant. He grinned devilishly, and his words sounded provocative, although Joy couldn't imagine why. She snatched the tray from his hands and marched back to the counter.

She didn't look at Elijah Perry again until she'd carried the tray to the kitchen, retrieved Mac's big ledger book and a box full of receipts, and dragged a high stool up to the mercantile counter. She sat on the business side of the counter, away from the floor of the mercantile, because she preferred having several feet of hard wood between her and the rest of this hostile territorial world. She'd rather have the continent between them but settled for what she could get.

Once she'd arranged herself on the stool she dove into her work, intending to ignore Mr. Perry. Against her will, her attention wavered, her pencil stilled, and her gaze stole over to him. Mr. McMurdo, she noted with displeasure, had brought Mr. Perry a mug of the devil's brew.

She'd never seen anyone take over a room with less effort than Mr. Elijah Perry did. In fact, he wasn't doing a thing except eating his stew, but his presence overwhelmed the small store. There was an almost unnatural stillness about the man; yet Joy sensed tension in him, as if he were a tightly wound spring that could explode into action any second. Mr. Hezekiah P. Thrash could take lessons from Mr. Elijah Perry when it came to capturing a congregation's attention.

On that thought, which she knew to be scandalous, Joy frowned, tore her gaze away from Mr. Perry, and directed it at the open ledger in front of her. As if the godly Hezekiah Thrash could benefit from a single thing learned from that dreadful sinner, Elijah Perry.

Joy was tapping the end of her pencil against her nose,

staring off into space, and contemplating the nature of evil when Elijah Perry looked up from his stew bowl. The movement drew her attention, and she turned to find him grinning at her.

"Lost in thought, Miss Hardesty?"

She frowned back. "Yes. Is there something I can do for you?"

He held up his bowl. Schooling his handsome face into a pleading expression that would have done credit to a grubby schoolboy, he said, "May I please have more, ma'am? This is right good stuff."

With a sniff to show him that she wasn't fooled by his pleasant demeanor, that she was made of impermeable rectitude and couldn't be beguiled by mere human flesh-pots, Joy slid from her stool and went to get his bowl. "Of course, Mr. Perry."

"Thank you kindly, ma'am."

He sounded intolerably meek and ever so polite. It was an act; Joy knew it. It was an act designed to catch people off guard and make them think there was some good in Elijah Perry. Joy knew better. Elijah Perry was a bad man, and there was no wrapping him up in clean linen or making anything else out of him. She thought Satan himself might have sounded thus when tempting Judas Iscariot into betraying his Lord.

Then she remembered that it wasn't her place to judge her fellow man.

Then she reminded herself that the only way a person had to ascertain the merits of his fellow beings on earth was by his actions—and Mr. Elijah Perry's actions proclaimed him to be a sinner.

Choose your company carefully, Joy Hardesty. Don't consort with the worldly. Your nature is too weak to withstand temptation.

Yes, Mother.

Bearing her mother's admonition in mind, and determined not to allow her weak nature to succumb to worldly lures, Joy was filled with righteousness and holy virtue when she bore Elijah's second bowl of stew out to him.

Another thought kept her visage grim. She didn't hold with giving people food without their paying for it. She knew, because her mother had told her so, that giving people things only taught them that idleness paid. But Mr. McMurdo had laughed when she'd told him the same thing. He'd said a nickel was plenty, and no man could eat more than a nickel's worth of his stew, no matter how many times she refilled his bowl.

She didn't understand his reasoning—after all, he put lots of meat in his stew—but she did as he'd bidden her. Her mother would have been able to come up with an argument that would have persuaded Mr. McMurdo of the faultiness of his reasoning, but Joy, unfortunately, was nothing like her mother. It was her primary failing in a life fraught with failings.

Holding her back as straight as a stick—not a difficult proposition given the tightness of her corset stays—she set the bowl in front of Mr. Perry in a manner calculated to let him know what she thought of him. And second helpings.

"Here's your second bowl of stew, Mr. Perry."

"Thank you, Miss Hardesty."

"You're welcome, Mr. Perry."

"It's very good stew. Did you make it, Miss Hardesty?"

"No, sir. Mr. McMurdo made it."

He looked up at her, a teasing expression on his face. "Think I'll quit while I'm ahead."

Joy frowned at him. Although she wrinkled her brow and thought and thought, she had no idea what he'd meant by that.

Chapter Two

Elijah sat back, sighed, and refrained from patting his belly only because he was a grown man and knew the habit to be childish. McMurdo's stew could almost reconcile a fellow to banishment in this godforsaken territory.

Perhaps not entirely godforsaken. He glanced in Joy Hardesty's direction and decided if that was godliness, he'd just as soon skip it. She sat hunched over a big ledger book behind the counter of the mercantile, and glared at the page upon which she worked as if she bore it a personal grudge. She looked like a missionary, all right—all vinegar and prudishness and austerity. Elijah couldn't understand what some females found so distasteful about human nature, but that one looked like she'd rather beat it off with a stick than succumb to anything human—or natural.

Not that he cared for human nature much himself, but

at least he had some fairly good reasons from which he'd forged his opinion. He'd bet any amount of money that Joy Hardesty had never seen so much as a small glimpse of the horrors men could perpetrate on each other.

He wondered how old she was, and wagered with himself on the answer. Twenty-five. He'd have to ask McMurdo. The only time Elijah, who made his living gambling, ever lost was when he bet against himself. He was too prudent to make shaky bets with other people.

He pushed his chair back until it was balanced on its rear two legs, and propped himself against the wall while he studied Joy Hardesty some more. Taking critical stock of her features, he guessed she wasn't really ugly—except for the expression on her face, which was ugly as sin. He grinned because the metaphor struck him as comically incongruous. A missionary lady who was as ugly as sin—*ha!* Sometimes Elijah was so damned clever, he amazed himself.

Her hair was brown. There was no way to tell if it was plain old brown-brown or if it had any interesting highlights, because there wasn't enough light in the room by which to study it. Besides, she had it braided into two skinny whips that were coiled up as tight as she was. She'd wrapped them around her head and pinned them down. Elijah bet they wouldn't dare try to get out of those pins, if they knew what was good for them. From what he could see, there wasn't anything about Joy Hardesty that wasn't coiled up tight.

The calico dress she wore was about as unbecoming as any Elijah'd ever seen. He wondered if she'd gone out of her way to select the least flattering color and style she could find, or if the gown's selection had been an unfortunate accident. It was brown, too, but the brown of her dress and the brown of her hair didn't look good together. Combined, they made the brown of her eyes look like mud.

Her complexion was pale. Sallow, actually. She looked skinny and sickly and altogether unappealing. Elijah, who liked most women a shade better than he liked most men, decided that if he'd met more women like Joy before this, his opinion of the two sexes would undoubtedly be different.

All that was beside the point. Although the prospect wasn't very attractive, Elijah guessed he'd have to deal with her again. With a sigh, he lowered the chair legs to the floor, picked up his empty bowl, plate, and beer mug, and carted them to the counter. He figured he might get a lecture if he left them on the table. He was kind of surprised she hadn't taken him to task for being free with the furniture when he'd tipped his chair back against the wall. On the other hand, it wasn't her furniture, so maybe she didn't care.

"Here, ma'am. Thanks for the chow."

She looked up with a grimace. Elijah wasn't surprised by that. Something else surprised him, however. He experienced a quick, sharp pang of pity for this unhappy woman. *That* surprised him. Hell, what did he care about her?

McMurdo's explanation for Joy's sour disposition rolled through Elijah's mind, though, and he wondered how life could have disappointed her so badly. After all, she wasn't that old. Not nearly as old as he was, for instance. Elijah figured he had good reasons for his own disenchantment. How could such a relatively young female have come by hers?

"Just put them down, please," she said crisply. "I'm busy right now."

His pity evaporated in a flash of irritation. "Yes, ma'am," he said, drawing the words out to annoy her.

29

He set the dishes on the counter, making as much noise about it as he could. "A pleasure doing business with you, Miss Hardesty." He had the satisfaction of seeing his barb hit home. Two bright patches of pink appeared on her pallid cheeks. He chalked up one for himself.

Because he'd been on the trail for a long time, and because he had nothing better to do, Elijah turned away from Joy and perused the shelves of McMurdo's mercantile establishment. He hadn't been this far away from a big city in a long time and was curious to see how things went forward here in the territory.

It was a well-stocked store for such an out-of-the-way place. He picked up a small, prettily decorated tin containing marzipan candies. *Shoot.* Now where had that old man come by these? The last time Elijah'd eaten marzipan had been when he lived in Maryland, before the war, a lifetime or three ago. He picked up the tin and weighed it in his palm. He did have a formidable sweet tooth. Maybe he'd just buy this candy and gobble it down.

With a grin, he wondered if he should offer some to Joy, and decided that was exactly what he should do. Maybe it'd sweeten her up, although he doubted it. At the very least, he expected that an offer of candy from a sinner like him would disconcert her—maybe make her blush and stammer—and would be worth it for that.

When he glanced at the counter, she still had her nose in her ledger. Elijah grinned. As it was the custom to barter for prices, he cleared his throat, anticipating a spirited exchange. "How much is this candy, ma'am?"

Joy glanced up, still frowning. She looked as though she didn't appreciate Elijah interrupting her perusal of that ledger, which must be either extremely fascinating or extremely confusing.

She squinted at the tin in Elijah's hand. It appeared to him as though she didn't want to look him in the eye. "I don't know. Isn't there a price marked on it? Mr. Mc-Murdo generally marks his unusual items."

Blast. And here Elijah had been looking forward to a battle. He turned the tin over and peered at it from all angles. His humor returned when he saw no price. "Nope."

She heaved an aggrieved sigh. "Oh, all right. Let me ask Mr. McMurdo." She slid off the high stool. Elijah guessed she was going to go looking for the proprietor of this establishment—and resented having to do so—when the old fellow himself walked through the door.

"There he is. You can ask him yourself." Joy climbed back up onto her stool.

Elijah shook his head and muttered loud enough for her to hear, "Hard to come by good help out here, I reckon." He gave Mac a grin to let him know he was teasing, although he really was irked by Joy's hostile attitude.

The old man chuckled. He seemed to do that a lot. Offhand, Elijah couldn't think of two less likely folks to have found each other than Alexander McMurdo and Joy Hardesty.

Joy, he noticed, had chosen not to react to his pointed comment about her rudeness. Her lips, however, looked like a couple of peaches that had been left out in the sun for too long and had wrinkled up. In fact, the whole picture Joy Hardesty presented was of something withered and lifeless. Elijah shuddered, the notion having reminded him of himself and unsettled him.

"Noticed you had some of my favorite treats on your shelves, Mac. How much for this tin of marzipan?"

The old man gave Elijah a broad smile. Now *here,* he thought, was a pleasant fellow. Nothing shrunken and tight and bitter about Alexander McMurdo. He looked as if he were about a hundred and ninety years old, but he was spry for all that, and his eyes were as blue as the sky outside and as twinkly as stars. Elijah found himself liking McMurdo enormously. He liked McMurdo, in fact, about as much as he disliked Joy.

"Great stuff, that," Mac said, pointing at the tin with the stem of his black briar pipe. "Hard to come by out here, but you can have the tin for four bits, Mr. Perry."

"Call me Elijah, Mac," he said, digging into his trouser pocket. He was about to hand the money to Mac when he caught the look on the old man's face, grinned, and turned to walk over to Joy. "Here, Miss Hardesty. Mr. McMurdo said four bits for the candy."

"I heard him." She sounded as ungracious as she looked.

Elijah held out the coin. Joy made a grab for it, but he palmed it and withdrew his hand. "You know, ma'am, pardon me for saying so, but for a Christian lady, you're mighty rough on us poor sinners. Aren't you afraid your meanness will turn us from the Lord's light and prevent us from ever being saved? I can tell you here and now that if everybody who preaches God's Word is as mean as you, I sure as good gracious don't want anything to do with Him."

Her face, already pale, bleached of color, and she looked stricken. "I beg your pardon. I didn't mean to be rude, Mr. Perry."

Still holding the coin, Elijah propped an elbow on the counter and leaned toward her. She backed up, almost fell off her stool, grabbed the counter with both hands, and held on tight. "Sure you did, Miss Hardesty. You took one look at bad old me and decided to teach me a lesson, 'cause I'm such a wicked man."

"You would, of course, know yourself much better than I."

Elijah raised his eyebrows in appreciation. "That's a

good one, ma'am. That's damn good." He took note of her recoil at his language and grinned his most ironic grin. "But it won't wash. You were as crusty as a loaf of week-old bread before you even knew my name. I think you're just mean through and through. You're mean to the core and don't like anything or anybody. Well, y'know what, ma'am?"

Joy's eyes had gone as round as billiard balls. She didn't answer him, but clutched the counter as if her life depended on it. She looked scared, which was a distinct improvement from her usual expression, in Elijah's opinion.

"I don't like you, either."

He flipped the coin insolently, and watched it wink in the dusty sunbeams. Joy didn't reach forward to catch it, but she watched, too, as it struck the counter, bounced, and rolled off onto the floor. Elijah heard it hit the ground, but didn't bother to watch where it went. "Better fetch it quick, ma'am. Otherwise Mac might take it out of your wages, and I'm sure he's as eager to see your backside as you are to get out of here."

With that, he turned and sauntered away from her, paused by the hatrack to pluck up his black hat and plop it onto his black hair, and left the store. Mac gave Joy a sympathetic smile; then he followed Elijah outside.

Joy watched the two men go. Her insides were squeezing and pitching so badly, she feared for a moment she might be physically sick. After taking several deep breaths, she decided her luncheon was safe.

She trembled all over when she braced herself with a hand on the counter and stooped to look for the coin. "Dreadful man," she whispered into the stillness of the mercantile.

Hatred stirreth up strife, Joy Hardesty. Your own be-

33

havior brought that man's censure down upon you. I do believe you're incapable of learning anything I try to teach you, Joy.

Her mother's voice, as clear as a bell, sounded the judgment, and Joy knew Elijah Perry had been right about her. She'd been rude to him—and for no better reason than that he was the sort of man her mother had cautioned her about. Yet her mother had also been very firm in her opinion that one must show sinners their way was not God's way, and that they should cease their wickedness and follow another path.

Joy sighed heavily. Another failure to add to her long, long list. If the ghost of Jacob Marley were to visit Joy, her chain of failures would be every bit as long as Marley's chain of miserly actions.

Her mother would have known how to deal with Elijah Perry, Joy thought dismally. Her mother had never been at a loss for anything. She'd always known what was right and what was wrong. Never had a moment's doubt sullied her mother's righteous thinking. She'd never shirked her duty to her fellows, either. A powerful woman, Joy's father had called her. And he'd been right.

Unfortunately, her mother wasn't here to guide her. And without her mother at her back, pushing her onto the proper path at every turn and scolding her for every misstep, Joy didn't know what to do or how to behave. She felt stuck, as if she were mired in quicksand.

Inertia. I do believe your middle name should have been Inertia, Joy Hardesty.

She couldn't find the coin. She searched and searched and searched, and it continued to elude her. It seemed typical of her life that so insignificant an item as a piece of gold should elude her in this persistent way. After searching for ten solid minutes, frustration, physical weakness, and a feeling of hopelessness overcame her

34

determination. Joy sat on the floor behind the counter, leaned back against the wall, and cried.

She knew her mother, who didn't have a weak bone in her body, would have looked on her with scorn and called her a pitiful specimen. She chalked up the way the dust motes in the air seemed to sparkle around her to her own imperfection of mind and spirit, and wished she could simply die now and get it over with.

Elijah stuck out his hand. "Pleased to meet you, Cooper."

The man to whom Mac had just introduced him shook Elijah's hand. "Likewise."

Curtis Cooper, according to Mac, was a hand on the nearby Blackworth ranch. Also according to Mac, the ranch was run by a woman, Susan Blackworth, who had built it up from ruin after her husband had met with an untimely death. From Mac's sparkly expression and meaningful wink, Elijah got the impression Mrs. Blackworth might be able to enlighten the world about her husband's demise should she ever care to do so. Elijah thought dryly that this territory seemed to be a magnet for unpleasant females.

Cooper had come to town with a couple of other cowboys, and had stopped by Mac's wagon yard to purchase some rope and lumber. Mac introduced all of them to Elijah.

Later Elijah was never quite able to figure out why he and those other three men had decided to set up a poker game in Mac's mercantile establishment, but he did know that it had seemed a perfectly logical thing to do at the time. He was pretty sure Mac had encouraged them, too, although he couldn't figure that out, either. If he ran a nice business like Mac's, Elijah was sure he'd not want a bunch of rough men with guns on their hips gambling in it while drinking beer.

Mac evidently didn't mind at all. In fact, he helped set out the table and chairs, smiling like an imp the whole time. He was an interesting fellow, Mac was. Elijah couldn't help but like him. He had a soft Scottish burr that treated the language more kindly than most of the twangs Elijah had heard since he'd left Maryland.

"And you can ask Joy here when you need refills," Mac said merrily, gesturing to his employee, who glared at the commotion from behind the counter.

She looked as mean as a snake. "You mean she'll condescend to serve a fellow beer if he gets dry?" Elijah scratched his head in a gesture he hoped conveyed doubt. The woman was getting to him. Whatever malevolence she radiated was starting to make his shoulder blades itch, and he wanted never to have to see her again. He couldn't, therefore, understand the urge marching side by side with the one about never seeing her again, which was to grab and kiss her, wrestle her to a nearby mattress, and make love to her until he'd conquered her sourness forever and replaced it with—joy.

He was just nuts, was all. Joy Hardesty was a disagreeable bit of goods, and that was that.

Joy's frown got meaner, and McMurdo laughed. "Sure, she'll serve ye beer, laddie. She's a good girl, Joy."

"Is she?"

Joy flounced into the back room with her ledger, ignoring Elijah so thoroughly, he knew he'd gotten her goat. He was surprised when a feeling of guilt overshadowed his satisfaction. When she returned, she bore paper, pen, and ink with her. She plopped these items on the counter and resumed her seat on the stool behind it, as if daring anyone to ask her to do anything. Elijah guessed she was going to write a letter or two.

She didn't say a word, but he felt her disapproval from where he sat shuffling cards. It pulsed in the air around him and made him shift his shoulders and twitch his legs more than once. He was a little puzzled that the other men didn't feel it. Or maybe they did. He didn't ask.

There was no reason for it, but Elijah found himself glancing at her quite often as the poker game progressed. He didn't care what she was doing or why she was doing it. She was nothing to him but a rude pain in the neck.

He got the impression she used that counter for the same reason she used her spiteful tongue—to keep people away. The notion didn't make him appreciate her to any greater degree. She was a dried-up, prune-faced old maid, was Joy Hardesty. Elijah decided he was glad she'd be waiting on them tonight. She'd hate it, and that made him happy.

Once during the evening, Elijah looked around to see where Mac was, but the proprietor of the store had evidently retired for the night. Seemed strange to Elijah. He'd want to keep an eye on things if this were his place, especially if there were four gambling gents being waited on by one single female. Not that any man would ever even think of doing anything untoward to Joy Hardesty, but still . . .

He didn't let himself worry about it.

When Joy got back to Auburn, she'd never complain about anything again as long as she lived. She vowed it on her mother's sainted memory. Once or twice in the several hours following the commencement of that ghastly poker game in Mr. McMurdo's front room, she wondered if she'd last out the night, much less ever see Auburn again.

She shouldn't be here. If God hadn't decided to punish her for her bloodless nature, she wouldn't be. She'd be in Central America with the Reverend Mr. Hezekiah P.

37

Thrash, saving souls. Sometimes Joy wondered why God's lessons had to be so very hard.

God has a plan for us all, Joy, and don't you ever forget it. It's not up to you to question God's intentions. It's up to you to fulfill them.

Yes, Mother.

She guessed this was God's test of her mettle. And, of course, she was failing again. For one thing, she should have refused to wait on those awful men while they were gambling and drinking. Her mother would, very politely, have declined the duty. Joy had been so astonished when Mr. McMurdo asked her, she hadn't been able to think fast enough to come up with a polite objection.

Such shilly-shallying is typical of your slovenly nature, Joy Hardesty.

Yes, Mother.

Yet McMurdo had asked her to do it, and he was her employer. Besides, no matter how much she deplored his sinful character, she owed him a good deal. He'd nursed her through her dreadful illness. She'd very nearly died, according to him, and she had no reason not to believe him, even though she didn't want to. It always confused her when sinners did good deeds and behaved like Christians.

His kindness shouldn't make any difference, however, and Joy knew it. No matter how benevolent a bad man seemed to be on the surface, iniquity was iniquity, and she should take no part in it. She knew the devil tempted people with soft words and presented quandaries as trials by which to temper the steel of their faith. Look at Job, for heaven's sake. Her mother had taught her that the truly worthy among God's creatures saw past surface goodness to the rotten cores underneath, and soundly rejected the lures of the world, no matter how benevolently offered.

On the other hand, Alexander McMurdo had been unrelenting kind to her, no matter how mean she was to him.

That was neither here nor there. A sinner was a sinner, and she shouldn't allow a sinner's charm to beguile her.

Yet this was her job.

That shouldn't matter. She should refuse to serve these men the devil's brew. She should avoid them as the transgressors they were.

But Mr. McMurdo was paying her to serve them.

But if she waited on them, serving them intoxicating liquors and knowing what they were, she was no better than Judas, who had accepted thirty pieces of silver to betray the Lord.

For a moment, Joy felt circumstances overwhelm her. She dropped her head into her hands and wished she were dead.

Why, oh, why did she have to be so irresolute and incompetent? She reminded herself of Nicodemus, the fellow who dared visit Christ only by night so that he wouldn't be condemned by his fellow Pharisees. Her mother had detested Nicodemus, calling him a lily-livered coward. Not for Mrs. Hardesty the comfort of sneaking around like a thief in the night, disguising her true colors or hiding her faith.

For instance, Joy's mother would never have let Alexander McMurdo's genial disposition and soft speech weaken her determination. Mrs. Hardesty would have remained resolute in the face of Mr. McMurdo's benevolence and dealt with him like the corrupt man he was. And her mother certainly wouldn't have allowed Elijah Perry to get the better of her in a battle of words—never in a million years. Her mother would not have let him cow her or make her feel guilty for demonstrating her repudiation of his wicked ways. Drinking and gambling!

They were the devil's work, and Joy's mother would have told him so.

Nobody had ever dared talk back to Joy's mother the way people did to Joy. Joy's mother couldn't be intimidated. Mrs. Hardesty had known herself to be right. Besides, her mother had been a saint. Everybody said so. No one disconcerted Mrs. George Quincy Hardesty, particularly not the late Reverend Mr. George Quincy Hardesty or his mousy daughter, Joy.

With a sigh, Joy turned her thoughts to her father. He'd been a weak-willed, ineffectual, irresolute man, according to Joy's mother, and Joy had never even thought about contradicting her. It was a shame he hadn't possessed more backbone. He hadn't, and he was, therefore, an unworthy vessel to have attempted to spread God's Word. By the time he had shuffled off this mortal coil, Joy, who when she was very small used to run to him for comfort from her mother's caustic tongue, thoroughly despised him.

Her mother, though . . . Her mother had truly been a saint. Everybody knew it. Even Joy did, although she invariably had to suppress a shudder when she thought about it, knowing as she did so that she herself was wicked beyond redemption.

Joy feared she took after her father. In fact, she was so unsure of herself that half the time she felt as though her insides had frozen solid. She never knew what to do. Or what not to do. If only her mother were still alive to guide her. Joy's mother had criticized her constantly for her lack of resolution, but she'd always been there to tell Joy what to do.

These men, for instance. In truth, Joy didn't even know them. Therefore, she felt uncomfortable despising them. She knew, however, because of the things her mother had taught her, that they exhibited all the trappings of evil-doers. If she possessed her mother's determination, she could have shown them, through her own strength of spirit, the error of their ways.

Joy hadn't done any such thing. Then, to compound her sins of omission and commission, she'd felt bad about her failure to judge and even worse about having been rude. This was no way to get on in life. Joy knew it, and she couldn't seem to help herself. Twenty-five years old, and already she was a disaster through and through.

Then there was the problem of Alexander McMurdo. For heaven's sake, the man smoked, drank, and swore. Any one of those behaviors was enough to condemn him to eternal damnation, according to the principles by which Joy had been reared. Yet he'd been so kind to Joy when she'd needed kindness most that she had a very hard time disapproving of him. Which only went to point out Joy's own inadequacies. Her mother would have said that what Joy perceived as kindness was merely frosting over filth, and that Joy was a fool to look upon him as anything more or less than a tool of the devil.

There are no two ways about it, Joy Hardesty. Either you follow the straight and narrow path, or you don't.

Yes, Mother.

At the moment, Joy was filled with such dreadful confusion she couldn't see any path at all, straight and narrow or otherwise. She felt like a machine whose gears had rusted in place. Half the time she couldn't even get her motor to whir. She was very depressed.

"Miss Hardesty, if it isn't too much trouble, could we have another round of beer over here?"

Joy's head snapped up, and she frowned automatically at the word *beer,* which she had been taught from the cradle was wicked. Although she guessed this was an-

41

other opportunity lost—her mother would have taken it to give these men a gentle lecture on the evils of drinking—she said only, "Certainly." She said it disagreeably to make up for her lack of resolution, then felt small-minded and puritanical. She wouldn't blame anyone for not welcoming the Lord into his heart if all of God's emissaries were like her.

Feeling even more discouraged than usual, she fetched the tray she used to carry dishes and waded into the hazy blue fog of cigar smoke surrounding the card table. The acrid smoke made her throat close up and her eyes water, but she did her job. This was a duty set out by her employer. She figured she could at least fulfill this function, even if her mother was surely frowning down at her in censure from her heavenly home and instructing Saint Peter to refuse her daughter admission through the Pearly Gates when the time came for Joy to knock at them.

She sighed heavily, and only realized how foolish she'd been to do so when smoke choked her lungs.

Quickly she snatched up the empty beer mugs and carted them to the back room. Once there, she realized she had no idea whose beer mug was whose. Then she thought it didn't matter. Those men out there were nothing but evil rogues who didn't deserve clean glasses.

Then she decided her thought had been a sinful one, and that she was shirking her duty to behave as a Christian, no matter what her circumstances. Turning the other cheek or something like that.

Then she remembered her mother's injunction against consorting with low company.

Then the thought occurred to her that, although those men were gambling, they might not be all bad—a shocking notion she'd heard her father suggest once or twice in her mother's presence, rather timidly.

Then the memory of her mother's voice fairly shrieked at her not to be Satan's dupe.

Then she shook her head and told herself to stop thinking. She was no good at it, and thinking only confused her. What she should do was pray for the good Lord to guide her. Maybe one of these days, He'd clear up all this perplexity for her. She hoped so, anyway.

So she washed the glasses, dried them, and refilled them. Beer smelled truly awful, she decided as her nose wrinkled. With another deep sigh—her lungs hurt from all the cigar smoke—she hefted the tray. It was heavier now, what with the four filled beer mugs balanced on it. With a sinking heart, she headed for the front room again.

"What the hell do you think you're doing, Cooper?"

Cooper looked at his inquisitor, a cowboy named Grant Davis, and frowned. "What the devil do you mean, what the hell do I think I'm doing, Davis?"

Davis slammed his handful of cards down on the table. "I meant what I said, damn it. What the hell do you think you're doing?"

Elijah didn't like this. He'd felt uncomfortable ever since this game started, and he felt even more uncomfortable now. Something ugly hovered in the air tonight, and it wasn't only Joy Hardesty's self-righteousness.

"Now, boys," he said lightly. "Let's not argue."

"To hell with that," Davis said with a snarl. "I say he's cheatin'."

Elijah slid a glance at the ceiling in what was, for him, a prayer of sorts. Then he said, even more lightly, "Now, now. Let's not be hasty."

"Hasty, my ass. Nobody calls me a cheater and gets away with it." Cooper slammed his own hand on the table. He scowled at Davis, who scowled back.

The fourth man in the game, an amiable fellow named

Pete Walker, pushed his chair back as though trying to distance himself from the blossoming hostilities. Elijah didn't blame him, although he felt sort of responsible in the present circumstances. After all, he was the professional gambler in the group. Also, he didn't want a fight to break out in the store and bust up McMurdo's merchandise.

"Yeah?" said Davis, more belligerent now. "What the hell do you aim to do about it, Cooper? I'm callin' you a cheater, 'cause you're a damn cheater, and I know it."

"Damn your eyes, Davis! You can go straight to hell."

"Okay, boys, let's calm down now," Elijah murmured. He tried to pitch his voice to a soothing timbre.

Neither of the combatants noticed. Pete Walker shoved his chair farther out, stood up, and began edging away from the argument. He didn't say a word, but his gaze darted between the two men, and he looked scared.

"I ain't goin' to hell, Cooper. You're the cheater, and you're goin' to hell."

"Yeah? Well, maybe you'd like to join me there, Davis."

Oh, hell. Elijah saw Davis reach for his gun a split second after Cooper reached for his. He grabbed for Davis, intending to shove him out of the way of a bullet.

Cooper's bullet hit Elijah on his upper arm, sending a jolt of pain through him and making him jog Grant Davis's gun hand. Davis, disconcerted by the noise and Elijah's shove and bellow of pain, pulled the trigger.

Elijah felt a second bullet strike his thigh. He spun around as his leg crumpled under him. A third bullet—he never did know from whose gun that one came—struck him in the ribs. He thought he heard one of them crack in the heartbeat's worth of time it took for his brain to register the disaster that had befallen him.

Damn. One of the last things he thought before the

pain overwhelmed his senses and he passed out was that he hoped somebody would post his letter to Virginia. He wished he'd left a note or something asking that his grandfather's watch be sent to her, too.

The *very* last thing he heard was the terrible crash of breaking glass, one more shot, and a woman's high-pitched scream. He welcomed unconsciousness as a relief from that piercing shriek.

Chapter Three

"But you *can't* just go away!"

"Shhhh. Best lower your voice and give the poor lad some peace and quiet, lass. He needs it."

That was unquestionably true, but Joy couldn't take it in right now. Mr. McMurdo had, only a moment before, told her he was leaving her alone, in charge of a man who might die at any second, and her wits had gone quite distracted. Heavenly days, how in the world was she supposed to cope if Mr. McMurdo just up and left her? It was unthinkable.

She pressed a hand to her head, disarranging her carefully pinned-up braids. "I'll give him peace and quiet!" she said less stridently, but with not a whit less sincerity. "But you *can't* simply go away and leave me to nurse him all by myself! You *can't!*"

Although Mr. McMurdo's wrinkled face appeared thoughtful through his whiskers—somber, even—his twinkly blue eyes looked as though they were laughing at her. Joy didn't appreciate it at all. That man lying on the bed in Mr. McMurdo's spare room might well *die*, for the love of mercy. Mr. McMurdo couldn't simply abandon her here with him.

"Pisht, lass, ye'll do fine. I dug out the bullets and stitched and patched him up. I even used some of my own special homemade medicine. There's plenty of it left in the cupboard to daub on the wounds when you have to change his bandages. And that willow-bark concoction will serve him fine if he turns feverish. And there's laudanum in the cupboard yonder.

"The poor fellow mostly needs sleep to heal, you know, and you can surely give him that. His body will do the rest, with the help of those medicaments, God's grace, and your gentle nursing. That good chicken soup will do the lad a world of good when he can take some, and you can find asparagus growing wild up by the river. And there's plenty of fish there, too." He nodded. "Fresh vegetables, fish. That's what the lad'll be needin' when he can eat solid food again. In the meantime, he can drink the soup."

"If the good Lord wills it," Joy said mechanically, without really meaning it.

"Of course," McMurdo murmured. "But I'd try the chicken soup anyway."

Joy saw him smile. She couldn't think of one single, solitary amusing thing about this situation. In truth, while she knew she wasn't a particularly sterling person, she wondered what she'd done to deserve this brand of revenge. It seemed too hard, too cruel.

She began to wring her hands. She didn't have any idea what Mr. Perry needed, but she had a strong feeling it was more than chicken soup and fresh vegetables. And, unlike her mother, Joy didn't have a direct connection to

God. She didn't know what He had in mind for the sinner lying unconscious on that bed, but she feared she was a poor excuse for an attendant by which to do it.

"Oh, Mr. McMurdo, please! *Please* don't leave me alone with him. What if he should take a turn for the worse in spite of your chicken soup and medicine?"

"I'm sure it wouldn't hurt to read the good Lord's Word aloud to him."

"Read the good. . . . ?" This time she knew he was amusing himself at her expense because he winked and grinned. She resented his attitude, and wondered if she were wicked to do so. Probably.

She thought of something else. "But where will *I* sleep? He's on the only bed in the back room."

"I'll set up a cot for you in the room with the lad, Joy. Ye'll be fine."

"You expect me to sleep in the same room with him?"

"Shhh, lass." Mr. McMurdo seemed to have to struggle to contain his merriment. Joy wanted to scream. "The poor boy's in much too bad shape to take advantage o' ye, lass."

"I suppose so." She frowned, and knew she should be putting up a stronger resistance. If only her mother were here. "Oh, but—"

"Joy, m'dear, there's truly no impropriety in the sleeping arrangements. The only thing you have to worry about is poor Mr. Perry. If the worst happens, well, if there's one thing you can do to a turn, it's pray over a body. If the poor fellow slips his hold on this world, ye're the best-qualified lady in the territory to pray him into the next, unless I miss my guess."

Joy was pretty sure the old man didn't mean his assessment of her qualifications as a compliment. She might have taken him to task if terror hadn't submerged her mother's principles inside of her and rendered her speechless. A soft groan from the insensible patient lying on the bed behind them made panic bubble up in her like boiling water. To her horror, she felt tears sting her eyes. Her mother would have been appalled. Joy was pretty appalled herself, but for a different reason.

Speech returned in a heartbeat. "But, Mr. McMurdo, I'm *not* qualified! Not as a doctor. I don't know what to do for gunshot wounds. Truly, you might be jeopardizing the poor man's life by leaving him in my care."

He winked again. Joy stamped her foot. "Stop that! I'm telling the truth! It's not fair to him to leave him with only me to watch over him."

"Tut, tut, child. Whilst you were sick, your friend Mr. Thrash told me you'd taken an intensive course of nursing in Boston."

"Well, yes. Yes, I did, but I didn't expect to have to use my skills all by myself. I expected to have someone supervising me. At least at first." *Jerusalem!* Without somebody at her back telling her what to do, Joy was good for nothing; her mother had told her so over and over and over. She'd never done anything all by herself in her whole life. She'd always had a strong presence behind her, pushing her, scolding her, giving her intricate instructions. How could she function alone?

Already she felt paralysis creeping over her. Her limbs felt like lead, her brain functions had congealed; she couldn't think; she was afraid to act. Mr. McMurdo *couldn't* leave her here to handle this crisis alone!

"Nonsense, child. You're as competent as the next person. More, probably. You merely have no confidence in yourself, but this experience will give it to you. You'll see how well you do. I trust you to do a wonderful job. You've had more medical training than most folks who pass themselves off as doctors here in the territory, I'll warrant."

But they'd had practice in their craft and trusted themselves. No matter how many complimentary words Mr. McMurdo used to make her feel better, Joy knew she was worthless without supervision. She didn't know how to say so, but only pleaded with her eyes. Her voiceless plea did as much good as her verbal ones had.

"If you found yourself under other circumstances with a wounded person, wouldn't you try to help even if there was nobody else around to assist you?"

"Well, of course. If there was no alternative."

"There. You see? Of course you would."

"But this is different!"

Mr. McMurdo reached into the cupboard and withdrew a pouch of tobacco, which he tossed into the bag he'd been packing. "Your Mr. Thrash said you were prepared to nurse the natives in Central America. Is poor Mr. Perry over there worth less than a jungle full of natives you've never met?"

Yes, Joy's brain shrieked. It did so silently, because Joy suspected she'd be showing herself up as a hypocrite if she said the word aloud. *Jerusalem!* To be thwarted in this manner by an old rogue like Alexander McMurdo maddened her. If only her mother were here. Her mother would know what to do.

"But—but Mr. Thrash had special medicines made in Boston for his expedition, Mr. McMurdo. He was prepared for all sorts of contingencies. I—I don't have anything with me here."

"Ah, but I do, lass. Ye'll do fine."

At once, a vision of her mother standing toe-to-toe with Alexander McMurdo entered Joy's head and made her heart spasm painfully. What a dreadful confrontation that would be. The thought made her cringe, and in an abrupt about-face, she decided she was glad her mother wasn't here. That poor man on the bed might die, but at least Joy wouldn't have to endure his death and her mother's condemnation both.

No matter what happened to Elijah Perry, in her mother's eyes it would be Joy's fault. Unless he recovered. Then it would be God's merciful will. Joy narrowed her eyes as the injustice of those judgments played at the corner of her brain. She didn't dwell on it because there was no time and she was so frightened.

"Please, Mr. McMurdo. Be reasonable. Can't you postpone your visit for only a little while? Even another two or three days? Until Mr. Perry's out of danger? Surely that family can spare you for the sake of a seriously wounded man, can't they?"

"Oh, aye. I expect they might, but I gave my word, you see. This is Cody and Mellie's first baby together, and I promised to stand godfather to the wee mite and take care of their little Katie whilst Mellie rests up."

Joy blinked, her chaotic thoughts diverted. "Their little Katie?"

"Aye."

"But you said this was their first baby."

"Together."

"You mean they have another child—separately?" How had the couple managed that? Adoption, perhaps?

"Aye, lass. Little Katie, from Mellie's first marriage."

"Oh. I see." Joy's heart hurt as she thought how sad it would be to be left a widow with a child, especially out here where there was no employment and perishingly few people. Women had such a difficult time in the world without a man or a family to provide for them. She couldn't even imagine being left a widow in Rio Hondo, in the middle of this hostile nowhere.

"Aye. Melissa divorced her first husband and married up with Cody a little over two years ago."

Compassion fled, a victim of shock. "Divorce?"

Mac winced, and Joy realized she'd spoken quite shrilly. But divorce? Divorce was disgraceful and sinful and went against everything she had ever been taught was right in the world. Her nose wrinkled in reaction.

Mac laughed at her. "Don't get prune-faced about our dear Mellie, lass. Ye're quite a one for the Bible. Recollect that verse tellin' folks to let the good Lord judge us." He tapped her on the head. "Ye've got enough to do what with takin' care of yourself, lass—and poor Elijah Perry over there—without goin' around condemnin' other folks before ye know them. Ye needn't be doin' the Lord's work for Him. He's plenty competent. He can judge Mellie for Himself, I reckon."

Joy experienced the strangest sensation when Mr. McMurdo's finger touched her once, twice, thrice, very lightly, on her head. It was a tingly feeling that started with his finger and sparkled through her body from top to toe. It was very curious, and the novelty of the physical sensation was only augmented by the sparkles she saw dancing in the air. She shut her eyes against them, shook herself, and prepared to argue some more.

Mr. McMurdo forestalled her. "Lass, I know ye'd like to quarrel with me for a few more hours, but I don't have time for it right now. I have to get to the O'Fannins' place before Cody sends out a search party."

Joy forgot about the bizarre feelings in her body and the odd sparkles in the air. "No! No, you simply can't leave me here alone with that man. I'm not fit to nurse him! Besides, it's . . . it's improper."

"Improper?" Tipping his head to one side, McMurdo looked at her with the kindest expression Joy had ever seen directed at her. There was something in his face that spoke eloquently, both of his faith in her and of his pity for her.

Nobody'd ever pitied her before. Especially nobody

53

like Alexander McMurdo, a canny old Scottish scoundrel whom her mother would stigmatize as a tool of Satan. Joy didn't like it.

Stiffening her spine, she said in a voice that was even stiffer, "Very well. I suppose you won't be swayed, and there's no help for it. I shall do my best."

"Ye'll do fine, lass. Trust yourself for once."

His smile was so sweet, and touched something so deep within her, that Joy felt a compelling urge to burst into tears. *Ridiculous!* She grimaced to make up for the emotions tumbling around in her belly. Her mother would surely berate her for displaying so fruitless a thing as sentiment when what she needed was resolution.

Don't waste your time in crying over the wicked, Joy Hardesty. The Lord expects action from his servants.

Yes, Mother.

Action be hanged. Joy was scared to death.

McMurdo finished packing his bag and loaded it onto his horse. The last thing he did before he left for the O'Fannins' ranch was show Joy a beautifully embroidered christening gown. He was taking it to the baby, a little boy they'd named Arnold after Cody O'Fannin's favorite cousin.

"What do you think, Joy? Think their newborn ranch hand will suffer embarrassment to be gowned in this thing?" He held the dress up for her inspection.

Joy's heart, which she generally tried to keep packed with cotton wool and hidden away so people wouldn't suspect how tender it was, melted, along with her panic. "Oh, how beautiful!" She reached out and fingered the fine embroidery. "Wherever did you get such a lovely christening gown?"

He winked at her. "I have me own ways, child."

She was so charmed by the idea of a tiny infant wearing that delicate gown for his christening that she forgot to resent Mac's wink and sly words. "Any mother would love to be given so beautiful a christening gown, Mr. McMurdo. I'm sure Mrs. O'Fannin will cherish it forever." Joy would have cherished it, had it been given to her for her own child. Not that she'd ever have a child. Who'd ever admire Joy Hardesty enough to plant a child in her?

"I'm sure she will, too. Y'know, Joy, I have a feeling you and Mellie could become fast friends."

Fast friends with a divorcée? Most unlikely. Joy pinched her lips together and didn't say so, feeling rather righteous about her forbearance. Instead, she asked, "But how do babies get christened out here, Mr. McMurdo? I didn't think Rio Hondo had a church." Which only went to show once more how depraved a place it was.

"Mr. Horgan, the circuit rider, pops by from time to time. He'll be here in a few weeks, and little Arnold can come to town and be christened then."

"A circuit rider. Oh, my." Never, not once, had Joy envisioned living anywhere in the United States or its territories so unsettled as to have no churches. Auburn, Massachusetts, fairly teemed with them.

"Well, I'd best be off."

Mac whisked the baby gown from Joy's slack fingers, sending up a puff of those strange sparkles. They must be a figment of her fevered brain—or dust particles shining in the sunlight. Of course. That was it. The wind blew constantly here, and there was always dust in the air. Those sparkles were the result of sun and dust. That was what they were. They weren't mysterious at all.

Then the import of Mac's words hit her.

He was leaving! In fact, he was walking out the door as she stood there contemplating dust. Her insides gave a hard twinge, and she hurried after him, wringing her hands. "I hope you won't be gone too long, Mr. Mc-Murdo."

He winked again. "Didn't know you cared, Joy, m'dear."

Unfamiliar with teasing, Joy sputtered several unconnected syllables. The old man patted her on the shoulder.

"Don't take on so, dear. Ye'll do fine with our poor Mr. Perry. You're just what the fellow needs."

She shook her head hard. "I don't think so."

"Sure, y'are." He turned and put his foot in the saddle. "And he's exactly what you need, too."

And then, before Joy could react to his appalling words, Mr. McMurdo kneed his mount and they trotted off in a cloud of dust. She stared after him, flapping the powdery earth away from her face and feeling almost too frightened to move.

She'd never had to shoulder so heavy a responsibility without a strong hand propelling her in the right direction and telling her what to do. Without her mother or someone almost as strong—nobody was quite as strong as Joy's mother—to guide her, she couldn't seem to focus her thoughts or her energy. She felt like steam from a kettle dissipating into the air; like a pile of beans without the bag around them. She was a glob of clay with no one to mold her. Clay couldn't mold itself, for heaven's sake.

"Oh, dear."

She walked to the wagon yard gate and watched Mr. McMurdo and his horse ride down the beaten stretch of earth the citizens of Rio Hondo had—in a fit of outrageous optimism, in Joy's opinion—named Second Street. It certainly wasn't like any street Joy had ever seen before. The settled part of town ended not far away from the wagon yard, and Mac rode on beyond it.

In Auburn, of course, the road would have curved, or trees and buildings would have obscured her line of sight, and Mac would have been hidden within minutes. In these parts the land was so flat, and there was so little by way of plant life or humanity between anything and anything else, that Joy could see him getting smaller and smaller and smaller, until he was no more than a tiny black dot moving against the anemic yellow-brown of the desert.

Eventually the prairie swallowed up the black dot, and she was left all alone, staring at nothing. With a gun-shot stranger whom she was required to nurse. With a man whose very way of life was anathema to her and who, moreover, might die any second.

She heaved a heavy sigh. "I expect there's no help for it."

Feeling overburdened and intensely inadequate, Joy shut the wagon yard gates, bolted them against visitors—she didn't feel up to nursing Elijah Perry and running Mac's business, too—and, with feet of lead, walked back into McMurdo's house.

"What am I supposed to do with you, Mr. Perry?" she muttered as she stared down at the wounded man.

His formerly swarthy complexion was a pale, sickly color today. His hair and mustache, which had seemed wickedly jaunty before, now lay limp against his skin. With trembling fingers, Joy brushed the hair back from his forehead and noticed that his hairline was receding. Leaning closer—but not too close, since the man was a miserable sinner and she didn't dare—she saw that his hair was thinning on top. This sign that he was a mere human male and, therefore, subject to the same mortification of the flesh as the rest of the world, comforted her strangely.

His skin had been tanned where the sun could reach it. The rest of him, Joy noticed, was more olive than pink.

She wondered if his ancestors had come from some sunny Mediterranean clime. His skin didn't have the pasty white pallor of her own. The white bandages Mac had wrapped around his wounds looked stark against his darker skin.

"Oh, dear," she murmured again. "Whatever am I supposed to do now?"

The notion of nursing this fellow all by herself had kept her stomach pitching uncomfortably ever since Mac had told her she'd have to do it. Now she pressed a hand to her midsection and commanded her innards to stop heaving. They didn't, and she sighed again.

"I suppose what I should do is think calmly about what Mother would tell me to do."

Her stomach rebelled violently. Joy shut her eyes and prayed for strength.

All right. Perhaps her mother was a little too potent an influence to contemplate at the moment. "What would the nursing teachers have told me to do at school in Boston?"

The teachers at the nursing school in Boston, while firm and demanding, had been much more soft-spoken and kindly disposed toward her than her mother had ever been. The thought of them didn't make Joy want to vomit. She took it as a sign that she should attempt to use them as her guides in this present instance.

"A sustaining broth," she muttered.

The nursing teachers in Boston had advocated broths and thin soups as preferable to solid foods for an injured patient. Water was best of all, but often patients—particularly male patients—objected to having nothing to support them but water. Thank heavens Mr. McMurdo had prepared some chicken soup already.

Joy went to the kitchen and found the pot simmering on the stove. She lifted the lid, sniffed, and decided it smelled quite tasty. "Good. I won't have to cook for a day or so."

She thought about the asparagus growing wild by the river and felt a sudden craving for fresh green vegetables. Frowning, she told herself not to be foolish. She couldn't leave this man by himself while she went sauntering off to the river.

"Later," she promised herself. If she managed to keep the poor fellow alive for another two days, she'd reward herself with a trip to the river. She'd walked up there before, when she was recovering from her own illness and feeling discouraged because Mr. Thrash and his party had ventured forth without her. The Spring River was only the equivalent of a couple of Auburn city blocks away, to the north, and it was surrounded by marshland and even some trees. She could catch fish there, too. Fish and asparagus would provide the patient with a light but strengthening meal when he could handle solid foods.

Because she anticipated fever, she mixed up some of the willow-bark tea McMurdo had recommended. She also got the bottle of laudanum down from the cupboard, and set a glass out so that she could mix some laudanum and water should it prove necessary. She pumped fresh water at the kitchen sink into a pitcher and set it beside the glass, just in case.

She rummaged through some of Mr. McMurdo's medical supplies a while longer and found some antiseptic tablets. *Good.* She could soak Mr. Perry's bandages after she'd laundered them. She was pleased that she'd thought of soaking the bandages, cleanliness being next to godliness and all that.

There. She was rather proud of herself that she was now prepared. Her mother would have commended her. Or, at least—Joy tried very hard never to be boastful— her mother wouldn't have chastised her for being *un*prepared. In any event, since most of her life had been spent trying with every breath to stay on her mother's extremely small charitable side, Joy experienced a feeling of relief, and that lightened her mood.

In furtherance of her need to stay in her dead mother's good graces, Joy made sure Mac's supply of bandages, pins with which to fasten them, and a crock of his healing balm were set out in case she needed them. She opened the crockery pot full of medicine, sniffed, and wrinkled her nose. What was in that stuff? It was greasy and smelled of herbs, and was nothing at all like the medicines she'd had access to in Boston. Well, that was nothing to the purpose. This was what she had, and this was what she'd use.

The idea of changing that man's bandages assaulted her and made her stomach heave again. She fought down her nausea with grim determination. She would do what she had to do, and that was that. If what she had to do entailed changing bandages on the nether limbs of a vile sinner, so be it. If it entailed touching all that naked flesh on Mr. Elijah Perry's body—*Jerusalem!* Joy controlled with difficulty the spurt of fright that ambushed her heart—but she controlled it.

All right then. She was prepared with broth and water, tea and medicine. Water and laudanum. Bandages and balm and antiseptic tablets. And training.

Ever since Joy had been old enough to understand the spoken word, she'd been taught, by look and tone, that she was intrinsically worth less than nothing—and Joy had been a good pupil. Now, in her twenty-fifth year, she knew she was inept and useless.

But she *had* gone to nursing school. She *did* know how to care for patients. She might very well be bad at it, but she knew how to do it. And she *would* do it. That man,

Elijah Perry, for all his immorality, deserved no less from her.

The idea that he might see the error of his ways and reform if she were to cure him occurred to Joy, and her mood lightened another fraction of an inch. Goodness, wouldn't that be something, if she, the least of God's creatures, led a sinner to the light?

Unlikely. But not impossible.

Besides, her mother wasn't here to berate her when she failed. That notion came to her out of the blue and made light explode within her.

Her mother wasn't here!

The only three human beings on the face of the entire earth who would know if she failed were herself, Alexander McMurdo, and Elijah Perry. And if she did fail, Elijah Perry would be dead, so that meant there were really only two.

She guessed she was being sinfully weak again, but the notion of having no witnesses to her undertaking of the nursing of that man in McMurdo's Wagon Yard suddenly appealed to her. She'd never been able to hide her flaws and errors before. Perhaps having been left here all alone to tend to the poor man wasn't such an awful prospect after all.

Joy felt, in fact, almost lighthearted when she finished taking stock of her supplies and tiptoed into the back room to check on her patient once more. Her relatively good mood vanished.

"Jerusalem. You look perfectly dreadful, Mr. Perry."

Joy felt his forehead with her hand. Thank heavens he didn't feel feverish yet. She prayed that would last although she didn't hold out too many hopes. From everything she'd been taught, a fever was to be expected in the case of sudden severe injury. She expected bullet wounds counted as sudden injuries, although the nursing teachers had been talking about carriage crashes or farming accidents or mishaps of that nature. They hadn't addressed gunfights. Of course, they lived in Boston. Boston was civilized. Not like Rio Hondo.

She decided not to think about that, but pulled a chair close to the bed. Picking up her patient's limp wrist, she found his pulse and counted the beats, measuring the time by the large clock on the dressing table across the room. "Fast," she murmured. "But not thready. You have a strong heart, Mr. Perry." Even if it was a black one. Presuming he had any heart at all. She decided not to think about that, either.

Mr. McMurdo had laid Elijah Perry's personal effects on the bedside table beside the kerosene lamp. Joy glanced at his belongings now, and felt a little spurt of sadness. How pathetic for a man to have only these few paltry earthly possessions to show for himself. Mr. Perry wasn't any spring chicken, after all. Yet a pair of spectacles in a leather case, a handsome silver-encased pocket watch, a folded piece of paper, some money, a multipurpose pocketknife, and a small leather-bound volume were all Joy discerned to mark the passage of the years of his life.

She picked up the book, wondering if it might be a Bible. "*The Moonstone,* by Wilkie Collins." A novel, with its pages neatly cut, all ready to read. She should have suspected as much from such a specimen as Elijah Perry.

Joy had never read a novel. Her mother said novels were works of the devil, and Joy, who had never considered doubting her mother, felt compelled to agree. Having nothing upon which to form an opinion by herself, she wondered about her mother's judgment now—and then reminded herself how easy it was to stray from the straight and narrow path.

The devil can make the most evil of things appear harmless, and don't you ever forget it, Joy Hardesty.

Yes, Mother.

She set the book down, determined to ignore it. Her mother would have burned it, and Joy supposed she should do likewise. Yet she couldn't quite make herself destroy someone else's property. Which only went to demonstrate another point of moral frailty in her character.

The watch was quite lovely and looked old. Its silver case was engraved with twining rose vines, and the initials *EJP* had been etched on the back. Joy smiled as she picked it up, intending to wind it. She could do this one small thing for Mr. Perry, if she could do nothing else. As she touched the stem, she was surprised to hear a tiny click, and the back of the watch opened up. She must have pressed a hidden catch.

"Oh!" A curl of fine blond hair fell out of the watch-case and landed in her lap.

In a fright borne of long experience, she glanced at Mr. Perry, hoping he hadn't seen what, to Joy, amounted to a terrible indiscretion if not an outright sin on her part. Then she sighed, annoyed with herself. How silly she was, to be sure. The poor man was unconscious. There was no way he'd even know she'd opened his watch case, much less be able to chide her for doing it.

She shook her head, dismayed that her first reaction to an accident was fear for her own hide. She should have had a care for Mr. Perry's property before ever thinking about her own culpability. Well, she'd always been incompetent; her every action merely emphasized the truth.

Still, she wondered about that lock of hair as she replaced it in the watchcase. Her heart was strangely touched to think that this man, this hardened reprobate, should carry such a token of affection around with him.

Who had given him the single tress? His mother? A sister or a sweetheart?

It was difficult for Joy to imagine a man like Elijah Perry as a member of a family, yet he must have been once. Was the person who'd given him that lock of hair still living? Did she await word from him? Was she dead? Was this a souvenir of a remembered and well-loved person from Mr. Perry's innocent past? If, of course, he'd ever been innocent. Joy had always assumed people were innocent until ruined, but she allowed to herself that she was no judge, the circles in which she'd traveled until now having been fairly circumscribed.

She shook her head, feeling unaccountably tender, finished winding Mr. Perry's watch, and set it back on the table. Her gaze fell on the folded paper as she did so.

"I wonder if this is something you intended to post," she murmured as she picked it up and turned it over.

"Miss Virginia Gladstone. In Baltimore, Maryland." She glanced from the addressed letter to Elijah Perry, frowning. "It looks to me as though you had intended to send this to Miss Gladstone. You've even affixed one of those newfangled postage stamps to it."

Oh, dear. This presented yet another problem. Joy hated having to make decisions on her own. She wasn't used to it. She'd never had to make so many decisions all by herself in her life. Tapping her cheek with the letter, she pondered her options. It did not occur to her to read the letter's contents.

"I wonder if Miss Virginia Gladstone is the one who gave you that lock of hair."

The notion appealed to Joy, although she didn't know why it should. "Perhaps she's waiting for you to return to her in Maryland. Maybe she's your sweetheart." She could imagine Mr. Perry having a sweetheart because, although he wasn't exactly young, he was rather attractive. He didn't look like the romantic sort, but that only intensified the incongruity of his having a sweetheart and, therefore, the appeal of the notion.

"If she *is* a sweetheart, or a family member, I expect she'd like to know you've suffered a serious injury." Of course, that meant Joy would have to do the telling, since Mr. Perry was in no condition to do so.

"Oh, dear. Such a letter will require great diplomacy in the writing." She couldn't imagine a sister or sweetheart taking comfort from knowing Mr. Perry had been shot all to goodness.

Her mother would have boldly but kindly told Miss Virginia Gladstone in Baltimore, Maryland, that Mr. Perry's sinful life had finally caught up with him and that he'd been shot while gambling, which was no more than he deserved, although the Lord might deem it advisable to spare him. Even though she knew her mother was right—her mother was always right—Joy couldn't make herself be quite that brutally honest.

No. What she would do was enclose Mr. Perry's letter to Miss Gladstone with a letter of her own, briefly stating that Mr. Perry had met with an accident, that he was currently being nursed by Joy in Rio Hondo, New Mexico Territory, and that Joy would keep Miss Gladstone informed of his progress. Yes. That should do it without worrying Miss Gladstone too much.

After another comprehensive check of her patient's condition, Joy decided there was nothing more she could do for him at the moment. She sailed out of the room and into Mr. McMurdo's parlor, settled herself at his desk, and set about writing a letter to a stranger in Baltimore, Maryland, about another stranger in Mr. McMurdo's back room.

Chapter Four

Elijah wondered if he'd gone to hell. His body burned with what seemed like unholy fire, and every joint, muscle, and tendon hurt, from his feet to his head. If this wasn't hell, Elijah hoped he'd die soon and get it over with. If it was hell, Elijah was sorry he hadn't believed in the devil sooner and spared himself this torment.

"Please don't wiggle, Mr. Perry. I know this hurts, but it can't be helped."

That voice didn't sound like a demon's. It didn't sound any too friendly, but . . .

"Aaaagh! Damn it, that hurts!"

"If you please, Mr. Perry, do try not to swear. I'm attempting to help you."

Oh, yeah. He remembered now. Cracking one eye open, Elijah discerned Miss Joy Hardesty, incongruously named would-be missionary and employee of Mr. Alexander McMurdo, proprietor of the wagon yard and mercantile establishment in which Elijah'd been shot.

She did something else to his chest that sent a shock of pain through him, and he groaned, squeezed his eyes tightly together, and tried not to cry. Since he thought it would be prudent not to rile her, he bit down on his tongue and didn't swear out loud again. *Damn, that hurt.*

At least he was alive. Elijah tested the knowledge and discovered it didn't thrill him. Frowning, he tried to recall why that should be. *Ah, yes.* He remembered that now, too. He was bored to flinders with life and everything in it. For good reason.

"Damn!" Making a tremendous effort, he pried his eyes open again and looked up at Joy, who frowned down at him in disapproval. No surprise there. "Sorry, ma'am. That hurts."

"I'm sure it does."

How in the name of mercy did she do that? he wondered. Talk without moving her lips. It sure made her look mean. He already knew she didn't like him and, he surmised, she didn't want to be helping him. But damn it, he was a wounded man and in pain. It occurred to him to wonder why she was helping him, but didn't dwell on the incongruity of her actions because his brain wasn't working right.

Instead of reflecting upon imponderables, he closed his eyes against the grim picture of Joy working him over and tried to remember what had happened. There had been a card game—which didn't seem right, somehow.

Oh, that's right. They'd set it up in McMurdo's mercantile; that was why it didn't seem right. Why had they done that? Elijah couldn't drum up an answer, although something made him think Mac had fostered the game. That didn't seem right either, so he stopped trying to muddle it out. There would be time for such discoveries later.

He moved on.

All right, they'd been playing poker. Somebody had cheated, somebody else had objected, and he—fool that he was—had tried to intervene before anyone got hurt. It went without saying that, for his efforts, *he'd* been the one who got hurt. Hell, when would he learn to mind his own business?

He cleared his throat. "How long have I been out, ma'am?"

"This is the third day since the . . . accident."

Diplomatic little prune, wasn't she? He tried to look around the room, but found his body didn't want to move. The least little twitch sent shafts of pain spearing him in every direction.

"Stop moving! Jerusalem, how do you expect me to change this bandage if you won't lie still, Mr. Perry?"

He moaned and shut his eyes again, too weak to answer. Her voice pierced him, and most unpleasantly. He managed to mumble, "Sorry."

Whatever she was doing to his chest was about to kill him. He wondered if the bullet had broken a rib, but was too weak to ask.

God, he was thirsty. He didn't mention it, because he didn't want her to shriek at him again. Damn, his head hurt. Everything hurt. Hoping he might get softer treatment from another source, after he'd rested up from his earlier attempt to move, he opened his eyes once more and croaked, "Where's Mac?"

Was it his imagination, or did her lips prune up even more than they'd already been pruned? His vision wasn't the best, and he couldn't be sure. She didn't sound happy, however, when she said, "He had to go away for a while. He left me in charge of you."

Glory. Mac must loathe him for causing trouble in his mercantile if he'd left him in the care of Miss Joy "Hates

Everybody" Hardesty. He sighed heavily and decided there was no justice in life. Or maybe there was, and this was it. What a discouraging thought.

Very carefully, using the politest words he could think of under the circumstances, when he could hardly think at all, he said, "May I please have a drink of water, ma'am?"

Speaking such a long sentence exhausted him, and he would have collapsed if he hadn't already been collapsed. His eyes closed, his head swam, and he subsided into a semiconscious wash of misery. His body felt like one enormous, bleeding wound.

How long he hovered between wakefulness and sleep, he didn't know. He had a feeling Joy had quit torturing him, although his chest still hurt like the devil. He wondered if she enjoyed hurting people and decided she probably did. She looked like the kind who would. After what seemed like hours, he felt a small hand touch his head. He cranked his eyelids up over eyes that felt as it somebody had thrown grit in them.

"Here, Mr. Perry. I brought you some nice, fresh, cold water. Perhaps this will make you feel more the thing."

The gentleness of her voice surprised him. He managed to slur a whispery, "Thanks."

She lifted his head—an activity that sent unspeakable anguish through his poor, wounded body—and he drank deeply of the water. She was right. It was fresh and cold and slid down his throat like heavenly nectar. He drank the contents of the tin cup greedily, dripping water onto his chin. He was too weak to wipe it away and felt foolish and unmanly when Joy gently mopped him up. Almost too exhausted to speak after having done so energetic a thing as drink water, he whispered, "Thanks."

"You're welcome."

She bustled off, and Elijah sank into sleep. He wasn't

sure how long she'd been gone when he sensed her at his side again. When he lifted an eyelid, he guessed she'd been gone only a minute or two, because she looked exactly the same.

"I know you're in great pain, Mr. Perry."

That was an understatement if he'd ever heard one. He didn't even try to indicate his agreement, but only blinked up at her. She reminded him of a drill sergeant, the way she stood so rigid and straight. Only the drill sergeants Elijah had known didn't fold their hands in front of them that way. Nuns did, if he recalled correctly. The ones he'd known were mean and seemed to enjoy torturing people, too. Maybe she was a nun in disguise.

"Mr. McMurdo left some laudanum, but I didn't want to administer it to you without asking if you'd like to take it first. The teachers at the nursing school in Boston said that some people react poorly to laudanum. I'm sure it would ease your pain, if you can tolerate it. Would you like me to mix you some laudanum and water?"

Laudanum. Thank God. "Yes, please," he whispered. Mary Ellen Loveless, the whore dearer to Elijah's heart than any other female of his present acquaintance, had been addicted to laudanum before Elijah had helped her dry out. Elijah wasn't about to scorn the drug on Mary Ellen's account. If it would ease his pain, he'd take it.

"All right. I'll stir some up for you."

He heard her counting drops, and could picture her intense concentration in his mind's eye. Her forehead would be wrinkled, her lips pinched, and her visage grim.

Not a cheerful specimen of womanhood, Joy Hardesty, whatever her name. He wondered if there was any joy in her at all, and decided there most likely wasn't. His conclusion gave rise to the speculation as to whether she'd been a morose, fretful baby, or if she'd had the ebullience of childhood whipped out of her. The thought occurred to him that perhaps her parents had meant her name as a cynical irony. He realized he was even weaker than he'd thought when the notion made him sad.

On the other hand, maybe she was one of those people who liked to see other people suffer. She sure stirred that concoction of hers with vigor. The spoon clanking against the tin cup as she whisked the mixture sounded like thunder to his tender ears.

"All right, Mr. Perry. I'm sure you'll find this an uncomfortable proposition, but I shall have to prop your head up again. I beg your pardon if I hurt you. I don't mean to do so."

Maybe she wasn't cold-blooded after all. At least her heart seemed to be in the right place in this instance. He managed another weak "Thanks" before the breath was punched out of him by the agony of her lifting his head from the pillow. Sweet Lord, have mercy, if he survived this ordeal, Elijah swore he'd never complain again. He knew he was lying even as the vow crossed his mind.

He got the medicine down, though. He only hoped it would stay down. The thought of being sick to his stomach on top of everything else held no appeal at all. Perspiration dripped from his body when the ordeal ended, and he sank back onto his pillow with relief. His eyes popped open when he felt a cool, damp cloth pressing against his head.

"I'm only bathing your forehead, Mr. Perry."

Joy's voice sounded strained. Elijah wondered if she hated hurting him as much as he hated being hurt. He didn't have strength enough to ask. He was feeling wearier than he could ever remember feeling in his life. One thing troubled him so much, however, that he felt compelled to speak again.

"Did anyone else get hurt when the shooting started, ma'am?"

She transferred her gaze from her cloth to his face. Elijah realized she had truly fine eyes—big and brown and soft. They didn't look like the eyes of a heartless woman; rather, they seemed to hold a world of doubt and trouble—unless it was his fevered imagination making him think so.

"No, Mr. Perry. You were the only one. I fear Mr. Davis and Mr. Cooper both drew their firearms, and you were hit by bullets from both of their guns."

Elijah sighed. That figured. If it wasn't just like him to try to bust up a gunfight and take bullets from both participants that had been meant for each other, he didn't know what was.

"Evidently there's no such thing as a lawman in this place, either, so I fear both men got off scot free."

That didn't bother him; he was used to it. One other thing did, however.

"How many times?" He was pretty sure he'd been shot more than once, but he couldn't remember. And, since every square inch of him hurt, he couldn't tell from the feel of things.

"How many times were you shot?"

"Yeah."

"Mr. McMurdo had to draw two bullets out of you. One from your leg and one from your upper arm. Another creased your skull. You were lucky in that the one that hit your chest didn't break any ribs, and only scored a rather deep rut in your side between two of them."

Lucky, was he? Elijah was in no condition to argue, no matter how much he disagreed. Hell, from the pain in his chest, he knew that if he'd turned just a little bit to the side, the bullet might have penetrated his heart and put him out of his misery forever. His luck remained unrelenting, though, and he still lived. There was obvi-

ously no easy way out of this life, at least not for Elijah
Perry.

He felt just as empty as ever inside, and very gloomy,
when he drifted off to sleep.

Joy was full of doubts when she handed her letter addressed to Miss Virginia Gladstone in Baltimore, Maryland, to the buckskin-clad freight-wagon driver. She'd
never succumbed to an impulse in her life before now,
and the fact that she'd done so this time frightened her.

What if Elijah Perry hadn't already posted his letter
because he hadn't wanted to? What if Miss Virginia
Gladstone hated him and never wanted to hear from him
again? What if—

"Oh, dear."

She pressed a hand to her forehead as she watched the
man slip her letter into his canvas mail sack. He tugged
on the brim of his hat and cocked an eyebrow in inquiry.

"Anything else you want posted, ma'am?"

At least he was polite. Joy managed a small smile.
"No, thank you."

She had acquaintances in Boston and Auburn, of
course, but she didn't have the heart to write to them.
The idea of explaining this latest of her failures to the
folks back home made her stomach cramp. They'd learn
soon enough, as soon as she managed to earn her passage
back east—or as soon as correspondence from Mr. Hezekiah P. Thrash reached them. The notion daunted her,
and she decided not to think about it. She had enough to
do, what with nursing Elijah Perry and running Mr. Mc-
Murdo's mercantile establishment. Confessions and self-
recriminations could wait.

On the second day of her ordeal, she'd opened the
wagon yard gates again. She knew it was her duty to do
so. After all, while she couldn't mend wagon axles or

repair broken harnesses, as Mr. McMurdo did, she could tend the store, and he would surely expect her to do so. The citizens of Rio Hondo, few in number though they were, relied on McMurdo's to keep them supplied with candles and kerosene and flour and molasses and so forth. Besides, clerking in his store was what McMurdo was paying her for.

She'd never agreed to nurse gun-shot strangers as part of her employment. Still and all, it was her Christian duty to do so, and Joy was nothing if not a slave to duty.

"The train runs from Albuquerque back east now, ma'am, so's this letter won't be too long in gettin' to Baltimore," the wagon driver said.

Joy knew he was trying to make her feel better, but his assurance only made her heart speed up and her stomach cramp harder. What if she'd done the wrong thing in writing to Miss Gladstone? She should have asked Mr. Perry, she supposed, but he was still so perilously weak. Joy couldn't make herself burden him with a decision under the circumstances. So she'd made the decision for him, and now she couldn't stop worrying about it. She said, "Thank you," because she couldn't think of anything better to say.

She hoped she'd done the right thing. She felt very low as the wagon driver tipped his hat again and drove off through the gates. She waved at him, and then felt silly. Waving good-bye to someone seemed like such a Massachusetts thing to do. It didn't seem frontiersy at all. The man smiled and waved back, however, and she felt a little better.

With dragging feet, she made her way back into Mr. McMurdo's house to check on her patient. He'd been shot five days ago, and it seemed to her that he was finally showing signs of improvement. At least she didn't fret about him dying on her any longer. That was a relief for several reasons.

For one thing, she really wanted to walk up to the Spring River and pick some asparagus and try to catch a couple of fish. She needed a small break from her nursing duties, which had consumed her life from the moment Mr. McMurdo had left her to them.

For another thing, and on a more practical note, she didn't know how she'd get rid of the remains if he were to pass over while under her care. She didn't know anybody else in town—not that there were very many people in town—whom she could call upon to help her bury him.

The mere thought of a corpse rotting on that bed for days and days until Mr. McMurdo came back made her feel sick. The only people she'd seen in Rio Hondo besides Mr. McMurdo and his customers were cowboys sent in from nearby ranches, the surly telegraph operator Henry Wiggins—and she didn't want to ask him—and the people who worked in the Pecos Saloon. She wouldn't—she *couldn't*—ask anyone at the Pecos Saloon to help her. She'd rather die than set one foot inside the vile establishment. She was sure her mother's spirit would send a storm of locusts down from the heavens to nibble her to death if she dared do such a thing.

She also didn't know if Mr. Perry belonged to any particular religious faith. She doubted it. If, however, he should be, for example, a Baptist, she wouldn't have any idea what sorts of prayers to recite over the grave. If she could get a grave dug in the first place.

Aside from all that, she already had serious doubts about herself and her nursing abilities. If Mr. Perry should die, she'd feel sure she'd done something wrong in caring for him. As it was, she was in a state of nervous excitement all day long, fearing she'd somehow damage

him. Every time she had to change his bandages, she
went through the torments of hell.

Of course, this was partly due to the indelicacy inher-
ent in such an activity. Mr. Perry's naked body was
enough to make a gently reared female faint dead away,
even one who, like Joy, had been trained in nursing.
Imagine a maiden lady peering at a man's naked thigh,
much less putting her hands on it! And his thigh wasn't
the only unseemly part of his body in view when she had
to change his bandages, either. The mere thought made
her blush. Yet she'd done it, and done it well, for five
whole days now, and she felt a certain satisfaction in
knowing it. Mr. Perry was getting better, and it was
partly, at least a little bit, due to her good nursing.

"And God's grace," she added conscientiously before
taking a deep breath and venturing into the back room
again. She found Elijah Perry scowling at the door. Her
heart executed a crazy plunge, she fought the urge to turn
around and run away, and she wondered—for at least the
thousandth time—if she was truly cut out for the nursing
life. Perhaps it was a good thing after all that Mr. Thrash
had left her behind.

Her hands began to wring each other of their own ac-
cord in response to her anxiety. "Is there something the
matter, Mr. Perry?"

"Oh, no," he said in the most sarcastic tone she'd ever
heard. She frowned in reaction. "Nothing's the matter.
I've just been shot all to hell, I'm stuck in this room and
unable to move, and I can't even see outdoors. I can't
tell if it's raining or snowing or sunny out there. Can't
you open the damned curtains at least?"

"Please don't swear at me, Mr. Perry." Joy used her
most severe manner, borrowed from what she remembered of her mother. She was proud that her voice didn't
shake. In truth, this man frightened her—which merely

pointed out another one of her myriad flaws. The fellow was helpless, for heaven's sake; there was no reason she should fear him. Except that she was a moral coward. What a depressing thought.

"I beg your pardon, Miss Hardesty." His voice conveyed no contrition at all. "But can you please open the blessed curtains so that some blessed sunlight can get in? It's blessed dismal in here."

"My mother always advised me to keep the draperies drawn during the sunlight hours, Mr. Perry."

"Why? Did she think gloom was good for recovering patients?"

Joy frowned harder. "Not at all. She always kept the draperies drawn so as not to fade the furniture and carpets."

She saw him roll his eyes, and irritation bloomed in her bosom.

"Damn it, ma'am, I distinctly recall that Mac had the curtains open in this room before my . . . accident. If he doesn't give a crap about his furniture and rugs fading, I can't imagine why your mother should."

Furious, Joy snapped, "Nevertheless, I shall keep the curtains closed." It didn't matter what he wanted anyway, because *she* was the only one in this house able to get around. A smug sense of triumph soothed her irritated nerves. She knew it was sinful of her to take pleasure in Mr. Perry's incapacity. She did it anyway.

"Blast it, Miss Hardesty, your mother isn't here, and I am, and I sure as the devil won't fade."

"You might not fade, Mr. Perry, but Mr. McMurdo left his home and business establishment under my care. I may not do the job as well as he does, but I'm trying."

"You sure as hell are."

Joy frowned again, and her sense of triumph crumpled. Since he was undoubtedly a master at trivial conversation, she decided not to bandy barbs with him, but turned to tidy up the medicines she'd laid out on the top of Mr. McMurdo's dressing table.

"I suppose you're just like your mother," Elijah muttered at her back.

"I shall never be the woman my mother was, Mr. Perry, but I'm try—That is to say, I attempt every day to live up to her memory." Joy sniffed, something her mother was wont to do when aggrieved, which was most of the time. "My mother was a wonderful housekeeper."

"Was she?"

"Yes. And she *always* kept the draperies shut."

"Yeah, I'll bet she did."

She turned around and glared at him. "That's what got you into this mess in the first place."

He squinted at her. "What are you talking about now?"

"Betting!" she said triumphantly, pleased by her own cleverness. "Your sinful life has led you to this pass, Mr. Perry, and don't you forget it. I should think you'd welcome advice from a person of my mother's caliber."

"My sinful life," he grumbled, as if too disgusted to argue. "Cripes."

"My mother was a saint, Mr. Perry. Everyone said so."

"Yeah, right."

"You don't see *me* in your predicament, do you?" She peeked at him over her shoulder.

"No, ma'am." It didn't sound as though he considered it much to Joy's credit. He scratched his chin. "I don't suppose you can bring me a basin so I can shave myself."

"Don't be any more foolish than you can manage to be, Mr. Perry. You're in no condition to shave yourself. I'm sure you couldn't hold a razor if you tried, and you certainly couldn't balance a basin of water on your lap or handle the shaving cream."

"Well, damn it, my chin itches. I'm uncomfortable enough without itching to death, too."

Joy drew herself up straight and folded her hands primly. "If you're truly uncomfortable with your beard, I shall be glad to shave you, Mr. Perry."

He squinted at her. "You? What do you know about shaving a man?"

It sounded to Joy as if Mr. Perry couldn't imagine her within fifty feet of a man. She wished she could find fault with his reasoning, but she couldn't. She could, however, set him straight. "I took an extensive course in nursing in Boston. The teachers had us practice shaving patients, since many men seem to find a growing beard uncomfortable."

He looked at her doubtfully. "I don't know. . . ."

"Of course, if you prefer, I shall be happy to let your beard grow. When your bullet wounds begin to heal, I'm sure their itching will take your mind off the itching on your chin." She gave him a tight smile and thought, *So there*. She knew she was being childish.

"You're mean as a cat, you know that, Miss Hardesty?"

"I didn't know that cats were particularly mean, Mr. Perry."

"Yeah. That doesn't surprise me. But they like torturing helpless animals, too."

"I am *not* torturing you! I'm attempting to help you get better, and I resent your implication."

"It's no implication, ma'am. It's a statement of fact."

"Fine." Indignation swelled within her, and Joy would have taken great pleasure in thumping Mr. Elijah Perry with one of his pillows. Since she couldn't do such a thing, she turned on her heel and resumed tidying up his room. *What an ungrateful, peevish man!*

She tried her best to ignore him—which was not unlike trying to ignore a hippopotamus that had found its way into the room—but at last his grunts and groans became too loud to ignore. When she turned around and found him grimacing horribly and with his feet on the floor, she shrieked, "What do you think you're doing?"

"Getting up." Perspiration poured from his forehead. Joy could see from across the room that he was in agony. The muscles in his arms quivered like the jellied aspic that used to swim around her mother's ham loaf.

She raced to the bed. "Lie back down this minute, Mr. Perry! You mustn't jar your wounds this way!"

"Damn it, I want some light in here. I'm bored. I want to read my book."

"You couldn't hold a book if you wanted to! I'll read to you, if you want entertainment."

"I don't want to hear the damned Bible. I want something interesting."

"Don't you dare use profanity in reference to the Bible!"

"Let go of me, damn it! I need some light. I'm turning into a mushroom lying here in the dark."

Frustrated and worried almost to death that he'd die because she was being stubborn, Joy cried, "Oh, for heaven's sake, I'll open the curtains. Just lie still."

He collapsed on the bed as if he'd been holding out for this. His legs still dangled over the side. Joy waited, but he didn't lift them.

"Get back into bed, Mr. Perry," she commanded severely.

"I can't move any more," he said in a whimper, sounding as if it took his last faint ounce of energy to do so.

"Well, you can't simply lie there like that."

"I'll lift 'em in a minute. After I recover."

"You wouldn't be in this fix if you hadn't been so obstreperous."

81

"I wouldn't be in this fix if you weren't such a sour apple."

Joy ripped the curtain open, and its wooden rings made a loud racket against the curtain rod. Although she was embarrassed about having made so much noise, she didn't want to give Mr. Perry the satisfaction of knowing it, so she ripped the second curtain back the same way. A sour apple, was she? Well, maybe she was, but she knew her duty as a Christian.

Still, she didn't like seeing his naked legs hanging outside of the bedclothes that way. She wished he'd cover himself. Exhausted or not, a decent man would do his best to hide his nudity in front of a maiden lady.

Mr. Perry had very hairy legs. They were exceptionally muscular, too, and looking at them made Joy feel . . . something. She wasn't sure what emotion they evoked, but it wasn't one she'd felt before. It was one thing to view a man's naked extremities when one had to do so in the pursuit of one's nursing vocation. It was another thing to see them on other occasions.

Oh, dear. She turned around and realized light from the window now poured into the room. She could see those long, hairy legs of his even more clearly than before.

Her mother had disparaged her father so often in Joy's hearing that Joy seldom sought memories of him when she was in need. She did so today, however. As she busied herself with preparing Elijah Perry's shaving gear while endeavoring to ignore Elijah Perry's legs, she recited some Scripture to herself. Her father had been used to reciting verses when he was upset.

The seventh chapter of the Song of Solomon tiptoed into her mind. *"How beautiful are thy feet. . . ."*

No, no, no. That one would never do.

Annoyed with herself, Joy backtracked and began silently reciting the Forty-seventh Psalm. It had been one of her father's favorites, and Joy liked it, too, even though she was sure she shouldn't. Her mother had sniffed and said it reminded her of the Holy Rollers, but Joy's mother wasn't here, and Joy said it to herself anyway.

"O clap your hands, all ye people; shout unto God with the voice of triumph. For the Lord most high is terrible; he is a great King over all the earth. He shall subdue the people under us, and the nations under our feet."

His feet were long and slender. Joy had seen calluses on his soles.

She shook herself mentally and forced her mind back into her psalm. *"He shall choose our inheritance for us, the excellency of Jacob whom he loved. Selah."*

Selah. Joy loved that word. With a sigh, she turned with her tray full of shaving gear.

There were Elijah Perry's legs, hanging over the side of the bed, big as life, as he lay on his pillow with his eyes shut. She couldn't stand it another moment longer. With a combination of fury and fear raging inside her, she deposited her tray on Mr. McMurdo's dressing table with a clatter. "Oh, for heaven's sake! I'll help you get back under the covers."

Elijah looked exhausted. At Joy's exclamation, he opened one eye and had the audacity to grin at her. "Can't take it, huh? Too much man for you, am I?"

Joy felt herself get hot and hoped she wouldn't perspire. She hated perspiring out here because dust clung to the sweat, and it was bothersome to have to wash five or six times a day, especially when one had to pump that hard, hard water. It formed such a crust on the cooking utensils that Joy had taken to using vinegar on them to dissolve the mineral deposits. Frowning to let Elijah

83

know his wit wasn't appreciated, she said, "Don't be ridiculous, Mr. Perry."

"I'll try."

He truly sounded as though he found it difficult to speak. When she lifted his legs, Joy felt his muscles tense and heard his sharp intake of breath. She knew how much it must hurt him to have his wounds jostled in this manner. It was his own fault, though, and she tried not to feel sorry for him. Her mother would never have spared any sympathy for a wicked transgressor like Elijah Perry. Joy wished she'd inherited her mother's strength of spirit instead of her father's soft heart.

After she'd settled him under the covers, she said, "I shall now fetch your shaving gear—if you believe I can be trusted not to cut your throat with the razor."

She noticed that Elijah Perry's eyes could twinkle almost as devilishly as Alexander McMurdo's and wasn't surprised. They were both wretched sinners.

All at once she wondered why sinners should have all the fun in life. Immediately she shoved the question aside. Such random thoughts were indications that Satan was here, in this room, working away at her resolution. With a sigh, she wished her faith were stronger.

"Thank you for opening the curtains, Miss Hardesty," Elijah said faintly.

She pursed her lips, surprised that he'd bothered to thank her. "You're welcome."

She hated knowing she'd given in and done something of which her mother wouldn't have approved.

She hated it even more when sunlight poured into the room and made everything seem bright and cheerful. It wasn't fair of God to make Elijah Perry's suggestion seem right.

It occurred to Joy in that moment that nothing in life was fair.

Chapter Five

"After you've been shaved, I shall read some passages from the Bible. Then I shall read to you from your"— Joy took a deep breath—"novel." She endowed the word *novel* with all the contempt she'd been taught to feel for works of fiction.

"What's the matter, Miss Hardesty? Are you one of those folks who think novels are wicked?"

Elijah cocked one eyebrow, which gave him an ironic look that Joy didn't appreciate. She sniffed. "My mother believed novels to be works of the devil, Mr. Perry."

"Actually, I think this one's the work of a gent named Wilkie Collins." His voice was as dry as the weather.

Joy sniffed again. "You know what I mean and are merely attempting to be clever. Novels are frivolous. They're not at all educational, and they promote sloth and indolence."

"Do they really? I never thought novels had so much

power. I'll respect 'em more now that I know."

Joy eyed him. "I don't believe sloth and indolence are characteristics for which one should strive, Mr. Perry."

"Balderdash. I've never once been slothful or indolent because of a novel, Miss Hardesty."

This time it was Joy who lifted one eyebrow. She was fairly certain her own expression didn't come near to matching his for irony, but she did her best.

He grinned. "It's true. I was indolent and slothful before I ever read a novel."

"I'm sure that's true."

"Novels are entertaining. Don't you ever feel the need to relax and stop working for a second or two?"

Yes. As a matter of fact, Joy felt such needs often. Now, for instance. Her limited energy was one of her many weaknesses.

Inertia. Your middle name should have been Inertia, Joy Hardesty.

"I try very hard not to succumb to such impulses, Mr. Perry," she said grimly.

"Oh, come on now. You can't work all the time. Everybody needs to rest every now and then."

"That's what prayer is for." Joy hated it when she sounded self-righteous, but she did then.

"Listen, Miss Hardesty, even the good Lord advised relaxing every now and then."

She scowled at him. "And how would *you* know?" She sounded nasty, and was ashamed of herself. She'd never let him know it.

"I know more than you give me credit for, Miss Holier-Than-Thou Hardesty," Elijah said with some asperity. "For instance, just take a gander at the Forty-seventh Psalm: 'O clap your hands, all ye people; shout unto God with the voice of triumph.' That doesn't sound to me like God expects us to do nothing but work and pray. It sounds to me as if he expects us to have some fun every now and then, too."

Joy realized her mouth had dropped open, so she shut it again and hoped Mr. Perry hadn't noticed. Good heavens, was he a mind reader as well as an unprincipled gambler? "How do you know that psalm?" she asked sharply.

"I told you. I know more than you think I do." He looked smug.

"Hmph." Annoyed, she tucked a cloth in at the neck of his nightshirt and spread it over his chest. Although she tried very hard to be gentle, he grunted when she smoothed it over his bandaged side. She would have apologized if he weren't such an exasperating man.

Because she was unsettled by his uncanny recitation of the very verses she'd been thinking herself, Joy said astringently, " 'In all labor there is profit: but the talk of the lips tendeth only to penury.' Proverbs fourteen: twenty-three."

Elijah clamped his chin down on the cloth where it had puffed up against his face. "Oh, yeah? Well, what about Psalm one-oh-four, Miss Joy Hardesty? 'Man goeth forth unto his work and to his labor until the evening.' Did you hear that? *'Until the evening.'* Not every second of every day. Even God rested on the seventh day, for Pete's sake."

"He didn't gamble during the rest of His days," Joy snapped. "He was doing something useful."

"Creating this blasted vale of tears and the people who clutter it up. Is that such a great thing?"

She looked up at him, stunned. She'd never heard such blasphemy. "Man is God's greatest creation, Mr. Perry. How dare you slander His work?"

"His greatest creation? Cripes, lady, it seems to me that it's all the earth can do to withstand the abominations

87

man perpetrates on it. And each other. Have you ever seen the coal pits back east? Or the slums in New York or Boston? Or the slaves' quarters on a Maryland plantation? Or are you going to try to tell me black men aren't human beings?"

"Of course I'm not. I have every admiration for the abolitionists who worked to free the poor creatures before the war began."

"I'll just bet you have." He glared at her before she could take him to task for betting again.

"Well, I do."

"From your safe little hidey-hole in Boston, I presume."

"My family lived in Auburn, Mr. Perry."

"Either way, a lot you know about it. It's easy to read about things. It's a whole lot harder when you see them. And I defy you to give me a sound reason why any merciful God in His right mind would have allowed people to come up with the institution of slavery."

"Don't you go putting the sins of the wicked upon the good Lord's shoulders, Mr. Perry."

"Wouldn't dream of it, Miss Hardesty. Nor would I dream of condemning the good Lord for having made man by calling us His greatest creation."

"He made man in His own image!" Joy cried, mortally offended.

"I'll believe that when I see Him."

"I doubt it will ever come to that."

He flashed her a sudden grin, and she felt a lick of pride. She wasn't usually so witty. Perhaps sparring with Mr. Perry was quickening her wits.

"I still don't believe He made us in His image, Miss Hardesty."

She sniffed. "Well, He did."

"Prove it."

"The Bible says so."

"The Bible's been translated a million times. Who are you to say all of those translators got it right?"

Joy huffed and turned away. She hated it when people offered her arguments she had no answers for. Her mother used to have an answer for everything. If only Joy thought as quickly as her mother used to do all the time instead of every now and then. But no; her own mind worked sluggishly most of the time, and it dwelled on unimportant matters. For instance, at the moment it was silently agreeing with Mr. Perry's foul assertions when she knew it shouldn't be. Joy couldn't think of a suitable argument to save herself.

She hated it when that happened. Her failure to argue effectively not only weakened her position, but it pointed out the peril in which her own faith lay. If she were a truly sound Christian, she should be able to whip out proof after proof in rebuttal to anything a trespasser against His Word might say to her. Her inability to do so made her very cranky.

"And anyway, what do you expect a body to do? Create worlds every day? For Pete's sake, I'm not God."

Joy gave a meaningful sniff.

"Yeah, I know. You've already consigned me to the fires of hell."

"It's not my job to do that, Mr. Perry, but I'm sure you know your worth better than I." That was pretty good, and she felt somewhat better about herself.

"Horsefeathers. You had me tried, convicted, and damned to the pit before you even knew my name. Tell me you didn't, and you'll be lying."

Fiddlesticks! He'd done it again. She couldn't think of a single thing to say to him—because he was right. It was excessively annoying to be thwarted by the truth in this way. Her mother had never let the truth stand in *her* way. Her mother had been above logic as other people were above the law. Joy envied her that.

She stopped in the act of carrying a basin of water to the bedside table, her prior reflection having sounded wrong somehow. She tried to fix it, but it wouldn't be fixed. *Well, rubbish.* She'd have to examine it later, when she wasn't so harassed. She set the water down and turned to fetch the shaving things.

"Leaving aside your penchant for damning everybody to the pit whether you know them or not, it all boils down to this, Miss Hardesty. Everyone works at his own job." Elijah gave her a sniff of his own. "I'm a gambling man. So what? It's honest work."

Joy gave him a look which she hoped was as skeptical as she felt, glad he'd directed the conversation back to a path with which she was familiar. "Honest work, my eye. Fleecing innocents is about as dishonest an occupation as any I've ever heard of." She set the shaving things down, bumping the basin and splashing some water out onto the table. Annoyed, she retreated to the bureau to fetch another towel.

"If you were a man, I'd punch you in the jaw for saying that, ma'am. I'll have you know, I'm the most honest gambler I know. I've never fleeced an honest soul in my life. Poker requires skill and patience, and I have both. I've worked damned hard, and I'm the best there is."

He sounded honestly incensed. Joy could hardly believe her ears. She'd never heard anyone try to justify gaming before. The people she'd known prior to coming to the territory had all deplored the activity as much as she did. "If you're so skillful, why don't you apply your talents to something worthwhile?"

"It *is* worthwhile. It buys my bread, damn it, and it's allowed me to put money in the bank."

Joy scrubbed up the spilled water, wishing she could be scrubbing Mr. Elijah Perry's tongue with soap and water, as her mother used to do to hers. A little home therapy might be good for him. "There you go, blaspheming again. Gambling is a sinful occupation. Calling it your job doesn't make it any less so, if you ask me."

"I didn't ask you."

"You didn't dare because you know I'm right."

"Folderol."

He eyed her keenly as she dipped the shaving brush in water and then whipped the shaving cream with it. It didn't look to Joy as if he were very happy about her being the one to shave him. *Good*. She hoped he'd worry so much that he'd be nice to her. It was exhausting, having to quarrel with him about everything.

It seemed that their argument had worn him out, too. He lay back on the bed with his eyes closed. His skin was as pasty as her own, and he looked mortally sick. Joy felt a tiny pang of compunction for having bickered with him. She never could tell where to draw the line; whether to point out to people the error of their ways or to turn the other cheek and leave them be.

"Are you sure you're up to being shaved, Mr. Perry? Perhaps you should rest a little first."

"No. I want to get this stubble off. It's driving me crazy."

Joy refrained from uttering the brilliant rejoinder that immediately sprang to her mind, and felt somewhat better about herself. "I'll have to help you to sit up. I can't shave you very well when you're lying down."

He cracked his eyes open and looked unhappy. After heaving a soft sigh, he said, "All right. Try to have some mercy on me even though I'm a sinner and you hate my guts, all right?"

"I don't hate your guts," she said, shocked into speaking before she thought. For heaven's sake, she was a Christian lady, and therefore filled with charity and love for all her fellow men, no matter how vile they were. Wasn't she?

"You could have fooled me." He shut his eyes again and seemed to be gathering his strength for the coming ordeal.

His words stung Joy. She didn't know why they should, either, because it was of no consequence to her whether the wicked man considered her hateful. Except that she didn't mean to be hateful. What she meant to be was helpful, and at the same time to point out the error of his ways. It was so frustrating not to be able to get it right. She just never got anything right.

In a voice tight with mental chaos, she said, "Tell me when you're ready, please, and I'll help you to sit up."

After another moment, during which she wondered if he'd dropped off to sleep, or into unconsciousness, he muttered, "I guess I'm ready."

"All right. I'll support your shoulders and you scoot yourself back against the headboard. I'll try to adjust the pillows as we work together." Reluctantly, she added, "I shall try very hard not to hurt you."

"Thank you."

She couldn't tell if his thanks were meant sarcastically. She suspected they were.

By the time she'd assisted him to sit up and plumped the pillows at his back, both Elijah and Joy were trembling, Elijah with pain and exhaustion, and Joy from the horror of having had to hurt him so badly. She truly hated hurting people, even when she had to do it in order to be of ultimate benefit to them, as in this case.

She even had tears in her eyes when she turned away from him and grabbed a small towel. Her hands shook. Her mother would have been disgusted with her. For only a second, Joy succumbed to her shredded nerves and sank her face into the softness of the towel. She never would have done such a lily-livered thing if she'd known Mr. Perry had opened his eyes.

"Are you crying?"

She jumped a foot and swirled around, yanking the towel from her face. "Of course not!"

"I'm all right, Miss Hardesty. Honest, I am. You didn't hurt me." His face was as pale as a shroud and drawn with pain, but his voice carried tenderness amazing in one so lost to goodness as he.

Joy didn't understand why he was being nice to her. She turned around again, because she didn't want him to see the tears his assurance had brought to her eyes. "Good." She would have said more, but didn't want him to hear her voice wobble.

Forcing her hands not to shake, she dipped the towel into the basin and squeezed it out. The water wasn't very hot, but one had to make do in cases like this. She concentrated on the duty before her and tried to forget how lifeless Mr. Perry's body had felt, how terribly wounded he was, how manfully he'd tried to help her help him, and how bravely he'd fought his pain. He was a wicked sinner. He wasn't supposed to exhibit any nobility of character.

Joy hated contradictions. She was confused enough already about Elijah Perry. She didn't need to have him to go and act all noble on her.

She heard him breathing heavily, as if he were trying to recruit his strength after the ordeal of sitting up. She was surprised when he said, "You know, I don't think you're as heartless as you want people to think you are."

Although she hated herself for it, she audibly sniffled back her tears. "I don't want people to think I'm heartless." She tried to make her tone severe.

He whispered, "Balderdash."

She slapped the towel over his face so he couldn't say anything else.

Elijah had never been so weak in his life. He was as weak as a kitten. As limp as a stalk of new grass. As wilted as a week-old flower.

He knew it must be his weakness that was making him reassess the sharp-tongued and self-righteous Joy Hardesty. He'd known women like her before—at least, he'd known women like what he'd assumed her to be. They hated everything and took pleasure in hurting people they considered beneath them—which was, it looked to him, like everyone who didn't belong to their own personal congregation.

Actually, most of them even liked hurting people *in* their own congregations. The females of Joy's stamp he'd met up with before now had delighted in picking holes in their friends. They propped themselves up by pulling the stuffing out of other people.

Elijah couldn't stand people like that. He'd been positive Joy was one of them. He wasn't so sure any longer.

It had actually been kind of fun when they'd fought their battle of Bible verses. She'd been surprised he'd known any. Little did she know he'd been force-fed Bible verses for the first ten years of his life. And the nuns who'd been lording it over him were every bit as cruel as he'd believed she was. Crueler, even. Poor Joy. No matter how much she tried to put up a good fight, she wasn't closed-minded enough to be a truly worthy opponent. Nor was she sure enough of her ground to make fighting with her really exhilarating.

No, as irritating and frustrating as she was, Elijah was beginning to suspect Joy of being more misguided than steeped in false piety and sanctimony. He'd have to think about this later, when he wasn't so tired, but he'd just about concluded that she was a fraud.

The warm, wet towel felt heavenly on his face. She'd put something in the water that smelled good and made his skin tingle. He'd have asked her what it was, but he was too enervated to speak at the moment. What with sparring with him verbally and manhandling him into an upright position, she'd managed to drain every ounce of strength out of him. If he'd had the energy, he'd have chuckled that such a tiny thing as she could have fatigued him so.

He wasn't sure he liked the idea of her wielding a straight razor anywhere near him, but he had no spunk left to object to that, either. He'd just have to trust her not to slit his throat. Actually, after the last half hour or so, he kind of did trust her. He didn't understand his revised opinion either.

As she shaved him, she was so gentle that he almost fell asleep. He'd never had such a delicate shave. As soon as she'd wiped him down, dried him off, slathered some soothing creamy stuff onto his shorn cheeks, and removed the cloth she'd draped over him, he drifted off to sleep under the influence of it.

When he awoke, the first thing he saw was Joy, sitting in the chair beside the bed, reading. His first reaction was pleasure that she hadn't drawn the curtains shut again as soon as his eyes were closed. His second was that she looked appropriate that way: quiet and serene. Gentle, reading a book.

The pose suited her. It suited her a damned sight better than the hostility and self-righteousness she projected most of the time. He wondered if she had to try to be as unpleasant as she was, then wondered why she'd want to do something so fruitless. He didn't wonder hard, since he didn't have the strength for it.

Making an enormous effort, he said, "What are you reading?" and fell back against his pillow, exhausted.

She uttered a small gasp and jumped in the chair. Elijah cocked one eye open and would have shaken his head in amazement if his head didn't hurt so much already. "Touchy little thing, aren't you?" His voice sounded too dry, and he wished he hadn't said anything when her lips pruned up.

He'd noticed as she worked on him that she wasn't as ugly as her standoffish demeanor had at first led him to believe. In truth, she had pretty eyes, nice hair, fair skin—although it was much too pale—and a nice, generous mouth when it wasn't all pinched up.

"I beg your pardon, Mr. Perry. I didn't know you'd awakened."

She sounded as stiff as a March gale, and Elijah sighed. He decided to be nice. "Thank you for taking such good care of me, Miss Hardesty." He had to fight his impulse to add something sarcastic, like, *I know you hate every minute of it.*

"You're welcome." She nodded. Her nod was stiff, too.

All right, they'd cleared that hurdle. What now? Elijah went back to his original question. "What verses are you reading?"

Joy looked down at her book. Elijah sharpened his gaze. Was she blushing? Or was it the bright sunlight making something reflect on her cheeks.

No, by damn! She was blushing. What in the name of holy hell was she blushing for?

She cleared her throat. "Actually, Mr. Perry, I felt the need to read the seventh psalm today."

He gave her a small grin. " 'O Lord my God, in thee do I put my trust: save me from all them that persecute me, and deliver me.' I don't mean to persecute you, Miss Hardesty."

Again she cleared her throat. "Of course not, Mr. Perry." Her gaze sharpened. "I must admit to a certain surprise that you know so much of the Bible."

His grin widened. "Fooled you, didn't I?"

She evidently didn't know what to make of him—whether to take the bait and snap back or humble herself and beg enlightenment. In the event, she did neither, but cleared her throat yet a third time. She was nervous about something, and Elijah wondered what. He didn't ask for fear a direct question would shut her up.

After a small space of silence she spoke again. "Actually, the truth is that after I'd read the seventh psalm, I decided to pick up your novel."

Elijah's eyes popped open. "No! You don't say! Has it corrupted you yet?"

Her eyes squinted and her lips wrinkled, and Elijah wished he'd kept his facetious comment to himself.

She surprised him again by being almost witty. "It hasn't had time to corrupt me yet, I fear. I'd only just begun to read it when you awoke."

Elijah watched her blush fade and decided she might be a genuinely fetching article if she hadn't been spoiled by her upbringing. He found himself curious about her, which was surprising all by itself, since he hadn't been interested enough in anything to be curious about it in more years than he cared to contemplate.

In his mind he tested various things to say to her before he spoke. He missed reading. Before heading out here to the territory, reading was about the only thing in the world that had been able to occupy his mind. Everything else had paled into boredom long since, but Elijah still found escape in books. He knew Joy had been correct when she'd told him he was too weak to hold that book in his hands, yet he wasn't sure he wanted to be read to like a little kid.

On the other hand, it would be a new experience to have a woman who might as well be one of the nuns he'd grown up with read a novel to him. The idea amused him. Little Sister Joy, reading to a black-hearted, scoundrelly gambling man, from a wicked work of fiction— *detective* fiction, what was more. "Miss Hardesty, if I let you read a Bible chapter to me, will you read a couple of chapters of *The Moonstone?* We can see if the Bible betters my evil ways before the novel decays your good ones."

She squinted at him, and Elijah got the distinct impression she was trying not to smile. Good grief, could it be that Miss Joy "Afraid of Fading Carpets" Hardesty had a sense of humor under all that whalebone and religion? The tiny spark of curiosity that had ignited in him earlier fanned higher.

"Well? What about it?"

"I do believe it is *you* who are trying to taint me, Mr. Perry, by proposing an underhanded wager to see which device can corrupt whom first."

Elijah was delighted. "By God, you're right! I didn't even see it that way until you mentioned it. You're a smart girl, Miss Hardesty. You might have been a good poker player if you'd ever taken it up, you know that?"

Evidently she didn't appreciate his levity in this instance. She tensed like a fiddle string. Before she could run out on him, Elijah said, "I didn't mean it, ma'am. Of course you wouldn't be a good poker player."

She relaxed slightly. "I should say not. However, I have a lot of work to do. I shouldn't be wasting my time reading novels."

"You said you would." Elijah frowned when he heard how whiny he sounded.

"And I shall honor my word. But I can't leave everything for the sake of entertainment."

"You were reading when I woke up," he reminded her.

"I had been reading the Bible, Mr. Perry. That's different."

"But you'd started the novel."

She sniffed. He'd gotten to her with that one; he could tell. "I felt it my duty to remain by your bedside, actually, since I know how drained you were after your shave—and after most injudiciously attempting to rise from your sickbed."

"Well, there. You can look at reading to me out of that book as part of my recovery, ma'am. I'd take it as a kindness." He considered offering to pay her to read to him, and decided against it, figuring he'd get farther by playing on her sense of duty—or martyrdom—than he ever would with cash.

He sucked in a breath and held it while Joy considered. After a moment, she said, "Oh, very well," in a voice that spoke eloquently of how put-upon she felt.

"You can read me two chapters out of the Bible first if it'll make you feel any better, ma'am." Elijah thought his offer quite generous, considering he'd hoped never to be read to out of the Good Book again after the nuns got through with him.

She inclined her head to one side. She looked regal when she did that, and Elijah's amusement bubbled up again. Poor little Joy. He wondered why her parents, who had obviously ruined her, had decided to bestow such a frivolous name on her. An expert at patience, Elijah decided he'd ask one of these days, after he got to know her better.

Joy selected her Bible verses carefully. Elijah would have bet she'd sought them out specifically for him, in order to get maximum use of the time allotted for the saving of his soul. He wondered if she'd bother if she knew he didn't have one. The notion depressed him, and he tucked it away.

Eventually she decided on John fourteen and fifteen.

" 'Let not your heart be troubled: ye believe in God, believe also in me. In my Father's house are many mansions: if it were not so, I would have told you. I go to prepare a place for you.' "

The language was beautiful and the words were soothing, even if Elijah didn't believe any of them. He decided to concentrate on the language, since that was less troubling than the emptiness of his life. It might have been fun to live back in old King James's time and use all that flowery language. On the other hand, the language would have been customary back then, and there would be none of the thrill of peculiarity that Elijah felt every time he heard it.

He was almost sorry when Joy finished reading chapter fifteen. " 'But that the world may know that I love the Father; and as the Father gave me commandment, even so I do. Arise, let us go hence.' "

With a big sigh, Joy shut her Bible. She lifted her gaze, and Elijah smiled at her. She blushed charmingly.

"Thank you, Miss Hardesty. That was nicely read."

"Thank you, Mr. Perry."

She picked up *The Moonstone* in both hands, as if lifting a very heavy boulder. She glanced at Elijah, who smiled his most devastating smile. She glanced away again quickly, drew in a huge breath—Elijah noted for the first time and with interest that she actually seemed to have a substantial bosom under all that whalebone— looked down at the book, opened it up, found the first page, and began to do her duty.

" 'Prologue. The Storming of Seringapatam—' "

"Well done."

She looked up at him in question, her pretty brown eyes huge. Elijah felt a funny catch in his chest. It was probably from the bullet hole. "You pronounced that Indian word beautifully, Miss Hardesty. I'm impressed."

"Oh." She looked down at the book, and Elijah was certain her cheeks had more color in them than they had had a second prior. She cleared her throat. "Actually, I—I practiced a little bit while you were asleep, Mr. Perry."

"Ah. I see." So she *had* been reading his novel, had she? And, from the blush in her cheeks, she'd been enjoying it, too. He felt better all at once. "Well, please go on. 'Seringapatam.' "

"Yes." She gave him one last quick peek, and began again. 'Prologue. The Storming of Seringapatam, 1799, extracted from a family paper. One. I address these lines—written in India—to my relatives in England . . . ' "

With a happy sigh—the first he'd breathed in years—Elijah relaxed back against his pillows and commenced enjoying himself.

Alexander McMurdo sat on Cody and Melissa O'Fannin's front porch swing, his feet propped up on the porch rail, two-and-a-half-year-old Katie in his lap, and smiled. The little girl was playing with an orange-and-white marmalade kitten, which tumbled with its brothers and sisters at their feet.

"You like that kitty, Katie, m'lass?"

"Like kee-kee." The little girl giggled as the kitten batted at the yarn doodad she dangled for it.

"D'ye suppose your ma and pa would let ye ride into town wi' me, Katie lass, so's we can take one of these fine kittens to a lady and gentleman residin' there?"

"Town?" Katie said, her big eyes widening with pleasure.

"Aye," said Mac. "There's somethin' I have to attend

101

to there." He didn't wonder at Katie's excitement about a proposed trip to town. Out here on her stepdaddy's ranch, she pretty much lived in the middle of nowhere. Going to town was an enormous pleasure for anyone who resided in the emptiness of southeastern New Mexico Territory's high plains.

Mac was pleased by the way things were going back in his wagon yard. He figured adding a kitten to the mix of Elijah Perry and Joy Hardesty would only move them along faster.

By Jupiter, he'd fix those two yet.

Chapter Six

"Thank heaven you're back!"

Forgetting dignity entirely in her elation at seeing Alexander McMurdo, Joy tore down the porch steps and raced out to the wagon yard gate. As little as two weeks ago, she wouldn't have believed she'd be happy to renew her acquaintance with so unworthy a specimen of mankind—according to her mother's wisdom, at any rate—as Alexander McMurdo. But she was ecstatic to see him now, her mother and her mother's opinions be hanged.

Her soaring heart took a nosedive when she saw that he had a small child with him. *Oh, dear.* The child in his lap must mean he was only visiting. Unless he intended to thrust this child into her care, to tend along with Elijah Perry. She wouldn't put it past him. Her pace slowed, and her smile had tipped upside down by the time she reached Mac's horse.

"Glad to see you, too, Joy, m'dear. This here's Katie,

Melissa's daughter." Mac lightly pinched the little girl's cheek. "Say your howdy-dos to Miss Hardesty, Katie, sweet."

"Ho, Miss Tee," Katie said obediently.

She eyed Joy curiously with big, bright, brown eyes. Joy didn't detect a hint of shyness in the girl. In spite of her wariness and mistrust, Joy couldn't help but be charmed by her. Katie was a tiny thing, and she couldn't be more than a couple of years old. It surprised Joy that she could say so many words. On the other hand, what else did a body have to do out here but talk?

Something inside of her, a compulsion with which she was unfamiliar, prompted Joy to don a beaming smile and hold out her hand to Katie. "Hello to you, too, Miss Katie. I'm very pleased to meet you." She shook the child's plump hand, and Katie giggled as if she'd been tickled. Joy's heart, usually bound around with the iron manacles of her mother's restrictive, exclusive philosophy, burst its bonds and expanded at least six sizes.

She surprised herself again when she exclaimed, "Oh, what a perfect darling, Mr. McMurdo. May I hold her?"

"Ye can lift her down off the horse, if you please, Miss Joy."

So Joy did as Mac had requested, and was amazed when the child gave her a big hug and a smacking kiss on the cheek. Joy had never experienced a spontaneous gesture of affection in her life that she could remember. Her father might have given her one or two when she was too young to know it and before her mother had terrorized them out of him. She hugged Katie back, and felt silly when tears pricked her eyes.

"I've got something else here for ye, too, Joy."

On the alert again in an instant, Joy's happiness in Katie transformed into suspicion. "You do?"

"Aye. You take Katie on in the house, and I'll fetch it in to ye."

Worried, Joy did as he asked. She couldn't imagine why Mr. McMurdo would bring her anything. Not anything she'd want, anyway. After all, she hadn't been particularly pleasant to him during their time together. Her mother's training took the opportunity to remind her that, while Alexander McMurdo was a misguided evildoer, and it was Joy's duty to display, in word and deed, how much she deprecated him and his behavior, she must never do so in anything but the kindest, most condescending manner. It was a fine line, and Joy had always found it an extremely difficult one to negotiate.

You look perfectly bilious, Joy Hardesty. It is a Christian's duty to act pleasant when carrying out the Lord's work. Smile! Show these sinners you're above them!

Yes, Mother.

Somehow the old refrain didn't sit as easily in Joy's heart today as it had before Mac went away. She wondered if this was an indication that she was becoming corrupted by earthly influences. With a heavy sigh, she decided it most likely was, and was struck yet again by relief that her mother couldn't see her now. That sentiment alone only went to prove how lost to goodness Joy had become.

Why, she'd even become so enamored by that wicked novel of Mr. Perry's that she'd initiated, on her own, two reading sessions per day, one in the morning and one in the evening. She always read Bible verses first, of course, but Joy knew—and she suspected Mr. Perry knew, too—that she did so only to give herself an excuse for reading from the vicious work of fiction. It was a lowering thought.

In spite of her troubled reflections, she carried Katie to Elijah Perry's bedroom door, intending, if he were awake, to shock him senseless with the introduction of an article of genuine purity. If he could withstand little Katie, the man was hardened beyond redemption.

She peeked inside the room and discovered him sitting up. She was happy to see him thus, because it meant he'd managed it on his own and was getting stronger. Not, of course, that she had any personal interest in Elijah Perry. It was, however, cheering to know her nursing hadn't damaged him. He still looked pale and exhausted, and Joy feared he wasn't out of the woods yet, but every day she was more encouraged about his ultimate recovery.

She refused to admit to herself that she'd begun to relish her encounters with him. In truth, although she wouldn't say so, she found him refreshing, like water to a thirsty man.

"Mr. Perry?"

He turned and smiled at her before he noticed the child. Then his smile faded and his eyes widened. "Good Lord, I didn't even know you were pregnant."

Joy gasped, scandalized, and wondered how she ever could have considered the man as anything but a tool of the devil. Then she remembered the baby in her arms and knew she'd have to take Elijah Perry to task for his indelicacy later.

"This," she announced frostily, "is Miss Katie Elizabeth daughter of Melissa O'Fannin, with whom Mr. Mc-Murdo has been staying this past week and more." It only occurred to her later to wonder where she'd come up with those names. They were correct, but she couldn't for the life of her remember when Mr. McMurdo had told them to her. At the moment she was too put out with Elijah Perry to marvel at her own feat of intuition.

She continued, pointedly ignoring Elijah's wicked grin. "Miss Katie, this gentleman—and I use the word even while knowing I may be giving him more credit than he deserves—is Mr. Elijah Perry. Can you say good morning to Mr. Perry?"

Katie was an adorable child. Her cheeks were pink and chubby, and her eyes gleamed with good humor and health. Her hair was apparently naturally curly, and curls flipped out from beneath her sunbonnet flaps, shiny and brown and as pretty as anything.

Joy understood with a shock that she loved the little girl. For heaven's sake, she hadn't known it was possible to love something or someone—wholly and unconditionally—before one even had a chance to judge his or her worthiness. Not, of course, that there could be anything coarse or impure about a mere baby. Still, the insight astonished her.

"Mor', Mippee," chirped the ever-cooperative Katie.

Joy laughed and hugged her. She paused to consider how out of character her impulsive gesture had been when she saw Elijah Perry gaping at her, goggle-eyed. Knowing how little she was given to spontaneous behaviors struck Joy as sad suddenly, and she wondered why it should do so. It never had before. Any tendency toward spontaneity had been driven out of her years before. She decided to ponder this later, along with all the other things she'd tucked aside to think about.

Elijah recovered from his start, and smiled at the little girl. "Good morning back to you, Miss Katie. You're a sweetheart, aren't you?"

Katie giggled again and nodded, and it was Joy's turn to gape. "Why, Mr. Perry, you sound almost as though you might like children. I'm perfectly astounded."

"No more astounded than I am that *you* should like them, Miss Hardesty, believe me." His voice was tart as a lemon. "I've always liked kids."

Although Joy experienced an almost ungovernable urge to argue with him about who should be nonplussed by whose affinity for children, she didn't, for the sake of Katie, who was obviously unused to people squabbling in front of her. Even the few sharp words Joy and Elijah had just exchanged seemed to bother her. Her sweet little lips lost their smile, her big brown eyes thinned, and she murmured, "Say happy tings."

Joy thought that was the most precious thing in the world and hugged her again.

"All right, darling, we'll say happy things from now on." She shot Elijah a speaking glance. "Won't we, Mr. Perry?"

More practiced in sneakiness than she, Elijah didn't even bat an eye or pause to consider. "We sure will." He spoke in the sunniest voice Joy had ever heard come from his debauched mouth.

"I see you've introduced yourselves."

Joy turned to find Mac behind her. "Indeed, we have, Mr. McMurdo. Miss Katie just delivered a lesson on manners to Mr. Perry."

"Hey!"

She gave Elijah a brilliant smile, and he shut his mouth. She knew he'd get her for it later, but she felt a glow of accomplishment that she should have put him in his place and assured his silence at the same time. She seldom won verbal bouts with him this easily, and chalked her present victory up to the influence of little Katie O'Fannin.

Useful weapons, children.

Her thought processes snagged instantly on the thought. With sudden, sickening clarity, she understood that she'd been the weapon of choice wielded by her own parents when it suited them.

How pathetic.

She decided to think about *this* understanding later, too, as it was revolutionary and she wasn't sure it was proper. Perhaps the unkind thought was a weapon of another sort, sent by the devil to tempt her into abandoning her early childhood training.

She wished all at once that life wasn't as complicated as it seemed to be.

"I've got something else here for the two o' ye, too," Mac said.

Joy noticed that he had his hands hidden behind his back. She had a premonition that she wasn't going to be thrilled with his *something else*. "You do?" she said cautiously.

"Don't worry, Joy, m'love," he said with a twinkle. "It's a good thing."

Katie nodded and announced happily, "Kee-kee."

Mac chuckled. "Aye. That's it, all right."

"Kee-kee?" Joy studied Katie's face, hoping to discern a clue in her expression. She didn't.

Kee—kee. Good grief. She refused to allow her smile to go sour. She would maintain her pleasant expression for the sake of the child in her arms, no matter how dreadful this alleged *kee-kee* turned out to be.

"May we see your kee-kee, Mr. McMurdo?" she asked, keeping her tone agreeable.

"Yeah, plop it down here, Mac. I haven't petted a kitten in a coon's age."

Joy spun around and stared at Elijah, who had the gall to wink at her. "Don't speak the language, I see, Miss Hardesty. Any of us who've been around children know that a kee-kee is a kitten."

Good heavens. Joy didn't answer, but turned to Mac again. Katie seemed unaffected by Joy's ignorance of the language of children.

"Aye, that's it all right, laddie." With a flourish worthy of a magician, Mac revealed a wicker basket containing an orange-and-white marmalade kitten.

"Oh!" cried Joy, who had always loathed cats on the principle—taught to her by her mother—that they were sinister and crafty. Today this kitten charmed her almost as much as Katie did.

"Hey," said Elijah, his voice cheerier than Joy had ever heard it. "I had a cat just like that when I was a kid."

"Not cah," corrected Katie severely from her perch in Joy's arms. "Kee-kee."

Joy hugged her. "That's right, darling. You tell that awful old man that this isn't a nasty old cat, but a darling, adorable kitten."

Chuckling as if he hadn't heard anything so witty in a dozen years, Mac carted the kitten over to Elijah's bed. He carefully lifted the kitten out of its basket and set it on the bed.

"Go ahead, Miss Hardesty. Be as spiteful as you want. You're not going to get a rise out of me today." Elijah lifted his unbandaged arm and tapped a finger on the counterpane to attract the kitten. "I like kittens. And kids."

Joy sniffed, feeling almost contrite that he'd pointed out her contrary behavior for what it was.

"Bring Katie over here, Joy," Mac suggested. "We'll see if this wee kitten will get along all right here."

Joy decided to put her own shortcomings and Elijah's gentle reproach aside. She could dwell on them both later, in private, and berate herself appropriately. "Yes, let's see the kitty, shall we, Katie?"

"See kee-kee," said Katie, ever agreeable.

Joy walked her over to the bed. Then, since there didn't seem to be anything else to do—Mac had appropriated the room's one chair—she sat on the bed, as close to the edge and as far away from Elijah Perry as she could get.

This seating arrangement was frightfully improper. She

knew it; she knew Elijah knew it, and she wasn't about to let him tease her about it. She ignored him, settled Katie on her lap, then looked at the kitten, who attacked Elijah's finger and turned a somersault in the effort.

Joy laughed, a perfect, happy, unrestrained laugh, and kept laughing until she noticed Elijah staring at her. Her laughter choked to a stop. Not only was he staring at her, but there seemed to be a strange phenomenon occurring right here in this room. She'd noticed it before, and it always startled her. The dust motes in air around them sparkled like floating diamond chips. It was a disconcerting spectacle, and one Joy had never encountered anywhere but here, in Rio Hondo. She wondered if it had something to do with atmospheric conditions on the high plains. And, in the meantime, Elijah kept staring.

Since Katie had crawled out of Joy's lap to move closer to the kitten, Joy stood abruptly. "What are you looking at, Mr. Perry?" Her voice was crisp.

"You." His sounded bemused.

She sniffed. It wasn't as imperious as one of her usual sniffs because she was flustered by sparkles and kittens and children. And Elijah Perry's expression. She endeavored to ignore them all.

"Why did you decide to bring us a kitten, Mr. McMurdo?"

Elijah patted the bed—using his wounded arm. Joy lifted her left eyebrow.

"Sit back down again, Miss Hardesty. I won't bite you."

She frowned at him, and then at the bed. Then, since Katie seemed to be getting closer to the bed's edge and Joy feared she might fall off, she did as Elijah suggested. It was shockingly unseemly of her to sit on a bed with a man in it, but he was wounded, and the chair was occupied, and this was the New Mexico Territory, and her mother couldn't see her.

Don't be a perfect fool, Joy Hardesty, she thought with some heat. *Your mother is dead and can't see* anyone *any longer. Thank God!*

This, her second revolutionary thought of the day, alarmed her. She reached out to Katie for comfort.

"Come along, Katie, dear. We don't want you to fall off the bed."

The little girl crawled onto Joy's lap. Joy felt . . . joy. It was a novel experience.

"I thought we could use us a mouser here in the store, Joy, m'lass. And since Cody and Mellie's barn cat had just had a litter a bit over a month ago, I brought one of 'em here."

Glad to have her thoughts diverted, Joy said, "I haven't noticed any mice here, Mr. McMurdo." She only realized how surprising that fact was when she said it aloud. All stores had mice. "Actually, I didn't even know you even had mice here in the territory."

Mac and Elijah laughed. She shared a scowl with both of them. "Well, I didn't."

"Yes," Katie confirmed with a firm nod of her small head. "I din."

So there, Joy thought, glad to have the baby as an ally. She gave Katie a hug, and the little girl returned it with gusto. Katie seemed accustomed to love and hugs, unlike Joy, and gave them freely. Joy couldn't remember a single other time in her life when she'd been this happy.

"Aye, we do have mice in the territory, Joy, m'dear. But this little fellow will keep 'em out. Both his mama and papa are great mousers, according to Melissa."

Melissa. The divorcée. Joy tried to drum up some condemnation for the mother of this beautiful little girl, but was unsuccessful. To distract herself from this, her latest shortcoming, she found herself asking, "How is their new baby getting along?"

Mac smiled broadly. "Oh, Arnold is a fine lad. A fine, bouncing baby boy."

Katie's ears perked up at the mention of her new brother's name. "Arr-o good bay."

"Aye, Katie, m'lass. Arnold's a very good baby. A strong, healthy lad. Got a good pair of lungs in him, too." Mac laughed heartily.

Katie joined him. Joy was sure Katie didn't have any idea what she was laughing about, and she thought how nice it would be to be able to laugh for no reason but the sake of laughter. She'd never done such a thing.

She felt the need to be able to see Katie's expressive face more clearly. "Shall we take your sunbonnet off, Katie?"

"Arrigh."

So Joy removed the girl's sunbonnet. She marveled at how small and cunningly made it was. Melissa O'Fannin, divorcée or not, obviously took pride in her daughter's appearance. Joy approved. Perhaps Melissa wasn't so *very* bad a person. There might have been a good reason for her to obtain a divorce, although Joy couldn't think of one offhand.

That woman made her own bed, Joy Hardesty. It was her duty to lie in it, and don't you ever forget it.

Yes, Mother.

She shook her head, trying to dislodge her mother's voice. It sounded excessively shrill and struck a discordant note in this small back room filled with invalid, sunshine, sinner, kitten, baby, and Joy Hardesty. She didn't want to think about divorce any longer. Or her mother.

"Right before you arrived, I was preparing luncheon

for Mr. Perry, Mr. McMurdo. Would you and Katie care to take luncheon with us?"

"Sounds delicious, Joy, m'dear. Want to eat some of Miss Hardesty's good cooking, Katie, darlin'?"

Mac chucked Katie under the chin, sending the child into a peal of giggles. Joy's heart melted. Try as she might, she couldn't recall anyone ever playing with her like that. She wondered if she'd be so nervous and frightened all the time if she'd been allowed some silliness during her childhood. Instead of games, she'd been taught Bible verses, guilt, and censure. She shook off the unworthy thought.

"Would you like to help me fix luncheon, Katie?"

"Fix 'unch," Katie chirped.

Immediately, she scooted off of Joy's lap and began climbing down from the bed. She was as limber as a monkey, and concentrated on the task she'd set for herself like a mountain climber conquering a difficult peak, and Joy laughed again, unrestrained and happy. She held her arms out, ready to catch Katie should it be necessary. Oh, my, her heart felt light. She'd had no idea children could foster such happy moods. She didn't recall her own mother ever seeming particularly happy. Of course, her mother had been stuck with Joy, not this adorable little darling of a girl named Katie.

She shook her head as Katie's dress bunched up around her bottom. Her chubby legs, encased in frilly drawers, strained to reach the ground, and Joy had a job of it to keep from pinching the dimpled pink flesh revealed. With a sigh, she rose from Mr. Perry's bed.

Then, surprising herself as much as she surprised Katie, she swooped down and scooped Katie up off the floor. Behaving in a manner of which she didn't even know herself capable, she tossed the little girl into the air, caught her, and then carried her, upside down, out of the room. Katie thought these antics hilarious, and laughed uproariously as she batted her petticoats out of her face.

Elijah Perry stared after Joy and Katie as if he'd never seen such a thing in his life. Which he hadn't. When he turned to look at Mac, he found the old man grinning like an elf, a knowing expression on his face and a marmalade kitten in his lap.

"Well, I never." Elijah knew it to be inadequate, but he couldn't find words to express his awe that Joy Hardesty had actually behaved like a normal human female. A *pleasant* normal human female.

Mac winked at him. "Aye, laddie. Our Joy's had a difficult life. She's learnin', though. She's learnin'."

Elijah turned his head to observe the retreating woman once more. "I reckon." He wasn't sure he believed it.

Joy washed Katie's hands and set her to counting out carrot sticks onto four plates. "See? You do it like this. One, two, three." She deliberately picked up a carrot stick as she recited each number.

Katie emulated her exactly. "One, two, fwee." She carefully arranged the carrot sticks into neat rows on each plate.

"You're doing a very good job, Katie." Although she didn't hover, Joy kept glancing away from her own chore, which was slicing cold beef for sandwiches. She couldn't keep her attention on her job; it kept sliding to the little girl helping her. Katie knelt on a stool, and her little brow wrinkled with the importance of her duty.

Spreading mustard on the bread she'd just sliced, Joy said, "Do you like carrots, Katie?"

The little head bobbed up and down. "Like cares."

Well, that put a new slant on things. Joy wasn't partial

115

to cares herself. She laughed, surprising herself. She couldn't recall when she'd laughed so much. Actually, she didn't think she ever had.

"Can you chew them? Do you have enough teeth?"

To demonstrate her dental assets, Katie turned and bared her teeth at Joy, who laughed again. "I guess you can chew any tough old carrot stick, can't you, Katie?"

The girl nodded and went back to her task. Joy sighed, and thought how delightful it would be to have a little girl of her own. It must be splendid to watch one's children grow from infancy, through all the stages of childhood, and into adulthood. Not, Joy told herself, that there weren't sure to be many heartbreaks and problems along the way. Still . . .

"Ah done!" Katie threw her hands out, peered over her shoulder, and gave Joy a smile she wished she could take down on paper with pen and ink.

She set her knife down, wiped her hands on her apron, and swept the little girl off her stool. "You did a wonderful job, Katie! A beautiful job!" She hugged Katie, who hugged her back.

Setting Katie down on the kitchen floor, Joy said, "I'm so glad you came to visit us today, Katie. Did you have a nice ride on Mr. McMurdo's horsie?" Her brows dipped. She'd never said the word *horsie* in her entire life until this moment. Not even when she was Katie's age. Her mother didn't approve of baby talk.

Still smiling, Katie nodded and announced, "We fie."

"You fie?" Now whatever did that mean? Perhaps she should consult with Mr. Perry, who seemed adept at childish talk. She grinned at the thought.

Katie nodded harder. "We fie," she repeated, and flapped her arms.

"Oh! You flew here, did you?"

"We fic." Katie smiled, pleased that Joy had finally understood.

"Mr. McMurdo must have a very fast horsie."

"Horsie fie."

"How nice for you. It must be nice to have a ride on such a fast horsie."

With her arms held out to her sides like wings, Katie toddled around the kitchen like a bird soaring through the air. Joy discovered herself laughing again, and resumed building sandwiches. She was taking forever preparing luncheon. The men were liable to start complaining soon.

"Need any help?"

Joy turned and found Mac watching her from the door of the kitchen. Katie had run over to him and was now climbing up his leg. With a jolt, Joy realized that, however much of a sinner Mr. McMurdo was according to Joy's mother's rules, he was a very nice man. She tried to remind herself that the devil was undoubtedly clouding her view of the matter and preventing her from recognizing that his niceness was a cover for evil, but the reminder didn't seem to want to stick and kept sliding out of her brain.

"Thank you, Mr. McMurdo. Perhaps you can carry another chair or two into Mr. Perry's room, so we can take our luncheon in there. I'm sure he'll be happy for the company."

Had she really said that? Joy frowned, but didn't have the leisure to dwell on it, because Mac said, "I'll be glad to do that, lass." He winked at her. "I see our Mr. Perry hasn't died from your nursin'. Reckon that school in Boston you went to did a good job."

She knew her smile quivered. She still resented him for running out on her, even though it hadn't turned out

117

to be the disaster she'd feared. "Yes. Yes, the school in Boston was very good."

Mac put Katie down, hooked two chairs, and started out of the kitchen. "I expect you're very good, too, lass. Don't deny yourself the credit. It's you who put their teachin' to the test."

He left, Katie bouncing along behind him. Joy's mouth hung open in shock. She searched and searched and searched, but her memory couldn't come up with such a nice compliment ever having been directed at her. Her mind formed several incomplete disclaimers, but she was too stunned to voice any of them.

Jerusalem! What a kind thing for him to have said to her. Even if he was wrong, of course.

A voice—not her mother's, but one that seemed deeper, gentler, and more soothing—whispered, *He's right, Joy. You've done a splendid job.*

The voice sounded in her ears so clearly that Joy jumped and shot a startled glance around the kitchen. She was alone.

"Jerusalem. Now you've started hearing things, Joy Hardesty. Next you'll start believing in little Katie's flying horsie."

She forced a chuckle. Then she shook herself, picked up the plates, put them on a tray with glasses of cool water, and carted everything into Elijah Perry's room. He gave her a sly wink, and she rolled her eyes in half-humorous disapproval. Rolling her eyes was something else she'd never done in her life before she came to Rio Hondo.

The horse plodded Mac and Katie out of town, away from Mac's wagon yard, Joy Hardesty, Elijah Perry, and the marmalade kitten. When Mac had left them, Joy and Elijah had been arguing about an appropriate name for the wee thing. Joy had favored Apricot. Elijah had propounded Killer. Mac had a feeling the dispute would go on for a while.

His grin broadened. Aye, things were going fine. Better than he'd expected, even.

"Did ye have a nice visit with Miss Hardesty and Mr. Perry, Katie, darlin'?"

The little girl nodded and knuckled her eyes. Mac laughed softly. "Aye, child, we've had a full day, haven't we? But we'll be back home in the wink of an eye."

They'd traveled about a mile past the outskirts of Rio Hondo by this time. Mac looked around to make sure nobody was in the vicinity.

It wasn't quite the wink of an eye, but as Katie nodded off to sleep in Mac's arms, he flicked his little finger. The horse upon which they rode lifted up from the desert floor and soared through the air toward the O'Fannin ranch. In a very few minutes, little Katie was home again.

Chapter Seven

Joy wiped her eyes. She'd just laughed so hard over a passage in *The Moonstone* that she'd made herself cry. She didn't pause to consider this phenomenon because she'd experienced so many unusual phenomena lately that this one hardly fazed her

"Oh, dear! I do love Mr. Betteredge, don't you, Mr. Perry? The way he phrases things is so droll."

"He's a good old guy, all right." In truth, Elijah had discovered that this morning he could scarcely make himself concentrate on the narrative Gabriel Betteredge had set forth on the loss of the moonstone. He was too caught up in watching Joy.

When he'd first set eyes on her, she'd looked like an emaciated pickle. She'd looked like the kind of female who'd live and die an old maid. She'd looked as if her sour, single state had already begun to wither her innards and dry her exterior into a forbidding shell of thwarted womanhood. He'd taken one look at her and judged that, in less than ten years, she'd be the kind of female who'd scurry around with a basket of good works slung over her arm, darting glances filled with fear and loathing about her wherever she went. She'd go around doling out her charity mean-spiritedly, not because she wanted to, but because she feared if she didn't, she'd go to hell.

When he'd first met Joy Hardesty, she'd given Elijah a sad, empty feeling in his middle. Granted, that was more than he usually felt. Usually he felt merely empty. But it hadn't felt good, the impression he got of Joy.

Since she'd started nursing him, though, she'd changed. Elijah couldn't put his finger on exactly how, but she'd changed.

Oh, she was still annoying as hell. And she argued with him about every little thing. But she wasn't pinched and huddled over any longer, and she didn't flinch every time she glanced at him, as if she feared his very presence might shatter her morals. She'd also gained a little weight and no longer looked like an animated stick. Her cheeks sported some color, even when she wasn't blushing over some outrageous thing he'd said, although he did try to say at least three outrageous things a day, to keep her on her toes.

She'd wiped her eyes and begun to read again, and he attempted to pay attention. He was distracted by her face, though, and his thoughts wandered again. The first time he'd realized she was actually quite pretty had been the day Mac brought Katie here. That was only about a week ago, and Elijah hadn't recovered yet. He didn't like thinking of the foul-tempered, dried-up spinster lady, Joy Hardesty, as a pretty woman, because her being pretty contradicted so many of the beliefs he'd adopted through the years. But she was pretty. And appealing. And feminine. He couldn't very well deny those facts, because they were true. Whatever else Elijah Perry was, he wasn't a liar.

Now, for instance, her skin looked pale and almost translucent where the sun's rays kissed it. She had fine bone structure, and a delicate pink flush delineated her cheeks. Of course, he'd almost had to kill himself to get her to open the curtains and let the sun in so he could see her.

Elijah pondered whether he should tell her how pretty she was. He was sure she had no idea. No, that would be too outrageous. He didn't want to make her run away yet, because he still needed her.

Suddenly she shut the book with a clap and looked straight into his eyes. "Do you think I'm like Miss Clack?"

Her question came to him out of the blue, as direct as an arrow, and the very nature of it rendered him speechless. Miss Clack, Wilkie Collins's own Christian spinster lady, had actually reminded Elijah very much of Joy Hardesty. As intolerant and bigoted as Joy herself, Miss Clack spread misery and Christian tracts among her acquaintances like a breeze scattering seeds, but with more calculated menace. The breeze didn't know what it was doing.

Miss Clack, however, unlike Joy, evidenced not a whit of uncertainty about her mission in life. One of the qualities that had finally endeared Joy to Elijah was her self-doubt. Not, he amended quickly, that he considered Joy endearing. *Endearing* was the wrong word. He couldn't think of the right one at the moment, but he knew what he meant.

After several seconds, during which he scrambled to get his thoughts to congeal into a coherent phrase of denial, Joy announced, "You do, don't you? You think I'm just like Miss Clack." She bowed her head. "I hate Miss Clack."

"You do?"

She nodded. "She's an awful person."

Well, this was interesting. Curious, he asked, "Does she remind you of anyone you knew back in Boston?"

She glared at him. "Auburn."

He knew she was from Auburn. He'd taken to saying Boston because it riled her. He wished he'd not done it today, because he didn't want to get off track here. He sensed this might be an important discussion. "Sorry. But does she? Remind you of anybody?"

"Yes."

"Who?"

She glanced away from him and gazed out the window. Elijah looked, too. The spring morning sky was as clear as crystal. Clouds mounded up in the west like shorn woolen fleeces. He wondered if they'd have a thunderstorm tonight. His glance returned to Joy, and he was sorry to see her lips pinched up tight, the way they'd been when he'd first met her. His heart, an organ he paid little attention to on an everyday basis, gave an odd little pitch—it was almost painful—and he cocked his head, unsettled, and wanting to make Joy feel better.

"You can tell me, Miss Hardesty. I won't tease you. Honest, I won't."

She turned and squinted at him again. He could tell she didn't believe him. "Truly," he said, trying to encourage her to spill her guts. "You may not think much of my morals, but believe it or not, I'm honest. I may gamble for a living, but I don't lie."

That was the truth. Elijah wasn't honest out of any inner sense of scrupulous rectitude. It was only that he'd discovered years before that honesty made his life easier. He'd seen scads of people get into trouble because they couldn't keep their lies straight. Most folks told lies so as not to hurt people or make themselves look bad, he'd realized. Since he didn't give a crap what anybody thought of him, and didn't care about anyone else, he found honesty an easy course to follow.

"Then you'll tell me the truth?"

"Yes."

"Am I like Miss Clack?"

He hesitated. He wouldn't lie to her, but he discovered he'd suddenly developed a strange, unexpected reluctance to hurt her feelings. *Odd.* This had never happened to him before. It must be because she'd nursed him so well that he felt this alien compunction.

"First tell me who Miss Clack reminds you of."

She turned her head again and mumbled something.

"I didn't hear you, Joy. Who does she remind you of?"

Her head jerked around, and she goggled at him. He realized he'd called her by her Christian name. With a grin, he amended, "I mean, Miss Hardesty."

He saw her swallow and nod, as if she were forgiving him the familiarity.

"Go on," he urged softly. "You can tell me."

"My mother."

She swallowed again. Elijah couldn't tell if she was swallowing tears or terror.

"Your mother is like Miss Clack?"

She nodded. Elijah suspected she didn't dare speak for fear she'd cry. Good God, if that was true, it was small wonder the poor girl was such a nervous bundle of reticence and rectitude.

He probed some more, gently, surprised he was bothering. What the hell did he care about this girl or her mother? Yet he probed. "She was as sure of her own righteousness as Miss Clack?"

Another nod.

125

"She thought everyone was going to hell but her?"

A quick glance up. A hesitation, as if she found his assessment somewhat harsh. Another glance away, and an expression telling Elijah that, harsh or not, his evaluation was on the money. Another nod.

He wasn't sure what to say. Wasn't sure he wanted to say anything at all. Yet she'd nursed him. In spite of her dislike of him and her obvious uneasiness around him, she'd nursed him. Hell, she'd even started reading a *novel* for his sake.

"Did she make you feel as though you weren't good enough for her, Miss Hardesty?"

Another nod. Sadder. Slower. Joy peered into her lap and fingered the pages of *The Moonstone*. "Yes. Always."

Curious—which was curious in itself, since he hadn't been curious about anything for years—Elijah asked, "Are your parents still living, Miss Hardesty?"

"No. They've both passed on."

Passed on. Elijah wasn't surprised she'd used the euphemism. He'd noticed before that the relatives of people who cared about things generally didn't just up and die. They *passed on,* or *passed away.* Not that he cared. He'd merely noticed. He also spared her his sympathy, judging she didn't need pity today, but was struggling with other problems.

He narrowed his eyes in thought. "What about your father? Was he the same as your mother? Was he, ah, very sure of himself?" He'd been going to ask her if her father was a self-righteous, overbearing bigot, too, but softened the question for Joy's sake.

"Oh, no." The response came in a staccato burst. It sounded to him as though she was glad to have something to talk about other than her mother. He hardly blamed her. "My father wasn't at all like my mother. In

126

fact, he was terribly misguided." She stopped speaking suddenly and frowned, as if she'd listened to herself and heard her judgment for the first time.

"Misguided?" Elijah shook his head. *Poor thing.* She must have had a hard time of it when she was a little girl. Not that it was any skin off his teeth. "Did your father drink or something?"

A gape of her mouth. A widening of her eyes. Damn, they were pretty eyes. A cock of her head. Now that the sunlight had been allowed into his room, Elijah could clearly see the red and gold highlights in her hair. Pretty hair. Thick hair. Hair that deserved better than those two tightly coiled braids.

"Good heavens, no! My father was a Methodist minister, Mr. Perry."

Elijah's shock drove Joy's physical attributes out of his brain. "A minister? But—"

"He was frivolous," Joy interrupted. "Mother used to say he'd never get anywhere because he lacked ambition and he was too fond of his little jokes."

"His little jokes?" If he'd taught his daughter any jokes, Elijah sure hadn't seen any evidence of it. "Did he, ah, shirk his flock or something?"

She frowned as she contemplated his question. "No— at least, I don't believe he did. Not in the way you mean."

Elijah tried to recall what he could of his Baltimore boyhood. "Did he pay calls on sick folks and preach sermons and so forth?"

"Oh, yes. I believe he was conscientious in his duties." She sucked in a deep breath and amended, "He was as conscientious as his capricious nature allowed, at any rate."

"His capricious nature? Was he irrational? Did he suffer crazy spells or attack his parishioners with sticks or something? Did his congregation dislike him?"

127

"Oh, no. Everyone seemed very fond of him." Her frown turned into a scowl. "They liked him because he was so easygoing, you see. He was permissive. He didn't take things seriously enough. He was much too eager to forgive and pardon people who strayed."

"He forgave people who strayed?"

"Well, yes."

"That doesn't sound like a bad thing. He sounds like a good Christian fellow to me." Not that Elijah knew anything about Christian fellows, good or otherwise.

She appeared to be confused for a moment. "Well, but . . . he was too easy. I mean, for instance, when one of the young women in town, ah . . ." She blushed bright pink.

Elijah was charmed. "When she strayed from the straight and narrow and got into trouble?" he suggested, using the time-honored affectation for pregnancy in an unwed female.

She shot him a grateful glance. Her blush remained hot. "Yes. When she, er, strayed, and brought her baby back to Auburn to live in her parents' home—they said it was an orphaned child they'd adopted, but everyone knew better—my father allowed her to remain in church as if she'd done nothing wrong."

"I presume your mother wanted him to kick her out?"

Joy cleared her throat. "Yes. That is, I don't know if she wanted him to expel her from the congregation, but she believed he should have made her pay for her misdeed. Somehow. Made her do some kind of penance or something." Her blush was gone, and her expression clearly conveyed her perplexity.

Elijah said, "Your mother, I presume, didn't think the poor girl had suffered enough humiliation and heartache already?"

"Um, no. I, ah, guess she didn't."

"She wanted her to pay in public? Maybe be locked in the stocks and have eggs thrown at her for a day or two. Or maybe wear a scarlet *A*, like Hester What's-her-name?"

"Heavens, no!"

Elijah could tell she'd denied it only out of habit. "Hmmm." He began to experience an intense dislike of Joy Hardesty's mother, and an equally intense sympathy for Joy's father. "Did your mother object to anything else your father did?"

"Um, well, yes. I think so. I mean, he used to visit the men in jail and speak to them, but Mother used to say he was too easy on them."

"Too easy on them?"

"I mean, she thought Father should . . . should condemn them for their actions. I mean . . . I don't mean condemn *them*, exactly, but denounce their actions. Or something. I mean—"

"I think I know what you mean."

She took another deep breath and straightened in her chair. Elijah had the strangest feeling she was gathering her mother's principles around her like a shield of righteousness. "He should have taken the opportunity to offer the Lord's Word as salvation to those men whose lives had diverged from the path of goodness and right. Instead he offered sympathy and kindness."

"Merciful heavens, what an evil man, to be sure."

Joy frowned at him, but offered no rebuttal to his sarcasm.

"And your mother didn't approve of that?"

She hesitated for a moment. "No."

"And she took him to task for his failure to live up to her firm principles, I suppose."

He sounded sarcastic again, and Joy appeared bewildered. "Well . . . yes."

129

"I see."

"Do you?"

Joy Hardesty's mother had been Miss Clack personified. The very idea made Elijah want to run away and hide. "So your dad possessed a sense of humor and some human compassion in his heart and your mother didn't?"

She opened and shut her mouth. "Well . . ."

"He was forgiving of his fellows and she sent 'em all to hell without remorse?"

"Well . . ."

"He liked to relax and be pleasant to people and she thought being pleasant was a symptom of moral weakness?"

"Actually, she said it was one's Christian duty to be pleasant to people, even sinners."

"How charitable of her. So it wasn't so much the pleasantness; it was the relaxation part she considered sinful?"

"Well . . ."

"In other words, your father was a nice man whose wife expected greater—or different—things from him than he expected from himself. Then, when he didn't turn out to be what she wanted him to be, she hated him for it? She belittled him?"

"Well . . ."

"I suppose she did it in public."

"Well, I wouldn't put it *that* way."

"I'm sure you wouldn't."

"My mother was a saint, Mr. Perry. Everybody said so."

"I'll bet they did. They wouldn't dare not say so."

"That's not kind. My mother tried very, very hard to live up to what the Lord expected of her."

"You mean she tried to live up to what she'd decided the Lord expected of her."

Joy frowned slightly. "I believe that amounts to the same thing."

"Do you? Did He come to Auburn, sit down to supper with her, and tell her so Himself?"

"My mother read the Bible every day. She prayed about it!" Joy was getting miffed. Elijah wasn't sure he gave a rap. He wished he had Joy's mother here. She wouldn't dare bully him. He wouldn't let her.

"I supposed it's your mother talking through you when you say your father was frivolous and unambitious."

"I . . . well—"

"Come on, now, admit it. You·didn't think that one up all by yourself, now, did you?"

"Well . . ."

"And I suppose she used to look down her nose at people who laughed at amusing things and had a good time when they weren't working, because she didn't have an ounce of amusement or restfulness in her."

"Um, she didn't approve of senseless amusements or frivolity. Japes and jests and so forth are tools of the devil, after all."

"According to your mother."

"I, well, yes."

"So in other words, your father liked to laugh, and your mother considered laughter sinful. Probably because she didn't know how."

Her brow furrowed, and Elijah imagined she was trying to figure out the flaw in his reasoning. He wasn't surprised when she couldn't do it.

"I suppose so."

"And I suppose she terrified any hint of a sense of humor out of you before you knew what it was, so you've always thought laughter was an act of evil."

"Now, don't you go putting words into my mouth, Mr. Perry."

"Wouldn't dream of it." Elijah couldn't understand the rage in his chest. It had built up during their discussion until he wanted to roar like a bull and gore Joy's damned dead mother on his horns.

As for Joy, she sat in her chair, *The Moonstone* on her lap, wringing her hands and looking as if she didn't know whether to whack Elijah over the head with the volume or burst into tears.

"Why'd they name you Joy? It sounds to me as if your mother had about as much truck with joy as she had with sin."

She jerked forward on the chair, and the book fell out of her lap. She leaned over, snatched it off the braided carpet, and snapped, "You needn't be unkind, Mr. Perry. My original question, if I recall, was 'Do I remind you of Miss Clack?' I fail to see what my being named Joy has to do with that."

"Yeah? Well, let me tell you something. Yes, you remind me of Miss Clack. You remind me of her a hell of a lot more than you remind me of joy."

She gasped. He glowered.

"You're trying your damnedest to hate everything and everybody, whether you want to or not. I think you were meant to be a nice person—maybe even a soft and gentle one—but your mother thrashed the instinct out of you. No wonder you're always bitching about having a stomachache. You're wound up so tight inside, trying to be the girl your mother wanted you to be, that you've twisted your guts up into little squeezy balls."

"How dare you!"

"I'll tell you how I dare, Miss Joy Hardesty. Because it's the truth!"

She gasped again. Her face had gone red with fury and embarrassment.

"Instead of taking a clue from your father, who sounds

like he was a nice guy, and being compassionate and forgiving, and laughing every now and then, you let your mother dominate you into being a foul-tempered, self-righteous, dried-up prig. You're as sour as vinegar and as dry as alum."

"Be quiet this instant, Mr. Perry!"

But Elijah was on a roll. He wouldn't be quiet. He was so mad at Joy Hardesty's mother, he wished he could rip her apart with his bare hands. "And let me tell you another thing. Your mother was a damned fool, Miss Joy Hardesty. She ruined you. By the time she was through with you, you hated yourself, you hated the world, you hated everyone in it, and you even hated your own father. If you want to nominate the woman for sainthood, go ahead, but she won't be getting my vote."

Joy stood, trembling with what looked like a potent combination of rage and humiliation. Her voice shook when she said, "If such things are voted on, Mr. Perry, I should be extremely doubtful if you'd be allowed to cast a ballot."

"Yeah, you're right, but let me tell you this, Miss Hardesty. You're about as far from joyful as anybody I've ever seen. I thought Christians were supposed to make a joyful noise unto the Lord. All you do is whine and moan and bitch and carp, and if your mother made you that way, she oughta be shot."

"She can't be shot. She's dead."

"And a good thing, too. How many other people did she ruin? You got any brothers or sisters?"

"No."

"*Damned* good thing! God alone knows what she'd do with a boy. You're bad enough."

"How dare you!"

"Don't give me that 'how dare you' crap, Miss Joy Hardesty. Your mother ruined you! She made you into a sour-faced prune! I'm sure as hell glad she's not here to nurse me, because you're bad enough. Neither one of you deserves to be called a woman. Hell, women are supposed to be soft and sweet. It seems to me the only thing soft about you is your brain. Thanks to your blasted mother, you're about as sweet as a long-horned steer. What's more, if you're a Christian, I'm glad I'm a heathen!" Exhausted from his emotional tirade, Elijah shut his mouth and sank back, breathing heavily, onto his pillows.

Pale and shaking, Joy glared at him for several seconds. Elijah began to wish he hadn't said all those things. He didn't really mean them in relation to Joy, exactly, but to her mother. He cleared his throat and wished he could live the last several minutes over again. He'd keep his fat mouth shut.

"Thank you *very* much, Mr. Elijah Perry. And why your own parents wasted such a noble, sainted name as Elijah on you is a mystery to me!"

A chuckle caught him by surprise. She was quick with a riposte, and he appreciated her for it. "I've always wondered about that myself."

"Good. Then I'll just leave you to wonder to your heart's content!" She turned and began to storm toward the door.

"Hey, wait! You can't just go away and leave me here all by myself."

"No?" She looked over her shoulder and gave him a nasty smile. "Watch me."

And with that she flounced out of the room, taking *The Moonstone* with her.

Chapter Eight

"Damn." Elijah hadn't intended to make her so mad she'd stop reading and leave him. He hoped she wouldn't continue reading the book on her own, because he was interested in finding out what happened next.

He stared at the door, wondering if she was going to come back and light into him some more, or if she was so angry she planned on staying away.

"Damn."

He missed her. She hadn't even been gone a minute, and he missed her. This was stupid.

He glared at the ceiling. Then he glared at the door some more. Then he decided, *to hell with it*, closed his eyes, and tried to nap. After a furious battle with himself—he *wouldn't* get out of bed, chase after Joy, and apologize—he finally slept.

* * *

Joy's anger lasted until she'd raced out of the house, made two furious circuits of the wagon yard, decided the yard was too small a scope for her fury, marched down Second Street, detoured north across the wooden footbridge and up Union, and walked all the way to the marshy land around the Spring River. There exhaustion and tight corsets got the better of her, and she sank down onto a fallen cottonwood log.

Because she wasn't sure if she was going to scream or weep, she looked around to make sure she was alone. She didn't fancy falling apart in front of an audience. Nobody else shared the secluded spot with her. Unsurprising. The wastrels, sinners, and debauched characters who lived in Rio Hondo were more apt to spend their daylight hours carousing in the Pecos Saloon than out in the open air by the river.

On the the other hand, Joy had no way of knowing such a thing for a certainty, since she hadn't met any of them, except once, when two of the girls from the Pecos Saloon had rather timidly braved Mr. McMurdo's mercantile store. They'd been quiet and subdued and Joy hadn't known who they were until afterward. Unless Mr. McMurdo had told her, she'd never have guessed they were . . . *those* kinds of women.

Nonsense. She was being ridiculous about the citizens of Rio Hondo. Of course they were wastrels and sinners! What else *could* they be out here in this wretched territory?

Well, they might possibly be ranchers, out tending to their cows and sheep on the range.

Fiddlesticks! The cattle and sheep ranchers in the area didn't live in the village of Rio Hondo. They visited only occasionally. No. The citizens of Rio Hondo were sinners.

Well, some of them were merchants, blacksmiths, and

other skilled craftsmen and laborers, seeing to the needs of the cattle and sheep ranchers.

Joy frowned. Perhaps. But she was pretty sure that, while some of them might be gainfully employed, the majority were still unchristian, rowdy characters.

Joy sniffed. All of which only went to prove how far superior her mother's teachings were to however the sinners inhabiting Rio Hondo had been brought up, no matter what Mr. Elijah Perry said.

Had her mother really taught Joy to hate her father?

The thought caught in her chest and made her sob out loud. Horrified, she snatched a hankie out of her pocket and pressed it to her mouth to keep any further stray sobs in.

Her father. Joy hadn't thought about her father for years. When she used to think about him, she'd done so with a combination of hurt and disapproval so powerful it had made her insides ache. Yet he'd been kind to her. In fact, now that she *did* think about him, his was the only smile Joy could remember from her childhood.

Was it so wrong to smile and laugh? Her mother had believed so. She'd taught Joy to believe it, too.

Now Joy wondered if her mother had been wrong. For the first time in her life, she wondered if her mother was really the saint Joy had always believed her to be.

She supposed it wasn't surprising that she had grown up believing her mother's teachings. The good Lord knew, her mother's personality had overpowered all the others in Joy's small orbit. Joy had grown up unaccustomed even to think about thinking for herself. Oh, dear, that didn't sound right. Was she really the miserable, tainted creature Mr. Perry believed her to be? She feared she might well be.

Feeling worthless and unhappy, Joy sank her head into her hands. "Oh, Father, I'm sorry." She wasn't sure if she was apologizing to her own father or to her Father in heaven, but she guessed either one would do.

She tried to picture her father in her mind's eye. She saw him, slightly overweight, a gentle-natured man with twinkling blue eyes. Eyes not unlike those of Alexander McMurdo. Joy remembered that once, a long time ago, she'd wished her own eyes were blue, like those of her father. They weren't. Joy had her mother's eyes. In fact, there wasn't a thing about herself that Joy could point to and say, "I inherited this from my kindhearted, good-natured father."

A powerful woman, Mrs. George Hardesty. Much more powerful than Mr. George Hardesty. So powerful, in fact, that when Joy contemplated her birth family, she and her father were mere specks of dust floating in the shadow of the massive personality of her mother. She had a vague recollection of standing, shaking, at her father's side while her mother ripped up at them both, and she shook her head.

How sad, she thought now. *How very sad. He* was *a nice man.*

It wasn't bad to be nice. Joy had suspected it for a long time, in her heart of hearts. She'd never experienced any sort of confirmation of her suspicion until this very day, when her mother's overbearing sanctity had been thrown in her face. By Elijah Perry, of all unlikely people.

Also for the first time in her life, she contemplated the battles her mother used to wage on a regular basis with some of the other women in town; women who were, ostensibly, her friends. Joy had always taken her mother's part in those little wars, believing—because it had never occurred to her not to believe—that those other women were wrong. Now she wondered if perhaps her mother had been a shade irrational in her beliefs and behavior.

"But if that's the case, then Mr. Perry is right, and I'm a living, breathing aberration—an unbalanced human being." What an appalling thought.

Her stomach hurt. She pressed a hand to it and remembered him telling her he didn't wonder that she always had a stomachache, because she was all twisted up inside. What was it he'd said? Her insides were twisted into little squeezy balls? Could he be right?

Joy, who often had to batter her internal self around viciously in order to bend her thinking to conform with that of her mother, realized she needed to do no battering at all in order to come up with an affirmative. Was it her own skewed thinking, her own true nature battling the austerity her mother forced on her, that caused her to feel sick all the time?

Although she didn't know it for a fact, she didn't *think* she was a naturally disagreeable person. In fact, when faced with dilemmas, her first instinct—like her father's— was to give people the benefit of the doubt. She had to fight her compulsion to be kindhearted—*foolish,* according to her mother—in order to criticize people's behavior.

She'd always believed herself to be a spineless weakling. Could it be she wasn't anything of the sort? Could it be that her inner nature was striving to be—Joy gasped at the thought—*friendly?*

What a revolutionary idea. Joy lifted her face from her cupped hands and used her handkerchief to wipe her tears away.

She experienced an impulse to race back to the wagon yard and apologize to Mr. Perry for being such a sourpuss, but she resisted it. She still wasn't sure about this new and radical line of reasoning. It wouldn't do to admit defeat too soon. Perhaps her mother had been right all along, and this was the devil tempting her into wickedness.

A spasm twisted her intestines, and Joy frowned. Had her mother done so much damage to Joy's basic good nature that even thinking like her made Joy's stomach ache? *Good heavens*. This bore further contemplation, although, while Joy was unsure of many things, she had a sneaking hunch that truly sound Christian behavior didn't foster dyspepsia. She also had a hunch that Mr. Perry was right, and her mother's way wasn't necessarily the only way. Or even the best way.

"Dear me," she muttered, wishing God would do her a favor and unscramble her brain for her. Or strike her with a falling tree and put her out of her suffering.

"But, oh, no," she grumbled, feeling aggrieved. "Nothing can be as simple as that, can it?" It didn't seem fair to her that being a good person should be so confoundedly difficult. Being good hadn't been difficult for her mother.

"Ha. But she only made other people feel bad, and I don't suppose *that's* difficult at all."

As soon as she heard herself, Joy sat up, shocked that those words had come from her mouth. She glanced around again, hoping no one had sneaked up behind her. She'd hate to be caught talking to herself, especially when she was saying unkind things about her own sainted—or not sainted; Joy was too confused to formulate a conclusive opinion—mother.

"Oh, stop it! Just stop it. You'd be better off not thinking at all if you're only going to confuse yourself, Joy Hardesty."

Fortunately, her mother's voice didn't chime in with a commentary on Joy's declaration. She braced herself for it, but it didn't come. She was profoundly relieved.

Out of the corner of her eye, Joy saw wild asparagus growing on the marshy bank of the Spring River and decided to pick some for supper. Among the ferny branches of the asparagus bushes, she discovered a fishing pole someone had left there. She picked it up and stared at it for several moments, puzzled. Why, the thing was even baited, and the worm still wiggled.

"Ew." Joy didn't enjoy baiting hooks. She glanced around and saw no one. Was this a sign from heaven? She shook her head hard and told herself not to be silly.

"Sign from heaven, my foot, Joy Hardesty. It's a fishing pole, and someone probably forgot it here. It means nothing more than that." She scowled at her own fanciful nature—and then remembered who had taught her that making up stories was wrong.

Joy squinted up into the heavens. Was her mother up there, glowering down upon her in disapproval? She remembered the stories her father used to tell her when she was a little girl and she'd been alone with him. He used to make up funny, whimsical tales that had kept her amused for hours, until her mother found out about it and put a stop to the practice. Her mother allowed her to hear only stories from the Bible—and even then, only the ones with the harshest moral messages.

She sighed. Those story hours with her father had been happy times for Joy. Strange that she had forgotten them for so many years. She frowned at the fishing pole. Then she stopped frowning and blinked when she perceived a faint glow of sparkles hovering around it. She blinked and stared harder, then decided she was seeing things, undoubtedly because she had lost what remained of her mind. Oddly enough, she didn't find the observation distasteful, probably because her mind had been nothing but a torment to her for two and a half decades now. She shook her head hard.

"Bother! I'm not going to waste a good worm on worrying about what you'd think, Mother."

And with that, she finished picking enough asparagus for a good dinner. Then she searched until she found a decent-size rock sticking far enough out of the slushy undergrowth to keep her bottom dry, hiked up her skirts, sat down, flung the line into the water, and waited for a fish to bite.

After a moment or two, Joy realized she was relaxing and frowned. What would her mother say? On the other hand, what did Joy care? Her mother was dead and couldn't see her, at least not in this plane. Anyway, perhaps relaxation wasn't sinful. Perhaps it was created by God to refresh a body when it had been through an ordeal.

She deliberately steered her mind away from her many transgressions. And from her mother's opinions. Instead, she concentrated on the beauty of the day, on how much fun one could have when one wasn't always judging one's own behavior and that of others, and on how very, very good the fresh air and sunshine felt on her face.

Elijah Perry awoke upon a prodigious snore. He felt something weighty on his chest, pried one eyelid up over a sleepy eye, and spied the little marmalade kitten curled up there like a cinnamon bun.

"Well, hello there, Killer." He grinned, lifted his good arm, and tried to find the kitten's chin tucked in somewhere in all that fur. The cat helped him out. When Elijah's finger stroked his neck, he purred like a Gatling gun. Elijah chuckled.

When he remembered the argument he and Joy had engaged in earlier in the day, his chuckle choked off, his grin faded, he opened his other eye, and he frowned. "Hell. I didn't mean to be so hard on her, Killer."

The kitten yawned, unimpressed, showing off two rows of sharp, white teeth.

"She's not equipped to fight with the likes of me. After all, I'm a lot older than she is. I've seen a hell of a lot more of the world, too. Besides, I've been verbally sparring with people since I was knee-high to a toadstool. She's never fought with anyone in her life, because her damned mother wouldn't let her. She equates disagreement with disobedience, I'll bet you anything."

The kitten yawned again.

Elijah's grin returned. "So I'm boring you, am I? Well, it makes me mad, Killer. I'd like to have that damned mother of hers here. I'd give her a piece of my mind she wouldn't soon forget. She wouldn't be able to push me around the way she did that poor kid of hers."

Joy Hardesty wasn't a kid any longer. Elijah scowled as he continued to pet the kitten. She was a woman—could even be a remarkably attractive one—but she had no idea what to do with her womanhood.

Damn that mother of hers. Elijah would wager almost anything that Joy would have been a nice person if she hadn't been so badly warped so young. It seemed a real pity to him. Not that he aimed to do anything about it. He was no do-gooder. Not Elijah Perry. And especially not for someone who wouldn't appreciate his efforts on her behalf. In fact, he thought with yet another grin, she'd undoubtedly fight him tooth and nail if he tried to instill some human charity into her.

The kitten got up, arched its back, and stretched, digging its back feet into Elijah's bandaged ribs.

"Ow! Dammit, Killer, I already took a whupping today from my nurse. I don't need one from you, too." He gently shoved the cat aside and struggled to a sitting position. He had to pee and looked around for the chamber pot Joy always had handy. He didn't see it.

143

Annoyed about having his bed get up and leave him, the marmalade kitten hissed once at Elijah, then burrowed into the quilt and shut its eyes again. Elijah smiled in appreciation. He liked cats. They didn't give a hang about anything but their own comfort.

"Joy Hardesty could take a few lessons from you, Killer."

Well, hell, he didn't know where the chamber pot was. He hoped to God it wasn't under the bed, because he was in no shape to bend over and fish it out.

"Blast it, I wish I hadn't riled her so bad. I need her." He didn't like admitting it. On the other hand, he'd ever been an honest man. "Reckon I owe her an apology, Killer. Especially for saying she was unfit to call herself a woman." His own words came back to him, and he winced at the memory. Then he swung his legs over the side of the bed and winced from the pain. He wasn't sure which felt worse, his guilty conscience or his healing bullet wounds.

"Well, if the dadblasted chamber pot isn't nearby, guess I'll just have to go out back and find a bush. I sure as hell can't hunker down and crawl under the bed."

With a heavy sigh he stuck his feet into the pair of Mac's slippers he'd been using. They were too small for him, but beggars, as the old saying went, couldn't be choosers. Then, taking a good deal of care since his side and his arm and his thigh still hurt, he shrugged into a bathrobe. With very small, very painful steps, Elijah limped through Mac's house, made his way to the kitchen door, and walked outside, thankful that the path was smooth and looked as though it had been raked recently. He relieved himself in some creosote bushes against the back fence.

"Reckon not even my pee can kill greasewood."

As he tucked himself back into his robe—rather, into

144

Mac's robe—he peered up into the blue, blue sky. There sure was a lot of sky out here in the territory. There was a lot of sky in Texas, too, but there were many more people in Texas than there were here. For some reason beyond Elijah's ken, all those people running around made their surroundings seem less vast than these. He took an experimental breath of fresh air. His chest wound didn't scream at him, so he took another, deeper one.

"Damn, it feels good to be outside." The sun felt warm on his shoulders. His skin felt as if it were sucking up its rays like a man dying of thirst might suck up water. He hated being laid up, even if he was having fun with his nurse.

The truth of his random thought rattled him, and his eyes popped open. He was having fun with Miss Grim-and-Proper Joy Hardesty? He tested the notion, rolled it around in his consciousness, and decided it was true. *Well, glory be.*

Because it felt good, if painful, to be out of bed, Elijah decided not to return to Mac's spare room immediately. Rather, he aimed himself at the mercantile, intending to sit beside the old potbellied stove for a little while. Maybe in a day or two he could spend an hour sitting in a chair outdoors. He'd see how this first excursion went first. With luck, he'd find that Joy had set *The Moonstone* on the counter, and maybe he could read ahead a little bit. God knew, there wasn't anything else for a crippled man to do around here.

Because he had to move so slowly, his progress was relatively silent. Therefore, when he shuffled into the store on his slippered feet, saw Joy behind the counter with her face buried in her hands, and stopped dead in his tracks to stare at her, his presence did not register with her. His heart flopped in his chest, and he pressed a hand to it, wondering if it was his wound acting up, or

145

if some unfamiliar emotion had made it squeeze so hard. He decided, to his astonishment, that it was emotion.

Unsure what to do, he paused, holding on to the door-jamb. Was she crying? Elijah's aching heart lurched even more painfully, and he strained to listen.

"Oh, dear Lord, please help me," he heard, uttered in a soft, almost strangled voice.

So she wasn't crying; she was praying. Elijah, who'd never had much to do with God, wondered if it was wicked of him to listen in as this poor, disturbed girl poured her heart out to the Almighty. Then he decided, since he was already damned for all eternity, if he were to judge himself by Joy's standards—or even his own— he guessed it didn't make any difference if he listened or not. So he did.

"Please, please, please show me what to do, Lord. I don't know any longer. I've always believed what my mother told me, but now Mr. Perry and Mr. McMurdo have made me doubt the correctness of my mother's teachings. Could she have been wrong, dear Lord? Could my father have been right all along, and not merely weak and misguided as Mother always said he was? Oh, I can't stand it! I hate this uncertainty, Lord! Please help me."

Elijah gritted his teeth, squinched his eyes, and grieved to hear his sanctimonious nurse express such anguished doubt. He wished he could remove the burdens from her heart and clear everything up for her, and marveled at the impulse. What the hell did he care about this starchy, overly religious old maid?

The problem, he realized the instant the question popped into his head, was that, however it had happened, he *did* care about her. Damn, how had that come about? She was as mean as a rabid dog and as bullheaded as a mule. The good Lord and Satan both knew she didn't *want* his assistance, much less his empathy.

Hell's bells. Elijah hated it when charitable urges struck him. Fortunately they didn't do so often. He leaned forward, trying to catch her next words.

"Oh, Lord, I'm so confused. Is Mr. Perry a tool of the devil?"

Elijah straightened up and frowned, Joy's question having stung him, although he could think of no good reason it should have done so. If he'd been asked if he was a tool of the devil, he might well have said yes. He'd have been making a joke, though, and he was positive Joy didn't consider it funny.

"My mother would say he was. I know she would."

Yeah, Elijah knew she would, too. And she wouldn't have considered it a joke either.

"But the things he said to me, while unkind, sounded terribly like the truth."

Damn right, they were the truth. Elijah told himself so, even as he continued to hurt for poor Joy and regretted having been so hard on her.

"But what if Mother was right, dear Lord?"

She wasn't Elijah wanted to shout. He didn't, because he didn't want to interrupt Joy's confession. He felt another minuscule pang of guilt about listening in on her conversation with God, but he could stand it. Hell, he was accustomed to doing much worse things than eavesdropping.

"If she was right, then I'm going straight to hell. I know it, because I can't fight against my weak nature any longer, Lord. Not without Your help, I can't. The things she taught me are beginning to make no sense to me. How can I denounce people I don't even know, Lord? I don't want people like Mr. McMurdo and Mr. Perry to hate me because I'm a self-righteous prig, God. And I don't believe it's my place to condemn them. Does that make me a sinner? Oh, Lord, I'm *so* confused!"

Elijah couldn't take any more. Shaking his head, he backed out of the store, making as little noise as he'd made coming into it, and limped back to Mac's house. He felt pretty rotten. He tried to tell himself it was because he was a wounded man, but he had a feeling his state of misery had more to do with Joy Hardesty's unhappiness than with his own physical condition.

Blast it, what did he care if the poor girl was suffering? She epitomized everything he'd ever hated in so-called *good* women.

"Hell and damnation."

His glance fell on Mac's desk as he passed through the parlor. He scowled. What in the name of glory was a Bible doing there, conveniently sitting on top of a pile of papers? Feeling as if the Fates were ganging up on him, Elijah tried to ignore the Bible and continue on to his room. His progress was hampered by the marmalade kitten, who took that moment to step into his path and then proceeded to rub against his legs, winding his fluffy tail around each of his calves in turn, and making walking impossible.

"Damn it, Killer, go away."

The kitten remained. He even looked up at Elijah and meowed, showing his sharp, pointy teeth. Elijah could have sworn the blasted cat was grinning at him. He sneaked another peek at the Bible. A breeze from somewhere—Elijah didn't see any open windows or doors— caused some papers upon which the book rested to slide, and the Bible fell open. Another breeze riffled its pages. The air around him bloomed with sparkling dust motes.

Elijah looked up at the ceiling. Then he looked down at the kitten. Then he sighed heavily and looked back at the Bible. As much as he tried to be honest with himself, still more did he try not to piss off the Fates.

"Aw, hell." As soon as he picked the book up, the

breeze stopped blowing, the marmalade kitten bounced off to chase a dust ball, and Elijah's scowl deepened. He looked down at the page to which the Bible had opened. "Aw, hell in a handbasket." He picked up the book and made his way back to the bed in his sickroom, holding it close to his chest.

Once he was comfortably propped against his pillows, he settled the Bible on his lap and began to leaf through it. Although the phenomenon fostered an uneasy sensation in his breast, Elijah wasn't entirely surprised when the Good Book seemed to fall open at passages extolling tolerance and goodwill.

He frowned heavily. "There's something more going on here than mere coincidence," he said to himself. He didn't expect the forces of nature to respond to his declaration, and they didn't.

That didn't mean, however, that he wasn't going to give Joy Hardesty holy hell for deserting him the next time he saw her. The marmalade kitten took that opportunity to jump up on his bed, climb on top of the Bible, and stare into Elijah's eyes.

"It's not up to you, damn it, Killer," he barked at the cat. "She ran out on me."

The kitten made a noise that was so near an aggrieved sigh as made no difference, and Elijah felt as if all the forces of nature were ganging up on him.

Joy pulled her already-damp handkerchief out of her pocket and blew her nose ferociously. "Blast! Why are you being such a morose, blithering simpleton, Joy Hardesty?" She frowned at her own behavior.

"Sulking and stewing never got you anywhere before, and they won't get you anywhere now. You have to deal with life as it is, and stop wishing it could be different."

She got up and fluffed out her skirt. Then she gave her

nose one more defiant blow, smoothed her hair back, and straightened her shoulders. "You have duties to perform—and don't you dare lecture me, Mother!"

Twelve miles from the O'Fannin ranch, Joy squinted at about a million sparkles that had suddenly burst into the air around her. They were just like the sparkles that had hovered over the fishing pole earlier in the day. "I've never seen such a curious phenomenon in my entire life."

She batted her hand in the air, but succeeded only in making the sparkles change color until she was staring at a veritable kaleidoscope of swirling shimmers. She blinked at them for a moment, enraptured.

Then she gave herself a brisk shake. "Stop mooning this instant, Joy Hardesty. Mr. McMurdo left you in charge of that man, and however much you disapprove of him, you still need to do your duty."

She turned abruptly and walked through the sparkles to the counter, where she picked up six fair-sized perch and a huge bunch of asparagus. Spying the provisions she'd provided by her very own hand cheered her up considerably.

"You might not know much, Joy Hardesty, and you might be as sour as a pickle—according to Mr. Perry. As if *he's* any judge—but you've certainly furnished the fixings for a very tolerable meal." Her smile faded. "Maybe a good dinner will make him forgive you for leaving him alone all day."

She felt guilty because she hadn't even prepared lunch for Elijah today. She'd just abandoned him in a snit. She hoped he hadn't hurt himself foraging for food.

"Good grief, you're thinking about him as if he were a wild animal or something."

Which, all things considered, wasn't a bad analogy. It made Joy grin again as she walked back to Mr. McMurdo's house with her armful of foodstuffs.

*   *   *

Elijah looked up when the door to his room opened. When he saw Joy back into the room, a tray of food balanced in her hands, his heart lit up as if somebody'd struck a match to it. Any idea he'd cherished of berating her for running out on him vanished in a spurt of happiness.

"You're back!" he cried, and then wished he'd kept his blasted mouth shut.

She turned around, opened her mouth, probably to shoot a retort at him, then stood still and goggled, her mouth hanging open. His happy smile evaporated. He squinted at her. "Something wrong?"

She gave a little jerk, as if awakening from a trance. "You're wearing spectacles," she said, making no move toward him.

Elijah reached up and fingered his eyeglasses. "Oh, yeah. I forgot I was wearing them. I wear 'em to read."

He saw Joy swallow, and his frown intensified. What the devil was wrong with wearing specs to read with? Lots of folks did. He opened his mouth to ask her, but didn't get the chance because she spoke first.

"And you're reading..." She paused with a gasp. "You're reading the *Bible!*"

Then she went off into such a peal of laughter that Elijah was afraid she'd drop his dinner tray before she managed to set it on the bureau. Damn, he was hungry.

Chapter Nine

"Well, I couldn't find *The Moonstone. Or* the chamber pot. *Or* my lunch."

Elijah sounded very crabby. Joy knew she should stop laughing, but she couldn't. It was as if all the laughter she'd kept bottled up for twenty-five years had popped its cork and was now rioting out of control. Tears ran down her cheeks. She managed to set the tray on a bureau before her knees gave out, and she collapsed into the chair beside Elijah's bed. Her whoops sounded improper and they embarrassed her, but she couldn't contain them.

He scowled at her. "What's so damn funny about me reading the Bible?"

"N-nothing. Nothing at all." She doubled over, helpless to withstand the power of her mirth.

"Is that food I smell there?" Elijah asked with some asperity. "Do you plan to feed it to me or torture me by making me smell it? I haven't eaten anything since breakfast, you know."

She nodded, and couldn't get any words formed. She needed to apologize for not feeding him sooner. She *would* apologize. As soon as she regained mastery over her giggles.

The only sounds in the room for several moments were Joy's unladylike snorts as she tried and failed to stop laughing, and the purr of the marmalade kitten snoozing on Elijah's blanketed legs. After several moments of this, Elijah said, "What do you think, Killer? Should I throw something at her? You suppose that'd make her shut up?"

Joy looked up, wiped her eyes with the hem of her apron, and gulped several times. After a moment she managed to choke out, "You're—you're *not* going to call that poor, sweet kitten Killer!"

"Oh, yeah? Says who?"

Oh, dear. He looked really quite exasperated with her. She could hardly blame him. She gasped twice, swallowed another laugh with a good deal of difficulty, snorted three times, and blurted out, "*I* say so!"

"You weren't here," Elijah reminded her coldly. "And I've already taught him his name, so there."

Joy sat up and gathered the shattered ribbons of her dignity around her. "Nonsense! I wasn't gone long enough for you to teach anything to anything." She frowned. "Or something like that."

"That's what you think. You were gone all day long, and he already knows his name is Killer."

"Fiddlesticks." Joy struggled out of the chair. She had a stitch in her side from laughing so hard. She couldn't remember such a thing ever happening to her before. Laughter had been frowned upon in her family, at least by her mother, whose will was so strong it had eventually choked the levity out of her father. Such a thing seemed a shame to her now, in light of the fact that her insides felt much less knotted up after her bout of glee than they had earlier in the day. Why, she could hardly feel the painful weight she always carried around in her chest.

Perhaps there was something healthful to this funning nonsense. Since she was pretty sure Elijah would make a big deal out of it if she mentioned her suspicion, she didn't. Instead, she folded her hands primly in front of her and lifted her chin. She forced herself not to give in to the bubble in her chest making her want to laugh some more. She cleared her throat, and stared at the wall behind Elijah's left shoulder. She didn't dare look him in the eyes for fear she'd burst out laughing.

"I owe you an apology, Mr. Perry. I should not have left you alone today, and I am sorry for my rash action. I was wrong to have lost my temper, and even more wrong to have left you helpless in your bed. I know my absence might have put you in peril, and I apologize. Although," she couldn't resist adding, "I see you ultimately found something useful to do with your time."

She lowered her gaze and stared pointedly at the Bible resting on his stomach. The incongruity of Elijah Perry, of all people, reading the Bible, struck her once more, and she snorted again. Her behavior embarrassed her, and she felt herself get warm.

Elijah stared at her. Joy, glancing at him briefly before resuming her inspection of the wall behind him, couldn't tell by his expression if he was annoyed or not. His continued perusal made her edgy, though, and she decided she didn't have to stand still for it. Ergo, she made a quick lunge for the bed and grabbed the kitten from his lap.

"Hey!" Elijah shouted.

"Killer, my foot. This adorable little thing's name is Apricot, and that's all there is to it." She stroked the kitten under the chin, and it purred louder. "Isn't that so, my precious Apricot kitty?"

"Dadblast it, you stole my cat!"

Joy smirked at him. "I did no such thing. I removed the kitten from your lap so that I may place your supper tray there."

"Oh. So you finally decided to feed me, did you?"

Elijah grinned, and Joy's heart executed a sudden flip-flop. *Good heavens.* He was a sinfully attractive man. Which, all things considered, made sense. Everything else about him was sinful, after all.

However, she couldn't allow herself to be distracted by such nonsensical attributes as human comeliness, which, her mother had always told her, only led the unwary to carnal urges and eternal damnation.

All inclination to laugh vanished in a flash, and Joy wished she hadn't thought about her mother.

Well, no matter. She determined to thrust all memories of her mother out of her mind this evening whenever they appeared. She might invite them back in later, if she discovered her mother had been right about everything. At the moment, Joy could only be glad her mother wasn't in Rio Hondo, or Joy would never live this day down.

"Yes, indeed. I am going to—Blast!" She dropped the kitten, who scrambled back onto the bed. "Come here, Apricot."

Elijah snagged the kitten and tucked it under his arm. "Don't pay any attention to her, Killer. You can help me eat my supper."

"Nonsense, Mr. Perry. Give me that kitten. It's unsanitary to eat with an animal on your bed."

"There are some people, Miss Hardesty, who believe it's unwise—even sinful—to take meals in bed anyway. What difference does Killer make?"

Joy planted her fists on her hips and squinted down at

him. "I'll tell you what difference Apricot makes, Mr. Perry. He makes the difference between your taking supper now, and your not taking it at all, because I will *not* serve you as long as Apricot remains on your bed."

Elijah frowned at her, then looked at her cat. "Damn it, Killer, I'm afraid she's got me there. I'm starving, thanks to her." He heaved a huge sigh that ended in a grunt.

Joy's humor returned with a thump, and she had to fight her smile. He'd evidently forgotten how tender his chest wound remained and had breathed too deeply. She held out her arms. "Please allow me to remove Apricot from your care, Mr. Perry."

He slanted a glance up at her. Joy's breath caught in her chest. He had the most beautiful eyes! She'd never paid any attention before, but his lashes were as dark and luxurious as anything Joy'd ever seen. He had fine eyes, Elijah Perry did. Fine, fine eyes. Even if he did need spectacles to read with. Recollecting this evidence of human frailty on her patient's part made Joy feel less breathless. She didn't lower her arms. "Give over, Mr. Perry. I demand you give me that cat. Apricot."

Elijah heaved another, softer, sigh. "Oh, all right. I'm sorry, Killer."

He handed Joy the kitten. She deliberately paid attention to the cat instead of the man when she took it out of his hands. She didn't quite dare look at Elijah until she'd gathered her wits back together. Strange, fluttering sensations had started dancing in her innards, and she had an unhappy suspicion they were caused by the sudden, electric, and wholly unwelcome attraction she felt for Mr. Perry.

This would never do. She told herself so at least fifteen times in the few seconds it took her to shoo the kitten out of Elijah's room and shut the door so he couldn't run back in again. She didn't trust little marmalade kittens in room full of freshly caught, freshly cooked fish.

Dusting her hands together, she steeled herself to withstand her uncooperative emotions and walked back to the bed. "There. I've put Apricot out of the room for the time being. I'll let him in again after you've eaten."

"Poor old Killer," grumbled Elijah. "I'm sure he could use some chow, too."

"Oh, I fed the cat." Joy shot Elijah a smug grin as she lifted his tray from the bureau. "It's only *you* I neglected."

Elijah gave her a good hot scowl. "Why doesn't that surprise me?"

"I have no idea, for I am a wonderfully capable nurse, you know. I had the best training in the world. Today's lapse was most unlike me." She expected one of her mother's rejoinders to kick her in the conscience after her uncharacteristic boast. It didn't, and she felt pretty cheerful about it.

With great care, she set the tray across Elijah's legs. She flapped open a napkin and tucked it under his chin. Touching his flesh made the flutters in her middle speed up and whirl like dervishes, but she refused to acknowledge them. Then she stood back and beamed at him. "There! I caught that fish today, Mr. Perry, after I deserted you. And I picked the asparagus, too. Mr. McMurdo already had the potatoes. And I found the pickled onions in his pantry."

Elijah scanned his tray with an appreciative eye. "Looks good." He glanced up at Joy and winked. "And so do you, Miss Hardesty."

Joy gasped, astonished, and almost fell over backward.

"This is the best chow I've had in years, Miss Hardesty. Of course, my opinion might be colored by the fact that you almost starved me to death today."

Elijah peered at Joy out of the corner of his eye, and was pleased to see that her cheeks remained pink. He squinted harder, and realized her high color was not due entirely to the blush she'd blushed when he'd said she looked good. By damn, she'd actually gotten some sun today after she deserted him. She looked much healthier for it, too. Not so washed-out and sickly. Good for her— even if her outdoor activities had left him perishingly hungry.

Actually, he realized—not for the first time—that she could be very attractive without half trying if she wanted to be. It was her pinched-up, withered, sourpuss expression that had originally put him off. If she continued to loosen up, she might turn out to be a genuinely pretty woman one of these days.

"I've already apologized to you, Mr. Perry, and I don't plan to do it again." She squinted at him. Elijah wasn't sure, but he thought there was still some humor lurking in her expression. "You can't milk an apology forever, you know, or the apologizer begins to feel put upon. Now that I've run away once and know I can get away with it, you'd best not tempt me to do it again until you're feeling stronger, don't you think?"

By God, it *was* humor! Elijah lifted his head and stared at her, a forkful of fish halfway to his mouth. "Are you teasing me, Miss Joy Hardesty? *You?*"

Her cheeks got pinker. Elijah was delighted. "You were! Well, by damn, I didn't think you had a tease in you, but you've proved me wrong. This *is* a red-letter day." He stuffed the fish into his mouth, pleased as punch. Maybe she wasn't such a starched-up old spinster, after all. There might be hope that she'd turn into a real human being yet.

"Don't take it too much to heart, Mr. Perry," Joy advised dryly.

"Don't worry, I won't. I'm sure it's a temporary aberration."

She gave him a glare that tickled his funny bone. "But really, this is mighty tasty, Miss Hardesty. I didn't know you could find asparagus out here in this crazy place."

"It grows wild in the marshes by the Spring River. There are even some willow and cottonwood trees up there."

"Really? I had no idea."

"Undoubtedly that's because you never get out of smoke-filled saloons, Mr. Perry." She gave him a superior smile and popped a bite of potato into her mouth.

He grinned at her. "Don't get too full of yourself, Miss Hardesty, or I might have to take you down a peg or two."

"Ha! I'd like to see you try, laid up as you are."

"I'm not as helpless as you think, Miss Priss. Just watch out, is all I have to say."

"Hmmm."

They ate in silence for a few minutes. Elijah kept sneaking glances at Joy, his amazement at the transformation in her boundless. He hoped she'd remain transformed. Why, she looked almost soft this evening, in the fading afternoon light leaking in through the window. Not at all the prickly, standoffish young woman he'd first seen sweeping off Mac's front porch.

Elijah's heart gave a sudden spasm. He stabbed another piece of fish and poked it into his mouth. Damn, it tasted good. As he chewed, he studied Joy's face some more.

By God, he did like her. In fact, even worse, he felt almost akin to her. *Blast.* How had that happened? He was supposed to be a coldhearted son of a bitch. He couldn't go around empathizing with troubled people—

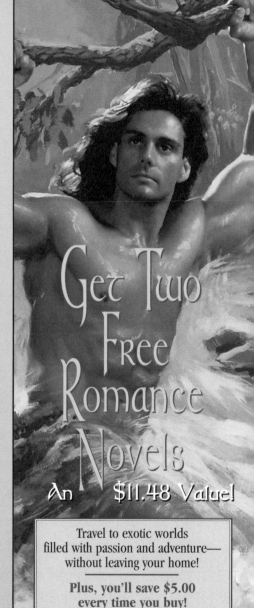

Thrill to the most sensual, adventure-filled Romances on the market today...

FROM ✦ LOVE SPELL BOOKS

As a home subscriber to the Love Spell Romance Book Club, you'll enjoy the best in today's BRAND-NEW Time Travel, Futuristic, Legendary Lovers, Perfect Heroes and other genre romance fiction. For five years, Love Spell has brought you the award-winning, high-quality authors you know and love to read. Each Love Spell romance will sweep you away to a world of high adventure...and intimate romance. Discover for yourself all the passion and excitement millions of readers thrill to each and every month.

Save $5.00 Each Time You Buy!

Every other month, the Love Spell Romance Book Club brings you four brand-new titles from Love Spell Books. EACH PACKAGE WILL SAVE YOU AT LEAST $5.00 FROM THE BOOK-STORE PRICE! And you'll never miss a new title with our convenient home delivery service.

Here's how we do it: Each package will carry a FREE 10-DAY EXAMINATION privilege. At the end of that time, if you decide to keep your books, simply pay the low invoice price of $17.96, no shipping or handling charges added. HOME DELIVERY IS ALWAYS FREE. With today's top romance novels selling for $5.99 and higher, our price SAVES YOU AT LEAST $5.00 with each shipment.

AND YOUR FIRST TWO-BOOK SHIP-MENT IS TOTALLY FREE!

IT'S A BARGAIN YOU CAN'T BEAT! A SUPER $11.48 Value!

Love Spell ✦ A Division of Dorchester Publishing Co., Inc.

Get Two Books Totally
F R E E —
An $11.48 Value!

▼ Tear Here and Mail Your FREE Book Card Today! ▼

PLEASE RUSH
MY TWO FREE
BOOKS TO ME
RIGHT AWAY!

Love Spell Romance Book Club
P.O. Box 6613
Edison, NJ 08818-6613

AFFIX
STAMP
HERE

especially troubled, starched-up spinster ladies—or his reputation would be ruined.

He investigated her and her personality some more as he took a bite of asparagus, understood something else—and hated it. Elijah shook his head and grimaced. Good God, he was like Joy Hardesty's damned mother.

Thunderation. It made him sick to admit it. But the conclusion he reached resonated, unfortunately, like the truth in his consciousness. Although they had tackled the problem from different directions, both Joy's awful mother and he, Elijah Perry, had come to the same conclusion about life. He stopped chewing and his eyes opened wide as he tried to wriggle out of this latest understanding. *Aw, hell, it couldn't be. Could it?*

Joy looked at him inquiringly, and he recommended chewing. *Damn it all to hell and back again.* He couldn't get out of it. No matter how much he hated admitting it, his intrinsic honesty wouldn't let him. Somehow or other, he had learned to mistrust the world every bit as much as Mrs. More-righteous-than-God-Himself Hardesty. What was more, he suspected he feared the world every bit as much as she had. He had come to consider the world an awful place filled with awful people, and had decided eons before not to trust it or them. Just, in fact, like Mrs. Hardesty.

Well, hell. He hated knowing he and Joy's mother had anything at all, even remotely, in common. But they did. And it wasn't all that remote, either. "Crap," he muttered as he stabbed a stalk of asparagus.

Joy arched an eyebrow. "Is something the matter with your supper, Mr. Perry?"

He hadn't meant to swear out loud. He mumbled, "No, ma'am. It's real good. Thanks."

Joy eyed him slantwise for a moment before she slipped a bite of fish between her lips. Elijah stared at her lips and realized something else. This realization shocked him even more than his last two had.

By thunder, he *wanted* her. As a man wanted a woman. *Good God.* He looked at his plate quickly, hoping she hadn't caught the expression of amazement he knew must be plastered all over his face.

"Um, may I ask you a question, Miss Hardesty?"

She shot him a suspicious glance, and waited until she'd swallowed before answering cautiously, "What question is that, Mr. Perry?"

"How old are you? If you don't mind my asking."

Her back went straight, her chin went up, the pink in her cheeks deepened, and Elijah, for all his emotional discomfort, grinned. "I know, I know: How rude of me, huh?"

"Indeed," she said in a frosty voice.

"I'll bet your mama would tell you not to be vain about your age, Miss Hardesty."

Her lips pursed for an instant. Elijah wished he hadn't brought her abysmal mother into the conversation, especially since he now suspected he was no better than she.

"Vanity has nothing to do with it, Mr. Perry. My mother would never have been so tactless as to ask another person his or her age."

Elijah had no reason to feel nettled by her frigid tone and starchy posture. After all, he was the one who'd mentioned Joy's old battle-ax of a mother. He frowned down at his supper again. "Yeah, right. I forgot. She was a saint." He wondered if he'd get a stomachache from all the bile the thought of Joy's mother was churning up in his stomach.

"Hmmm. Yes. Perhaps."

His head snapped up. "Perhaps? You mean you're not sure about her sanctity any longer?"

Joy laid her fork down beside her plate, set her plate on the table beside the bed, and stood up. "Are you finished, Mr. Perry? I made some apple dumplings for dessert if you're ready for one. There's even some cream to pour over them."

"Coward," he said, grinning, as he handed her his empty plate.

There went her lips again, pursing up all hard and pinchy. Elijah wished he were a well man; he'd kiss them soft again. His eyes popped open when he realized what he'd just thought. *Good Lord!* Was his brain going soft, or what?

"I am not a coward," Joy said crisply. "And there is no reason for you to look so surprised that I made apple dumplings for dessert. I am a very good cook."

Elijah swallowed hard, and could only be glad she'd so completely misunderstood his expression. "Er, yes, I know you're a good cook, Miss Hardesty. I'd love an apple dumpling for dessert. With cream. Thank you."

He guessed she wasn't used to his being polite to her, because her eyes narrowed as she examined him. She looked as if she expected him to pop out of the covers and shout "Boo!" As if he could. He tried on his blandest, least offensive smile. Joy's distrust didn't appear to abate significantly. She did, however, nod once briefly, and turn.

Right before she got to the door, she turned around and said, "I am twenty-five years old, Mr. Perry."

Then she twisted the handle, opened the door, and the marmalade kitten dashed into the room and made a flying leap onto Elijah's stomach. He'd opened his mouth to speak to Joy, but the sudden pain of the kitten's attack made him grunt instead. As he pressed a hand to his wounded ribs, he heard Joy go off into another peal of laughter right before she shut the door.

In spite of his pain, Elijah smiled. Damn, he'd never in a million years have guessed he'd actually be having fun with Miss Joy Hardesty.

Joy had pulled the bedroom curtains closed over the windows and had finished lighting the kerosene lamps when she discovered that the marmalade kitten had curled up in her chair. Still feeling lighthearted—how long the condition would endure, she had no way of knowing, but she intended to savor it while it lasted—she jammed her fists on her hips and pretended to frown at it.

"Well! Turn my back for one little minute, and look what happens." She turned her head slightly and squinted in Elijah's direction. She didn't quite dare look him in the eye, because she feared what she might see there. "I thought you were supposed to be taking care of Apricot, Mr. Perry."

"I tried."

His voice, low and teasing, made something funny happen in Joy's chest. *Jerusalem!* This was perfectly shocking. At least, it should be. This evening Joy discovered nothing shocked her very much. *Merciful heavens.* What did this mean? It wasn't anything good, she was sure.

"Well!" she said again, striving to maintain her tone of mock outrage.

"Come here, Killer. Come here, boy." Elijah kissed his lips together, calling the kitten, and Joy's innards took to swooping and diving like sparrows that had overindulged in fermented berries. She took a deep breath, and commanded herself to cease this outrageous internal dithering.

"Shoo," she said, and fluttered her hands at the cat. It propped one eye open and grimaced at her. She grinned in appreciation. "Apricot looks like he's telling me to go away and leave him alone."

"*Killer's* telling you to go to hell, actually."

She shot him a sidelong glance. "I see. And do you speak cat fluently, Mr. Perry?" She might have dipped her comment in sugar before she gave it to him, it sounded so sweet.

He barked out a laugh. "The good Lord knows, I've known enough of 'em in my time. Both the feline and the human variety."

Joy sniffed, reminding herself of herself, and unsettling her. She hadn't realized how obnoxious she sounded when she sniffed like that. Nevertheless, she persisted in a teasing voice, "I'm sure that's true."

Elijah patted a spot on the bed at his side. "Why don't you leave poor Killer alone and sit here by me."

"*Apricot* considers such a suggestion as outrageous as I do, Mr. Perry."

"Horsefeathers. There's nothing improper about sitting next to a wounded man, Miss Hardesty. It's not as if I'm fit enough to do anything to you. Bore you to death, maybe, but that's about it."

Joy tried to keep from giggling, and couldn't. She knew that if her mother *was* watching from her heavenly home, she would probably send a bolt of lightning down from the skies and fry her on the spot for what she was about to do. She did it anyway.

Heaving a sigh and muttering, "What a sane Christian woman won't do for the sake of being kind to dumb animals," she sat on the spot Elijah had just patted. Then, because her own behavior shocked her, she scooted to the very edge of the bed.

"Don't fall off, Miss Hardesty," Elijah advised acidly.

"I'll try not to," she responded. Her tone was quite snappy, and she was proud of it. In truth, her heart had taken to thundering like an avalanche, and she hoped to goodness Mr. Perry wouldn't notice the heat in her cheeks. With luck, she'd been toasted enough by the warm spring sunshine this morning that her blush would pass for sunburn.

She sneaked a peek at him from out of the corner of her eye, and was relieved to see him staring up at the ceiling. Maybe her high color would fade by the time he looked at her again. She also noticed that he had his hands folded over his stomach.

At least he wouldn't be attempting to do anything improper to her person. No man would want to. What a relief that was.

Joy knew she was sliding down the slippery slope of sin and depredation and into perdition when she realized she was lying to herself. It wasn't a relief at all. Rather, she experienced a strong, ardent wish that she, Joy Hardesty, could inspire lust in the male breast. At any rate, she wished she could inspire lust in *this* male breast. *Jerusalem!* What kind of fallen, immoral woman did that make her? She didn't want to think about it now.

Instead she cleared her throat and said, "Would you like me to read another chapter from *The Moonstone,* Mr. Perry?"

He lowered his head, and Joy saw that his brows had creased into a frown, cutting two deep ruts in his forehead. His face reminded her of a weathered board. Elijah Perry evidently had lived hard in his life. Unlike Joy herself, who'd been too scared to live at all. She sighed, wishing suddenly that she'd been born into a different family, a family that had cherished laughter and openness as much as her mother had deplored them. What a wicked woman she was turning out to be. Joy tried to be appalled and couldn't.

"Actually, I think I'd rather just talk this evening, Miss Hardesty, if you're game."

At once Joy's heart gave a hard spasm, and all of her inhibitions and trepidations stampeded back into her head like rampaging longhorns. "Talk?" The word popped out like a bullet. "Talk about what?"

He shrugged and grimaced, then rubbed his wounded arm. "I don't know. About anything. You know, just talk. You tell me about your life, and I'll tell you about—" He stopped talking and grinned suddenly. "Well, I'll think of something to tell you about, anyway."

She squinted at him. "If I tell you about my life, you have to tell me about yours, Mr. Perry. Fair's fair."

He tilted his head to one side, and his grin turned devilish. "I might shock you."

She sniffed. "I sincerely doubt it. I'm not *that* innocent, you know."

"You're not? I don't believe it."

"Hmph. Well, I'm not."

"I don't know. I'll have to think about this."

Joy, feeling nervous, let her gaze scan the room. It landed on the table beside Elijah's bed, and fastened on the lovely old silver watch in which she'd found the lock of hair. Before she could think about what she planned to do, she leaned over and picked up the watch. "This is a beautiful old thing, Mr. Perry. Did it belong to your father, by any chance?"

When she made herself glance at him, she saw his expression had softened a good deal. He looked younger and less bored with life. "No," he said, his voice gentle. "My Uncle Luke gave me that. It belonged to his father."

"Was your uncle Luke your father's brother, or your mother's?"

"Neither, actually. He was just a close friend of the family's, and I always called him Uncle Luke." Elijah took the watch from Joy's fingers and gazed at it lovingly. "He owned a hotel in Baltimore. I think the only times I was ever happy was when I was working in my Uncle Luke's hotel."

"Really? What did you do there?"

He sighed deeply. "Oh, anything. Everything. Whatever he wanted me to do. I would have scrubbed the stairs with a toothbrush if he'd asked me to, but he didn't. He was always nice to me."

His voice had taken on a puzzled quality, as if he didn't know why his Uncle Luke had bothered to be nice to him. A scrap of sadness nestled in Joy's heart. She looked at the strong brown fingers loosely clasping the watch, and tried to imagine the little boy Elijah Perry used to be. Her imagination, not having been given any scope to operate in her life, failed to produce an image.

Elijah sighed again. "Luke's son and I were good friends, though."

"Really? Were you about the same age?"

He nodded. "He was little older than I was. Luke Junior. He married my sister Eliza, and they had the prettiest little baby girl." He shook his head, and Joy could tell he was remembering something very old and very dear to him. "Prettiest little thing, she was, all blond curls and blue eyes. Virginia, her name was. Is. Virginia Gladstone."

Joy tried to stifle her gasp.

Chapter Ten

Elijah heard Joy's short gasp and turned to look at her. "What? What's wrong with Virginia Gladstone? It's a perfectly good name."

She smiled. She had a damned fine smile for a pickled old maid. "There's nothing wrong with Virginia Gladstone, Mr. Perry. I'm only surprised to hear you say such nice things about a baby, is all."

He gave her a sniff that sounded amazingly like one of hers. "Yeah? Well, it just so happens that I like kids, Miss Joy Hardesty. What's wrong with that?"

"Not a thing. In fact, I think it's a charming trait, considering you're not exactly the type of fellow a person would normally associate with such soft emotions."

His frown deepened until his honesty tapped him on the shoulder and told him to admit she'd spoken nothing but the truth. He released his scowl with another sigh. "Yeah. You're right." He fingered his Uncle Luke's watch. It meant a lot to him, although he seldom allowed himself to think about it. "She's almost your age now. I've been writing to her since I was sixteen."

He wasn't surprised when Joy blinked at him. "You mean she's all grown up now?"

He nodded. "I haven't seen her since she was two years old. Damn, she was a cutie-pie."

"My goodness."

He pressed the clasp, released the latch, and gently opened the watch. Carefully he lifted out the lock of hair he kept in there. "This is hers."

Joy didn't reach for the tress, but eyed it wonderingly. "That's a lock of hair from a little girl?"

He nodded. "She'd barely turned two when she gave it to me."

"Merciful heavens."

He smiled, remembering. "I was planning to leave home for good. I didn't tell anyone my plans, but I asked her mama if I could have a lock of Virginia's hair as a keepsake, and she gave it to me. Once I left, I never went back again, but I kept writing to Virginia. I send her things from all over. Everywhere I land, I'll send her a letter and a little keepsake. I sent her an arrowhead from Mexico once. And a gold nugget from California." He smiled at the memories, and then his smile turned into a frown. "To tell the truth, I'm not even sure Virginia's alive any longer."

"Good gracious. Do you mean to tell me she's never written you back?" Joy's eyes went as round as copper pennies. She had gorgeous eyes, really, when they weren't squinting at the world suspiciously.

"I honestly don't know, Miss Hardesty. I've never given her an address where she can reach me."

"Why not?"

"I move around too much." It was an evasion and

didn't tell anywhere near the full story, but he didn't feel like elaborating.

She puzzled over his half answer. "I'm . . . surprised, I suppose is the right word, that you've never gone home again."

He shrugged, being careful not to jar his wounded shoulder. "There wasn't anything in Baltimore for me. I loved staying with Uncle Luke and his wife, but they were getting old. Luke Junior was married to my sister and growing a family. I couldn't impose on them any longer."

"What about—where were your parents?"

He felt his features harden as they always did when he thought about his parents. "Oh, they were there. In Baltimore. Still are, I reckon."

"Oh."

From the expression on her face, Elijah knew Joy wanted to ask him about his folks but was too polite. Her mother's training again. He shook his head, exasperated. "Go ahead, Miss Hardesty. Your mother isn't here to spank you if you get nosy." Not that he wanted to talk about his parents. In fact, at the moment, he wasn't sure whom he disliked more, Mrs. Hardesty or his own father. They were nothing alike, but they'd both been poisonous parents.

Joy looked indignant for a moment before her expression relaxed into a small, sweet smile. Elijah felt something catch in his chest. "Well, I *am* curious. After all, you're very unlike the men—the *gentlemen*, I hasten to elaborate—to whom I was exposed in Auburn."

He chuckled. "I imagine I am."

She looked at him expectantly, and he sighed. "All right. My parents. Well, let me think for a minute."

Joy sat patiently on the edge of his bed—he didn't know how she kept her balance, poised like that—while

171

Elijah tried to find words with which to describe his feelings about his parents. It was a new experience for him, attempting to explain his innermost thoughts and emotions, and he discovered it wasn't easy. His brow furrowed. Joy cocked her head and lifted her brows. Her hands were folded in her lap, and she presented the very picture of the kind of lady his mother pretended to be and wasn't. Joy didn't have to pretend. If it weren't for all the false pieties her own mother had crammed into her, she'd actually be an ideal lady. Interesting notion, that, but nothing to the point.

Elijah muttered an oath under his breath. Joy primmed her lips; he could tell she did it comically, as if she were attempting to find humor in her own foibles as well as his. He grinned in reaction. "Aw, hell, Miss Hardesty, I'm trying to find something to say about my parents that won't shock you."

Joy peered coyly at her lap and pinched a pleat in her skirt between two fingers, smoothing it down flat. "I'm sure there's nothing you can say that will shock me any more than anything else you've ever said to me, Mr. Perry."

His crack of laughter made Joy's eyes sparkle. Damn, she had pretty eyes.

"All right, all right. I expect you're right. Then it won't mortify you unduly to learn that I didn't like my parents—mostly because they didn't like me."

Her eyes stopped sparkling. "They didn't like you? How can that be?"

The bitterness he tried to keep locked away leaked into his chest and made it ache momentarily. "Damned if I know. Sure as hell, if I ever had a kid, I'd love it and want to get to know it."

He sucked in a breath and told himself to stop swearing. After all, even though Joy knew he was a hardened sinner, he didn't have to sully her ears so brutally. He cleared his throat. "My sister was ten years older than me, and I guess they figured their job was done when I came along and spoiled everything. They never wanted me around. I guess I got in their way. So, as soon as I outgrew my nannies, they sent me away to school."

"My goodness." She thought that one over for a moment. Her brows knitted. "How old were you when you went to school?"

He shrugged. "I dunno. Five or six."

"Five or six! Good heavens. You must have missed your home terribly."

"Oh, I don't know. When I was at home, they kept me tucked away so I couldn't bother them. There wasn't much to miss."

"Mercy."

His lips twisted into their customary cynical grin. "There isn't much of mercy in either one of my parents, I fear."

"I should say not. I can't imagine sending so very young a child away from home. I should think your parents would have missed you dreadfully."

"My mother might have. My father didn't want me, Miss Hardesty."

"He *what?*"

"He didn't want me. My father even told me so." Knowing it did him no credit to whine about his childhood—after all, he was a grown man now—he tried to keep his voice light.

"Why, I never! I've never heard of anything so horrid in my life!"

Her indignation on his behalf pleased him, although he would have been hard-pressed to say why. "I fear not all folks are cut out to have children. You must have figured that one out by this time."

He had the satisfaction of seeing his remark register. Her eyebrows rose again into two high arches, and she let out a small gasp. "Do you think my mother was like that? Unfit for motherhood, I mean?"

"From what you've told me about her so far, it sounds like it to me." He refrained from saying that she, herself, and the way she behaved, had told him as much as he needed to know about her mother before he'd spoken a word to her. He didn't want to wound her. Not now that he'd come to like her, he didn't.

"Anyway, when I was in Baltimore, I didn't stay at my parents' house. During summers, I used to hang out at Uncle Luke's hotel. I loved that place." He stared over Joy's shoulder, remembering the fine times he used to have. "I worked, you know. I didn't shirk. Uncle Luke used to let me do things. Damn, I loved it there."

"Did you used to spend the night there, too?"

"Yeah. Uncle Luke and Aunt Genevieve didn't mind having me around like my parents did. I've liked hotels all my life because of Uncle Luke."

"I can understand that, I guess."

"I used to wish I could stay with Uncle Luke at the hotel instead of going off to school. I didn't mind being away from my parents and their house, but I sure missed that hotel."

He cocked his head as an amusing thought struck him. "Y'know, actually, you might have been better off if your own mother had sent you away to school. I don't think the nuns twisted me up inside as much as your mother twisted you, all things considered. At least I never expected the nuns to love me, so I wasn't disappointed when they didn't."

"Nuns! Good heavens! You mean to tell me you went to a *Catholic* school?"

She sounded more shocked about the Catholic part

than when he'd said his father didn't love him. Her judgments—courtesy of her mother, Elijah was sure—tickled him enormously. "Is that bad? Are Catholics wicked sinners, Miss Hardesty? Well, if it's any comfort, I haven't set foot in a Catholic church since I was sixteen years old and left home. Or any other church, for that matter."

There went her eyebrows again, arching over her pretty eyes like rainbows. Elijah was charmed.

"You left home when you were *sixteen?*"

"Yeah. That was before the war. I went west. Then, when the war started, I joined the army."

Her eyes widened until he wasn't sure they weren't going to pop out of her head. "Oh, hell, Miss Hardesty. I was a man grown by the time the conflict began. There were a lot of boys younger than me dying for the right to own slaves."

She blinked at him, and he wished he he hadn't allowed his bitterness to taint his opinion of the great Confederate cause.

"Oh, but . . . but . . ." She swallowed. "Yes, I know many young men died."

"They weren't all young. I was—shoot—twenty-three or twenty-four when I joined."

"That's still awfully young, Mr. Perry. I'm twenty-five, and I only recently found a calling."

"The missionaries," he said, trying not to sound contemptuous.

"Yes. The missionaries." She frowned down at the pleat in her skirt. She'd been running it between her fingers for several minutes now. Elijah figured it would never uncrease at this rate. "But war seems like such a dreadful waste of life and energy. My goodness."

"Maybe, but it was the patriotic thing to do." Again he regretted his sarcasm, but realized almost immediately that Joy hadn't noticed it.

"Oh. Well, but you were so young when you left home. And even when you joined the army—such a young man as you were. And boys even younger than you! Why, I think I'd die if any son of mine ever had to go to war, no matter how old he was."

"That's because you have a heart tucked away somewhere in that prim and proper body of yours, Miss Joy Hardesty. Neither my mother nor my father seemed to possess such an article. Anyway, nobody expected the war to last more than a few weeks."

She thought for a moment. "Yes. Yes, I remember hearing that, too. It did last, though. For a long time."

"It sure did." His shudder was brief and involuntary. "I, ah, still have dreams about it sometimes. Nightmares, I guess is what they are."

Her sympathy was almost palpable. Well, fancy that. Miss Joy Hardesty really *did* have a heart. Elijah was strangely moved.

"I'm sorry, Mr. Perry. It must be awful to carry those memories around with you."

The topic was making him feel uncomfortable. "I guess."

Conversation lagged for a few minutes as he thought about the war and Joy thought about whatever she was thinking about. Because he was afraid she'd get nervous and bolt, Elijah decided to initiate another subject. "So, tell me, Miss Hardesty, do you think your father was the sinful weakling your mother considered him? Or was he merely a nice, placid fellow who couldn't stand up to his overbearing wife?"

That jolted her. Elijah saw her give a start. There went her frown. And her eyebrows dipped into a harsh vee. He grinned. "What's the matter, Miss Hardesty? Can't stand to hear the truth? She *was* overbearing. You'd admit it if she hadn't browbeaten you into a quivering, quaking pudding."

She opened her mouth to spew bile at him, but shut it again before anything emerged. Elijah wondered what was going on in that spinsterish head of hers. She gave him one of her patented sniffs. Damn, she was fun to rile.

"My mother was a strong woman," she said, her voice tight. "That doesn't mean she was overbearing. Exactly."

"No?" His skepticism rang loudly in the one syllable.

She squinted at him from under her brows. "Well, no, it doesn't."

He tipped his head and squinted back, letting all of his incredulity show.

Joy heaved an aggrieved sigh. "Well, she might have had a"—she was obviously searching hard for a word— "powerful personality." She nodded, pleased with herself. "That's what my father said, anyway."

Elijah let out with a bark of glee. "Powerful!"

Joy scowled at him. "Yes. Powerful."

"Powerful, my ass. She was impossible. Admit it, Miss Hardesty. She made you hate a man you loved. She made you hate your own father."

"She—"

"She did! You loved your father, who sounds like he might have been a real nice man. But your mother turned your love around and made you hate him. That's not power; that's spite."

"But—"

"But nothing. She was pernicious."

She wouldn't admit it without a fight; Elijah saw it in the set of her jaw, and he was delighted. Hell, they could keep this going for days. He hadn't expected his convalescence to be so entertaining. She sniffed again, and he laughed, a big, booming laugh that he suspected she resented like fire. She glowered at him for a full minute before she spoke again.

"Perhaps you might have a point." Her admission was grudging. "But you didn't know either of my parents, so I don't think you're any kind of judge."

"I don't have to know them. I know you."

He had her with that one and was proud of himself.

Lifting her chin, Joy said, "Well, then, I presume what you said about your own unkind parents is correct, then, because *I* know *you*."

Elijah grinned, acknowledging her barb. "Good one, Miss Hardesty."

She preened. "Thank you, Mr. Perry."

Again, conversation flagged. Joy took the watch from Elijah's slack fingers and turned it over in her hands. "This is a truly lovely old thing, Mr. Perry."

"I like it."

He saw her frown. He saw her lips pinch. He saw her squint. He sighed and waited for whatever she aimed to fling at him this time. It didn't take her long.

"I think you should write to Miss Gladstone, Mr. Perry. I'm sure she would like to know that you've been injured. She must love you very much. After all, if I had a mysterious uncle who had been writing to me and sending me things from all over the United States and its territories since I was two years old, I'd have endowed him with almost mythical properties by this time."

"I'll write her, don't worry." He frowned at the nightstand. "In fact, I had a letter with me when I got here, but I guess it got lost when I was shot."

She glanced nervously at him from under her lashes. "Er, yes, perhaps it did."

He nodded. Joy collected herself. He guessed she didn't like to remember about when he'd been shot. It must have scared the tar out of her.

"But you need to write her now, so she can send you her best wishes. I know it sounds odd, but I believe it helps to have people wishing you well."

What he wished was that she'd drop the subject. "I said I'd write to her. Besides, I'm sure she wishes me well all the time."

"That's not the same, and you know it. You need her to wish you well *now*, when you need it! I'm sure you'll sneer at me for saying so, but it wouldn't hurt to have another couple of people praying for you, Mr. Perry."

His right eyebrow arched. It did that when he was surprised. "Do you pray for me, Miss Hardesty?"

She looked peeved. "Of course I do! But that's not the point."

Elijah thought it was very much the point, but he didn't feel like arguing. He liked knowing Joy Hardesty prayed for him, though. Damned if he didn't. "What's the point, then?"

"The point is that you should establish contact with her now, when you'll be someplace for a considerable length of time—"

Elijah snorted.

"You'd better be here for a goodly length of time, anyway, or you'll never heal." Her voice was as sour as an unripe crabapple. "Then she can write you, and you can establish a relationship with her. Wouldn't that be nice? To have someone—a relative—to care about you?"

Elijah wasn't prepared for the cold dread that crept over him when he heard Joy's suggestion. He said, "No."

It didn't surprise him when she looked puzzled. "But why not? Don't you think she'd like to know what's happened to you? I'm sure she'd want to know you've been injured. I know I would."

"No."

"But why not? Don't you think it would be nice to get

to know her now? When you're both grown up? I'm sure she'd be delighted to meet you in person at long last. Why, you were younger than she is now when you left home. And you're neither of you getting any younger, you know."

"I know it. And no, I don't think it would be nice." He'd begun to growl and couldn't seem to help himself.

"But why not?"

"Because I don't want to know if she's grown up to be a simpering, silly, stupid, worthless female, damn it! And I don't want her to know me, either. Damn it, leave me alone about it."

Joy eyed him consideringly. He expected her to give it up, because she generally did when he got mad. Her mother's training again, he supposed. He didn't expect Mrs. Hardesty had tolerated dissension in her household, especially not from the daughter she'd bullied so hard. He was, therefore, unprepared when Joy kept it up.

"You're being ridiculous, Mr. Perry. The poor girl doesn't even know what you look like." She glanced down at the watch in her lap. "I'm sure she'd be pleased to see for herself that she has such a dashing uncle writing letters to her."

"Dashing?" Incredulous, Elijah could only stare at her. Did she really consider him dashing?

She lifted that little chin of hers again. "Well, you're certainly not dull and boring. And you're also rather good-looking." She frowned at him defiantly. "As I'm sure you know good and well."

Caught between astonishment and immense self-satisfaction, Elijah could only open and close his mouth uselessly for a moment or two. Then he recalled the people with whom Joy had spent her life, and his vanity collapsed with a bang. "Balderdash." Feeling abused, and with cold fear still clutching at his heart, he turned to

180

stare at the wall next to his bed. "Besides, she knows what I look like."

"How can she possibly know that? You were sixteen when you left home, and she was only two. I don't know about you, but I don't recall a single thing from when I was two—well, except for my mother making me sit at the breakfast table until I finished my oatmeal porridge."

His head swiveled around and he gazed at her again. "What? Why'd she do that? You didn't like porridge?"

She wrinkled her nose, a gesture that made her look more like a young human female than anything she'd done yet in his presence, save laugh her head off. "It made me sick to my stomach."

"So why did she make you eat it?"

She heaved a sigh. "It was good for me."

"It made you sick. How could it be good for you?"

Her eyes thinned. "Well, but—"

"But nothing. The old battle-ax was trying to force you to do something she was determined was good for you, whether it was or not, because she wouldn't brook defiance in any form. She was mean as a snake, Joy Hardesty. If she thought you should eat pig slop or soap, she'd have made you do that, too."

She opened her mouth and shut it again. She reminded him of a sparrow when she tilted her head to one side and pursed her lips. "She did wash my mouth out with soap and water when I was bad."

"Bad? How can a kid be bad? Ignorant, maybe, but that's as far as I'm willing to go."

Shaking the moment off, Joy said, "All this is totally beside the point. We were discussing you and Miss Gladstone. You were going to explain to me how she could possibly know what you look like." She gave him a good hot glare to let him know she wasn't going to accept any more waffling on his part. He grinned. She was getting to be more and more fun with each passing minute.

Then he remembered Virginia, and his amusement faded. "I sent her a tintype a few years back."

Joy nodded. "That was nice of you."

"Yeah. I figured she'd want to know what her black-sheep uncle looked like. I used to cut a fine figure of a fellow, you know."

She smirked. "I'm sure you did. How long ago was that?"

He gazed at the ceiling as he counted back through the years. "Must have been right after the war started, because I was in my brand-spanking-new, shiny gray uniform." He shook his head and a soft sound of regret escaped his lips. "That didn't last long."

"What didn't last long? The uniform?"

"Its niceness. By the end of the war we were in tatters. Nobody'd seen gray wool for two years or more. We were in butternut rags, and most of us were barefoot."

He saw her shoulders twitch with her shudder. "How dreadful." Her head lifted and she peered closely at him. "But that was—what?—eight years ago? Eight years ago! Do you mean to tell me she hasn't seen a likeness of you for eight years?"

"Damn it, I don't want her to see me now. I want her to remember me with hair!" Damn, he hadn't meant to say that. He felt very grumpy that Joy Hardesty should have wrung such a confession out of him. He frowned at her to let her know it.

She giggled. Why wasn't he surprised?

"You have hair!"

He lifted his good hand and ran his fingers through his thinning hair. "Not as much as I used to have." Damn, he hated getting old.

"I believe that's a fairly universal complaint among men, Mr. Perry."

"How would you know?"

There went her giggle again. Even if it did prick his vanity, he liked hearing it. "I've seen men worry about their hair before. The organist's husband, Mr. Crowder, used to brush five thin little strands of hair across his perfectly bald head every morning of his life. It looked silly, but I expect those five hairs made him feel more the thing."

Hell, at least he didn't do that. "Yeah, I expect you're right."

She aimed a smile loaded with sympathy at him. He didn't know whether to be appreciative or resentful. "So you don't want Miss Gladstone to know that her devil-may-care, dashing, romantic uncle is a human male, just like all the rest of the human males in the world. Your vanity is pricked by the notion that she might find out who you really are. Is that it?"

Elijah considered his slight paunch and the gray in his sideburns. *Yeah, that's it, all right.* He'd never admit it. Not out loud and to Joy Hardesty, he wouldn't. "Don't be ridiculous." The words rang false in his ears.

Joy heard the falseness. Her smile broadened and she tipped her head to squint at him harder. He felt like a side of beef hanging in a butcher's shop, awaiting her judgment. It was a very uncomfortable feeling.

"I don't think I'm being ridiculous at all. I think I just hit upon the truth."

He snorted. "A lot you know about it." It wasn't one of his more forceful rejoinders.

She lifted a finger and shook it in front of his face. "I may not know much about men, Mr. Perry, but I know *all* about not wanting people to know what's inside of me, or to perceive my weaknesses."

Her words must have startled her because she shut her mouth and looked as if she hadn't expected to say them, at least not out loud. Elijah, who must have been even weaker than he knew himself to be, felt a clutching in his chest when he saw her eyes widen.

He cleared his throat. "Well, then, you see? We have something else in common, Miss Hardesty. Who'd have thought it?"

Her gaze dropped immediately. "Certainly not I." Her voice had gone soft.

Elijah discovered his good hand reaching out and his fingers tucking under her chin and lifting it. "Are those tears I see in your eyes, Miss Hardesty?"

She jerked her chin from his fingers. "Certainly not!"

"Don't fib, Joy. You mother wouldn't like it."

"Oh, bother my mother!" She reached up and dashed her hand across her cheek to catch the tears.

He chuckled. "Good idea, my dear. But you know, Joy, you're not a bad person. Or a weak one. Your mother tried to turn you into one, but you're stronger than she was. You've never been comfortable trying to be the mean old prune she wanted you to be. Admit it. Your mother was a hard-hearted woman, and you're not."

For a second he could see the struggle going on inside her. Then she heaved the biggest sigh he'd ever heard. "You're right." She had to wipe her eyes again.

"There's no reason to cry, Miss Hardesty." His own gentleness surprised him. "You're a better person than your mother ever could have hoped to be, because you're kinder than she was, and you see goodness in people she wanted only to condemn. See? You're much more like Jesus than your mother ever was."

"What would you know about Jesus?"

"The nuns taught me all about Him. Trust me. And I know He didn't go around making people miserable like your mother did."

She sniffled. "Do you really think so, Mr. Perry?"

"I really think so, Miss Hardesty." He reached for a clean handkerchief in the drawer of the table beside his bed. "Here. Use this. Blow your nose now."

With a small show of reluctance, Joy took his handkerchief and did as she'd been told.

"There," said Elijah. "That's better."

In a little voice, she said, "Thank you."

"Thank *you*, Joy. I'm pleased to have gotten to know you."

"You are?" He could tell she didn't believe him.

"I am."

Because he suspected she needed more convincing, he took her by the hand and gently tugged her into his arms. His brain registered its extreme shock when his lips settled on hers and a fire ignited in his loins.

Chapter Eleven

Alarm bells sounded in Joy's head. This was wrong. It was wrong, wrong, wrong. It was . . . it was . . .

She sighed. It was delicious. The clappers on her alarm bells took up soft leather pads. The clangs they made softened and lengthened until they refashioned themselves into the gentle cooing of doves. Her mother's admonitions, which had taught her that kissing a man, any man, and especially a man like Elijah Perry, was an unconscionable iniquity, sagged and wobbled and melted away.

Her body, which had gone rigid with bewilderment and fright, relaxed. She swayed into Elijah's embrace until her very bones seemed to thaw, and her torso molded against his. A tender sweetness filled her. Her skin tingled all over. Her nipples tightened. Lightness buoyed her spirit. She felt as one with Elijah. All of her senses responded and thrummed with a delightful, liquid heat.

A deep, primitive pulse throbbed through her.

Desire. She was feeling human desire for the first time in her life. How perfectly astonishing.

And there was more to this than mere desire as well. His strong, long hands held her close. Everywhere he touched her, her skin vibrated with life. She no longer felt isolated and alone in the universe, a stranger in an alien, hostile land she didn't understand. Rather, she had become part of a pair with Elijah Perry. She was half of a wonderful partnership; she had become part of a luscious, intimate blending of bodies; a melodious duet. A—

"Good Lord!"

She yanked herself out of his arms.

"Ow! Damn it, be careful of my arm! I'm a wounded man!"

Joy pressed her hand to her lips and stared at Elijah. His expression was that of a man in sore pain, and he was rubbing his gun-shot arm with the hand that had lately been tenderly cupping the back of her head. He looked both surprised and, to her surprise, offended.

"I'm sorry," she whispered before she could stop herself.

Sorry? You're sorry, all right, Joy Hardesty. You're the sorriest excuse for a Christian woman I've ever seen. You're fallen past redemption now, you scarlet hussy!

Oh, no. Not her mother again! Joy clapped her hands over her ears.

Elijah frowned at her. He still rubbed his shoulder. She must have really jarred it when she pulled away from him. "What's the matter, Joy? Did I hurt you?"

Listen to him, Joy Hardesty; all sweetness and light now that you've come to your senses. The vile sinner is trying to lure you back into his clutches, you foolish, foolish girl! I knew you were no good, Joy Hardesty. I could tell you were wicked from the moment you were born.

"No! That's not true!"

Elijah peered at her, puzzled. "What's not true? That I didn't hurt you?"

Butter wouldn't melt in his mouth, Joy Hardesty. Just look at him, the wicked bounder. And you! You're such a fool, child!

Joy shook her head hard, hoping in that way to exorcise her mother's relentless, scolding voice. She wanted to shut her eyes and scream and scream and scream until that voice in her head was drowned out forever.

"Well, I'm glad of that, but you don't have to look so scared, Joy. I'd never hurt you on purpose."

She stared at Elijah. What was he talking about?

He wouldn't hurt you? Her mother's voice mocked her in her head, dripping with malice and disgust. *He already did hurt you, Joy. He took advantage of you because you let your vigilance flag. It's as I always told you, you stupid girl!*

"No." Joy shook her head again, trying to oust the spiteful words. "No."

Elijah eyed her strangely. He left off rubbing his shoulder and held out his hand. "Here, Joy, what's the matter? I didn't mean to frighten you."

She couldn't stop shaking her head. She stared at his hand as she might stare at a coiled rattler. She whispered, "No," again and scooted farther away from him. In the endeavor, she put her hand down on the apricot kitten, which had been curled up next to her.

He gave a howl of indignation, sprang up onto all four feet, arched his back like a witch's familiar, bared his teeth, hissed, and swiped at Joy with sharp, daggerlike claws. Four red welts appeared on the back of her hand, and the pain rattled her. She leaped to her feet.

189

"Joy!"

Elijah looked alarmed now. The shaking in her head had engulfed the rest of Joy's body, and she trembled from tip to toe. Tears she couldn't stop washed her cheeks. She pressed the palm of her scratched hand to her face and cried, "No!" She backed up, staring at him wild-eyed.

"Joy!" His voice had an exasperated edge to it. "Come back here. I won't hurt you. For God's sake! I only kissed you!"

Listen to the villain now, Joy Hardesty. It was only a kiss to him! I told you so. No one would ever want you. You're too weak, Joy. You're too feeble a vessel. Your precious Mr. Thrash didn't want you, and now even that sinful gambling man doesn't want you. What did I tell you, Joy? What did I tell you?

"No!"

"Joy. Please come back here. Let's talk about this."

Talk! Are you going to fall for that one, you stupid girl? Talk? Bah! If you go back to that man's arms, you're no better than you ought to be, Joy Hardesty. You're no better than I always feared you were.

Joy couldn't take any more of this. Between her mother in her head and Elijah Perry on the bed, Joy's emotional state was teetering on the verge of collapse. Even Apricot had turned against her. With a gasp borne of pure agony, she whirled around and ran to the door.

"Joy!"

She heard the distress in Elijah's voice. She didn't understand it, but she knew she had to get away from him. Slamming the door behind her—something she hadn't dared do before in her entire life, at least not since her mother beat her the first time—Joy ran out of Alexander McMurdo's house and raced to the huge double gates of his wagon yard. It took her three fumbling attempts before she managed to lift the heavy bolt and push it back. Then she flung wide the gate and ran down Second Street, stumbling and tripping and weeping, as if all the demons in hell were after her.

Elijah pushed himself out of bed. As quickly as he could, he shoved his feet into Mac's slippers and limped after Joy. There was no way he could catch her, but he had to try.

"Damn." He saw her struggling with the gate, and winced when she yanked it open. It crashed against the wooden fence, which shook as if a wild bull had rammed it. Then she disappeared into the darkness of the night. "Damn it all! What the devil's gotten into you, Joy? I kissed you. Was it that bad?"

Evidently it was. Elijah's heart felt heavy as lead when he made his limping way to the gaping gates. By the time he got there, Joy was nowhere to be seen. "Damn it. How the hell can I even tell which way you went?"

Scared to death for the poor girl, and feeling inexplicably guilty for having frightened her, Elijah pondered what he should do for several seconds. Then, even though he knew he was being a damned fool—again— he slowly and painfully hobbled down Second Street. He headed away from the lights of the Pecos Saloon, because he had a feeling Joy would have tried to get as far away from humanity as she could. Not that there was much humanity to be found in the Pecos Saloon.

With a sigh that fell halfway between terror for her safety and exasperation that she should have become panic-stricken at so trivial a thing as a kiss, Elijah scanned the darkness of the night. He wished he still had the eagle-eyed vision of his youth.

* * *

Several miles to the southwest of Rio Hondo, Alexander McMurdo frowned into the starry night sky. "Your kiss was no trivial thing to her, lad, and ye ought to know it." Mac pondered Elijah's heart as he puffed on his old briar pipe, then nodded. "Aye, I thought ye knew it, lad. And it were no trivial thing to you, either."

He nodded again when he divined that Elijah did know it, and that the defense of denial, which Elijah had developed almost to perfection during his life, was again being called into play.

Good. The magic was working. It would take a while yet, but Mac would see to it that one of these days, Elijah Perry would admit himself to be a lonely man in need of Joy.

Joy was going to need more work than Elijah, because she'd been more damaged by her upbringing. Mac pondered the best course for him to follow. Should he return to Rio Hondo or remain here for a while? The O'Fannins would be happy to have him stay with them forever, but Mac didn't aim to do that. He was a mighty wizard, after all, and however much he loved Cody and Melissa and their growing family, his skills were needed elsewhere.

"Poor lass," he murmured into the heavens as he contemplated Joy. Her heart had been twisted unmercifully by her mother. It was a pity, that, but not an irreversible one. Mac moved his little finger.

Several miles away, Joy Hardesty stumbled over a creosote bush and fell, panting, to the ground. Winded, she pushed herself into a sitting position, braced herself with her hands, and peered up into a sky as thick and black and velvety as anything she'd ever seen. It looked to Joy as if someone had tossed a bucketful of diamond chips into it. Stars winked and twinkled down at her with a vigor approaching mania.

Then, to her astonishment, a cloud of what looked like

a swarm of minuscule fireflies floated over her head. She stared at them, mesmerized. Then the sparkling mist descended upon her, and Joy realized they weren't fireflies. They weren't anything she'd ever seen before except, once or twice, in Mac's store and up by the Spring River.

As she blinked into the legion of sparkles and they settled on and around her, she felt a strange sensation, a tingly but oddly peaceful one. It filled her starting from every place the sparkles touched her. Her brain calmed. Her heart stopped racing. The echo of her mother's voice faded into a distant, unlamented memory.

She heard another voice supplant her mother's. This voice wasn't shrill and hateful; rather, it was deep and rich and soothing. And it told her she wasn't a sinful weakling at all. In fact, as Joy half listened, half intuited, this voice told her she was nothing of what her mother had tried to convince her she was.

Ye're a good girl, Joy. A kind girl. Ye're just fine, child, and ye're gettin' better every day. Everything's going to be grand in your life. Just grand. It's past time ye let a little happiness bloom inside ye, Joy. Don't let the old witch fool you.

The old witch?

Joy stared into the darkness surrounding her, wondering if she'd truly lost her mind this time. Lunatics were said to hear voices, weren't they? Yes. She was sure of it. She waited for the horror of this new revelation to hit her, and it didn't. She closed her eyes for a moment, trying to rid herself of the latest manifestation of her mental instability. Voices. Lord, Lord, she was hearing voices.

The new voice laughed gently, and her eyes flew open. She looked around, but saw nothing but the earth stretching out into the pitch-blackness of the night. A coyote yipped in the distance. Joy sighed. If she sat here long enough, maybe a cougar would find her and put her out of her misery.

Ah, child, don't wish for the end at this point. Ye haven't even lived yet.

Joy frowned slightly. Why did this new voice have a Scottish accent? Had Alexander McMurdo returned? Was he now teasing her? Was he out here, hiding in the darkness? The notion didn't disturb her as much as she expected it should. She heaved an enormous sigh.

"Joy? Joy! Are you out here?"

"Good heavens! Is that you, Mr. Perry?"

"Damn it, where are you?"

He sounded extremely irked. Joy scrambled to her feet, dusted off her hands, and whacked at her skirt, an assuredly fruitless gesture. "What are you doing out here, Mr. Perry? You shouldn't be out-of-doors! You should be in bed recuperating!"

"Don't you lecture me, damn it! You ran off, and I was worried about you. What was I supposed to do?"

"As to that, I have no idea, but I'm sure you shouldn't be up and around. Why, that leg wound isn't half healed enough for you to be wandering around in the desert."

"Blast it, you scared the devil out of me when you took off like that. I—" His voice cracked as if broken by emotion, and he stopped speaking.

How strange. Mr. Elijah Perry had been worried about her welfare? Joy thought and thought, and couldn't recall another single instance in her life in which someone had actually worried about her. Her mother used to revile her constantly, but Joy didn't think it was because she worried about her; it was more because she didn't like her.

"Merciful heavens!" The thought, new and radical, hit her in the chest like a fist.

"What? Where are you, blast it?"

She could see him now, a barely discernible black

patch against the twinkling night sky. "I'm right here, Mr. Perry. I'm sorry I caused you concern."

"Concern? Damn it, you scared the hell out of me!"

She smiled. "Yes, you said that before. You needn't swear at me, Mr. Perry." She walked over to him and took his arm. "Here, let me help you back to your room."

He was breathing hard, short, gasping breaths. Joy was touched that he'd headed after her, even if she thought he'd been foolish to risk his health.

"Here," she said. "Lean on me and rest for a moment before we go back."

Her heart had been feeling lighter and lighter ever since that cloud of sparkles had descended on her. She figured this was merely a manifestation of her incipient lunacy, but she couldn't deny that she felt much more cheerful than she had when she'd run away from Elijah Perry a few minutes ago. In fact, she decided, insanity wasn't half-bad if this was what it did to one.

She smiled at the idea. Elijah still panted at her side.

"Thank you very much for worrying about me, Mr. Perry."

After a second or two, during which Joy figured he was struggling to contain either his fury or his suffering, he said, "You're welcome."

"Are you in very much pain?"

"Some." The word was clipped, and Joy was pretty sure he was lying.

"Oh, dear, you *are* in pain, aren't you? I'm really terribly sorry, Mr. Perry. You shouldn't have tried to find me, you know."

"Like hell. I was the one who drove you off."

"No, you weren't." Surprised by her own statement, Joy only had to think about it for a split second before she realized it was the truth.

"I wasn't?"

Mulling over this new and interesting concept in her head, Joy was slow to respond. After a moment she said, "No, I don't believe so. I do believe it was fear and surprise at my own boldness that sent me running."

"Boldness?" He sounded crabby. "What boldness?"

She giggled. "Well, I suppose *boldness* is a relative term, Mr. Perry. For me, that was bold."

His chuckle was deep, and it filtered through Joy much as had those strange sparkles several minutes earlier.

"I didn't mean to frighten you, Miss Hardesty."

She sighed. She was back to being Miss Hardesty. Well, she supposed that was as it should be. After all, she hadn't given him leave to call her by her Christian name.

"I know you didn't, Mr. Perry. Are you fit to walk back now? We'll take it slowly and carefully."

"Yeah, I guess so. I probably should practice walking more often."

"I'm not sure about that."

"Balderdash. Of course I should. I can't lie around in bed for the rest of my life."

"A couple of weeks is hardly the rest of your life."

"It feels like it."

"According to the nursing teachers in Boston, a person who has sustained a serious injury—"

"To hell with the nursing teachers in Boston. I'm sick of lying in bed."

For some reason, this argument struck Joy as funny. She laughed out loud.

"What?" Elijah, on the other hand, sounded extremely annoyed.

Her shoulders started shaking with her mirth. Elijah muttered, "Ow! Stop that. You're making my bad arm jiggle."

She made a huge effort and managed to suppress her laughter. "I beg your pardon, Mr. Perry."

"I don't see what's so funny."

"No, I can tell you don't. You sound excessively peeved, as a matter of fact."

"Well, damn it, I'm in pain!"

"I'm very sorry about that, but it's your own fault, you know. After all, how could I get lost here? There's nothing around but . . . nothing."

"Damn it, there might be anything out here. Bad men. Indians. Cougars. Hell, for all I know, there are bears out here."

"Bears?"

"Well, maybe not bears."

Joy's smile seemed a mile wide on her face. It was a face, after all, unused to smiling. "Thank you for worrying about my welfare, Mr. Perry."

He heaved a big sigh. "You're welcome."

"I believe we should give you a small dose of laudanum when we get you settled back in bed."

"Laudanum. Humph."

In spite of his *humph,* he sounded a little more hopeful. Joy perceived that he was merely being cantankerous in scorning medicine. The nursing teachers had told her how men could be. Insufferable patients, most of them. Mr. Perry definitely could use a dose of laudanum, poor fellow.

"Tomorrow, if you're not too indisposed from tonight's exercise, perhaps we can stroll up to the Spring River. It's really quite pretty there."

"Is it?"

"Yes, it is. There are even some flowers blooming on the riverbanks."

"Flowers?"

He sounded skeptical, which tickled Joy. "Yes, I know.

197

The scenery around Rio Hondo isn't exactly the stuff of great landscape paintings, is it?"

"What scenery? The only thing worth looking at around here is the sky."

Joy tilted her head back and gazed into the heavens. Lord above, they were gorgeous. God had done a remarkable job with the sky in New Mexico Territory. "Yes. Yes, the sky is beautiful out here, isn't it?"

He didn't answer for a minute. Joy wondered if his wounds were very painful. She expected they were. When he spoke, though, she heard gaiety in his tone. "*Beautiful* isn't the first word that sprang to mind, actually."

She laughed softly, trying not to jar his shoulder. "Perhaps there's another word that more accurately describes them. Vast, certainly. Majestic? Yes, I do believe the sky in the New Mexico Territory could be deemed majestic."

He said nothing, but Joy could feel him shake his head. His deep, rumbling laugh didn't surprise her. "Miss Hardesty," he said a moment later. "You are a very surprising female."

She was? There was no reason Joy could come up with to explain the burst of happiness Elijah's statement ignited in her, but it was there. And she decided to cherish it while it lasted.

They walked the rest of the way back to McMurdo's Wagon Yard in silence.

Mac watched in his mind's eye, and was pleased. He decided to visit an extra dose of his special wizardly healing on Elijah Perry as he slept tonight, because tomorrow he wanted Elijah and Joy to walk to the Spring River together.

Mac had plans for them.

* * *

As soon as Elijah opened his eyes in the morning, he remembered what had happened the night before, and he braced himself. Joy was right: he had most certainly been in no condition to have hared out after her. He wouldn't have if he hadn't felt responsible for her having bolted. He fully expected the result of his foolish and unnaturally noble gesture to punish him this morning.

He frowned at the ceiling, waiting for the aches and pains to begin.

"What's the matter, Mr. Perry? Are you feeling poorly?"

Joy's question surprised him, because he hadn't known she was in the room. He turned his head on the pillow and saw her straightening her nursing utensils around a jar of wildflowers on a table on the other side of the room. He squinted at her. She looked softer this morning. Prettier. Not as tense as usual.

He had, however, as yet no answer to her question. Very gingerly, he moved his wounded arm. He frowned. Even more gingerly, he moved his wounded leg. His frown eased. As carefully as if his body were made of spun glass, he turned onto his side—the one without the bullet-scraped ribs. *Well, what do you know?* He felt no more or less pain than if he'd stayed in bed all night long.

Joy stopped puttering and turned to peer at him. Her brow furrowed, and she began to look worried.

He grimaced at her anxious expression and said, "No."

Her eyebrows arched. "No? No, what? No, you don't feel poorly this morning?"

His grimace turned into a smile. "No. I don't feel poorly at all. As a matter of fact, I'm not very sore at all, hardly." He bunched his right hand into a fist. "Much."

"Truly?"

His smile vanished. "What do you mean, *truly?* Do you think I'd lie to you after you ran out into the night and I had to chase you down? If I'd suffered agonies this morning, it would be your fault. Do you think I'd lie about that?"

Holding a roll of gauze, Joy walked over to the bed and stared down at him. Elijah stared back, marveling at the change in her. Damned if she didn't look downright mischievous this morning. If anyone had asked him three weeks ago if he thought Joy Hardesty had a mischievous bone in her body, his answer would have been an unqualified no. Yet, here she was, big as life, and looking like a kid who'd just hooked a doughnut from the cookie jar.

"No, I expect you'd relish a chance to hold any anguish you were suffering against me," she said, her tone jolly.

Good God. She was capable not merely of mischievousness, but of jollity. Elijah could scarcely fathom these new revelations. He also had a hard time tearing his gaze away from hers.

Damn, she had pretty eyes. And they were—saints be praised!—*sparkling* this morning. Had she been visited by some divine manifestation in the middle of the night or something? He figured he'd better not ask. She'd probably accuse him of blasphemy.

He cleared his throat. "Where's Killer this morning?"

"*Apricot* is in the kitchen eating his breakfast. I expect he'll come bounding in here any minute."

She turned away from him, but Elijah caught her hand. Her cheeks held heightened color when she turned around again. "Yes, Mr. Perry?"

"Don't leave me. Please?" He hoped he sounded pathetic.

She grinned, evidently not fooled by his show of pathos. "I'm only going to the kitchen to fetch your breakfast."

"Oh." He reluctantly released her hand. It had felt good in his, a circumstance that astonished him almost as much as the change in Joy from grim and determined do-gooder to humorous and lovely friend. The word took him by surprise, and he said it aloud, softly. "Friend."

"I beg your pardon?"

Her big, luminous eyes held all the innocence in the world. Elijah shook his head, baffled about this latest understanding that had weaseled its way into his head. "I do believe we're becoming friends, Miss Hardesty."

Those eyes of hers opened wide. "Friends?" She blinked down at him, obviously as startled as he. "My goodness."

"I haven't had very many friends in my life." He hadn't known he was going to say that. It sounded pitiful, no matter how true it was.

She blinked a few more times. He expected her to say something sarcastic. Instead she said, "I don't believe I have, either, actually."

Her smile came out of nowhere. So did his. "Well, then, what do you know? Amazing things happen sometimes, don't they?"

She turned around again, all efficiency. "Indeed they do. And now, since you were so kind, albeit foolish, as to run after me last night—*run* being a euphemistic term under the circumstances—I have prepared you a delicious meal this morning." She turned around and shot him a smile that was at least as delicious as anything she might have cooked up in the kitchen. "After expending all that energy chasing after me, I expect you need a sustaining meal."

"My mouth's watering already, Miss Hardesty."

She left the room laughing, and Elijah felt better than he had in years.

Apricot batted at the wad of paper Joy had tossed at him, then chased after it, tumbling ears over tail as he leaped into the air and pounced on his toy. Joy was having a hard time catching her breath, she was laughing so hard. Elijah was eyeing her as if he'd never seen her before.

She tossed her head, a saucy gesture she hardly recognized as belonging in her own personal repertoire. "Stop staring at me that way, Mr. Perry. I will *not* assist you in pulling on your trousers."

His grin was a work of art. "Please? I promise I won't kiss you again."

Her cheeks must be bright red, because they burned like fire. "Stop it this instant, Mr. Perry, or I shan't walk to the river with you." She snatched up *The Moonstone*. "Or, better yet, I'll give you a lesson in proper manners the way my mother used to do to me. With a hard swat where it will do the most good."

She thought she had him with that one, but learned her mistake in a second when his eyebrows waggled suggestively.

"Promise?"

"Oh, you're impossible!"

"I know it. Impossibility is one of my many charms."

"Charms? Ha!" She sniffed. Somehow this sniff didn't sound as obnoxious to her as had all the other sniffs she'd sniffed in her life. "I shall leave you to your own devices now, Mr. Perry. When you've managed to dress yourself, I shall accompany you to the river. There I shall read to you if you like, or we can fish silently and enjoy the beauties of this lovely spring day." She inhaled deeply until she realized Elijah was staring at her swelling bosom. Then she uttered a short, sharp, "Oh!" and fled, Apricot trailing in her wake,

She heard Elijah call after her, "You're both deserting me!" and smiled to herself. Offhand, she couldn't recall a single other time in her life when she'd felt this chipper.

Sucking in another deep whiff of the crystal-clear air of southeastern New Mexico Territory, she told herself it was the atmosphere that had invigorated her so. She had a feeling she was fibbing.

Chapter Twelve

Joy matched her steps to Elijah's so she wouldn't race ahead of him to the river. She carried her fishing pole and a bundle of things wrapped in a faded old quilt. She aimed to make a day of it, complete with a picnic.

And, by heaven, she'd even take a nap if she felt like it. In the middle of the day. Like a complete and absolute lazybones—her mother and her mother's voice be hanged. Apricot danced beside her, galloping off every now and then to investigate interesting things along the way.

Joy wanted to run with the kitten. She wanted to leap and skip and whirl around and dance in the spring sunshine. She'd never done any of those things as a girl. Now that she was five and twenty—an old maid by anyone's reckoning—she wanted to do them. Here. Now. In Rio Hondo, New Mexico Territory, of all unlikely places. She laughed at herself.

"What? What's so funny?"

She glanced up to find Elijah grinning down at her, his eyes twinkling in a manner her mother would have stigmatized as brazen and unseemly. Joy found the effect of his twinkle charming. "Oh, nothing."

"You're laughing because I'm crippled, aren't you? You think it's divine justice that I should be laid up after being shot during a poker game, don't you?"

"I? Why, I'd never be so petty, Mr. Perry."

"Ha. A likely story."

His show of mock annoyance made her giggle again.

"You can't mean to tell me you're just laughing for the hell of it?"

"I never do anything for the hell of it, Mr. Perry. I thought you knew that by this time." She gave him an arch look, and was pleased as punch when he smiled back at her. He had a lovely smile, Mr. Elijah Perry, even if he was a sinful gambling man.

The notion of Elijah being a sinful gambler, and of her, Joy Eloise Hardesty, having been alone in a small house with him for nearly four entire weeks tickled her. Why, back home in Auburn, Massachusetts, she'd have been ruined beyond redemption after the first night. She'd be the talk of the town—if anyone believed it. She was such a sour old stick, they probably wouldn't. That thought tickled her, too. Everything tickled her today.

"Yeah, I know you'd never do anything for the hell of it. Silly of me to say such a thing."

His grin was almost as perfect as the day. Joy sighed happily.

"You're full of beans today, aren't you?"

She threw a stick for Apricot, who bounded after it and attacked it as if it were his mortal enemy. Joy laughed. "No one's told me I was full of beans since I was six years old, Mr. Perry."

"Oh? Who did it then?"

She sighed again, remembering. "My father. We'd gone to the pond, because my mother was sick."

"Sounds like the two of you had a good time together."

"We did." She realized the warmth in her chest had melted the lump of pain usually residing there. *How strange.* It was also strange to recall the great pleasure she'd taken on that day, almost twenty years ago, when her father had tended her and they'd gone to the pond. He hadn't criticized and belittled her; rather, he'd laughed with her. Joy had listened for hours, enraptured, as her father had spun yarns for her amusement. She wondered if she'd be a different person today if her father had had the tending of her more often. But he hadn't, and she was now whatever it was she'd become.

"Your father sounds like a nice fellow, Joy. I wish I'd known him. The preachers I used to know were more like your mother than your father."

She glanced up at him. The twinkle in his eyes made her look away again quickly. "They were? What do you mean?"

"Oh, they were judgmental and harsh and cruel for the most part."

"Cruel? You think my mother was cruel?"

"Think it? I know it."

She pondered that one, frowning. Her pleasure in the day faded slightly.

Elijah must have noticed the change in her mood. "But I don't want to talk about the old bat today."

"No, indeed," she agreed readily, finding that relegating her mother to the back of her mind cheered her considerably. Even thinking of her as an old bat felt right.

When they got to the marshy area surrounding the river, Joy took Elijah by the hand and guided him along firm ground to the place where she'd caught their supper a few days earlier. She wouldn't let him sit on a fallen log until she'd spread the old quilt on it. "We don't want the dampness to creep into your old bones and give you rheumatism, now, do we?"

"Old bones? Hell, I'm not *that* old."

She laughed at him. "And I'll settle myself here, beside you."

Apricot made a flying leap for the quilt and started digging at it with his sharp little claws.

"Looks like Killer's trying to murder it."

"Apricot is merely fluffing your blanket for you, Mr. Perry."

"Fluffing it, my eye. He's trying to rip it to shreds. And my name's Elijah, *Joy.*"

The notion of calling this man by his Christian name gave Joy a warm, gooey feeling in her middle. Because she didn't want him to know it, she said, "All right, *Elijah,*" and flounced off to the river's edge, where she picked up a stick and poked around in the mud.

She heard his soft laugh at her back. "What are you doing now?"

"Looking for worms. Ah, here's a nice fat one!" She picked it up and dangled it for him to see. She even made a smacking sound with her lips, as if she aimed to pop the juicy wiggler into her mouth and eat it.

His laugh got louder. Joy was pleased with herself as she baited her hook with a grimace and tossed the line into the river. Then she returned to the log, held the fishing pole with one hand, flipped *The Moonstone* open with the other, picked it up, and began to read. She heard Apricot purring like an engine, and thought the day couldn't get any finer.

She cooked fish for lunch, and couldn't recall ever having eaten a tastier meal, even if she and Elijah did have to fight Apricot over their plates. Feeling extravagant and happy, Joy finally gave up and let the cat have an entire fish for himself. Elijah laughed at her. She was neither surprised nor dismayed. In fact, she stuck her tongue out at him. She could hardly believe it of herself.

After lunch she read *The Moonstone* until she caught sight of Elijah shifting his position on the log and trying not to appear uncomfortable.

"All right," she said in the voice her mother used to use to intimidate her into obeying her commands. "It's time for your nap, Mr. *Elijah* Perry. You're going to have to stand up now, and I'm going to find a flat, dry place and spread the quilt on it."

"Yes, ma'am." He saluted her sharply. Joy was delighted.

It didn't take long for her to find a suitable spot in a patch of dappled shade near a young cottonwood tree. Then she had to hold the kitten, who seem to feel it his privilege to curl up in the center of the blanket, thereby rendering the napping place unsuitable for human occupation. It took Elijah a few grunts of pain and a minute or two, but he eventually managed to lie down and arrange himself in a nappable position. Joy frowned down at him, petting Apricot distractedly.

"Are you comfortable? I have a cushion for your head."

"That would be nice."

He smiled up at her, and Joy's heart flipped and flopped like one of the fish she'd recently caught. She wished Elijah Perry weren't such a devilishly attractive man, and that her heart would behave itself.

After she'd positioned the pillow under his head and watched Apricot maneuver himself into a ball on Elijah's stomach, Joy sat on the quilt, too. She propped a second cushion against a fallen cottonwood log, leaned back, closed her eyes, and let the fresh spring sunshine wash her cheeks with its warmth.

Right before she dropped off to sleep, she realized the knot of pain she'd carried around in her chest since she was born hadn't yet returned to bother her, and it must have been well past noon.

A whole battalion of Yankee bluecoats, mounted on fresh horses, surged toward the ragged band of Confederate soldiers trying to hide themselves behind a sparse stand of elms and firs. Elijah's heart banged against his breastbone like the entire Confederate drum corps. It seemed strange to him that he should feel such exhilaration in what might well be the last few seconds remaining to him in life. The ground rumbled like thunder, and he braced himself for the barrage of gunfire sure to come.

It didn't. Nor did the horses get any closer. Elijah squinted into the line of mounted soldiers and wondered what was holding them back. By rights they should have run him down by this time. The ground rattled his very bones, yet the line of Yankees stayed as far away as ever. What the hell was going on?

His eyes opened and he gazed up, disoriented, into a canopy of cottonwood leaves. Where the devil was he?

Something stirred at his side. He glanced over, saw Joy Hardesty sleeping sweetly, her head cradled in her open palm, Killer curled up at her waist, and everything came back to him in a rush. A flood of contentment filled him. Before he gave himself time to think about it, he reached over and smoothed Joy's cheek with his fingers. Her skin was as soft as a baby's.

Damn, he wished they were alone in Rio Hondo, and that Joy wasn't quite who she was. He'd make slow, sweet love to her right here, right now. Then they could nap again, or make love again, or laugh together and tell tall tales and play with the kitten, and—

Hell, you wouldn't be able to make love with a woman,

Elijah Perry, and you know it. Especially not Joy. She deserves better than you.

He blinked, astounded about the truth he'd just told himself.

Then he realized the ground still shook. Hard. What in the name of holy hell was happening? Did New Mexico Territory get earthquakes? Did earthquakes last this long? He yanked his mind away from what he'd like to do with Joy and painfully pushed himself up until he was sitting, his wounded leg stretched out straight, his other knee bent. Killer opened one eye and peered at him malevolently, as if he didn't appreciate having his nap interrupted.

"Get over it, cat," Elijah advised the kitten. "You're only an animal, and you'll do as I say." He didn't believe it, but he figured Killer could use some discipline.

Joy slept on, her dreams undisturbed by Elijah's erotic fantasies or the rumbling of the earth beneath her. She slept the sleep of the innocent, which was appropriate enough. She seemed happy today, resting on the quilt he'd been sharing with her. He wondered if she knew she'd stretched out beside him. Probably not. He reached over again to brush a stray lock of hair away from her eyes. She was a very pretty girl when she wasn't attempting to be what her mother had tried to make of her.

Before he knew what he was doing, Elijah had leaned over and softly kissed her forehead, where the lock of hair had been. Joy stirred and smiled in her sleep. A charge of something primitive roared through Elijah, and he was hard-pressed to keep from drawing Joy into his arms and ravishing her. As if he were fit to ravish anyone at all, much less a corseted spinster lady with strong Christian principles and a solid right hook. He sighed, feeling old and useless, and not liking it.

And in the meantime, the distant thundering seemed to

be growing louder, and the earth rattled as if God had dumped the planet into a sieve and was now attempting to separate the chaff from the wheat by shaking it to death. "What the hell *is* that?"

Neither Joy nor Killer had an answer for him, but the kitten evidently didn't much like the way the earth was behaving. He looked around as if startled and leaped onto his feet, arching his back and hissing at Elijah.

"Hell, it's not my fault, Killer. I don't know what's happening, either."

Joy yawned hugely. Elijah chuckled, sure she'd never have done such a thing if she knew he was watching. Her eyes fluttered open, and his heart gave a twinge of appreciation. Before he knew he was going to do it, he'd reached out and cupped her soft cheek in his big, rough hand.

"Good afternoon, sleepyhead." His voice had gone low and seductive. He never talked like that except when he was trying to get into a lady's drawers. Those blasted bullets had apparently damaged more than his flesh. His mind was shot too.

"H'lo," she said, her voice thick with sleep. She smiled lazily up at him, and Elijah spared a moment to be grateful he wasn't a well man, or he'd have pounced on her. Joy Hardesty. Right here. By the banks of the Spring River. In broad daylight.

Her eyes narrowed, and Elijah expected her to object to the hand he still held to her cheek. Her skin felt warm with spring sunshine and soft with her own peculiar femininity—especially peculiar because he hadn't expected to find it in her.

"What's that awful noise? Why is the ground rumbling?"

As if she didn't even know his hand was there, she sat up, and Elijah's hand fell away. He sighed. "I don't

212

know. I thought it was part of a dream, but it wasn't."

"No. It's definitely not a dream."

By this time the kitten had taken all he intended to take on the ground. With several bounds and a flying leap, he dug his claws into the trunk of the nearby cottonwood, yowling as he went. Joy giggled. Then she frowned. "Whatever it is, it's frightened Apricot."

"Whatever it is, it's not doing my peace of mind much good, either."

She stood up and shook out her skirts. Elijah wanted her back at his side again. Lordy, this was bad. He was developing a schoolboy crush on his nurse.

Joy shaded her eyes with her hand and peered past the scanty stand of trees beside the river and into the distance. She pointed. "There's a huge cloud of dust over there, to the east."

"Is there?" Elijah left off staring up at Joy's bosom and decided his fun was over for the day. With another sigh and a large grunt, he struggled to his feet. Damn, he'd be glad when he healed. If he ever did. He told himself four weeks wasn't an eternity by any means, but he couldn't help but be impatient. He wasn't used to being laid up.

"You don't suppose it's a hurricane or a tornado or something, do you?" Joy sounded doubtful.

She did so for good reason, in Elijah's estimation. "They don't get hurricanes this far inland, Joy. And it's not a tornado. People call 'em twisters for a reason, you know."

Her lips pinched up. "Well, I've never seen either one before, so how am I supposed to know that?"

He laughed. "Anyway, if it were a weather-related phenomenon, don't you think it'd be coming down from the sky rather than starting up from the plains?"

She snorted. "How should I know that either? I haven't

lived long enough in this vile place to know what happens here. Except for gambling, cursing, and shooting, of course."

"Good one, Joy." Elijah squinted off to the east, wishing his eyesight were better. "I wonder if someone's running cattle."

"Running cattle?" Joy left off staring at the cloud of dust in the distance and commenced staring at Elijah. "What does that mean? Why would a body want to make a cow run?"

He laughed again, harder this time, until the wound in his side stitched and he had to press his hand over it. Joy, he noticed, didn't appreciate being laughed at. She'd planted her fists on her hips, and her glare got hotter. "Don't hit me, sweetheart. What you said struck me as funny, is all."

"Yes. I can see that." With a sniff, she whirled around and stared at the cloud of dust some more. The noise was getting louder and louder. The cat screeched. Joy walked to the cottonwood and tried to pluck it from the trunk, but it dug in its claws and wouldn't budge.

"Careful," Elijah advised. "Killer might up and take a swat at you. He's scared, it looks like."

"I don't blame him. It's disconcerting to have that big noise and big cloud of dirt heading at one."

"Yeah, it is." Elijah thought he could make out what looked like the familiar curve of cattle horns amid the dust. "Hey, come here for a minute. Are those longhorns I see?"

"Where?" Joy ran back over to Elijah, abandoning the kitten, who stared after her as if he considered her a base deserter. He hissed to let her know it. Joy ignored him, and peered off to the east.

Since she was standing right in front of him, Elijah rested his hands on her shoulders and drew her back slightly so that her back barely rested against his chest. He felt content this way, and smiled to himself. He hoped she wouldn't up and slap him for taking the liberty.

"I do believe you're right." Joy was evidently too caught up in the distant phenomenon to notice how close she stood to Elijah, or that he was resting his hands on her shoulders. "I think I see animals. A whole bunch of cows. Running straight toward Second Street."

"It's a herd of cattle, Joy, not a bunch of cows."

"Well, whatever it's called, I think that's one."

"I think you're right." Sounds started to distinguish themselves from amid the thundering hooves. Elijah heard whistles and whoops and moos. "It's a cattle drive."

"My goodness. I've heard about cattle drives."

"That's why this place is here, I reckon. It's a stopover for ranchers driving herds up north."

"Is it? I didn't know that. I wondered why anyone would want to build a town out here, in the middle of nowhere."

"Let's mosey on down to McMurdo's. We'll be able to see it better from there."

"Hmmm. I'm not sure I want to."

Nevertheless, Joy packed up their picnic things quickly while Elijah tried to pry the kitten from the tree trunk. Since he was a wounded man, he couldn't very well bend over and help Joy, but he did enjoy the way her little rump stuck in the air as she folded the quilt. With a sigh, he contemplated what she'd do if he put his hands there. The consequences would undoubtedly be painful to him, so he didn't do it, but he wanted to.

They made their slow way back to the wagon yard, Elijah cradling Killer with one of the cushions to protect himself from the frightened kitten's claws. As soon as they were safely inside the gates, he let the cushion go, and the cat dashed into the barn. Elijah figured he'd be safe from cattle hooves and longhorns in there.

"Better go inside and get us a couple of bandannas, Joy. There's going to be a lot of dust kicked up when the beasts run down Second."

"All right." She started for the house, then stopped and turned around. She looked worried. "They aren't going to chase all those cows into Mr. McMurdo's yard, are they?"

"Naw. They wouldn't all fit. They'll probably run them through town and pasture them somewhere to the west of us. Then some of the cowboys will watch 'em while the others come into town and buy supplies—and get drunk."

Joy sniffed and lifted her chin. "What a deplorable waste of a man's life."

God, he loved the way she did that; went all pruney with indignation whenever anyone did or said something she didn't approve of. With a cheerful laugh, Elijah said, "Don't worry. You can lock the gates so they can't come in and get you."

She scowled at him. "I'm not worried about that!"

He tilted his head to one side and watched as she stomped to the house. "You should be," he said softly. She couldn't hear him. "I do believe you should be."

Elijah got tired of watching the enormous herd of long-horns being driven down Second Street before Joy did. He'd seen such nonsense before. She hadn't, and was obviously fascinated. So he took to watching her instead. She'd dragged some crates over to the six-foot fence, and had scrambled up onto one of them. Even so, she had to stand on her tiptoes to watch the passing herd. Elijah was glad he'd suggested the bandannas, because they'd have choked to death on flying dust and grit without the ban-dannas covering their noses.

"I'm going to need a bath after this," Joy said, laughing.

The thought appealed to Elijah. "I'll be happy to help you wash up."

She smacked him playfully. He was glad she didn't know he wasn't joking. The idea of soaping his hands and lathering Joy's slender body was an extremely appealing one, however, and he had a difficult time letting it go. Eventually, he contented himself with appreciating how Joy's shapely ankle rounded into her calf and disappeared under her petticoats. He was sure she'd be offended if he told her how pretty he thought her legs were.

Life at McMurdo's Wagon Yard perked up as a result of the spring cattle drives. Several more herds were driven through the town after that first one as the nearby ranchers prepared to drive their cattle to market.

Joy was kept busy in McMurdo's mercantile with cowboys coming in for supplies. Since Elijah was now fit to be up, if not around, by this time, he took to reading to her from *The Moonstone* while she scurried about restocking shelves and taking inventory of supplies. When he finished *The Moonstone,* he started in on *The Woman in White.* Joy forgot to make him read Bible verses before reading from the novel.

The mail pouch arrived on a freight wagon from Santa Fe. Joy searched through it for a letter from Miss Virginia Gladstone, but there wasn't one. She figured Miss Gladstone hadn't yet had a chance to receive and respond to the letter Joy had written her. She contemplated telling Elijah what she'd done, but their rapport had become so easy, she didn't quite dare for fear a confession would cause constraint between them. She waited for one of her mother's lectures to attack her, and was glad when it didn't.

Her mother's condemning voice, in fact, came to her less and less frequently as the days turned into weeks and she continued to nurse Elijah Perry and work in Alexander McMurdo's store. She almost forgot the place belonged to Mr. McMurdo. Her days took on a tranquil, isolated, golden-edged quality in her mind, and she sometimes thought she wouldn't really mind staying here like this forever. Two weeks had passed since her picnic by the river with Elijah and Apricot, and she was enjoying herself for the first time in her life.

The overall politeness of the cowboys who did commerce in Mr. McMurdo's small mercantile establishment surprised and gratified her. She stared after one young man who'd just stammered out his thanks to her, bowed from the waist, blushed, and departed, his high-heeled boots sounding like cannon fire on the scarred wooden boards.

"My goodness, I do believe that fellow is shy. Either that, or he's terribly sunburned."

Elijah sat on one of the wooden chairs in front of the potbellied stove. He'd watched Joy conduct business with the young man, and hadn't liked what he'd seen. Now he stuck his finger in *The Woman in White* to mark his place and scowled after the departing cowboy. He wasn't sure he liked all these men coming into the store and doing business with Joy. She wasn't up to dealing with a bunch of men who hadn't seen a lovely young unmarried female in months. "That's not sunburn. He was shy with you."

Joy peered at the back of the retreating man and muttered, "How strange."

Elijah transferred his scowl from the cowboy to her. "What's strange about it? You're a young, pretty woman, and he's a young, randy cowboy. He fancies you. That's not strange. That's normal."

"*What?*" She stared at Elijah as if he'd suddenly grown a second head.

Her incredulity irked him. "What, what? It's the truth. For God's sake, Joy, you're a young, pretty, unmarried girl. There's not another young, pretty, unmarried female within two hundred miles of here." Elijah's thoughts turned to the Pecos Saloon, and he amended grumpily, "Leastways, not another one like you."

"But . . . but . . . ." Her words stuttered to a halt.

"But what?" He couldn't have explained why he was suddenly so peeved, but he was. And he didn't appreciate Joy's pretense of surprise, either. Hell, wasn't she the one who thought all men were beasts? Wasn't she scared to death of her essential feminine nature, and what men and women did together? Why should she be surprised that these lonely cowpokes should lust after her?

The notion occurred to him that he wasn't so much annoyed with Joy as with the men who wanted her. They were all more nearly her age than he was, after all. Probably any dozen or two of them would make her a fine husband.

A fierce urge to strangle something swept through him.

"But—" She tried again, and again she failed. Elijah glowered at her. His obvious rancor apparently goosed the words out of her mouth. "But . . . but, I'm *me*. Nobody wants *me*."

Elijah's rancor evaporated. He stared at her, confounded. Then he set *The Woman in White* on the table beside the potbellied stove, stood up, and went over to her. He grabbed her by the hand. "Come with me."

"Why? What are you doing?"

He didn't answer, but pulled her toward the corner of the store where Mac kept stacks of blue flannel work shirts, leather vests, trousers, hats, and so forth. She tried to dig in her heels, but Elijah was relentless. His strength

219

was returning, and she wasn't powerful enough to resist him. Her heels screeched across the floorboards. "You're probably scratching Mac's floor all to hell, Joy."

"What? Oh!"

She stumbled and almost fell. When he looked, Elijah wasn't surprised to see her peering anxiously at the scratches her heels had made on the floor. He didn't care. "Come here."

"What are you doing?" Since she couldn't screech with her heels, she'd started using her voice. Elijah wasn't surprised about that, either.

"I want you to look at something, Joy Hardesty."

"What?"

He stopped in front of the scratchy mirror Mac had hung on the wall next to a rack of hats. "That." He jerked her around to stand in front of him, facing the mirror. He held on to her shoulders so she couldn't escape. He wanted her to look at herself, honestly and without prejudice, for once in her life.

She came up only to his chin, so he could peer into the mirror with her. Her reflection stared back, wide-eyed and scared, pink-cheeked, and very, very pretty.

"I want you to see you, Joy. I want you to look at yourself without filtering your image through your mother's malicious fog. I want you to see yourself for what you are."

He saw her swallow. She still looked scared.

"You're a young, pretty woman, Joy. Lately you've even become vibrant. Vivacious, even."

"V-vivacious? Me?" She sounded as shocked as if he'd told her Jesus had returned to earth and was prepared to take her up with Him to heaven.

"Yes. Vivacious. You. Pretty. You. Young. Appealing." He thought for a moment, and decided to toss in a few more adjectives. "Nice. Kindhearted."

She swallowed again. Her eyes started to glitter, and Elijah was afraid she might cry. She didn't. Instead she whispered, "But you used to say I was mean and spiteful and hateful."

He grinned at her in the mirror. "That's because you used to be mean and spiteful and hateful. You're not any longer."

"Honestly?"

"Honestly."

She gazed at his reflection in wonder. "You mean it? Really?"

"I'm not in the habit of lying, Joy, whatever other bad habits I might have."

"And you really think I'm pretty? Truly?"

Elijah shook his head in mock disgust. "For the love of God, Joy, *look* at yourself."

She did, and her smile broke out like the sun after a rainstorm. She turned in his arms and glowed up at him for a split second before Elijah couldn't stand it any longer and drew her into his embrace.

Chapter Thirteen

The emotion that washed over Joy in that moment surpassed anything she'd experienced before. She felt joy. She, whose name had always seemed like a cruel joke, felt joy fill her completely.

When Elijah kissed her, she hungered for him. Everything in her body responded. She'd been here alone with him for six weeks, and she had fallen head over heels in love with him. In those very few seconds, while he kissed her, she admitted it to herself. The admission felt wonderful. Freeing. Exhilarating.

Her head felt as if it were filled with stars. Her blood ran hot with passion. Her bones turned to jelly, and she clung to Elijah Perry as if to life itself. He was so strong. His arms felt like steel around her, keeping her upright, protecting her from life's storms. And he was wise—in a way she'd never understood as wise before she'd met him. She wanted to stay in his arms forever.

His tongue slipped between her lips and into her mouth, and Joy greeted it with her own. His hand splayed across her back at her waist, drawing her against his hard, warm body. In that moment she felt protected. Wanted. Loved. The combination was a heady one indeed.

She'd had her arms wrapped around him in a crushing embrace, shocked by the newness of the experience into immobility. After a moment, when she'd almost accustomed herself to the thrill of being in Elijah's arms, she let her hands wander up and down his back. She felt the hard planes of his body, so different from her own, and wanted to feel his bare flesh with hers. She wasn't even shocked. Her nipples tingled with need, and her skin felt flushed.

She wanted to rip her clothes off and play naked on the floor with Elijah Perry. She wanted to run in the sunshine with him, as bare as a newborn baby. She wanted to frolic on the banks of the Spring River with him, to make slow, lazy love under the shade of the cottonwood trees. She wanted him to teach her the joy of love, as he'd taught her the joy of life.

"Well, well, well, I see the two o' ye seem to have overcome your dislike of one another."

Alexander McMurdo's voice and soft chuckle filtered over Joy like those sparkles had done weeks ago on the prairie. She jerked in Elijah's arms, and her eyes flew open.

Elijah groaned. Immediately contrite, she looked up at him. "Did I hurt you?"

He shook his head, but his face held a pained expression. Joy laid her hand lightly over his wounded ribs. She felt his heart hammering like a piston in his chest. He'd squeezed his eyes shut, and tiny wrinkles radiated from their corners. He looked healthier than he had when he'd first come here, even before he was shot.

"Are you sure?" Because she couldn't seem to help herself, she lifted her hand and smoothed her fingers over his crow's-feet. She loved those crow's-feet. She loved everything about him.

"I'm sure." His voice was hoarse. He heaved a big sigh.

Joy felt bereft when he took a step back, away from her, and his hands fell from her waist, leaving a cold spot there across her back. She stared up at him, blinking as a sprinkle of sparkles wafted in front of her eyes, blurring his face for an instant.

Good heavens, he looked as though his head were framed by a halo. The phenomenon was so unexpected and so incongruous, she laughed once, sharply. She'd never drunk champagne in her life, but she'd heard it was bubbly, and that was what she felt like in that moment: bubbly.

"Do you really think I'm pretty, Elijah?"

He looked down at her and shook his head, as if he couldn't understand why she'd still question him after that kiss. Joy took a step back—and her left boot heel landed on Apricot's tail. The kitten yowled. Joy jumped a foot. Elijah jerked.

"Well, well, well," Mac said again. "In fact, I'd venture to guess that the two o' ye might even have decided that ye like each other, after all."

Both Joy and Elijah turned toward the voice.

Standing in a puddle of sunlight and sparkles at the door, and observing everything with his twinkly blue eyes, Alexander McMurdo took his old black briar pipe from between his lips, threw back his head, and laughed.

Joy served up a nice dinner of chicken, fricasseed with onions, potatoes, and carrots. The apricot kitten, who'd grown quite a bit in the several weeks since Mac had brought him into her life, sat on the floor next to Mac's chair, his expression one of happy expectancy. Mac reached down and scratched him behind the ear. "Cute little guy, this. Has he caught any mice?"

Not having anticipated the question, Joy paused on her way to the table with the bread basket. "Mice?" She glanced at Elijah.

He said, "Mice?" and blinked. "Er, I don't know. Joy?"

When her gaze locked with his, she felt a rush of heat spread through her body. What a fool she'd made of herself in front of Mr. McMurdo with Elijah Perry. She was surprised, albeit grateful, that neither man had teased her about the kiss she and Elijah had shared in front of their small audience.

She had a difficult time tearing her glance away from Elijah and aiming it at Mac. She knew it was sinful, but she was sorry her idyll with her patient had come to an end at last. A small arrow of disappointment pierced her heart, and she wondered if she'd ever experience joy again. She shook herself and set the bread basket on the table.

"I haven't seen him catch any mice, but he's out in the barn a lot. I suspect he's hunting in there."

Mac nodded. "I expect so. What did you name him?"

"Killer," Elijah said promptly.

"Apricot," Joy said at the same time.

Mac laughed and peered down at the kitten. "So you're a Killer Apricot, are you? I'd say that's a fine name for an orange kitten."

"Killer Apricot?" In spite of all her doubts and insecurities, Joy broke into laughter.

Elijah grinned. "I like it."

Joy filled a plate and handed it to Mac. "I think I do, too. How funny." She stopped carving and gazed at Mac closely. "How's little Katie doing, Mr. McMurdo? She's such an adorable little girl. Does she like her new brother?"

Elijah waggled a finger at the chicken. "Keep carving, Joy. Can't you work and talk at the same time?"

She stuck her tongue out at him, realized immediately what she'd done, and blushed. She carved the chicken, however, keeping her head lowered and hoping neither man had observed her lapse in manners.

Mac pretended not to notice this display of pleasantries between two people who, when he'd last seen them, had been on the verge of killing each other. "Oh, aye, wee Katie loves her brother. Arnold's fond of her, too. Already knows when she's there and goos at her."

With a sigh, Joy handed Elijah his plate. "It must be wonderful to have two such sweet children." She wished she hadn't said that out loud when Elijah shot her a curious—it actually looked cynical to her—glance. She wanted to stick her tongue out at him again, but restrained herself.

"Aye, Cody and Mellie are happy about it, that's for sure. It's a grand place to start a family, out here."

Joy looked up from carving her own piece of chicken. "Is it? It seems rather, ah, far removed from the rest of the world."

Mac grinned broadly. "Oh, aye, it is that. But that's one of its beauties, you see. There's lots of wide-open spaces for children to run around in. Mellie likes it because it's so clean. She grew up in a rough neighborhood in Boston, y'know, and the sanitation wasn't the best back there."

Joy frowned. "But there isn't any sanitation at all out here. At least none that I've seen."

Mac's grin widened still further. "Aye, that's true, but there's plenty of unpopulated space to dump your garbage in."

"I suppose so." Joy took a bite of chicken and was happy that it was so tasty. She might not be good for much, but at least she could cook a decent meal. She ought to be able to cook well. The good Lord knew, her mother had browbeaten kitchen skills into her for years. By this time, Joy could make bread blindfolded and wring a chicken's neck, pluck it, and cook it without blinking an eye.

"This place needs a hotel."

Both Joy and Mac stopped chewing, looked up from their plates, and stared at Elijah. He gazed back, his brow beetling with his frown. "Well, it does."

Joy swallowed her bite of chicken. "Do you really think Rio Hondo could support a hotel?"

His frown deepened. "I don't see why not. It's not going away, you know. And it's growing all the time. It's not like one of those California gold camps that dried up as soon as they'd dug all the gold out of the surrounding countryside. This is turning out to be great cattle country. Rio Hondo will only get bigger. The ranchers need it because there's no place else to stop over for hundreds of miles. Businessmen will be investing down here more and more, and they're going to want to come out to investigate their investments. And I'm sure the cowboys and ranchers would like a decent place to stay when they come to town." He shot a glance at Mac. "I mean—not that your wagon yard isn't useful and decent—"

"I know what you mean, lad." Mac grinned at him.

"Well . . ." Elijah cleared his throat. "Anyway, I think Rio Hondo could use a hotel."

Mac nodded soberly. He reminded Joy of Solomon, and for some reason she recalled the passage out of the Song of Solomon that had plagued her when she first began tending Elijah: *"How beautiful are thy feet."* She

tucked her chin in again so neither of the men eating
with her could see the color blooming in her cheeks.

"Aye, laddie, I expect you're right. More settlers are
moving to the territory all the time. Pretty soon we'll
even have churches and schools."

Elijah smiled and nodded. Joy lifted her head and
gaped at Mr. McMurdo. "Churches and schools?"

"Aye. Why not? Folks need such things when they set
out to civilize a place. Women and children, especially,
like to socialize. Where better to do it than in church?"

"I, ah, had never thought about churches in exactly that
light, Mr. McMurdo."

Mac laid his fork on his plate and reached over to pat
Joy's hand. "I'd consider it a kindness on your part if
ye'd call me Mac, Joy. I truly would."

"You would?"

"I would."

Joy believed him. *How odd.* She said, "Mac," and
smiled at him. He smiled back, and she felt perfectly
wonderful all of a sudden. She attacked her chicken with
renewed vigor.

"Well? So you want to open a hotel here, do you,
Elijah, m'lad?"

"*Open* one? Me?"

When Joy glanced up, intrigued by Mac's suggestion,
she saw that Elijah was staring at the old man, a look of
wonder on his face, as if he'd suddenly been blinded by
a heavenly light. She peered quickly from Elijah to Mac
and back again. "Why, what a splendid idea, Mr. Mc-
Murdo—Mac. You told me once that the only time you
can recollect being happy was when you were helping
out in your uncle's hotel, Elij—Mr. Perry."

Elijah turned his head and looked at her as if she were
a total stranger who'd spoken to him in some foreign
language.

Mac said, "I don't think the fellow minds if you call him Elijah, Joy, m'dear."

Joy hardly heard him. She was too busy trying to figure what was going on in Elijah's handsome, albeit graying, head. She saw him tilt it to the right. His eyes took on a glassy cast. She saw that his chewing slowed and then stopped. She hoped he wasn't feeling ill. He swallowed, reached for the glass of water Joy had set at his place, and took a hearty gulp.

"Open a hotel," he murmured, set his eating utensils on his plate, and stared at the wall behind Joy's shoulder. "*Build* a hotel."

Joy and Mac exchanged a glance. Mac's eyes shone like blue diamonds. "I do believe the lad's given himself something to think about, Joy."

She peered at Elijah for a couple of seconds. "I do believe you're right."

Elijah's head jerked, as if he were shaking himself out of a dream, and he went back to his dinner. "Anyway, this place needs a hotel."

"Indeed it does." Mac reminded Joy of a cheerful elf.

"You may be right." She wanted to ask Elijah about hotels. She wanted to know what he thought would go into the building and the running of one out here, in Rio Hondo, in the great emptiness of southeastern New Mexico Territory. Did he really think so many people were going to populate the area that they'd actually need a *hotel*? The notion seemed unlikely to her, but what did she know about it? Or anything else, for that matter? She'd been so sheltered from the real world in her lifetime that she knew little about it.

"Have you heard from your missionary friends, Joy?"

Joy's head snapped around so quickly, she nearly broke her neck. "What?"

Mac's twinkle became more pronounced. "Your missionary friends. You know, the ones who went to preach to the natives in South America. Surely you remember Mr. Thrash?"

Mr. Thrash. Joy gulped. *Oh, yes.* How could she have forgotten Mr. Thrash? She'd believed herself to be in love with him, hadn't she? "N-no. I haven't heard from them. Yet. I—I guess they'll write." She glanced at Elijah for some reason she couldn't put a name to. "I think they will, anyway. At least, I hope so." With a shock, she realized she didn't care if she never heard from Mr. Thrash or the rest of those people again as long as she lived.

Elijah frowned. "You're not going to tell me you still want to tramp off to the jungles and make those poor Indians miserable, are you?"

She bridled. "We didn't intend to make them miserable, Mr. Elijah Perry. We intended to show them the glories of God's healing light. And medicine. And anyway, why shouldn't we? Don't you think they deserve to hear the Word of the Lord?"

With a shrug, Elijah buttered a piece of bread. "I expect they have their own religion, Joy. Why do you want to mess up whatever works for them with Jesus and Mary and all that?"

Suddenly all of Joy's recent happiness fled. The ache in her chest, which she hadn't felt for almost two solid weeks now, returned like a sour stomach. Her mother's voice came out of her mouth: "Because Jesus and Mary are the truth!" She slapped a hand to her lips, appalled. Had that awful sound come from her? Her gaze flicked from Elijah to Mac, who grinned as if he'd never seen or heard anything so funny in a month of Sundays.

"Ah, leave them alone, for the love of God. I'll never understand why folks are so eager to go where they don't belong and tell the people who live there how they think

231

they should live. As if your preacher friend knows anything about South American Indians." Elijah poked a
hunk of chicken into his mouth to keep his buttered bread
company and chewed on them hard.

"I . . . I . . ." Joy didn't continue because she realized
with horror that she wanted to agree with him. *Good
heavens!* She glanced up at the ceiling, almost expecting
to see her mother there with a hairbrush in her hand,
ready to paddle Joy's behind with it. She cleared her
throat. "I don't believe I want to talk about it at the supper table, Mr. Perry."

He slammed his fork onto his plate. "Elijah! My
name's *Elijah,* Joy. You've been calling me that for three
weeks now."

"Elijah," she muttered, feeling confused and beleaguered.

Mac beamed at the two of them, as if he were presid-
ing over a comedy of his own making.

Which he was.

The next morning, Mac and Joy stood behind the counter
of Mac's mercantile store, where Joy had dragged him
right after breakfast. Conscientious to her toenails, she
wanted to explain to him how his business had prospered
during his absence.

She'd kept the books up-to-date, and was actually
rather pleased with herself, although she'd never say so
aloud. Her mother's lessons in how worthless she was
still haunted her to that degree, even if they didn't intrude
into her thoughts more than five or six times a day anymore.

"Ye've done wonders, Joy, both with my store and
with our patient there." Mac gestured with his pipe toward the potbellied stove, where Elijah sat on a chair,

fingering *The Woman in White* and brooding about something Joy couldn't imagine.

She dragged her attention from Elijah to Mac. "Thank you. The spring cattle drives have started, and the business has been booming."

"I can see that."

"I've kept track of all the sales, and made notes about the kinds of supplies I believe you need to order from Santa Fe and Saint Louis."

Mac nodded contentedly. "You're a good businesswoman, Joy. You'd be a fine at running a business of your own someday."

A business of her own? Startled, she couldn't think of a thing to say. She'd never considered herself to be much good at anything. Sure as sunrise comes after sunset, nobody had ever complimented her on her business acumen before.

"Aye. Maybe ye can partner up with Elijah over there. When he builds his hotel, don't ya know."

Joy's glance shot to Elijah, whose head had snapped up. "What?" He looked grumpy. Joy frowned. What did *he* have to be grumpy about?

"I was just tellin' Joy here that you could use her when you open your hotel in Rio Hondo, laddie. She's good at keepin' the books, and she's smart as a whip."

Joy felt her eyes widen. Smart as a whip? Joy Hardesty? Her mother used to tell her she was as useless as dust balls. She'd probably have compared her to something even less useful than dust balls if she could have thought of anything. Her mother had never visited anyplace as wild as Rio Hondo. Joy spared a moment to be glad her mother's sphere of operation had been the relatively small township of Auburn, Massachusetts, or she might have compared Joy to a yucca pod or something.

"Yeah, she's pretty smart. She did a good job on me, anyway." Elijah smiled at her.

She stared at him, too astonished for words. He must have noticed her discomposure, because he winked. Then his eyes took on an abstracted cast, and he returned to brooding. Joy wondered what he was thinking about, but she didn't ask. She and Mac still had some accounts to go over.

"Aye, and the place looks neat and tidy, too. It's hard to keep anything looking spiffy out here, where the wind blows all the time, and there aren't hardly any trees to catch the grit."

Trees. Of course. That was it. Joy wondered why she'd never considered the absence of trees as she'd battled the dust. Trees would make the place look less uncivilized, too.

"But folks're beginning to plant 'em," Mac continued. "Why, I understand Mr. Chisum has two long rows of sturdy oak trees leadin' up to his ranch house. And Cody and Mellie have planted a whole orchard full of apple trees at their place."

"An apple orchard? Out here? For heaven's sake." Joy had a sudden burning desire to meet the O'Fannins, even if Mrs. O'Fannin had been divorced. An apple orchard. How . . . how optimistic of them. She realized for the first time that she'd never been optimistic about anything at all, let alone the future of a newly developed territory. A tiny flicker of ambition, banked since she was an infant by her mother's disparaging opinion of her worth, sparked to life in Joy's heart.

"Oh, aye. They're not the only ones, either. Why, the Partridges have planted one field with pecan trees and another with apple, apricot, and peach trees. They live on a rise out beside the Pecos, and they've planted mulberries and live oaks to shade their house, too."

234

"Pecans. Peaches. Apricots. Mulberries. Live oaks." They sounded lovely to Joy, who missed the forests of her New England home. They were about all she missed about the land of her birth, but—

Good Lord on high, did she really mean that? Mac began speaking again before she could muddle through her confused thoughts to find an answer.

"Aye. And Mellie was telling me she has a right fair corn patch going, too. In fact, she's quite the gardener, our Mellie."

"My goodness. I didn't know anything grew out here but sagebrush and cactus." Trying to be fair, she murmured, "Yucca, of course. Creosote."

Mac let out with a hearty chuckle. "Oh, aye, we've got plenty of them things growin' out here, too. Mellie says all you have to do is stick something in the ground, and it'll grow."

"Mercy sakes."

"The place needs a hotel," Elijah announced out of the blue.

Mac and Joy both turned to look at him. Joy noticed a strange light in his eyes, which were directed straight at her.

"Aye," said Mac. "Reckon it could use a hotel, all right."

Elijah's intense expression once more faded into abstraction. "A hotel," he muttered, to himself this time. "The place needs a hotel."

Mac gestured at him with his pipe. "I think the boy's growing some ideas in that handsome head of his."

Joy smiled at Elijah. "It is a handsome head, isn't it?" She realized what she'd said as soon as the words were out, and she jerked back to her business. "Anyway, let me show you this, Mac. I think you're going to need more lumber. Several of the cowboys have come in asking for lumber and wire for fences."

From his laugh, and from the look he gave her, Joy feared Mac hadn't missed her absurd comment about Elijah Perry's looks. *Blast!* What was the matter with her? She used to be so good at guarding her tongue. She sniffed. If she hadn't been good at guarding her tongue, her mother would have been at her twenty-four hours a day instead of merely twenty-three. She decided she didn't want to think about it.

Joy sat on her bed in the back of Mac's store—Elijah had kept the bedroom in Mac's house at her insistence—and stared at the money in her lap. Mac had paid her well for her service in his mercantile establishment during his absence. She might even have enough money to get herself back to Auburn now. She went over a possible route in her head.

First she'd have to hire space in a freight wagon to get her from Rio Hondo to Santa Fe or Albuquerque. Then she'd either have to take a stagecoach somewhere or, if Albuquerque had a train station, catch a train there to take her back east. When she'd traveled out here with Mr. Thrash, the group of missionaries had traveled by wagon train. And extremely uncomfortable it had been, too.

At any rate, whatever train she caught in New Mexico Territory probably wouldn't take her any farther than Kansas City or Saint Joseph. Maybe Saint Louis. From there she'd probably be able to catch a train to Philadelphia, if there wasn't one that went all the way to Boston. The railroad lines went clear across the continent now.

Her heart felt heavy, and tears backed up behind her eyelids. Whatever did that mean? Joy thought she knew, and it made her angry.

"Don't be any more of a fool than you can help being, Joy Hardesty."

Letting her head fall back, she stared at the ceiling, knowing it was already too late for her not to be a fool.

"Dear Lord, how could you let something like this happen to me? Wasn't I enough of a mess already, without adding this burden to my life?"

The dear Lord didn't answer. He didn't have to. Joy already knew the answer. Yes, she was enough of a mess already. And yes, she didn't want to leave Rio Hondo. Because—saints preserve her!—she had managed to fall madly in love with Elijah Perry, gambler, womanizer, sinner, and rambling man.

"Oh, dear Lord, this is terrible!"

Her mother was probably laughing herself sick up there in heaven.

Elijah Perry sat on his bed in Mac's back room, leaning against the headboard with his hands cupped behind his head, as he pondered the strange and unusual ideas that had been playing tag in his head all day.

Aloud, he said, "You're getting old, Elijah Perry. You aren't going to be able to keep wandering around forever."

He frowned, testing the truth of those two sentences. With a sigh, he decided they were, indeed, true. What a pain in the neck the truth could be sometimes. He tried again: "Putting down roots doesn't have to be all *that* frightening."

Discovering he wasn't sure about that one, he decided to overlook it for a while and forge onward. "You used to like the hotel business, remember." He did remember, and he felt better.

"Besides, the place *does* need a hotel. Mac's wagon

yard won't be able to fill the needs of the community forever."

That truth, while it didn't strike him with as much pleasure as the one about the hotel business, didn't bother him as much as the ones about his getting old or setting down roots.

The one that popped up next was too bizarre even to consider in his current state of debilitation, so he skipped over it and tackled another one. This one wasn't as thorny as the prior one, but it did make his stomach hurt and his heart thump as if he were having a seizure: "If you stop moving around, you might have to learn what's happened to Virginia."

He waited for the sick feeling in his stomach to settle. He knew he could probably get out of having to come to grips with an adult Virginia by simply ignoring her and never writing to her again. Whatever else he'd been in his life, however, Elijah had never been a coward. He guessed he'd have to live with facing the truth about Virginia, even though he feared that discovering she'd grown up to be a simpering, foolish female might well kill him. The image he carried in his head of her as a darling two-year-old was precious to him. It would break his heart to have it shattered.

He scowled at the ceiling. "So be it."

Hell, he'd survived worse in his day, hadn't he? And he never knew. Maybe Virginia had grown up to be a charming and delightful young lady.

"Don't be stupid," he advised his fanciful self. Where had this ridiculous whimsy suddenly sprung from, anyway? He never used to be afraid to face hard facts.

"Like hell."

Rattled by the latest words to leap from his mouth, Elijah started slightly and looked around. No one was in the room but him. He must have said it.

With a heavy sigh, he admitted that perhaps, once or twice—maybe—he'd tried to duck out on facing unpleasant facts.

"Damn. It's been more than once or twice, you damnfool liar. You hate facing ugly facts and always have. Hell, man, grow up."

Elijah wasn't generally so hard on himself and wished he hadn't begun to be now. It seemed that he'd opened the floodgates, however, and the miserable details of his life kept pouring into his head. Exasperated, he went on to further franknesses.

"You might have to deal with the rest of your family if you keep in touch with Virginia. Even your mother and father, if they're alive."

He shuddered and squinted into the dim bedroom, lit at present by a single candle. The one candle was having a hard time fighting the gloom now that the sun had almost set. The prospect of reacquainting himself with his family didn't give him the stomachache he'd expected it to. *Good.* He brightened a fraction.

"Hell, you don't have to have anything to do with them. It's not like any of 'em are likely to come out here for a visit."

For all he knew, his parents were dead. And maybe his sister had died years since and was buried in the graveyard next to them. The possibility didn't cause him so much as a twinge of grief. He considered that a good omen, and kept thinking.

Mary Ellen Loveless.

The name exploded into his brain like a firecracker, and Elijah winced and then sighed again, more heavily than before.

"Hell, you don't owe her anything. She'd probably be dead by now if it wasn't for you."

It didn't work. Mary Ellen Loveless still troubled him. *Damn it.*

A perplexing complication, Mary Ellen. Always before in his life, Elijah had settled such complications by simply walking away from them. If he stuck around in Rio Hondo for however many days remained to him, however, doing so permanent a thing as running a hotel, the loose ends he'd left behind in his decades as a rolling stone might well find him out.

"God, what a thought!" He shuddered again.

All right. He had to face facts someday; he might as well start now. If he did decide to settle in Rio Hondo, he'd have to think long and hard on what to do about Mary Ellen.

Mary Ellen had been a worse-for-wear, albeit very young, wretchedly laudanum-addicted sporting girl when Elijah first met her in San Francisco. As he'd had nothing better to do with himself at the time, and since he liked her pretty well, he'd helped her overcome her addiction. She'd been half in love with him ever since—and he'd been half in love with her, too, if he aimed to be brutally honest with himself. And, since this evening seemed to be the time for such truth telling, he admitted it. He'd only ever been half in love with her, however.

Mary Ellen was the only human being Elijah had kept in touch with—more or less—in the past fifteen years. Actually, she'd had more to do with the keeping-in-touch part than he. He'd run into her every now and then. She seemed adept at tracking him down, because she'd shown up three or four times in places he'd stayed for longer than a week or two. Elijah had always been happy to see her, and she hadn't ever made a fuss when he'd moved along. She knew he wasn't the settling-down type. Or hadn't been, rather. Before he got shot here in Rio Hondo.

If, however, he settled down the way he wanted to settle down, here, in Rio Hondo, he'd have to deal with Mary Ellen. Permanently. He didn't want to do it. He feared he'd hurt her feelings. What an odd concept: Elijah Perry worrying about hurting a whore's feelings. He snorted derisively.

"You can be one hell of an ass without half trying, Elijah Perry."

That truth didn't bother him. He'd known it for years.

"So that's that."

Elijah felt something kick at his conscience and resented it. Hell, for twenty-one years now he'd been doing his best to rid himself of a conscience, but the damned thing wouldn't die no matter what he did to it. He'd even gone out of his way, once or twice, to do something he considered downright evil in an attempt to put his conscience to rest once and for all. It hadn't worked.

That wasn't the end of it. The question of Joy Hardesty remained.

Elijah uncupped his hands, dropped his chin to his chest, and let his arms fall to his sides. He closed his eyes and shook his head. Damn it, this wasn't fair. He grabbed one of his pillows and punched it hard. It didn't help.

When the glory of his hotel concept had burst into his brain, it had done so fully grown—and with attachments.

No matter which way he'd looked at it, Joy was there. Only she wasn't Joy Hardesty in his mind's eye. No. Nothing could be that simple, could it?

"Damn it."

Elijah slammed one pillow down on top of the other and gave them such a hot glare, he was surprised they didn't burst into flames.

He knew God was getting back at him for his wicked ways when his mind's eye pictured Joy standing on the porch of his fine new hotel, holding the hands of a little girl and a little boy, and smiling at him. Because—God save him—she was his *wife!* And those kids—Lord, he couldn't stand it—were his children.

That wasn't even the worst of it. No. He buried his head in the top pillow and wished he could simply smother himself and get it over with. This final truth was so awful, he'd been avoiding it all day, and now he was trying to avoid it through the night. But it wouldn't go away, and it refused to be ignored any longer.

He was in love with her.

Chapter Fourteen

Joy smiled at the freight-delivery man as he lugged the heavy mail pouch into Mac's store. "It looks like there's lots of mail this time," she said, because she felt the need to say something.

He heaved the pouch onto the counter with a grunt. "Yeah. More folks movin' out here all the time, I reckon."

"I suppose that's true." Joy spent a moment missing her population-dense home in Auburn, Massachusetts. In Auburn, there were all sorts of people to talk to, anytime she wanted to. Of course, the only ones she knew had been connected with her mother's religious enterprises and were, therefore, not the most comfortable communicants in the world. She shook off the moment and nodded brightly at the freight man. "It's a warm day and you have a hard job. You must be thirsty. Would you care for a cool drink?"

"Yes, ma'am. Thank you kindly. A glass of Mac's beer would be right welcome."

Joy hadn't thought about alcohol when she'd offered the man a drink. She'd been thinking more on the order of water or apple cider or lemonade. Not that there was such a commodity as a lemon to be had within hundreds of miles of Rio Hondo. She didn't think about protesting, though, but only nodded, smiled again, and went into the back room to procure the beer. In spite of her mother's endless homilies, she now knew that not every single person who took a mug of beer after performing a hard task was necessarily wicked and depraved.

She pulled the handle on the beer keg, watched the beer foam out of the spigot, and half expected to hear her mother's voice spout a lecture on the evils of drink, and how weak-willed and sinful Joy was for contributing to the freight driver's downfall. A lecture didn't materialize, and she was pleased.

Instead, while she was in the back room, she decided the poor man might appreciate some bread and butter and a hunk of cheese, so she took a minute to prepare him plate of food, then carried the small repast out to the store on a tray. The freight driver had strolled over to the pot-bellied stove, where Elijah Perry was stationed again today. The men were exchanging pleasantries. Joy braced herself and tried to ignore the battering of her heart as she took the tray to the stove.

"Here you are, sir."

"Thank you, ma'am." The man bobbed his head and looked happily at the food. "Thank you very kindly. I am a mite peckish, and that there food looks real tasty."

Joy pretended not to see Elijah's arched eyebrows and his expression of feigned shock when he realized she was giving food away. As sweetly as she knew how, she said, "You have a very difficult and demanding job. I'm sure you deserve at least this much in refreshment."

Because the snort Elijah gave irked her, she kicked him lightly on the shin as she turned to take the tray to the back room.

"Ow!"

She fluttered her eyelashes. "Oh, my dear goodness gracious! Did I kick you, Mr. Perry? I'm ever so sorry. Pray, forgive me!"

Elijah rolled his eyes, and Joy smirked as she swished away from him and headed for the counter. She heard him mutter, " 'Pray forgive me.' I can't believe you said that."

"Pretty gal, that. Nice, too. Don't see too many pretty gals out here in the territory."

This remark came from the freight driver. Joy almost bumped into the pickle barrel. As soon as she'd made her way into the back room, she peeked around the doorjamb and strained to hear whether Elijah would say something; perhaps agree with that excessively kind and perceptive man. She should have known better.

"She's pretty enough, but she's prickly as a cactus."

Joy scowled, and her pounding heart stumbled. Then Elijah looked at her before she could duck behind the door, and winked. She jerked her head away and felt herself flush from her toenails to the part in her hair.

Well, she had no business playing coy games with Elijah Perry, even if she did care for him more than she knew was good for her. She was gainfully employed in Mac's store and had work to do. Part of that work was sorting through the mail as quickly as she could when the pouch was delivered. The whole of Rio Hondo and its surrounding ranches knew when the freight driver came to town, and they'd soon be rushing to Mac's wagon yard to pick up any letters from home. Joy knew better than to expect any mail herself. No one she knew in Auburn liked her well enough to write.

Considering that thought too depressing to dwell upon, she set her tray in its proper place, and went back out to the mail pouch resting on the counter. Climbing onto her high stool, she refused to look toward the potbellied stove, and tried not to listen in on the conversation Elijah and the freight driver were engaged in.

Not eavesdropping became easier when she realized they were discussing baseball, a sport she knew less than nothing about, if such a state of ignorance was possible. Her mother, needless to say, had considered baseball frivolous and sinful. Mrs. Hardesty hadn't allowed Joy's father to organize a church baseball team for the young boys who attended Sunday school there. As Joy recalled her parents' arguments about the baseball issue, she decided that, given several alternatives, a baseball team for young lads seemed preferable to most of them. It would certainly have been more productive than tipping over outhouses, throwing dice, and soaping windows, three activities the young men in Auburn had favored.

That, however, was neither here nor there. Joy wasn't in Auburn any longer, her parents were dead, and she still didn't know one end of a baseball bat from the other. She quickly became engrossed in sorting the mail.

Not many minutes later, Joy realized to her considerable surprise that she enjoyed the job of sorting mail. Many of the letters had been folded and sealed with wax, and she liked trying to decipher the various seals. Most of the wax globs had been pressed with a button or a ring or some other mundane household item. Still others bore the imprint of more impressive stamps.

Of the letters that hadn't been merely folded and sealed, some had been stuffed into ready-made envelopes and gummed closed. Several of them had obviously been sent from post offices, and bore inked stamps. Quite a few had the more newfangled gummed postage stamps on them. Joy was intrigued by those stamps, which she considered a clever idea, especially if one didn't live near a post office. One could purchase a supply of gummed stamps and have them on hand whenever one wanted to write a letter.

Correspondence to Rio Hondo, New Mexico Territory, boasted postmarks from everywhere in the United States, its territories, and even overseas. Even the least exciting piece of mail, a letter to John Chisum, had been posted in Texas, a place that had always evoked thoughts of the wild and woolly frontier in Joy's mind. And now she herself lived in a place even more wild and woolly than Texas! All at once, Joy felt like a daring pioneer; a rugged adventurer into new and untried lands.

Perhaps not exactly daring and rugged.

Still, the notion appealed to her, and she was smiling when she came across a neatly addressed missive, sealed in pink wax with a thistle print embedded in the wafer, and directed to—*her*. She had to stare at the letter for several moments before the words on the outside registered fully. Somebody had written her a letter! She turned the envelope over twice, studying it. Squinting at the postmark, she pondered. She didn't know a single soul in Maryland. Did she?

Then it dawned on her: Virginia Gladstone had responded to Joy's letter about Elijah's accident! She glanced at him. She still hadn't told him she'd posted his letter to Virginia. At the moment he and the freight driver were laughing about something, and Joy could only be glad Elijah wasn't looking at her. She knew guilt must be plastered all over her face.

Because she didn't trust herself not to reveal her feelings if this letter contained something dreadful—although she couldn't imagine what Virginia Gladstone might have written to her that could be dreadful—Joy turned away from the men and broke the seal as quietly as she could.

Virginia Gladstone had neat, precise handwriting that appealed to Joy's orderly soul. She read quickly.

Dear Miss Hardesty. Thank you very much for taking the time to write to me, and for forwarding Uncle Elijah's letter to me.

Uncle Elijah. Joy smiled. *Uncle Elijah, indeed!* She read on.

It was very kind of you to do so. I pray nightly that my dear uncle is recovering from his accident. I have often wished to thank him for his great kindness to me over the years, but he has never given me an address so that I might do so. If he is well enough, please give him my deepest love, and tell him that I wish he would visit Baltimore. We would all be so thrilled to see him again! Thank you again, very much. Yours sincerely, Virginia Gladstone.

"How nice of her." It was a short letter, and it said no more than Joy herself might have written under similar circumstances. She couldn't understand why it should make her want to cry.

When she glanced over at Elijah again, he was still holding forth with the freight driver. They were discussing something called a foul ball—Joy presumed they hadn't yet exhausted the subject of baseball—so she tucked Virginia Gladstone's letter into her pocket. She really ought to tell Elijah she'd written Virginia.

It occurred to her that Virginia might well have written

her "Uncle Elijah"—she grinned again at the appellation—a letter, so she resumed sorting through the pile of mail.

Some of the envelopes were very battered. It looked to Joy as though mail sent to the western territories had to be nearly as tough as the people who resided in them to survive the ordeal. She held up a parcel and had to squint to read the address. It looked as though it had weathered a war on its way west from New York City. It was addressed to Mac, so she set it aside.

The next envelope she picked up had her name written on it. She started violently, not having expected to find even one piece of correspondence addressed to her, much less two of them. She gasped when she realized this particular missive had been posted from south of the border, in Mexico.

"What's the matter, Joy?"

Elijah's voice nearly startled her off of her stool. When she glanced at him, she saw that both he and the freight-wagon driver had stopped speaking and were staring at her. She licked her lips.

Elijah rose from his chair. She saw from his expression that he was concerned about her, and thought it was sweet of him to care. She couldn't recall anyone ever having been concerned about her before she came to the territory. She waved at him to sit down again.

"It's nothing. It's just that I received a letter, and I hadn't anticipated one." She smiled to let him know she was all right, even though she wasn't sure she was. A cold feeling, for which she couldn't account, had begun creeping up her spine and coiling around her heart.

"You sure?" Elijah cocked his head and studied her face. "You look scared. Did you get some bad news?"

"Of course not. That is, I don't know yet. I haven't even opened it." Drat him, why was he turning so perceptive all at once? He was supposed to be a black-hearted, heedless, devil-may-care gambling man. He wasn't supposed to be able to read her mind so easily—and then worry about her. "I'm fine," she said, summoning up a smile. "Go on back to your conversation."

After eyeing her for another moment or two, he did as she'd bidden him. Joy stared at the envelope in her hand. She didn't know if it contained bad news, good news, or no news. Whatever it contained, she assumed it was correspondence from Mr. Hezekiah P. Thrash or one of the missionaries who'd gone to Central America with him. Joy hadn't become very well acquainted with any of them. She hadn't dared.

As she'd traveled across the country in their company, she'd been reluctant to reveal too much of herself for fear they'd discover she was a fraud and send her packing. Although, as she mulled over the matter now, she knew of no reason to have feared being thought a fraud. After all, she was a fully trained, able-bodied nurse and a God-fearing Christian. She frowned at the letter and realized her pervasive feeling of incompetence was yet one more legacy from her dear, departed mother.

She shot a quick peek at the ceiling, sure she'd witness some sign of disapproval—a lightning bolt, perhaps—directed at her from the late Mrs. Hardesty. All she saw was ceiling. And it looked as if she ought to take the broom to it, too, because there was a cobweb dangling from a rafter right above her head. She frowned at the web, wondering how a spider could work so fast. She'd swept all the cobwebs down no more than a week ago.

Well, that was nothing to the purpose. She had a letter to open. Her fingers trembled when she broke the wafer, spread the single sheet open on the counter, and read the few words written thereupon.

Mr. Thrash wanted her to join his company. Joy stared

at the paper before her, hardly comprehending the message it contained. Mr. Thrash not only wanted her, he was sending an emissary to escort her into the jungle where the missionaries had set up their medical station and church.

"We have but a tent for holy services," the letter informed her, "yet our mission prospers."

"Good," she whispered, wondering why her heart felt like a lump of coal. She was supposed to be thrilled that Mr. Thrash had remembered her and had cared so much that he was now sending someone to fetch her. She should be elated. She should be jumping for joy. This was what she'd wanted all along.

Wasn't it?

"Of course it is." She spoke the words aloud, trying to convince herself. She realized her mistake when Elijah spoke to her again.

"Of course what is?"

She glanced at him quickly. "Er—nothing. I was just . . . talking to myself."

He gave her a strange look, but Joy was befuddled and couldn't think of anything else to say. Besides, her mail was none of his business. Her mail was no one's business. There wasn't a soul in the entire world to whom she meant a hill of beans; why should anyone care about her mail?

On that depressing note, she put Mr. Thrash's letter aside and determined to think about it as she sorted through the rest of the mail. There were several letters for the O'Fannins and the Partridges and Susan Blackworth, the neighbors Mac spoke about most frequently. Joy hadn't seen any of them except from afar, although cowboys from their various ranches had been in and out of the wagon yard in the weeks since her arrival.

Life out here was so strange. Until she came to Rio

Hondo, Joy would have been unable to imagine not visiting a store or a neighbor for months on end. She shook her head, and decided the notion didn't appeal to her now, either.

As little as she'd had to do with her fellow creatures on this earth until now, still less did she want to live apart from them. In fact, she realized as she culled through all shapes and sizes of correspondence, what she *really* wanted was to feel as though she belonged. She wanted to be accepted by her fellow men and women naturally, as if she were inherently no different from anyone else. She was sick to death of feeling like an interloper into human society.

Her mother had taught her she wasn't worth the space she took up on earth. *How kind of her.* Joy slammed a letter down onto the pile she'd designated for Mac, and decided that if she was ever blessed with children—and she couldn't imagine any man wanting her to bear his children—she'd rear them to accept themselves as worthwhile people. No child asked to be born. It was the parents' responsibility to teach their children self-worth. Joy would *never* deliberately set out to destroy her child's self-respect.

"That's exactly what she did to me, the miserable old sourpuss."

"I beg your pardon?"

Joy jumped on her stool and again glanced at the men who'd been chatting by the potbellied stove. Elijah was looking even more concerned than he had before. Joy smiled at him, gratified that he seemed to care for her, at least a little bit—and she'd been meaner to him than to anyone else in her recent memory. Maybe there was hope for her yet.

"I beg your pardon. I was just thinking."

"Don't look like they was happy thoughts, ma'am,"

the freight driver said. "Anything I can do?"

How sweet. Joy gave him an especially friendly smile. Elijah, she noticed, had begun frowning at him, and she wondered why. "Thank you very much, sir, but no. I fear I was merely talking to myself. It was a silly thing to do."

"If she needs anything, I'll help her." Elijah's words came out as hard and cold as ice chunks. Both Joy and the freight driver were taken aback.

Joy saw the freight driver blink at Elijah several times and then nod slowly. "That's how it is, eh? Well, I reckon I should have guessed."

The man smiled at Elijah, who held on to his pose of anger for another moment and then relaxed. He nodded. Joy had no idea what they were agreeing on. Baseball, perhaps. She went back to her sorting.

One thing was good about this latest development: if she joined Mr. Thrash and his missionaries, at least she wouldn't have to go back to Auburn a failure. She expected her mood to lighten on that note and was disappointed when it didn't. What was wrong with her?

Don't be an idiot, Joy Hardesty. You know very well what's wrong with you.

She did know what was wrong with her, and it annoyed her. She had allowed herself to become infatuated with Elijah Perry, was what was wrong, thus proving herself to be foolish beyond redemption. Even if she stayed in Rio Hondo for the rest of her life, what good would remaining do her? As soon as he was fit, Elijah Perry would move on. He wasn't a settling-down sort of man.

Well, now, that may no longer be true, Joy. Recall the hotel, if you will.

Joy dropped the envelope she held and whipped her head back and forth, looking for the source of this latest voice. It wasn't that of her mother. Actually it reminded her of Mac's. She shook her head, wishing she'd stop hearing voices. From all she'd ever read, hearing voices was a sure sign of insanity. Would she begin seeing things next? She remembered the sparkles that occasionally manifested themselves to her, and her insides gave a hard spasm.

She'd better not go back to Auburn if she'd lost her mind. It would be terrible enough to be a lunatic out here in Rio Hondo, where one could hardly tell the lunatics from the sane people. It would be downright humiliating to be considered a lunatic in front of her mother's old cronies. Or old crones. Joy grinned, proud of herself for that one.

The hotel. Joy read addresses and thought about a hotel in Rio Hondo. It seemed to her that if one did have to remain in this godforsaken place, it would be more pleasant to run a business in the town, such as it was, than to live out there on those empty windswept plains, miles and miles removed from one's neighbors. If one operated a business in town, especially a hotel, one would always have people with whom to converse. Not that Joy was an adept conversationalist—her mother had thrashed the words out of her as well as the spirit—but she might learn one day if she practiced long enough.

The word *thrashed* struck her as appropriate to her present circumstances, and she considered how her life might go on as a missionary in Central America. As little as six months ago, the opportunity had seemed like her salvation. It didn't any longer. Joy heaved a sigh and wished life could be easy. Just once.

"Thanks again for the food, ma'am."

Again Joy jumped on her stool, startled. She looked up from her letters to find the freight-wagon driver holding his empty plate and beer mug. She smiled and took them from him. "I hope you enjoyed it. It wasn't much."

"It was kind of you to offer me food, ma'am. Not everyone's so considerate."

How sweet. Joy liked being thought considerate, even if the behavior was new to her. She climbed down from her stool, took the dishes, and carried them into the back room, thinking all the way.

Being considerate to one's fellow man was a virtue, wasn't it? Why had she grown up feeling that it was foolish to be considerate? Her mother used to grumble about having to give alms to the poor, and had cautioned her over and over again against being hoodwinked by unscrupulous folks looking for a handout. That attitude didn't speak very well of Christian charity to Joy as she looked back on it from her new adult perspective.

She sighed. One more thing to contemplate. There were so many of them, sometimes her head spun with the impossibility of sifting everything out.

"All right, Joy. What's wrong?"

She whirled around, almost dropping the dishes. Elijah Perry stood at the open doorway, a scowl on his face, his fists on his lean hips. Good heavens, he was a large man. He must have been devastatingly handsome in his earlier days. Not that he was old now, exactly, but he did have a few years on him. And a few pounds. And a few gray hairs, what there were left of them. Joy grinned when she realized that going over Elijah Perry's more human attributes made him seem less intimidating. She set the plate and beer mug beside the washbasin.

"Nothing is wrong, Elijah. I'm fine." She added, "Thank you," because she truly did appreciate his caring whether she was perturbed.

"Horse patties. Something's happened to upset you, and I want to know what it is."

Horse patties? Joy giggled. "I'm not upset."

"The hell you're not. Listen to me, Joy. I've had to put up with you for weeks and weeks now, and I can tell when you're worried or upset. For God's sake, I've spent more time with you than with any other human being on the face of the earth since I was sixteen years old. Don't tell *me* you're not upset, because I know better."

He stomped over to her. She turned around and almost bumped into him. She'd have backed up, but she had no room in which to do so. Tilting her head back, she gazed up into his face. It was, she realized, not nearly so forbidding-looking as she'd at first considered it. In truth, Joy now believed it to be a good face; it was certainly one that had become dear to her. Lord, Lord, how had she let that happen? She'd been weakened from illness and abandonment, she supposed, and hadn't guarded herself well enough. Too late now. She sighed again.

"There," he said, almost triumphantly. "You see? You just sighed. I *know* there's something wrong when you sigh, and I want to know what it is."

His eyes were so pretty. Especially when he felt intensely about something, they had a certain light to them. They didn't dance, exactly, like Mr. McMurdo's did, but they shone with a fire Joy hadn't encountered before. The people she knew back home in Auburn would have died sooner than be fiery about anything. Tepid. They were all tepid. Except her mother, who was an iceberg.

"It's really nothing, Elijah. It's only that I received a letter from Mr. Thrash."

His frown faded, but his eyebrows didn't lift. He looked puzzled. "Mr. Thrash. Who the hell's—Oh, hell. You don't mean to say Thrash is the preacher man, do you?"

His phrasing tickled her. She giggled again. "Well, actually, yes, I do mean to say that, because it's the truth."

Elijah dropped his arms and unclenched his fists. "Oh."

Deftly Joy stepped around him. She'd begun to feel a terrible urge to fling her arms around him, and knew she'd do it if she stood so close to him for very much longer. What would happen if she were to do so brazen a thing, she didn't even want to contemplate. She heard him turn behind her.

"What did he have to say?"

She continued on her way to the counter, where stacks of mail still awaited her disposition. She glanced at him over her shoulder, and decided she was interested in his reaction to her news. Ergo, she maintained a noncommittal tone when she told it to him. "He wants me to join his mission work in the jungles of Central America. They've set up a church 'and a medical mission there."

"The hell you say!"

His roar nearly deafened her. She climbed onto her stool and frowned at him. "There's no need to make such a fuss, Elijah. It was for the purpose of becoming a missionary that I came to Rio Hondo in the first place, you know." She didn't admit to him that the idea of being a missionary in the South American jungles no longer held any appeal to her and that, in fact, the thought of rejoining Mr. Thrash made her blood run cold.

He stormed up to her, and his heavy steps sounded like a series of thunderclaps in the confined area of Mac's small store. Joy flinched, wishing he weren't quite such a noisy man sometimes. Now, for instance.

"You can't go down there and join up with that gang of meddlers, Joy. You know you can't!"

Although she'd been telling herself almost exactly the same thing not two minutes earlier, his attitude irked her. "I don't know why not. He's sending someone to guide me to the mission."

"He's *what?*"

She clapped her hands over her ears. "Please! There's no need to shout. I can hear you."

"Damn it all, Joy, you can't be a missionary. You'd hate it, and you know it!"

She did know it, actually. Nevertheless, his domineering attitude reminded her of her mother, and she discovered her perverse streak being activated. "I've been trained as a nursing missionary, Elijah Perry. What do you mean, I'd hate it? What do you know about what I hate and don't hate, you wretched man?"

"I know you'd hate it, because I know you!"

"Nonsense!" Something genuinely relevant struck her, and she added, "Besides, I have to earn my living somehow, and I don't particularly care to remain working in Mr. McMurdo's store. He doesn't need me, you know. He was only being charitable when he offered me this job."

"That's not the point!"

All right. Enough was enough. Elijah's show of temper was beginning to seriously annoy her. "The point is, I was trained as a missionary nurse. I have to earn a living, since I don't have any other source of income. I can't remain here, because Mac doesn't need me. Ergo, I suppose I shall have to join Mr. Thrash in Central America." So there, she thought peevishly.

"That's stupid!"

"What's stupid about it?"

"Everything! You'd be totally out of place among a batch of missionaries, and you know it!"

"I do not know it! I was trained for it!"

"That was before you knew better, when you were pretending to be like your miserable mother. You'd hate it now that you've changed."

Changed, had she? And she had a miserable mother, did she? Well, maybe he was right, but he had no right to say so. "You're being ridiculous, Elijah Perry."

"I am not!" Furious, Elijah turned away from Joy, cut sharply around the end of the counter, and stalked over to the stove. There he picked up *The Woman in White*, scowled at it, slammed it back on the table, and jerked around.

Joy sniffed. "Don't damage the book, if you please, Mr. Perry."

"Don't 'Mr. Perry' me, Joy. And I'll damage the book if I damn well please. It's my book!"

Joy shook her head, exasperated. "Very well. Ruin it if it suits you."

"I don't want to ruin it!"

Good heavens, he was in a vile mood. "This is a stupid conversation," she muttered.

Striving to ignore him, she went back to sifting through the mail. She heard him coming back to the counter. Since she didn't trust him not to do something she'd regret while he was in this mood, she spread her arms out over the already sorted piles of correspondence. She wouldn't have put it past him to sweep it all onto the floor, and then she'd have to pick it up and sort it all over again. She glared a warning at him.

He stopped short of the counter. His hands had bunched into fists again, but he held them rigidly at his sides this time. Joy felt anger radiating from him like waves of heat from a fire. She held her ground, staring back, daring him to do his worst.

He did.

"Damn it, you can't go to Central America with that idiot Thrash. You're going to stay right here in Rio Hondo and help me run my hotel. You're going to marry me, damn it!"

In the end, it was Joy who started so violently, she scattered mail all over the floor.

Chapter Fifteen

Joy stood stock-still amid a flutter of falling paper and stared at Elijah, her mouth gaping open.

Elijah stared back, his gape matching hers and then some. Hell fire, had he really, honestly and truly, just asked the woman to marry him? From the expression on her face, Elijah feared he had. What in the name of mercy was he thinking?

"What did you just say?"

Joy's voice had gone so small and squeaky, Elijah barely heard her. Because his senses had obviously become deranged, and because he could scarcely comprehend the enormity of the blunder he'd just committed, and because his brains refused to unscramble, he remained silent. He did manage to close his mouth.

So did Joy. Then she opened it again. Her eyebrows began to lower into a frown. These were bad omens.

Even in his present state of bewilderment, Elijah could tell that much.

She cleared her throat. "Excuse me, Elijah, I don't believe I heard you properly."

An out! She'd just offered him an out. He could deny she'd heard him propose. *Brilliant.*

He couldn't do it. Elijah Perry's conscience, an untrustworthy item that had seldom before interfered in his life, today stared him straight in the face and refused to allow him to lie. *Damn it!* Why was he developing scruples now, of all inconvenient times?

Joy squinted at him. Her hands went to her hips. She was getting mad; he recognized all the symptoms. "I, ah, I . . ." *Oh, hell.*

He heard footsteps on the wooden boards of the porch. Could reprieve actually be at hand? *Voices!* He heard voices. *Thank God, thank God!* Joy heard them, too. Elijah saw her stiffen, then huff with frustration. He turned around, wondering if he was wise to turn his back on her under the circumstances. On the other hand, how much damage could she do with a piece of paper?

He heard Joy mutter, "You haven't heard the last of this, Elijah Perry. I plan to hear your excuse for this latest outrage before I'm very much older."

Oh, yeah? Elijah might have something to say about that—or he might not, depending on how he deemed best to preserve his health and his single status. He faced the door, smiling for all he was worth, ready—nay, willing—to embrace his salvation, in whatever form it presented itself.

He had it backward.

"Elijah!" the newcomer cried. "Elijah! Darling!"

It was Mary Ellen Loveless, and she embraced him. Ran right up to him and flung herself at him, in fact. Elijah, who had believed himself to be beyond shock after having proposed to Joy Hardesty, discovered he was wrong. He was so surprised by Mary Ellen's sudden appearance that he almost fell over backward. If he hadn't stumbled into Joy, and if she hadn't shoved him, hard, in the back, he'd have ended on the floor with Mary Ellen crawling all over him.

Instead she crawled all over him while he remained standing, wild-eyed with shock. Over Mary Ellen's dyed-blond hair, Elijah saw Joy stiffen to attention, and heard her gasp with indignation. He saw her eyes narrow as she witnessed the extremely painted Mary Ellen plant kisses all over his face. He'd have sworn on a stack of Bibles that he witnessed fury rise within Joy, changing the color of her flesh by inches until the very part in her hair glowed red with rage.

He also saw Mac, behind Joy, chuckling with unfeigned humor, his pipe clamped between his pearly teeth, and his blue eyes twinkling up a storm. Mac winked at him. Hell of a lot of good that did him.

"Well! I never!"

"Joy! Wait!" Elijah wrested a hand free from Mary Ellen's grip and waved it wildly in the air as Joy stalked past him, her back as straight as a lance, her lips pinched up so tightly he could hardly see them.

Mac stepped aside to let Joy pass, a wise move on his part since she didn't seem inclined to take note of any impediments in her way. Elijah watched her storm out through the door, and his heart, almost as unreliable a commodity as his conscience, sank down into his boots. In the split second he had to think about anything at all before she disappeared with a swish of skirts, he realized he *had* meant it when he'd proposed.

"Elijah, honey, I'm so damned glad to see you again!" Mary Ellen gave him a fat, wet kiss on the lips.

Sweet God in heaven, what was he supposed to do now?

Mac burst out laughing, then turned and followed Joy out of the store, leaving Elijah to deal with his past by himself.

To the best of her recollection, Joy had never thrown a temper tantrum before. As she sent a glass jar hurtling across the room to smash against the wall, widening the splotch the jar of ink had made, she realized she'd denied herself a good deal of relief in her life. Of course, if she'd thrown an ink bottle at home in Auburn, her mother would have killed her.

"If she'd killed me, she'd have spared me this!" she cried, hurling a flatiron against the wet spot, and gouging a hole in the wall. She'd fix it later. Mac would understand.

"Aye, child, I do understand."

Joy whirled around, barely keeping her grip on the rock that she'd expected to hurl after the flatiron. She blinked at Mac, who stood in the door of her room, a halo of sparkles wreathing his head. He nodded at her.

"Go ahead, child. Fling it. It'll make ye feel better."

Perceiving the sense in Mac's suggestion, Joy spun around and heaved the rock. Adobe plaster exploded from the wall, exposing the wooden framework underneath. Joy drew the back of her shaking hand across her forehead, wiping perspiration away. She did feel moderately better. Except for the huge, gaping, bleeding, throbbing hole in her heart.

Damn Elijah Perry to perdition for all eternity. She turned back to face Mac.

"He proposed to me not ten seconds before that . . . that . . . that . . . *hussy* showed up, Mac! He *proposed* to

264

me! I *know* he did! I *heard* him! It *wasn't* my imagination! It *wasn't!*"

"Aye, child, I'm sure he did. He meant it, too. He loves ye, Joy."

"Ha!" Feeling tears sting her eyes, Joy whirled around, mortified that she'd want to cry over such a pernicious, deceiving, foul, base, beastly, dishonest man as Elijah Perry—who'd proposed to her and then fallen into the arms of a . . . a . . . Joy wasn't sure what one called women like that, but she knew whatever one called them, they weren't good women. Not like her. Not that she was good.

All at once the anger drained out of her. Deflated, she sank onto her bed and drooped there like a wilted lily. She peered at the mess she'd made of her bedroom wall.

"I'm sorry, Mac. I'll clean it up."

"There's nothing to be sorry about, lass. You sustained a big shock, and you deserve to be upset."

Upset? That was one word for it. Maniacal was another. Hurt. Sad. Angry. Offended. Outraged. All of those, and more. "I've, ah, never done anything like this before." She waved a hand at the glass shards and plaster dust littering the floor.

"Then it's about time ye started, child. There're a lot of emotions piled up inside o' ye. Ye've got to let 'em out, or they'll eat at your liver."

She looked up at him. He truly was a kind man. How strange that it should have taken her so long to recognize the genuine goodness in him. She shook her head, feeling bitter and beaten. *Thank you so much, Mother, for making me as blind as you were.* "Thank you, Mac. I appreciate your understanding."

"Oh, aye, lass. You and Elijah both have a lot of ground to make up, y'know."

Joy snorted before she could stop herself. "Elijah!"

Ooooh, she'd like to have a minute alone with him. With another flatiron in her hand. She'd throw that one at his fat head.

Laughing, Mac sat next to her on the bed and put an arm around her shoulder. Unused to people touching her, Joy was surprised she didn't flinch away from the contact. Instead, she felt a tingling warmth invade her body, making her relax and easing the turmoil raging in her heart and brain.

"It'll all be fine, child. Soon. Ye'll see. Give the lad a chance, Joy. He's no more acquainted with deep human emotions than ye are. Your mother tried to ruin you, and his father tried to ruin him, and they both almost succeeded. He had help from the war, and from the freedom the world grants to men to run away from their problems. Ye weren't so lucky, lass, but ye'll be better soon. And so will he. Ye'll see."

"Will I?" Joy didn't believe a word of it, even if she did appreciate his saying so. Her heart sat in her chest like a lump of cold, lifeless dough. Dough whose yeast had died. Dough that would never rise again.

Mac's soft chuckle seemed to penetrate her barren dull places, and Joy couldn't stand another minute of this terrible anguish. With a choking sob, she turned and wept onto Mac's shoulder. He patted her back and mouthed soothing words into her ear, and Joy, whose eyes were squeezed shut against the ache in her heart, didn't see the showers and showers of healing sparkles rising from his hands every time he touched her.

"Mary Ellen?"

Elijah knew it was Mary Ellen, of course, but he couldn't think of anything else to say. *Let go of me*, occurred to him, but not even he was mean enough to say that out loud. Mary Ellen cared for him. Hell, he even cared for Mary Ellen, and he didn't want to hurt her feelings. Not the way he'd just hurt Joy's.

His blasted heart reminded him of its presence again when it gave a hard spasm. Damn it, he had to go after Joy and explain everything to her.

How could he explain this?

Elijah heard a crash that sounded as if it came from the back room. What the hell was that?

There was another crash, louder this time. It sounded like someone was heaving heavy objects against the wall. He hoped that wasn't Joy cutting loose in there. Damn it, if Mary Ellen would just let go of him for a second, he could go back there and check up on Joy. Of course, if he did she'd probably start heaving heavy objects at him. And he wouldn't blame her.

Aw, hell.

Elijah couldn't for the life of him perceive an easy way out of this one.

"Oh, Elijah, honey, I'm so glad to see you!"

Damnation, now Mary Ellen was crying. Elijah wasn't sure he could stand dealing with two hysterical women. Hell, he'd managed to avoid hysteria all his life; why had it chosen to besiege him now, when he wasn't in full health?

The term *poetic justice* occurred to him, and he resented it.

Mary Ellen pushed herself away from him, nearly sending him reeling backward. She caught him by the shoulders and, sniffling, stared at him, her makeup streaming down her cheeks, her blue eyes reminding Elijah of marbles in a river.

"Oh, Elijah, I got so scared when they told me you'd been shot."

"You heard about that?" How the hell had she heard

about that? If he weren't so confused, he'd have asked. Mary Ellen spared him the necessity.

"I was in Albuquerque, you know, because I knew you were headin' west, when this cowboy came into the saloon where I was workin' and told us you'd been shot all to hell. Oh, honey!"

Before Elijah could brace himself, Mary Ellen had pulled him to her bosom again. She had a substantial bosom. He very nearly bounced off of it, but she also had a grip on her, so he didn't. She was squeezing the hell out of his scarcely healed wounds, however, and he murmured a tentative, "Ow."

She let him go immediately and slapped a hand to her painted lips. "Oh, Elijah, darlin', did I hurt you?"

He cleared his throat, thanking God—if there was such an entity—she'd released him. "A little." Mary Ellen was a mess with that paint running all over her face. He groped for his handkerchief and dangled it out to her. She grabbed it, offering him a shaky smile.

"Thanks, honey. I was so worried about you."

"Er, yeah, I can see that. Um, why did you decide to come here, Mary Ellen?" Had that been tactless? Well, Elijah was too rattled to worry about it now.

Her laugh wobbled. "Why did I come here? God Almighty, Elijah, I thought you were dead!"

"Oh. Well, um, I'm not."

She smiled and sniffled. "I can see that. I'm so glad."

"Yeah. Me, too."

"I come down here to see for myself, because I didn't trust nobody else to do it for me. Rio Hondo ain't exactly an easy place to get to."

"You're right about that."

She blew her nose and wiped her eyes again. "I decided, if you were still alive, maybe I could take care of you, if you wanted me to."

Her eyelashes fluttered. Elijah sighed and wished he could see his way out of this. But with Joy smashing things in the back room and Mary Ellen fluttering her eyelashes at him in this one, damned if he didn't feel like a bear in a trap. He hated feeling trapped.

What did men do in situations like this? Something startling occurred to him: perhaps he should tell Mary Ellen the truth.

What a novel idea. Honest in all other aspects of his life, Elijah had discovered that, when it came to women, honesty seldom served. However, in the few brief seconds of silence that followed Mary Ellen's offer to tend his wounds, Elijah mulled over the notion of truth telling and decided a dollop of truth in this instance, while guaranteed to be painful, might make things easier in the long run. He took a deep breath.

Mary Ellen laid a hand on his chest, over his heart. Until today, he'd not been sure he possessed one. At the moment it was battering against his ribs like a herd of wild buffalo, and he couldn't have ignored it if he'd tried.

"What is it, honey? I figured I could check this place out. Maybe open a saloon here. Rio Hondo's gonna grow, according to all the men in Albuquerque. Even though there's hardly anything to it, they say the ranchers need the place."

"Yeah. I reckon they do."

"Even if it is ugly as a mangy dog and a hellhole."

Stung, Elijah muttered, "It's not so bad."

Mary Ellen shrugged, obviously unconvinced.

Elijah braced himself. "Mary Ellen . . ."

"Yes, sweetie-pie?"

"I, ah . . . I aim to settle here. In Rio Hondo."

Her eyes went wide. "You? You're aimin' to settle down? *Here?*"

She smiled hugely. Elijah realized his mistake. He

should have opened his truth-telling session another way. *Damn it*. Feeling like a fly struggling in a sticky web, he tried again. "That is, I aim to open a hotel here. Build one."

"A hotel? You?"

"I used to work in my uncle's hotel in Baltimore. I liked it." He wished he didn't feel so defensive about his proposed enterprise. It should be nobody's business if he wanted to give up the chancy life of a professional gambler and take up hotel keeping. Why did he expect her to laugh at him?

She cocked her head, interested. Elijah was relieved when she didn't so much as crack a smirk.

"Sounds like a fine idea to me, Elijah, honey. Sounds right up my alley." Her smile this time was conspiratorial, as if she expected him to let her set up a brothel in his hotel.

Aw, hell. "Mary Ellen, you see, it's like this . . ."

"Yes?"

It's like what? Elijah let his head fall back. He stared at the ceiling and prayed for inspiration. It didn't strike. No surprise there. God was probably laughing his head off at him. Fancy Elijah Perry, of all people, praying for something. "You see, I've met someone."

She drew back an inch or so. "I beg your pardon?"

Hell, this was awful. "Well, I didn't intend to. I mean, I didn't mean for anything to happen."

Great, now he was whining. Elijah told himself to get a grip. "That is, Miss Hardesty nursed me when I was laid up, you see, and, ah, we've become, ah, sort of fond of each other."

Fond of each other? Elijah cursed himself as seven kinds of a fool. He was fond of Joy Hardesty. He had no idea what Joy thought of him, although he had a feeling *fond* didn't describe it. Not at the moment, anyway. He heard another crash from the back room.

"I see." Mary Ellen took another step away from him, her eyes narrowing ominously. She didn't look like she was going to cry again anytime soon. Beat the crap out of him, maybe.

Elijah shot a hand out to grab her wrist. "Listen, Mary Ellen, I didn't mean for anything to happen. I mean, I was wounded. I'd just taken three bullets—or was it four? I forget—anyway, it was real bad there for a while. Joy and I were, ah, sort of left alone together for a long time. I . . . we . . . it just . . . well, sort of happened."

"Of course. It just happened."

Elijah had never heard Mary Ellen sound like that. She didn't sound any better when she continued.

"Naturally, a body couldn't expect Elijah Perry, of all people, to keep his pecker in his pants. Not even if he'd just got shot all to hell."

Couldn't expect him to keep his pecker in his pants? Elijah gaped at Mary Ellen very much as he'd gaped at Joy several minutes earlier. The thought of him having seduced Joy Hardesty—of having overcome her rigid moral principles so far as to have lain with her in a carnal manner—was so absurd, he actually barked out a short, harsh laugh before he caught himself. Mary Ellen straightened and took another step backward.

"Was that her in here when I came in?" Mary Ellen gestured to where Joy had been standing.

Elijah nodded. He couldn't think of anything to say that didn't sound stupid.

"That dried-up old maid?"

"She's not a dried-up old maid, Mary Ellen."

Mary Ellen sniffed, sounding remarkably like Joy. "Oh, of course not. I suppose *she's* a *lady,* unlike some of us."

"Now Mary Ellen, there's nothing wrong with you. I didn't expect to fall—" Elijah caught himself before he

271

could say *fall in love*. Good God, had he really almost said that? "I didn't expect to come to care for her." *There*. That was better.

Mary Ellen turned to survey the little mercantile. She frowned. "This place is a dump."

Elijah looked, too. It wasn't exactly like some of the places he'd been to in San Antonio, he reckoned. Or back home in Baltimore. Still, for a frontier outpost, it was a tidy little store. "It's not so bad." *Lukewarm, Elijah. You can do better than that.* He cleared his throat again. "Actually, it's pretty well stocked, considering there's not another town in any direction for two hundred miles or more."

She sniffed again and wandered over to the leather goods. She ran her finger over a saddle displayed on a sawhorse. Her nose wrinkled when she gazed at the clear path her finger had made in the dust, and then when she looked at the blot on her finger.

Because he didn't want to hear any more animadversions on the place in which he hoped to settle, Elijah said, "There's no way to keep the dust down out here. No trees. Folks are planting 'em. There's trees up by the Spring River. Lots of the ranchers are planting trees."

The expression on Mary Ellen's face reminded Elijah of Sister Mary Emanuel's. Sister M. E. used to look like that when Elijah said things she considered silly. He sighed. "More folks are moving here every day, Mary Ellen. The town is growing all the time. It'll be a fine place to live one of these days."

She wiped her finger on Elijah's handkerchief. "Next thing you'll be telling me is you and your little lovey-dove are aiming to set up a nursery. I can't believe it." She shook her head, staring at him in disbelief. "I just can't believe it."

Kids? Elijah goggled at her. Until he'd begun contemplating a hotel, he'd never thought about having kids of his own in his entire life. Not that he didn't like kids, but . . . Hell, this was too much to take in all at once.

He heard a small mew and turned to see that Killer—Apricot—whatever in hell the kitten's name was—had jumped onto the counter and was eyeing Mary Ellen suspiciously. Sensing an ally, Elijah said, "H'lo, cat." He walked over to pet him.

Killer Apricot swished his tail and uttered a louder, more menacing meow.

"I hate cats." Mary Ellen wrinkled her nose again.

The kitten hissed at her. Elijah said, "Oh, Killer's all right, for a cat. Ow!" He glared at the kitten, who'd just taken a swipe at his hand. Killer Apricot leaped off of the counter and scampered behind a shelf.

"He don't like bein' two-timed any more than I do, I reckon."

Beleaguered, Elijah blotted a tiny spot of blood on his trousers. "Mary Ellen, I didn't two-time you. We had no agreement between us. It was always friendly and happy and no strings attached. I never once made you any promises or guarantees, did I?"

She expelled a huge gust of air. "No, of course you didn't, damn it. You'd never offer anyone anything if you could get out of it, or get what you wanted for free. I guess I'm just a fool, is all." She flounced over to the counter and leaned over it. "What's all that stuff on the floor there?"

Elijah looked, too. "Uh, it's mail. It . . . fell."

"Oh. Well, somebody better pick it up before the cat pees on it."

She sounded malicious. Elijah wished he could fault her for it, but he couldn't. "Listen, Mary Ellen, I'm really sorry about this—"

"Sure you are."

"I am, damn it. I didn't mean for this to happen—any of it. I mean, I sure as hell didn't intend to get shot, and I couldn't stand Joy when I first met her. She couldn't stand me, either." He grinned, remembering. His grin faded when he recalled that she probably still couldn't stand him, thanks to Mary Ellen's untimely arrival. Hell, he hated having his hand forced. He'd have taken care of Mary Ellen. Managed to explain her to Joy eventually. Somehow or other.

Liar.

Elijah jerked his head around, looking for the source of that voice, before he realized it was probably his blasted conscience talking to him. Once he'd allowed it a toehold, the damn thing had started working overtime.

All right, so he'd probably have avoided saying anything about, or having anything to do with, Mary Ellen if he could have avoided it. That wasn't such a major sin, was it?

Yes, it is a major sin. You owe Mary Ellen Loveless, Elijah Perry. If you owe her nothing else, at least you owe her your friendship and some explanations. It's not her fault you fell in love with Joy.

He winced. There was that word again. *Crap.* All right, so he owed Mary Ellen. He was paying up now, wasn't he?

His conscience snorted at him. Derisively.

He saw Mary Ellen's shoulders sag. The sporting life was hard on a woman. It had aged Mary Ellen before her time. Hell, she wasn't anywhere near as old as he was, and she looked ancient and wrung out. He felt sorry for her. "Listen, Mary Ellen, maybe I could help you out— you know, help you set yourself up somewhere. Get a business going or something. A saloon, maybe? Maybe I can help somehow."

She eyed him coldly. "Help how?"

He shrugged. "I don't know. Money. I've got money you can have."

"In other words, you want to pay me to go away and not sully your little lady's eyes and ears with my vulgar self, is that right?"

"I didn't mean it that way." Or did he? Hell, he didn't know what he meant anymore.

No, damn it, he didn't mean it that way. "That's not true. I care about you, Mary Ellen. We've been friends for years."

"Friends!" She made the word sound like a curse.

Elijah, who hadn't had very many friends in his life, didn't appreciate it. He frowned. "Yes, friends. We were friends. I'd like to think we still are."

"Ha!"

All right, so they weren't still friends. Still . . . "Listen, I feel bad that you feel bad." He tested that one and discovered it was true. "If it would make you feel better about all of this, I'll help you financially. It's about all I have to give you, is money, Mary Ellen. I can't offer you anything more than that, except my friendship, and I can see you don't want that. At least not now. Maybe you will later."

Her lips squeezed together until they were a straight, white line against what was left of her paint. "I'll think about it." She gripped the counter as if it were the only thing holding her up.

Relief washed through Elijah. "Good. You think about it, Mary Ellen. I—I'm really sorry about this."

"Yeah. Sure."

He heaved a sigh and guessed it was foolish of him to expect her to forgive him yet. Not that he had anything to be forgiven for. Exactly. It was just that—

He heard a soft thump and turned to see that Killer

had jumped onto the counter again. Mary Ellen heard it, too. She looked down—and screamed.

Killer Apricot dropped a fat, deceased mouse onto her painted fingernails. Mary Ellen's grip on the counter eased, and she slid into a dead faint on the floor.

"Aw, hell."

It had needed only this.

Chapter Sixteen

"Of course," Joy said, her lips hardly moving. "I'm sure I don't mind giving up my bed for your . . . your *friend* there." She glared daggers at Elijah. Her quivering finger pointed at Mary Ellen's body draped in his arms. "I suppose you want me to nurse her, too?"

Elijah stood in her open doorway, blinking at the mess she'd made of her room. Shoot fire, was that a flatiron on the floor there? No wonder there was such a huge hole in the wall. He was surprised she could have thrown it with such force. She wasn't very big, after all. Not nearly as big as Mary Ellen, whose weight was about to bust his bum arm.

"You don't have to tend her," he ground out through gritted teeth. "Killer dropped a dead mouse on her hand, and she fainted."

"He did?"

"I just need somewhere to store her until she comes to."

"Meow."

Elijah peered down toward his boots and saw Killer weaving his tail around his calves. Damn cat looked proud of himself. He glanced up at Joy again.

She looked proud of the cat, too. "What a discerning animal you are, Apricot. Come here, boy." She knelt and kissed her lips for the kitten, who trotted over and began to purr. Elijah felt as though he'd been deserted in a battlefield—with a battle raging around him. Joy picked up the cat and started stroking him.

"Very well, Mr. Perry. You may lay your friend on my bed. I shall leave you to tend her while I pick up the mail scattered on the floor of Mr. McMurdo's store."

"Joy—"

He didn't get to say any more because she marched past him. She didn't look at Mary Ellen. Two blazing patches burned on her cheeks. Elijah didn't want to think about them. He glanced up and saw Mac grinning at him from the chair next to Joy's bed.

The old man patted the counterpane invitingly. "Why don't you set her down here, lad. There's some water on the nightstand there." He gestured at the pitcher and glass next to the bed.

What the hell was Mac doing in Joy's bedroom? Well, Elijah didn't suppose it much mattered. He'd trust Mac with his life; Elijah was sure Mac wouldn't do anything to harm Joy. Not like Elijah himself, for example, who seemed to trample women under his feet without half trying. He carried Mary Ellen to the bed and plopped her down. She sank into the soft tick mattress like a stone. Elijah imagined Joy lying there, her body making a much smaller dent than Mary Ellen's. Unless, of course, Elijah were lying on top of her, pressing her into the mattress, their bodies joined in the timeless embrace of—

He blinked, shocked out of the trance he'd momentarily lost himself in. Lord God Almighty, where had that image sprung from?

Mac laughed again. Elijah glanced at him sharply, wondering if the old man could read his mind.

"Your face is an open book, lad."

It was? *Terrific.* And a pornographic one, at that. Elijah didn't say a thing.

"Why don't I tend Miss Mary Ellen here, whilst you go out and try to talk to Joy. She needs ye, lad."

"She does, does she?" Elijah stared at the inert form on the bed, and wished he believed it. His head jerked up. "How did you know her name was Mary Ellen?"

Mac didn't answer. He only laughed again, and a great swarm of sparkles filled the air. *Wonderful.*

Joy didn't bother to sort the mail again. She scooped it up by the armful and dropped it on the counter. She'd go through it later, after she'd come to grips with Elijah Perry's asking her to marry him a mere minute or two before that . . . that . . .

"*Blast* it!" She wished she'd learned some curse words when she was young; she'd delight in using them now.

"Other children rebel. Why didn't I?"

Smack! Another stack of mail hit the counter.

"But, oh, no, not Joy Hardesty. I was too *afraid* to rebel. My mother would have skinned me alive if I'd rebelled—after she'd humiliated me in every way she could think of. By the time I was old enough to rebel, I didn't have enough spunk left to sneeze in her presence, much less mount a rebellion. If the founding fathers had been like you, Joy Hardesty, the United States would still be a British colony!"

Thwack! The package Mac had received from New

279

York made a loud thump as it hit the counter. The noise satisfied something primitive in Joy's soul. She picked it up and slammed it down again, and only then wondered if the wrinkled brown wrapper surrounded anything breakable. Too late now. She didn't even care. Much.

Like a bird swooping for a worm she dove for the floor again and retrieved the last of the scattered mail. She hurt her hand slapping it onto the counter.

"Ow! *Damn* it!"

So shocked was Joy at having uttered a swear word that she went still for a second before a sensation of utter triumph filled her. "Damn!" she cried again. Then, louder, "*Damn!*"

She could do it! She could swear! In fact, if she emptied her mind of everything and concentrated only on the tumult within her, Joy had a feeling she might even be able to holler. She tried it. She shut her eyes, threw her arms out and her head back, and shrieked at the top of her lungs.

What a glorious sensation. Thrilling. Fulfilling. Why had she never tried this before?

"Don't be an idiot, Joy. You never tried it before because your mother had you cowed and bowed down before you were old enough to know what a yell was."

Well, those days were gone for good. To seal their end, Joy shouted loud enough to wake the dead, "Go straight to *hell,* Mother! That's where you belong! And you can take Elijah Perry with you!"

She ran out from behind the counter when she heard the door to the back room open. Right before she made it to the front door of Mac's mercantile, she looked back and saw Elijah Perry standing there, staring at her as if she'd lost her mind. Which she might well have done. She didn't care.

"Go to *hell,* Elijah Perry!" she advised him right before

she opened the door. She stuck her tongue out and blew a raspberry at him, another thing she'd never done before in her life. "And you can take that painted trollop with you!" Then she darted, lickety-split, out the door, and tore like a jackrabbit to the open double gates.

Joy had no idea where she was going. Maybe up to the Spring River. If no one was there, she could practice cursing and shouting. Or maybe she'd run out onto the desert and pick some wildflowers. Why not? What else did she have to do? She wasn't beholden to anyone. She even had enough money to get herself back to Auburn if she wanted to.

For the second time in her life, she blew a raspberry, this time at the notion of returning to Auburn.

"To *hell* with Auburn," she muttered, feeling proud of her new range of language. "I shall go to ... to ... to *California!*"

What a marvelous idea! From everything Joy had read about it, California was the very place for an independent female to make a living. It was a virtual haven for every sort of eccentric individual. All kinds of strange behaviors were tolerated in California, and the citizens evidently welcomed women, single or otherwise. The stupid *men* who lived there had no idea how to take care of themselves. Why, she could set herself up as a visiting nurse! Become a laundress! Open a bakery! Or work in a hospital! Or work with orphaned children; giving them the love that Joy herself had never received. Or do something even more innovative.

Her mind ran blank for a moment, but Joy didn't despair. She'd finished with despair in this life. She'd think of something to do that would enable her to earn a living. Why, she might even become a female preacher! Wouldn't *that* be something! Her mother would faint dead away, if she weren't already dead.

Since cognizance of her own personal independence had struck her after she'd dressed this morning, she was still corseted up tightly. Therefore, she was unable to run for more than a very few yards before her breath gave out, and she had to stop running or pass out. Winded, she stopped still, leaned over, braced her hands on her knees, and tried to catch her breath.

"I shall never lace my corset tightly again," she vowed to her new self. "Never."

When she straightened after a few moments, she discovered herself in the middle of Second Street. Fortunately, traffic in Rio Hondo was never heavy. This afternoon, as the temperature hovered in the mid-eighties, most folks and animals were lounging in the shade or indoors.

Nothing ran her down, at any rate, so she glanced around and tried to decide what to do now. She figured she deserved some time off. She'd been working like a slave seven days a week for weeks now, what with Mr. McMurdo leaving her to tend Elijah Perry and his store. *The rat.* Mr. Perry, not Mr. McMurdo. Mac was such a kindhearted fellow, he'd probably applaud her for taking some time off to cut loose.

Joy sniffed, her insides roiling with a bizarre combination of liberty and remorse. Well, so she didn't aim to go back to the wagon yard anytime soon. Let Elijah and Mac handle it—and that female, whoever she was. Joy aimed to please herself.

She saw a buggy being pulled by a fine-looking gray horse trotting down the roadway. Such a conveyance wasn't customary in this out-of-the-way place, where folks were more apt to travel on horseback or in rustic wagons. Intrigued, she decided to see who was commuting in such style. If this were a civilized town, she'd assume the buggy belonged to the local doctor, but Rio Hondo didn't possess one of those.

"They have me instead—a trained nursing missionary," she muttered, and sniffed again, this time with something verging on pride. She'd done a good job nursing Elijah Perry. "A *damned* good job, in fact." She grinned, wondering if she'd ever tire of that word. Probably. She knew it was juvenile of her to take such pleasure in saying naughty words, but she'd never been allowed to be juvenile before and figured she was entitled.

Because the horse and buggy were traveling at a steady clip and she didn't want to breathe in all the dust the horse's hooves were kicking up, she stepped up onto the wooden boardwalk to watch it pass. She retrieved her handkerchief from her pocket, and held it over her nose and mouth. She'd never understood why pictures of western men invariably showed them wearing bandannas until she came to Rio Hondo, but she did now. Any man brave enough to ride a horse in the middle of a herd of cows needed something to pull up over his nose and mouth, or he'd choke to death on the dust.

Good heavens, there was a young woman in that buggy! Joy wondered if she was another one of Elijah Perry's old flames. But no, this woman looked respectable. The man driving the buggy seemed vaguely familiar to Joy—from a description perhaps? After mulling it over for a moment, she decided it was either Mr. Partridge or Mr. O'Fannin. Probably Mr. Partridge, since Mr. O'Fannin would want to be home with his wife and newborn son. *He,* unlike some men Joy could mention, evidently cherished the women in his life. *Woman* in his life. It was only men like Elijah Perry, the rat, who had more than one of them.

Having been taught from the cradle not to be snoopy,

Joy decided, as long as she was in a rebellious mood, she aimed to pry. She might as well take advantage of this daring spirit while it was in her. For all she knew, she'd suffer another attack of her mother's voice and lose heart again. Besides, how often did a new female come to Rio Hondo?

Twice, today.

Her heart gave an enormous pang, and she snorted, furious with herself for having her feelings hurt because Elijah Perry had a lady friend. Not that *that* female, back there on Joy's bed in the wagon yard, bore much resemblance to any lady Joy'd ever seen before. *Ha!* If that was a lady, Joy was a hussy. Anyway, Elijah probably had any number of females in his life. He was, she reminded herself, a rambler, a gambler, and a no-good wandering rogue, and she'd best never forget it.

Feeling not much better for having cleared up that point in her mind, Joy walked quickly to where the buggy had come to a stop, right in front of the wagon yard gates. Mr. Partridge, if that was he, got out of the buggy, walked around to the other side, and assisted the woman to alight. A gentleman, he. Joy approved.

The woman was young. Younger than Joy, by the looks of her, and she appeared bewildered.

Emboldened by the startling events of her day, Joy walked up to the pair, as fearless as anyone. The man turned and watched her approach, his face expressionless. Joy stuck her nose in the air, refusing to be daunted by a man, any man, even one as remote and cold-looking as this one. She ignored him completely and strode up to the woman, holding her hand out and smiling in what she hoped was a friendly manner. She had very little experience with being bold—or friendly—and she didn't want to make a botch of it.

"Welcome to Rio Hondo. You look a little lost. May I help you?"

"Oh, thank you."

Taller than Joy by a good four or five inches, the young woman had a brilliant smile. When she smiled, she reminded Joy of someone, but she couldn't come up with a name to go with the impression. The woman took Joy's hand gladly and shook it with enthusiasm.

"Mr. Partridge here was kind enough to bring me to town." The newcomer glanced around uncertainly, and added, "Such as it is. This is Rio Hondo, isn't it?"

Joy laughed. "Indeed it is. Rio Hondo isn't much to look at, I fear."

"Er, no." The young woman blushed. "Not that I mean to disparage it in any way."

"Of course not."

"Oh, dear. I always say the most awful things. It's because I speak before I think, you know."

"I wish I did that," Joy said, meaning it sincerely.

"You do?" The young woman eyed her in some surprise.

"Yes, I do. My name is Joy Hardesty, Miss—"

"Oh!" The young woman clapped her hands in delight. "You're *exactly* the person I came here to find!"

"I am?" Joy was so startled, her voice squeaked. This couldn't possibly be the emissary from Mr. Thrash.

"Oh, yes! I owe you so much. I'm Virginia Gladstone!"

Joy went numb with wonder. For several seconds she was unable to do more than gawk at the woman to whom she'd written about Elijah's accident.

The man who'd brought the newcomer into town saved her the necessity of speaking. He cleared his throat. "Well, Miss Gladstone, if you've found the party you need, maybe I should get on home again."

Emma Craig

"Oh, yes." Virginia Gladstone turned to the driver and shook his hand. "Thank you ever so much, Mr. Partridge. And please convey my regards to Mrs. Partridge and your beautiful children."

Joy watched with interest as Mr. Partridge's hard, cold eyes went soft and warm at the mention of his wife and children. She considered it remarkable that a happy family life could have such an effect on a man. She'd never known a happy family in her whole life. The realization came as yet another blow in a day filled with them.

"You're welcome, Miss Gladstone. Don't hesitate to have Mac send for us if you need a place to stay or anything."

"Thank you very much."

After he'd unloaded Virginia's carpetbag, Noah Partridge tipped his hat, climbed back into his buggy, and took off for home. Joy watched him go, a small ache in her heart, wondering if a man would ever be so eager to get back home to her. She doubted it.

"His wife is such a kind, lovely person," Virginia said, dragging Joy's attention from the retreating buggy.

"Is she? I've never met her."

"Oh, yes. She quite took me under her wing. And their two children are really beautiful."

"How nice of her."

"Yes, she was awfully kind to me. To tell you the truth, I didn't know exactly what to do once I got to Santa Fe."

"Yes, I can imagine." Joy wondered how Mac was going to accommodate yet another stray female. The men who stayed overnight at the wagon yard generally camped outside, but Joy didn't believe such an arrangement would be appropriate for Miss Gladstone, who seemed very much a city girl. Well, that wasn't her problem. She'd be happy to have Virginia sleep in her room, but they'd have to dislodge Elijah's other woman friend first. Joy sniffed.

"May I help you with your bag?"

"Oh, no, thank you. I can carry it if you'll show me where to go. Are, er, are there any hotels here in town?" Virginia glanced around doubtfully.

Joy laughed, discovering she didn't have to force it. "I'm afraid not. Your uncle has been talking about building one, but there are no such accommodations yet, I fear. Don't worry, though. Mr. McMurdo will be happy to put you up."

"Thank you."

Joy had felt dreadfully out of place when she'd first arrived in Rio Hondo, even though she'd headed west expecting to endure hardships. She could tell, both from Virginia's expression of trepidation and from her traveling costume, which was much more fashionable than anything Joy had seen on a woman in the territory, that Virginia hadn't been prepared for the frontier. The young woman's concern engendered a surge of protectiveness in Joy.

"This is so kind of you. Fancy you walking up to us that way. I must tell you that I was becoming somewhat frightened. This trip to the territory was, well, rather impulsive on my part."

Impulsivity was something else about which Joy had no knowledge. It sounded nice, though. "I'm awfully glad you came."

"My mother and father thought I was insane," Virginia admitted with a little laugh. "And I have to admit, when I arrived in Santa Fe, I feared they might be right."

"I know exactly what you mean," Joy said feelingly. She well remembered her anxiety when Mr. Thrash's band of missionaries had arrived in Santa Fe. Joy thought she'd never seen an uglier, dustier place. That was before they'd made their way to Rio Hondo. She almost laughed at the thought. "I trust you aren't so discouraged any longer."

"Not anymore. Between you and the Partridges, I do believe I've never encountered kinder, more generous people."

"Where did you meet Mrs. Partridge?"

"Well, you know, it was the strangest thing. After I received your letter, I decided to come out and meet Uncle Elijah for myself. I figured that if he was laid up, he couldn't escape before I had a chance to thank him for his kindness to me over the years."

Joy did laugh at that. "No, he hasn't escaped yet." She'd bet anything—if she were ever to do so sinful a thing as bet—that he was going to wish he had, however, if he didn't already.

"I'm so glad!"

Joy wished she was glad as well, but gladness didn't precisely describe the emotions churning within her at the moment. Although, it must be admitted, she was looking forward to the meeting between Elijah Perry and the niece he'd been avoiding for so many years.

Perhaps she was glad. In fact, she decided defiantly, she *was* glad she'd written to Virginia Gladstone. Not only did Virginia seem to be a very nice person, but Joy took satisfaction in knowing she wasn't the only one who was going to be forced to deal with the unplanned surprises of life. Let Elijah Perry stew some, too.

Besides, Joy had written to Virginia from the noblest of motives. If Elijah didn't like it, he could lump it. She straightened, feeling smug.

Virginia continued, "Anyway, I was in Santa Fe, you see, wondering what to do, and just happened to meet Mrs. Partridge by accident. She and her husband drove me all the way from Santa Fe to Rio Hondo in their wagon. It was quite a treat to be able to chat with someone. I'd begun to question the advisability of my trip out here, you see."

"It was a brave thing to do," Joy observed, admiring Virginia's resolute spirit. Joy herself had never set out to accomplish anything, really. When she'd joined Mr. Thrash's missionaries in Boston, she'd been, in truth, running away from home. She thought Virginia's adventure was ever so much more exciting than her own had been.

"Oh, dear, I hope I did the right thing."

The worried timbre in Virginia's voice melted Joy's heart. She took Virginia's arm, taking comfort in giving the other woman a measure of her own strength, such as it was. "I'm sure you did the right thing. I do believe it's past time Mr. Perry came to grips with his life." Heaven only knew, he'd forced her to come to grips with hers. Turnabout being fair play, it was his chance now. Joy was going to watch with relish as he did it, too.

As they approached the mercantile, Elijah stepped out onto the porch and caught sight of them. Joy's chest went tight. She didn't know if it was with apprehension, grief, vindictiveness, or a combination of all three.

She muttered, "Brace yourself, Miss Gladstone. You're about to meet your uncle."

"Is that him?" Virginia sounded breathless with fear or excitement. Probably both, Joy decided.

She was beginning to feel a pinch of consternation herself. She'd forgotten how intimidating a figure Elijah Perry could be if one didn't know him. Or even if one did. Nevertheless, she did not flinch. Rather, she marched Virginia Gladstone right up the porch steps and drew her to a halt before Elijah, whose brow had furrowed in puzzlement.

He didn't even know this was his niece! Joy considered such a state of affairs deplorable. She released Virginia's arm and folded her hands primly in front of her.

In a voice as demure as a nun's, she announced, "Miss Gladstone, it is my great pleasure to introduce you to your uncle, Mr. Elijah Perry."

Elijah's mouth fell open.

Virginia gasped and dropped her carpetbag. "Uncle Elijah!"

"Virginia?"

Until that second, Joy didn't know Elijah could sound so unsure of himself. She stepped back a pace in order to give these long-lost relatives an opportunity to do whatever it was they aimed to do. Elijah, she noted with interest, didn't seem inclined to do anything at all but stand there as if he'd been turned to stone.

Virginia, on the other hand, whooped, "*Uncle Elijah!*" and threw herself onto his chest. Joy tilted her head to one side and wondered for a moment if Elijah was so shocked he was going to tumble over backward or if he was going to recover his composure.

He did neither, but that was only because Virginia propelled him into the wall behind him. He staggered backward, and felt much as he had when the first of those three bullets had struck him. Shocked didn't half describe the state of his mind.

How the hell did you find me? his brain shrieked. Fortunately, he was too dazed to utter the question aloud. His arms closed around Virginia automatically, and only because they'd learned a long time ago to do that with women who flung themselves at him.

"Virginia," he whispered through lips that were as dry and gritty as sandpaper. This was Virginia. His niece. His sister's daughter. Virginia. The one he'd been writing to ever since he left home a million years ago. The one he didn't want to know for fear he'd learn that she'd become a ridiculous fool like all the others of her sex. Over Virginia's head, Elijah caught sight of Joy. Like *almost* all the others of her sex.

He'd seen a picture of the *Mona Lisa* once or twice. The painting had a smile exactly like the one now decorating Joy's face. Enigmatic. Faintly amused. Unmerciful.

Virginia tore herself away from him as precipitately as she'd thrown herself at him. Snatching a handkerchief from her sleeve, she blew her nose with a vigor one didn't generally encounter in proper young ladies.

"Yes, Uncle Elijah. It's I! Virginia!"

Her voice was shaky, but Elijah clearly detected elation in it. Was she happy to meet *him?* Elijah Perry? The despair of his family?

"I'm so *happy* to meet you at last!"

Son of a bitch, she was. Elijah opened his mouth. Nothing emerged.

Virginia didn't seem to notice. "And wasn't it kind of Miss Hardesty to write and tell me about your horrible accident, Uncle Elijah? I might never have been able to meet you in person if she hadn't!"

Elijah snapped to attention. Joy! Joy was the author of this debacle! He shot her another glance, but her expression hadn't changed an iota. She still wore the *Mona Lisa* smile that Elijah couldn't decipher. Before he could react to this latest disclosure, Virginia attacked him again. Again he bumped against the wall. He realized both bumps had jarred his wounded arm, and it hurt. He said "Ow," halfheartedly. Virginia didn't seem to notice.

"Oh, I've been wanting to know you forever, Uncle Elijah! Mother said you were always so kind to me when I was a baby. She wanted me to know you better, but you never came home after the war, she said. She said your parents were so awful to you!"

"She did?" Elijah tried to remember what his sister looked like, and was unsuccessful in drawing her image in his mind's eye.

"Oh, yes! And I've been wanting to know you for so long! I've longed to make up for the meanness of Grandmother and Grandfather Perry, and to bring you back into the family! They're both dead, you know."

They were? Dead? His parents? Elijah tried to assimilate the information, but it sat there in his brain, as dead as his parents, and refused to be assimilated.

"Oh, I'm so sorry! Of course, you didn't want to learn about their demise in this way." Virginia stepped away from him once more and brushed tears from her cheeks. "I'm such a dimwit! I always blurt out the wrong thing. I'm so sorry!"

Elijah heard a noise and eyed Joy again. Except for having compressed her lips—Elijah suspected she was trying not to laugh at him—she looked much the same.

"Ah, no. No, that's fine. It's not the wrong thing at all."

"You must be very sad, though, and I should have broken the news to you in a more gentle and dignified way. I fear I'm not dignified at all, Uncle Elijah. In fact, my mother says I'm just like you. She usually laughs when she says it, because she was ever so fond of you, you know. I hope you don't mind."

Just like him? And his sister was fond of him? His head awhirl, Elijah didn't know what to mind or not mind. Nor did he know what to say.

Stepping into the breach at last, Joy murmured, "I'm sure your uncle is quite happy to know his parents are deceased, Miss Gladstone." She sniffed, and if Elijah hadn't already divined the truth by the cattiness of her statement, he'd have known by the sniff that she was still mad as hell at him.

Virginia blinked, confused.

"I'm not either glad to know it," Elijah lied.

Joy gave him another one of her patented sniffs.

A swarm of sparkles suddenly filled the air around them. Elijah shut his eyes against them and knew without looking that Mac had just joined them.

Chapter Seventeen

Later on that evening, Elijah, Joy, Virginia, and Mac sat at Mac's small kitchen table, dining on stew and corn bread. Virginia and Joy drank apple cider. Mac and Elijah took beer.

Virginia looked with some confusion at her uncle, her big blue eyes wide. "You mean, that woman truly *is* a friend of yours, Uncle Elijah?"

She was, of course, referring to Mary Ellen Loveless, who had stormed out of Mac's store not long before. It had taken a good deal of persuasion on Elijah's part to get her to do so, but Mary Ellen had at last been persuaded to give up Joy's bed. She had originally wanted to stay and berate him for the rest of the year. At least that was what it had felt like to him. It had been embarrassing, too, since he knew his niece could hear every word Mary Ellen screeched at him. And Joy. Joy heard them, too.

Elijah didn't really blame Mary Ellen. It was his fault he'd never explained his true feelings for her. He really did like her. But he didn't want to spend the rest of his life with her, the way she evidently wanted to spend the rest of hers with him. He felt honestly wretched about having hurt her feelings. He felt even more wretched about having to explain Mary Ellen to Virginia. And to Joy.

"Er, yes. Yes, Miss Loveless and I go back a long way, Virginia. We met, oh, ten or eleven years ago, I reckon." He wasn't about to get into how they'd met or what Mary Ellen's profession, then and now, was. Poor Virginia had her hands full merely coming to grips with her reprobate uncle.

Elijah scowled at Joy to let her know he'd deal with her later. Imagine Joy having the guts to write to his niece! If she'd planned and connived for a hundred years, she couldn't have come up with a better way to get back at him for all the teasing he'd done to her since they'd met.

She smiled back at him, a smile so honey-coated and serene, Elijah knew it was a mockery. *Damn it.* How'd she get so uppity all of a sudden? He used to be able to reduce her to tears with a couple of winks or a leer or two. He huffed, aggravated, and was galled to see an expression of satisfaction spread across her face, as if she knew he was caught in a corner and she was gloating. Let her gloat. He'd get her later.

"This is delicious stew, Mac," Virginia said. She'd not experienced one iota of hesitation about calling the wagon yard owner by his nickname, Elijah noticed. Unlike some pinched-up, starchy, too-good-for-this-world females he could mention.

Mac nodded. "Thankee, Virginia. We're proud to share it wi' ye."

Virginia gave Mac one of her glorious smiles and turned again to Elijah, who heaved a large internal sigh. God, he wished the inquisition would end. It was his fault, he supposed, for not having had the nerve to meet her in person earlier. Although he wasn't ready to admit it, he was glad to have done so at last. Virginia was a niece to make any man proud.

She opened her mouth to speak, and Elijah revised the opinion he'd just formulated. She'd be a great niece if she weren't so damned curious about his personal life. And blabby. The woman was blabby.

"I'm sure she must be a lovely woman if she's a friend of yours, Uncle Elijah, but I must admit I've never met anyone quite like her before."

"I should hope not," Joy said—the first words she'd spoken since they sat down to supper.

Virginia's pretty blue eyes went round again. "Mercy sakes, do you mean she's a woman of . . . of . . . questionable character?"

Joy stabbed a carrot out of her stew. "Oh, I don't think there's any question about her character, Miss Gladstone." Butter wouldn't melt in her mouth.

Virginia said, "Really?" in an awed-sounding voice. Her smile was huge, as if she'd been longing to meet such a woman for years.

"Mary Ellen's character is fine," Elijah ground out between clenched teeth. "Miss Hardesty doesn't cotton to anyone who doesn't share her strict moral views, is all."

"Oh." Virginia sounded disappointed. "I was hoping Miss Loveless might be one of those saloon women one reads about in yellowback novels. I've always wanted to meet one." She popped a piece of corn bread into her mouth and chewed happily.

Joy choked on a bite of stew.

Elijah beamed at Virginia. A girl after his own heart, his niece.

Pausing only to pat Joy on the back, Virginia went on. "Rio Hondo is such an intriguing place, Uncle Elijah. I've never seen anything quite like it. The novels don't do the West justice, you know. I've read a million of them, too, trying to imagine you doing some of the things the heroes in them do."

Since she was smiling sweetly at him and sounded utterly sincere, Elijah did not snort or gag in disgust. Maybe she wasn't a girl after his own heart, after all.

"Your parents don't object to your reading novels?"

Virginia and Elijah turned to look at Joy, who evidently realized she'd all but shouted her question. She stammered, "I—I mean . . . well . . . but . . . Oh, bother. I beg your pardon, Miss Gladstone, but my own parents would have died sooner than let me read a novel. I'm only surprised that some parents don't mind, is all." She glanced around the table and her gaze stuck on Elijah, as if daring him to say anything, anything at all, about her or her parents or novels.

He gave her a treacly smile, and then turned to Virginia. "Miss Hardesty had a rather strict upbringing, you see, Virginia."

"I see. I'm glad my parents weren't strict with me, because I do so enjoy doing new things and learning about the world. And reading novels. I truly adore novels." Virginia popped a bite of stew into her mouth, chewed it energetically, and swallowed.

"My parents would have killed me if I'd even looked at a novel." Joy sounded disgruntled.

"My goodness. Your youth must have been rather, er, circumscribed, Miss Hardesty."

"It was."

Virginia and Joy were polar opposites when it came to

personality, Elijah decided. While every single move Joy made was weighed and deliberated over for fear someone would pounce on her and berate her for it, Virginia had no qualms about forming, holding, and speaking her opinions, no matter how bizarre they might be. She was a bold bit of goods, too. Imagine her coming all the way out here by herself. By damn, his sister had done a good job with her. He ought to write and tell her so.

"I'm awfully glad my parents didn't hold such strict notions," Virginia went on. She laughed gaily. "Although I must say your parents might be right about refusing to allow you to read some of the novels I've come across."

Joy tried to recover her composure. "Actually, Mr. Perry and I have had an opportunity to read two novels during his convalescence." She hadn't been smiling much since she'd met Mary Ellen Loveless, but she doled out a smile to Virginia now. "We read *The Moonstone* and *The Woman in White.*"

"Oh!" cried Virginia. "Didn't you simply adore *The Moonstone?*"

"Yes, indeed, it was most entertaining."

If Joy got any more demure, Elijah thought sourly, she'd sprout wings and a halo.

"And I liked *The Woman in White,* too," said Virginia. "Although I thought that schoolteacher was silly to have chosen Laura over the other sister. I mean, the one— drat! I can't recall her name." Virginia demolished another bite of stew while she frowned and thought.

"Marian?" Joy offered helpfully.

Virginia smacked her hand on the table, making Joy jump and Elijah grin. "That's it! Oh, I beg your pardon, Miss Hardesty. I really should try to control myself. My mother would lecture me roundly for getting boisterous at the dinner table."

"Please, Miss Gladstone, think nothing of it. I'd give

my eyeteeth to have a single ounce of exuberance inside me."

Elijah smirked at Joy. She made a face at him, and his smirk turned into a goggle. Damn, maybe she was learning *too* fast.

"Would you really?" Virginia seemed puzzled, but quickly put the emotion behind her. "At any rate, I liked the sister who ferreted out the villain, even if she wasn't pretty and rich, not the one who was the victim. Victims are so boring, don't you think?"

"Er, yes," said Joy. "Yes, I do believe victims are a trifle boring."

"Exactly! I thought that schoolteacher fellow—"

"Mr. Hartwright?"

"Yes, that's it. I thought he really ought to have fallen in love with the daring, bold sister who did all the work instead of the one who got locked up in the asylum. Laura was such a prim, silly little thing, don't you think so?"

"Yes." Joy's forehead wrinkled as she pondered Virginia's assessment of Wilkie Collins's sisters. "By Jupiter, I do believe you're right, Miss Gladstone."

"I know people are always saying that young ladies should be proper and demure and sit in the corner and knit, but I have more exciting things planned for my life."

"Do ye now?" Mac's eyes twinkled like candles.

"Oh, yes. This is part of it, actually. Seeing the West."

"My goodness." Joy stared at Virginia as if she hadn't considered her own trek west in the light of an adventure. "You mean you'd have come out here even if you hadn't been trying to meet your uncle? You mean to say you *wanted* to?"

"Miss Hardesty came here originally to be a missionary." Elijah dropped that tidbit into the conversation in order to see how Virginia would react to it. Joy shot him a scowl, so that was good. He resented her attitude about Mary Ellen, even though he knew his resentment to be irrational. Hell, any well-brought-up young lady would resent a fellow's whore girlfriend showing up right after he'd asked her to marry him. Damn it, what was wrong with him, anyway?

"A missionary? How fascinating. Did you perceive a vocation, or feel a call, or something like that? I've always been interested in how people choose the religious life."

"Er, not exactly." Joy frowned at Elijah, as if she expected him to say something derogatory about missionaries—or her. He didn't. Rather, he donned his most ingenuous expression and smiled a smile of pure innocence at her. From the way she shot a look at the ceiling and grimaced, he guessed she didn't believe it. *Smart girl, Joy.*

"Not exactly? I don't believe I understand, Miss Hardesty."

"Ahem. I don't know that I felt a calling, exactly. . . ." Joy's voice trailed off.

"Oh." Virginia tilted her head and looked perplexed. "Yet I should think missionary work would be quite a bold step in a person's life. Did you plan to establish a church in Rio Hondo or something?"

"Lord, no," Elijah cut in, hoping to irk Joy further. "She and her missionary friends were aiming for the Central American jungles, where they were going to plague the natives into believing in Jesus."

"We weren't planning to plague anyone!"

Elijah was pleased she'd grabbed his bait. He offered her another toothy smile, and had the satisfaction of seeing her stiffen in her chair like water freezing. She turned to Virginia and pretended to ignore him.

"The Reverend Mr. Hezekiah P. Thrash—"

Virginia burst out laughing. "Mr. Thrash? What a droll name!"

Joy appeared displeased, although she tried to hide it. A tickle of appreciation made Elijah chuckle. Joy shot him a glare hot enough to boil water before she continued.

"Yes, well, I don't suppose he could help his name. Anyway, he has set up a medical mission in the jungles of Mexico, and has asked me to join him." This time her scowl held a ton of defiance.

Elijah almost dropped his fork. Hell, he'd forgotten all about the letter Joy'd received today. If he goaded her too hard, she might just up and go off to her Mr. Thrash to spite him, and Elijah couldn't allow that to happen. Backpedaling furiously, he said, "But she's decided the missionary life isn't for her."

"And how, pray, did you come to that conclusion, Mr. Perry?" Joy set her fork on her plate deliberately, and glowered at him.

"Because it's the truth." Elijah set his fork down, too, and glowered back.

"Nonsense."

"It's not nonsense. You've said as much."

"No, I haven't."

"Yes, you have."

"No, I haven't."

"Yes, you have. You'd hate it, Joy, and you know it."

"I *don't* know it. Who are you to tell me what I'd hate and what I wouldn't hate?"

"I'm me, and I know you, and I know you'd hate it."

"Jerusalem! You're the most exasperating man in the universe. Did you know that, Elijah Perry?"

"I don't care how exasperating I am, damnit. You're not going down there to Mexico to torment the Indians!"

302

"And why not? I have to earn a living somehow, and you know it!"

"Damnit, you can earn a living anywhere, doing anything! You don't need to go to Mexico!"

"Oh? And what if I want to? What then, Mr. Know-it-all?"

"You *don't* want to!" Elijah had begun to holler.

"How would *you* know?" So had Joy.

"Because I know *you,* damnit! You're not going to any damned Central American jungle, and that's final!"

"You don't have any say about what I can and can't do!" Joy stood, pressed her hands on the table, and leaned toward Elijah as if a hard wind were blowing at her back.

"I do too have a say about it, damnit!" Elijah rose as well, slammed down his linen napkin—Mac had set out the best dinnerware this evening—and his voice became a bellow.

"You don't either! You don't have one single, little, tiny *thing* to say about what I do!"

"I do too!"

"Do not!"

"Do too!"

"Do not!"

"Do too!"

"Oh, this is ridiculous. You don't have a single, solitary thing to do with my life, Elijah Perry. You never have, and you never will."

"Damn it, I do too have something to do with your life, Joy Hardesty!"

She crossed her arms over her breasts and frowned at him as if she hated him more than bugs and snakes and lizards. "Oh? And just why do you think *that,* pray tell?"

Elijah shouted so loud the windows rattled, "Because I'm the man you aim to marry, damn it!"

Joy's mouth dropped open. So did Virginia's. It was

a struggle, but Joy managed to say, in a voice shaking with rage, "I wouldn't marry you if you were the last man in the entire world, Elijah Perry!"

She turned and stormed out of the house. Elijah, feeling helpless and hating it, watched her go. Virginia's eyes were so big they looked like they might fall out of her head. Mac sat back in his chair and laughed and laughed. The air around him filled with sparkles.

"Damn it, I know I made a mess of it," Elijah grumbled. He hadn't been able to find Joy, although he and Virginia had been searching for her for an hour or more. Thank God the days were long in the late spring, because Elijah's heart went cold with fear whenever he thought about Joy being caught out on the plains at night. Anything might happen to her. Hell, a cougar might get her. Or a bandit. Or a coyote. Or the weather. The weather was unpredictable in these parts. It might take it into its head to snow, and then where would they be? Elijah feared that if he lost Joy, he'd be left with nothing but the insufferable emptiness that had ridden into Rio Hondo with him all those weeks ago.

"Do you really want to marry Miss Hardesty, Uncle Elijah?"

Virginia was panting from trying to keep up with him. Elijah's terror for Joy was so great, he hadn't slackened his frenzied pace for Virginia's sake. "Yes." He didn't elaborate, mainly because he couldn't explain it.

"I think that's sweet."

Sweet, was it? Elijah could think of lots of words to describe his state of mind, but *sweet* wasn't one of them. Deranged, perhaps. Foolish. Idiotic. Unwise.

"Do you love her?"

Elijah stopped walking so abruptly, Virginia bumped into his back. He mumbled, "Beg pardon."

"Think nothing of it." Virginia pressed a hand to her heart and tried to catch her breath.

Did he love her? Love? What was that?

"I suppose that was a silly question," said the chatty Virginia. "Of course you love her, or you wouldn't want to marry her. She does seem to be an awfully nice person. And so funny! Why, I don't believe I've ever met anyone with such a splendid sense of humor. Except you, Uncle Elijah."

Elijah turned and stared at her. He didn't think he could possibly have heard her correctly.

Virginia gazed up at him, apparently bewildered. "What? What did I say?"

There was no point in arguing with the girl. She was obviously suffering from the effects of her long journey to the territory. What else could account for her mistaken belief that Joy Hardesty possessed a sense of humor? "Nothing."

He turned again, and resumed his search. After exhausting all the other places in Rio Hondo, he decided to lead Virginia to the Spring River, recalling the pleasant picnic he and Joy had shared there.

Lord, he wished he'd made love to her then, when he'd had the chance. Then she wouldn't balk at marrying him, and he wouldn't have to be going through this torture now. Of course, Joy probably wouldn't have let him, but . . .

Elijah wished he could stop thinking about all the things he wished he'd done before Joy ran away from him.

Joy had never climbed a tree before, and was no expert. She'd ripped her skirt on the rough bark of the cottonwood and wasn't quite sure how she'd manage to get down again, but the view was certainly spectacular from up among the branches. She swung her feet back and forth, feeling a sense of freedom as foreign to her as tree climbing.

"Children climb trees all the time. What a shame I had to wait until I was five and twenty to discover the sport." She laughed at herself and allowed her mind to wander.

Did Elijah Perry really want her to marry him? Such a scenario seemed incredible to her, mostly because, while he infuriated her more than any other human being on the face of the earth—now that her mother was dead—she loved him. Joy couldn't fathom anyone she loved loving her back.

"Of course, he hasn't declared his love," she reminded herself. "He's only demanded that you marry him. He probably only needs someone to help him run his hotel, and you're handy." She sniffed, feeling cynical and slightly world-weary, two emotions every bit as unfamiliar to her as the sense of freedom.

"Joy! Joy Hardesty, where the hell are you?"

Joy's lips pursed. She'd been listening to Elijah and Virginia holler for her for almost an hour now, but she wasn't about to show herself yet. Let them worry. Not that she wanted Virginia to worry, but Virginia was with Elijah, so there wasn't anything Joy could do to alleviate Virginia's worries without also informing Elijah. As far as Joy was concerned, Elijah could just suffer. It would do him a world of good, after all the suffering he'd put everyone else through in his life.

Self-righteous prig, she thought suddenly. "Good heavens, I sound just like Mother. What a horrible idea."

"Where else could she have gone, Uncle Elijah?"

"I don't know. There's nothing here but nothing."

Joy was pleased to hear the apprehension in Elijah's voice.

"Haven't we looked everywhere?"

Virginia sounded tired. Joy felt a little guilty. On the other hand, it wasn't her fault Elijah had all but driven her out of Mac's house. Nor was it her fault that Virginia had opted to go with him when he barreled out after Joy.

I hope his leg isn't paining him.

Irked with herself for worrying about Elijah, Joy reminded herself that his having gone and gotten himself shot wasn't her fault.

Two wrongs don't make a right, Joy Hardesty, and there's no wrapping your sins up in clean linen.

Joy was so startled to hear her mother's voice in her head after several blissful days of silence that she almost fell out the tree.

Be quiet, Mother. I don't need another lecture from you. Joy looked around, frowning, as if her mother were there and could see her.

It seems to me you do need a lecture, Joy. You're behaving in a very childish manner.

So what? Joy demanded childishly. *At least I'm not sniveling in a corner like I used to do, thanks to you.*

There was a long pause during which Joy heard nothing, not even the rustling of leaves or the howling wind or Elijah and Virginia trying to find her. The sensation was eerie, and Joy wondered if something strange was going on in the atmosphere, or if she was merely out of her mind.

After what seemed like hours, she heard, *I never meant you any harm, Joy.*

Joy whipped her head back and forth, her mother's voice having taken on an edge of remorse she'd never heard in it. Was this some sort of parlor trick?

Parlor, shmarlor. She was sitting in a tree beside the Spring River. How could it be a parlor trick? Still and all, Joy's mother's voice had never sounded like this before. Because she was disconcerted, Joy said aloud, "Go away!"

"Joy!"

Oh, bother! She'd forgotten all about Elijah. She drew her feet up so they wouldn't show through the branches of the tree. She didn't want to be discovered quite yet.

It's true, Joy, I know now that I was unkind to you, but I never meant to be. I only wanted the best for you.

A great sense of injustice welled up in Joy. *You wanted what* you *thought was best for me. You never bothered to find out even who I was. How could you* ever *know what might or might not have been best for* me?

Oh, Joy, I'm so sorry. Please forgive me. I understand how wrong I was. But please don't reject everything I tried to teach you. Surely you value some of the lessons I taught you.

This was insane. Joy knew it was insane, yet the voice was as clear as the New Mexico sky.

To err is human, Joy. To forgive is divine. Please forgive me. I never meant to hurt you.

Good heavens, could it be true?

Elijah's voice came again, jarring her out of communication with her mother's voice—or her own insanity. She wasn't sure which it was; wasn't even sure she wanted to know.

"Joy! Damn it, reveal yourself! We've been looking for you everywhere!"

Wouldn't you know it? At the very moment Joy felt she might be making a breakthrough in her troubled relationship with her mother, another dominant force—this time an arrogant, sinfully handsome, and utterly bothersome gambler—interrupted. Peeved, Joy tried to reestablish whatever mood she'd been in a second before, knowing somehow that it had been important.

"I see her!"

It was Virginia. *Blast!* She'd been found. Would she never come to terms with her mother's legacy? It didn't seem fair to her, although one of her mother's admonitions, this one against self-pity, asserted itself, and Joy decided to accept discovery with good grace.

"I'm up here," she called.

"Up where? I can't see you, damn it!"

"Stop swearing at me, Elijah Perry."

"Yes, Uncle Elijah. Nobody likes to be yelled at."

Perceptive girl, Virginia. Joy liked her. "That's right," she said.

"Well, damn it, I've been scared to death! What do you expect me to do when I'm that scared? Walk around whistling 'Dixie'?"

"You might try prayer," Joy suggested. "It works for many of us."

She heard Elijah grumble something under his breath. She could see them now. Virginia had evidently lost sight of her in the branches again, because she was squinting up into the wrong tree.

"I'm up here," she called again.

"Oh, what a lovely place this is!" Virginia possessed an excitement and exuberance that Joy couldn't help but envy. She didn't expect she'd ever be as free as Virginia, although she aimed to try.

"It's even nicer from up here," she said, parting the branches and peering down at her two pursuers.

Elijah jerked to a halt right under her tree and craned his neck to find her. His scowl was ferocious enough to have scared her if she'd been within his reach. Since she wasn't, she waved and smiled at him, feeling safe and superior for once in her life.

"What in the name of holy hell are you doing up a tree, Joy Hardesty?"

His voice was so loud it made her ears ring and the

leaves rustle—unless that was the wind. Virginia clapped her hands over her ears.

"There's no need for such a horrid noise, Mr. Perry. I can assure you I'm not deaf. At least, I didn't used to be." Joy liked the way she sounded, tart but not sniveling. She'd have to practice that tone some more, in private. Or on Elijah.

He sucked in a breath big enough for her to hear, and used it to say, in a much calmer voice, "I beg your pardon, Joy."

Joy could hardly believe her ears.

"But would you please come down now? I promise you I won't holler anymore."

Joy considered it. "Well, I don't know. . . ."

"Please, Miss Hardesty? There are so many things I want to ask you about life here in the territory, and about your missionary work—"

"She doesn't have any missionary work," Elijah snapped.

Virginia glanced at him and didn't reply. "And all sorts of other things. I think what you've done is so exciting!"

"Climbing a damned tree?"

Virginia gave him a soft whack on the arm, and he said, "Ow," but it didn't sound as if he meant it.

"Actually," said Joy, trying to sound nonchalant, as if she climbed trees every day, "I'm rather enjoying the view. Won't you climb up and join me, Miss Gladstone? I assure you, a body can see almost forever from this altitude."

Virginia's expressive face brightened right up.

Elijah shouted, "No! Damn it, Joy, you come down here right this minute!"

Joy eyed him for a moment, feeling defiant as anything. "I'm sure there's room for you, too, Mr. Perry, if you'd care to join us." Then she smiled, hoping this particular smile of hers was even half as wicked as one of his.

"I couldn't climb that tree if I wanted to, and you know it, Joy."

She could tell his teeth were clenched, because the words came out strained. "What a pity."

Suddenly a huge clap of thunder shook the air around them. Joy started and almost fell from her perch.

"There's a thunderstorm brewing, Joy," Elijah said. "Quit playing now, and get down from there. A tree's the last place you want to be in a thunderstorm."

He was, unfortunately, right. Joy knew it. And she didn't fancy getting fried merely for the sake of annoying Elijah Perry, no matter how richly he deserved it. Maintaining a haughty demeanor, she said, "Oh, very well. Stand aside, if you will."

In truth, she wasn't sure how she was going to maneuver her way down the tree. She'd almost killed herself climbing it. She'd rather die than tell him so.

"Stand aside, my ass. I'm going to stand right here so I can catch you if you fall."

Another boom of thunder rattled Joy's nerves. *Bother the weather!* The weather back east might be bad more often than not, but at least it was dependable. Out here in the territory you never knew from one second to the next what the weather might do. It was a characteristic she'd not found particularly annoying until this minute.

On the other hand, she didn't trust Elijah Perry not to do something despicable. "Close your eyes, please, if you insist upon standing beneath the tree."

Virginia made a choking sound in her throat. Joy endeavored to ignore her.

Elijah yelled, "For the love of God, stop being stupid, Joy! I'm not going to shut my eyes, because that would defeat the purpose."

311

"I will *not* have you peering up under my petticoats, Mr. Perry, so don't you even think it."

"Oh, for God's sake. All right, I'll close my eyes."

Joy didn't trust him. "Don't peek."

He let out an exasperated huff. "I won't peek."

Joy still didn't trust him. "Miss Gladstone, will you please keep an eye on your uncle for me?"

"I'll be happy to, Miss Hardesty."

Thank heavens for Virginia Gladstone! "Thank you very much."

She took a deep breath and surveyed the tree. How ever had she managed to get up here in the first place? It seemed an awfully long way down.

A crash of thunder smote her ears, and at the same time she heard a tremendous crack. Her eyes opened wide when she saw, about fifty yards downstream, a tree split in half and, smoking, fall into the river, creating a wave that splashed water over the riverbanks on both sides. *Merciful heavens.* She stopped thinking, grabbed onto her tree limb, and carefully wriggled herself to a lower branch.

"Hurry up," she heard Elijah mutter. He sounded worried, and she appreciated it, but she didn't dare hurry up. She wasn't about to tell him so.

A few fat raindrops splattered onto the leaves beside her.

Wonderful. Just what she needed was for the sky to open up and drench them all. She wished they hadn't come after her. This would be much less embarrassing if she were by herself.

As if the devil's minions had heard her, the sky opened up. She heard Virginia squeal when a torrent of rain gushed down from above. It sounded like a delighted squeal, which didn't surprise Joy as much as it would have coming from anyone else. Virginia seemed to take a good deal of pleasure from the oddities of life, a characteristic Joy both envied and appreciated.

Oh, Lord, she hadn't realized how slippery a cottonwood tree could be when it was wet. For the first time Joy felt some trepidation. She grabbed another branch, and her hand slipped. She managed to catch herself on another branch. Fortunately, she didn't weigh much. Unfortunately, the little she did weigh was too much for the branch she was using as security. It broke off against the trunk with a noise like a whip cracking. Joy was too surprised even to scream.

It seemed like an eternity that she flailed there in midair, trying and failing to grab another branch. And then she was falling, scraping herself against tree limbs, reaching wildly for purchase, grabbing at branches and sliding off, her hands scraping against wood as she stripped leaves from the tree and the leaves stripped the skin from her hands.

She heard Virginia scream and cry out, "Uncle Elijah, she's falling!"

Elijah shouted, *"Joy!"*

And then she heard a terrible crunching sound, pain ripped through her body, and everything went black.

Chapter Eighteen

Joy decided she must be in church, although she didn't remember seeing a church in Rio Hondo. Being in church would account for the choir she heard singing. It was a wonderful choir; much more tuneful than the one that used to sing in her father's church.

But if she was in church, why did she feel so wonderful? She never felt wonderful in church; she only ever felt guilty. She tested the sensations flooding her body, and decided she must be dreaming. Her mother would kill her if she discovered Joy sleeping in church.

Her eyes wouldn't open. *Hmmm.* Joy pondered this phenomenon, and then realized she was in Elijah Perry's arms. She was in his arms, and they were in the softest, most comfortable bed Joy had ever slept in.

So she must have married him. She didn't remember having done so, but she was very happy she had. She really did love him awfully. And, in spite of his background—and hers—he loved her too. The sweetness of this awareness filled her, and she sighed.

He was going to make love to her now. Sweet, beautiful love. In spite of her mother's lectures, Joy knew the marriage bed wasn't meant to be one of suffering. It was meant to be shared by two people who loved each other and who had committed themselves to each other. If anyone could teach her how to enjoy the act of love, it was Elijah Perry. The good Lord knew he'd had plenty of practice. Joy considered writing to Mary Ellen Loveless and thanking her for her part in Elijah's education.

Alive with anticipation, Joy sank into Elijah's arms, longing to feel his big, strong hands stroking her naked skin. They were going to be the happiest couple in the territory. She knew it in her bones. And they'd ask Mac to stand godfather to their first child. And Virginia could be godmother.

On that delightful thought, Joy sank further into the soft comfort of unconsciousness.

"Drink it, lad. It'll do ye good."

Elijah squinted at Mac and clamped his teeth together so he wouldn't bellow at the old man. It wasn't Mac's fault Joy was hurt. Yet Elijah's nerves were strung like an acrobat's wire, and he had a struggle maintaining his composure. He wanted to break things. To shriek and scream. To stamp his feet and then throw himself on the floor and drum his heels. In fact, he wanted to throw a temper tantrum.

Instead, he drank the tea Mac handed him.

Oh, God; oh, God. Joy had to get better. She *had* to. Virginia laid a hand on his shoulder and he jumped a foot off his chair and sloshed his tea. He wanted to holler at her, too.

316

"I'm sure she'll be all right, Uncle Elijah. Mac said she would be."

What the hell did Mac know about it? Elijah grunted out a "Huh," and didn't ask the question. Joy was still unconscious. The only sounds she'd made since she hit the dirt beneath that damned tree were a few pitiful moans and a groan or two. She'd been silent the whole time he carried her back to the ranch. Elijah had never been so scared in his life.

He looked at the clock ticking away on the bedside table. Almost nine o'clock. Nine o'clock, and she hadn't opened her eyes yet. What did it mean? *Oh, God, please don't take her away from me.*

"Looks like it's past time for a bite of supper."

Elijah jerked his head up and frowned. Supper? Why the hell was Mac talking about supper when Joy was in such a terrible predicament?

"I'll help you, Mac. I'm sure we all need to keep up our strength."

Strength. Strength? What the hell did Elijah need with strength if Joy died on him? The thought sent a wave of anguish through him, and he let out a choked noise that didn't mean anything except how frantic he was. Mac gave him a compassionate smile, and Elijah wanted to belt him. He didn't need compassion; damn it, he needed Joy.

He watched Mac and Virginia leave the room and buried his face in his hands. "Damn it, Joy, don't leave me. You *can't* die on me, damn it. Who'll I fight with if you die?"

Elijah heard a chuckle from the direction of the door and whipped his head around. *Damn.* He'd thought Mac had already left. Elijah frowned at him to let him know there wasn't anything funny about this catastrophe. Joy might *die,* for the love of God.

"I've often heard Joy say that a good prayer helps in times of trouble, lad."

Elijah muttered, "Prayer. Hell."

Another chuckle. Elijah's nerves screeched like seventeen untuned violins.

"Prayers go in the other direction from hell, lad."

Elijah shook his head, feeling horrible despair. Mac left, thank God, and he was alone with Joy.

"Prayer." The only time Elijah had prayed was when the nuns had made him pray in school. He'd had all the prayers memorized back then, and he tried to remember one of them. He'd never uttered a spontaneous prayer in his life, and wasn't sure he could make one up on the spur of the moment.

"Hell, Perry, Protestants do it all the time. What's the matter with you?"

Criminy, things were rough if he was talking to himself. Elijah muttered a soft "Damn" and got down on his knees. He folded his hands together, leaned on the bed, and endeavored to ignore the pain shooting through his body. Mac had tried to dose him with laudanum after he'd carried Joy indoors, but Elijah wouldn't have it. He wanted to be awake for Joy if she regained consciousness.

When she regained consciousness, rather. *Oh, Lord; oh, Lord.*

That was a start. Elijah managed to murmur, "Oh, Lord," before his imagination went dry. He tried again. "Oh, Lord, please don't let her die." That sounded negative. He had an intuitive suspicion that God appreciated positive thinking. He cleared his throat.

"Oh, Lord, please keep Joy safe."

She wasn't safe already. She was lying here, in this bed, as pale as a snowdrop, unconscious. Hell, Elijah wished a priest would pop up from somewhere and rescue them all from this crisis.

"Damn it, God, I don't know how to ask for this. Make Joy better, damn it. It would be too damned unfair of you to take her now, when she's only beginning to understand how to enjoy life, damn it!"

Frowning fiercely, he suspected he'd made a botch of his prayer already, and he had hardly begun yet. On the other hand, what the hell did he care if God got offended? Elijah had been offended by God often enough—or at least by His representatives here below.

"And, damn it, God, what about me? I know I haven't been the best man in the world but, damn it, you wouldn't have been either if you'd had to live the life I've lived."

That didn't make a lick of sense, and Elijah knew it. He thumped his fist on the bed, scared and frustrated and mad as hell. "Damn it, God, *help* her!"

"Stop—"

The soft, breathy word startled Elijah so badly, he jerked away from the bed and wrenched every single one of his already-sore muscles. He stared at Joy, scarcely daring to believe the word had come from her. Her eyes remained closed. She looked as close to dead as made no matter. He leaned closer, ignoring his screaming muscles, and squinted into her face.

"Joy?"

". . . swearing . . ."

It was her! He'd seen her lips move! Elijah shouted, *"Joy!"*

She flinched at the noise. ". . . at me, Elijah Perry."

Speaking so many words at once evidently exhausted her, because she didn't even purse her lips after admonishing him, but lay there, breathing shallowly, her lips parted. Elijah, unable to help himself, whooped again,

319

leaned over, and kissed her parted lips. "You're alive!" he cried when he came up for air.

One of Joy's eyes opened halfway. "I won't be if you smother me."

"Hallelujah! Hallelujah!" Elijah shouted. "She's alive! She's alive!"

The clatter of running feet announced Virginia and Mac before they charged into the room. By the time they got there, both of Joy's eyes were open, and Elijah was doing a limping jig around the room.

"Joy!" Virginia cried.

"Lass!" Mac cried.

"She's alive!" Elijah cried.

"I have a perfectly dreadful headache," Joy announced in a voice that sounded as if it had been ripped apart by strong hands. "Please keep your voices down."

Elijah flung himself onto his knees beside her bed so hard that a cry of pain was wrenched from him involuntarily. He didn't care. He took her hand. The palm was scraped raw and had been washed and anointed with healing balm by Mac. Elijah kissed her hand with a fervor he hadn't felt for anything since he was born. "You're alive!" he said again.

And he burst into tears.

"I can feed myself." Joy sounded short-tempered and snappish. She sounded, in fact, quite like her old self.

"I don't care. You're going to let me feed you until you're well."

Elijah knew it was unmanly of him to have cried, but he didn't give a crap. When he'd realized Joy wasn't going to die on him, all the emotions he'd had bottled up inside of him for almost forty years had burst out in a flood.

"It's only a headache. I assure you, my hands work perfectly well."

"They don't either. They're scraped all to hell and back."

"Stop swearing at me, Elijah Perry!"

"I'm not swearing at you. I'm just swearing for the hell of it."

Joy uttered something that sounded like a snarl, but she allowed him to lift the spoon to her lips and drank the broth it contained. Elijah watched her avidly. Joy eyed him back, a wary expression on her face. Elijah tipped the spoon to her lips again.

"Why are you looking at me like that?" she asked after she'd swallowed another sip of broth.

"Like what?"

"Like you're only waiting to spring something on me."

"The only thing I'm going to spring on you is me, Joy, as soon as you're better."

She looked worried.

Virginia, who was sitting on the chair beside Joy's bed and petting Killer Apricot, laughed. "He was so worried about you, he almost died himself, Miss Hardesty."

Joy still didn't look as though she understood anything going on around her. Elijah, who didn't appreciate Virginia's announcing his weakness so bluntly, shot her a look and hurried another spoonful of broth to Joy's mouth. She drank it because it was either drink it or wear it. She frowned at him. He was used to it.

"You're on your way to a full recovery now," he said, hoping to forestall any further revelations on his niece's part. Shrewd woman, Virginia. Elijah wasn't sure that was a good thing under the present circumstances.

"I don't know why he was worried. I should have thought he'd be pleased that I finally made a complete fool of myself." Joy lifted a bandaged hand to her bandaged forehead.

"Does your head still ache?" Elijah asked gently.

Joy slitted her eyes and squinted at him, and he guessed she wasn't used to his being nice to her. She'd get used to it.

"Of course my head still aches, Elijah Perry. I fell out of a tree, if you'll recall."

Elijah shuddered, dripping broth on Joy's quilt. She gave a little hiss of disapproval. "How could I ever forget it? I thought sure you were dead."

"Well, I'm not. You can't get rid of me that easily."

The sourness of her words astonished him. "Get *rid* of you? For the love of God, Joy, I was scared for you!"

Her slant-eyed look didn't soften. Rather, her expression looked more incredulous than ever.

Virginia laughed at them both. Elijah swiveled his head to frown at her, but she ignored him. It figured. He was definitely losing his magic touch with the ladies. He braced himself when he saw Virginia take a breath with which to speak again.

"Far from wanting to get rid of you, Miss Hardesty, Uncle Elijah wants to marry you. He's fallen deeply in love with you, you know."

Joy's eyebrows arched like soaring larks. "He *what?*"

Her screech hurt Elijah's ears. Because he didn't want Virginia to reveal any more of his secrets, he said, "You already know I want you to marry me, Joy. I've asked you sixteen or seventeen times."

"You didn't!" She sounded indignant.

Elijah didn't understand. "I did too."

"You did not. You *told* me I was going to marry you, Elijah Perry. That's a far cry from asking a woman for her hand." She gave him one of her sniffs. God, he loved her sniffs. "And you never once mentioned a single, solitary word about"—she paused, her mouth open, before she muttered—"affection."

Damn. Elijah feared they'd come to this. Well, he guessed he was up to it. "That's only because . . ." Because what? *Crap* "Because I hadn't gotten around to it yet."

"Nonsense." Joy turned her head away from him and glared at the wall beside her bed.

Virginia giggled. *Wonderful.* Why the hell didn't she leave the room? He might be able to declare himself if he didn't have an audience. He heard Killer Apricot purr. It sounded like a mocking purr, and Elijah reckoned his mind was going. He sucked in a big breath, but he didn't get to use it, because Joy faced him again.

"And besides, I haven't decided what I'm going to do yet. Mr. Thrash's agent will be here soon, and it would be a shame for him to come all this way to fetch me only to discover that I've changed my mind."

"To hell with Thrash!"

"Will you *please* stop swearing!"

"Not until you promise you're not going to join that idiot in Central America, damn it!"

Virginia went off into a gale of laughter. This time Elijah and Joy both frowned at her. She rose from her chair, lifting Killer Apricot and setting him gently on the floor. "I think I'm in the way here. I'll just go see if Mac needs any help while the two of you thrash"—she giggled at her pun—"out your problems without an audience."

"Thank God," Elijah grumbled.

Joy shot him a look. "Please don't feel driven out, Miss Gladstone. I don't believe your uncle is dangerous."

"Dangerous?" Elijah muttered. "Good God."

Virginia bent to kiss Joy's cheek. "No, I'm sure he's not. But he does love you very much, you know, Miss

Hardesty. And I should be very happy to have you as my aunt."

Joy looked surprised. Elijah wasn't sure if it was because of Virginia's claim that he loved her or if it was merely that Joy had never considered being anyone's relation before, by marriage or any other means.

Deciding to ignore the love issue for now, Elijah said, "There. You see? Virginia knows what you should do."

That broke the spell for Joy. She was back to scowling at him in less than a second. "That's as may be, but *I* don't know what I should do."

"What would be so bad about being married to me? We could run a nice hotel here in Rio Hondo. The only time I was ever happy was when I was helping out in my uncle's hotel."

"Yes, so you've told me."

"And you'd love it, Joy. There would be people in and out, and you can leave Bibles in all the rooms and try to convert everyone."

The scowl she gave him should have pickled his gizzard, but it only made him smile. God, he loved her!

"Humph," she said.

"So, just say yes, Joy, and we'll get married and live happily ever after."

"What about that woman?"

"What woman?" Elijah racked his brain, and couldn't think of any other woman but Virginia, and she was his niece. Surely Joy couldn't have any objection to—Then it struck him. Mary Ellen. "Oh, her."

"Yes. Her."

Shutting his eyes and lifting his head, Elijah contemplated his many sins for a moment in silence. Then he decided, *To hell with it,* and told the truth.

"Mary Ellen and I have known each other for years, Joy. We were, ah, lovers for a long time. Sporadically."

When he opened his eyes, he saw the hurt and disbelief in her face. "We were more like friends, Joy. Honestly. I cared for her, but . . ." He didn't know how to explain it.

Joy turned away from him for several moments. Elijah felt misunderstood and abused and sorry for himself. "Damn it, it's not like you didn't already know I was a sinner, Joy! I never tried to hide it. Besides, I had no reason to reform until now, because I'd never contemplated marriage to anyone, but I sure as hell didn't aim to live celibate. Women like Mary Ellen are the salvation of men like me."

That was the wrong thing to say. He knew it as soon as Joy turned her face his way again. "The salvation of men like you, my foot. You exploited that poor woman, Elijah Perry, and made her think you cared for her. Small wonder she was angry with both of us."

"I didn't exploit her!"

"You shared her bed!"

"Damn it, she was a whore!"

Oh, Lord, he'd gone and done it again. He wished he still possessed even a tenth of the manners those nuns had tried to beat into him in his youth.

Joy's gasp was followed almost immediately by a furious spate of words. "If you don't watch your language, I shall never speak to you again in this life, Elijah Perry! And it's only because of the vile appetites of men like you that women like that poor, misguided creature are forced to do the kind of work they do!"

"Vile appetites?"

"Yes! Vile appetites."

"Of men like me?" Elijah wasn't sure he could stand it.

"Yes. Of men like you. Do you think that just because you're *men* you have the right to slake your lust on any available female? Don't you think *women* have passions, too? But do *we* sink to the depths of depredation men sink to? No, we do not! We require affection before we give our bodies to men. And furthermore—" She stopped speaking abruptly, evidently taken aback by Elijah's sudden change in demeanor.

"You have passions?" Elijah felt the grin spread over his face even as he watched the heat staining Joy's cheeks. "I always knew you did."

"Oh, you're impossible!"

"But listen to me, Joy. You *need* to marry me. I mean, you're becoming almost human. If you run off with those missionaries, you'll revert."

"Revert?"

"Yes. You'll revert to your old self, and then you'll hate yourself again. I'm good for you!"

"You're a boastful cad!"

"And you're just the one to reform me. You're good for me, too, Joy. I mean, I never would have even thought about settling down if I'd never met you."

"*That* was a black day, indeed."

"No, it wasn't. It was the best day in our respective lives."

"I suspect we shall just have to disagree about that, Mr. Perry."

"You don't disagree. You're just being stubborn."

"Stubborn? Me? You're as stubborn as an army mule. And you have no sense of fair play! A gentleman would never harass a woman about marrying him when she's suffering with a headache like mine. You're no gentleman, Elijah Perry."

He felt a lick of encouragement and grinned at her. "Yeah, and you love me for it, too."

"Ha!"

"Just like I love you for your priggishness." Oh, hell,

he hadn't meant to say that. He realized what he'd done when the color drained from Joy's face as fast as it had bloomed.

"You what?"

There was no getting away from it now. He'd cooked his own goose. He cleared his throat. "I, ah, love you, Joy. Very, uh, much."

The only response he received to this alarming declaration was a perceptible widening of her eyes. She had truly lovely eyes. And she no longer had that pinched-up look she'd had when he'd first met her, either.

"And, ah, I have plenty of money. I've been saving for years, you know, because I didn't really have anything to spend it on." He gestured with his hand helplessly. "You know, no family or anything—well, except for back in Maryland, and I guess we should go back there. My sister's all right, I guess, and I know she'd like to meet you. We can honeymoon back there. Even take Virginia back with us, maybe. But that won't take very much money. I figured we can use the money I have saved up to start our business."

No answer from the bed. *Aw, hell, now what?* He sensed it was too late to take anything back—besides, he didn't really want to. Or if he did, he knew the desire to be cowardly, because he meant every word. He didn't seem to be making much headway with Joy, however. He plunged blindly onward. "So you don't need to think I can't take care of you the way you deserve to be taken care of. I can support you. Maybe we won't ever be rich, but—"

"Be quiet this instant, Elijah Perry, and kiss me."

It took Elijah only a moment to assimilate the import of Joy's command, and when he did, he didn't bother to analyze it but took her literally. When Mac and Virginia tiptoed back into Joy's room with the agent Mr. Hezekiah P. Thrash had sent from the Central American jungles, Elijah and Joy were locked in an embrace that looked as if it would take dynamite to break apart.

Chapter Nineteen

Mr. Thrash's agent, Mr. Farthingale, picked up his teacup with two fingers and sipped delicately before he resumed frowning at Joy.

"I'm not sure I entirely understand you, Miss Hardesty. Mr. Thrash sent me here—a long way, I can assure you—because he said you were strong in the faith and desired to join his mission."

"I am strong in the faith," Joy said, striving with every nerve in her body to maintain her ladylike manner. "I fear my life has taken a turn, however, and I shan't be joining Mr. Thrash's fine work."

Mr. Farthingale eyed her with distaste. "Mr. Thrash isn't going to like this."

"Mr. Thrash has nothing to say about it."

Joy turned to scowl at Elijah, whose expression was stormy. Mr. Farthingale looked fairly stormy himself when he glanced at Elijah. Joy sighed. "I fear Mr. Perry

329

is correct, Mr. Farthingale, even if he wasn't very diplomatic. If Mr. Thrash had waited a while before he sent you to Rio Hondo, he would have received the letter I planned to write him explaining the change in my circumstances."

Still looking annoyed, Mr. Farthingale said, "Which are?" He appeared almost as disapproving as Joy's mother used to.

Joy reacted to his expression more strongly than she intended. "Mr. Perry and I are going to be married, Mr. Farthingale, and we plan to settle here, in Rio Hondo. I fear Mr. Thrash made a false assumption about my willingness to join him after he deserted me here without so much as an explanation to me. He didn't even see fit to write me an explanatory note." She sniffed and glared at Mr. Farthingale, daring him with her eyes to take issue with her assessment of Mr. Thrash's behavior.

Farthingale sat up straighter in his chair. "Well! I never."

"I'm sure that's true," said Joy.

Elijah gave a quick snort of amusement and stepped forward from where he'd been leaning against the wall of Joy's room, next to the door. "Listen, Mr. Farthingale. You're not going to change Joy's mind, so you might as well take the news with good grace. There's no reason to go away mad."

"That's true, Mr. Farthingale." Joy offered Mr. Thrash's emissary a conciliatory smile, which he did not return.

"Right. As long as you go away, everything will be just fine."

Joy wished she were fit enough to be out of bed. She'd stomp on Elijah's foot for being so outrageous. "He didn't really mean that," she muttered, glaring at Elijah.

"I did too." He glared back at her.

Mr. Farthingale set his teacup down with a clink. "I see. It seems to me that I've wasted my time and that of Mr. Thrash by coming here. His time is valuable, you know, Miss Hardesty. As is mine. We're both needed in Mexico."

"I'm sure that's true," she murmured, wishing he'd shut up and go away. "Er, I'm sure Mr. McMurdo will be pleased to give you some stew and corn bread, Mr. Farthingale, before you have to set out for Mexico again." She decided they'd all be better off if she didn't mention the beer.

With a somewhat bitter-sounding huff, Mr. Farthingale bowed formally and left the room, brushing by Elijah without comment. Joy was interested to notice how insubstantial Farthingale looked next to Elijah. She sighed heavily and closed her eyes. Her headache was almost gone by this time. She was surprised her confrontation with Farthingale hadn't brought it thundering back.

"How are you feeling, Joy?"

She started, not having anticipated Elijah's voice coming to her from so close. The last she'd seen him, he'd been nearly across the room. Opening her eyes, she saw him standing at the head of her bed, gazing down at her with an expression she'd never seen on his face before, and had never expected to see on any man's face directed at her. She smiled up at him, feeling tender and full of love.

"I'm much better, thank you."

"I'm glad of that." The soft expression vanished and was replaced by a frown. "If you ever do anything so harebrained as climb a tree again, I swear I'll turn you over my knee and paddle you."

She felt her lips pinch up. "You will do no such thing, Elijah Perry. You have no right to paddle me. Or to do anything else to me, for that matter."

"I will have." He yanked over the chair Farthingale had lately vacated and straddled it. "As soon as we're married, I'll be able to beat you every day if I want to."

"You wouldn't dare."

"Try me."

"If you ever so much as lay a hand on me, Elijah Perry, I'll shoot you where you stand."

They glared at each other for a full minute before Elijah threw his head back and roared with laughter. After another tense moment, Joy joined him.

That night, Joy felt restless. She'd slept most of the day since her accident, and now that her headache was gone she was discovering sleep difficult to find again.

Not only that, but in a shocking statement of freedom from her mother's dicta, she'd taken off her corset. She aimed to sleep without it on for the rest of her life, too. Elijah would be pleased, she was sure.

Joy was pretty pleased herself. She felt brave and daring, even though she thought the feeling was probably ridiculous. After all, it was only a corset. Existing sans corset was more comfortable than trying to live with it, to be sure. Removing it, however, was so absolutely contrary to everything she'd ever been taught that she felt funny about it. But free. She even did a few deep-breathing exercises as she sat in bed, and smiled all alone in her bedroom. It felt delicious to be able to draw in big breaths without whalebone stabbing her in the ribs.

"Learn something every day," she muttered to the ceiling.

She'd also come to the conclusion that, as hard-headed and beastly as her mother had been, she truly hadn't meant to crush Joy's spirit. In fact—Joy sucked in a gigantic breath—she'd only had Joy's interests at heart.

"I forgive you, Mother." It was the hardest thing Joy had ever had to say in her life.

When she received no answer from her mental mother and her stomach didn't begin cramping, she breathed a sigh of relief and decided she could live her life quite well without her mother's constant lectures always sounding in her head. She hoped her mother, as much as she forgave her, would stay away. And, while Joy would probably never love her mother as a daughter ought to love a mother, at least she could forever after this moment be free from the paralysis of fear and indecision her mother's influence had created in her. She tested the knowledge, discovered she was happy, and grinned at the ceiling. Freedom! She loved it.

An early summer thunderstorm raged outside her window, crashing and banging for all it was worth. Intrigued and not a little alarmed by the commotion, Joy finally gave up on sleep, climbed from her bed, dragged a chair to the window, and sat.

She pulled back the curtains, recalling with a smile the day Elijah had bullied her into opening his curtains for the first time. How long ago that seemed. And how frightened of him she'd been. And now they were going to be married. It didn't seem possible.

Elation filled her as she watched the lightning bolts light up the sky. They were coming so fast and furiously that the entire universe seemed bathed in white light. The noise was tremendous. Joy wondered if battlegrounds sounded like that. The ground here was so hard, the water had a difficult time sinking in, and it had already made a lake of Mr. McMurdo's wagon yard. She was glad he'd had the foresight to build his house and store up from the flat of the plains, or his store would be flooded.

The violence of the storm thrilled her, even if it was incredibly noisy. Here was another indication that she wasn't the daughter her mother wanted her to be. She didn't flinch from thunder and lightning, as a properly submissive female should do, but gloried in the ferocious display of nature. Tonight she didn't give a rap—even half a rap—about how disappointed her mother would be in her. She was disappointed in her mother, if it came to that, and·she'd never, ever, treat any children she and Elijah were blessed with as her mother had treated her.

"Whether you meant it or not, Mother, you were a beast to me, and I resent you for it." She even blew a raspberry at her mother's memory, and giggled at herself. Then she decided she wasn't going to waste a perfectly good thunderstorm pondering her mother.

With her elbows propped on the windowsill, Joy recalled her day. She'd actually enjoyed climbing that tree. And, really, if it hadn't begun to rain, she expected she'd have been able to get down safely. Of course, women were hampered a good deal by their corsets and petticoats. Next time she tried to climb a tree, Joy decided, she'd wear breeches. The notion of Joy Hardesty donning breeches and climbing trees was so radical, she giggled again.

"What are you laughing about?"

Joy jumped up from her chair, sending it toppling over backward, and whirled around to find Elijah standing in the doorway, his hand still on the knob, watching her. She slammed a hand over her heart. "You scared the tar out of me, Elijah Perry! What are you sneaking up on me for?"

"I was worried about you, Joy. You ought to know that by now. You suffered a terrible fall, and now it's raining cats and dogs. I was afraid you'd be scared."

Oh, how sweet. Memories returned in a rush, and Joy smiled at the love of her life. He'd actually gone so far as to cry over her. She held out her hand to him. "Come

334

over here and help me watch the storm. It's beautiful."

Flashes of light from the storm illuminated his face and form in unforgiving brightness. She saw the lines on his dear countenance, and the gray in his receding hair. She even noticed his slight paunch, back again since he was nearly recovered from his terrible injuries. She was pleased as punch to see it, too. She wanted him whole, as he was. She didn't want any artificiality between them. The good Lord knew, he'd known her at her very worst, and he loved her anyway.

"The storm's not the only beautiful thing around here tonight, Joy."

Merciful heavens, did he mean her? Suddenly shy, Joy didn't dare ask. She did, however, toss her head in a pert, womanly gesture wholly unlike the Joy Hardesty she used to be, but very much like the Joy Hardesty she'd become.

Without another word, Elijah walked over and took her hand. He stood gazing down at her in a way that unsettled her, until she got nervous and turned again toward the window. "See? Isn't that something?"

"It is."

She wasn't sure he was talking about the storm, but decided to pretend he was. "Nature's putting on quite a performance out there."

He sighed. Joy got the impression he'd given up on something, but she wasn't sure what. "Yep. It's a real show, all right."

In a quick move, Elijah picked up the chair, sat on it, and pulled Joy into his lap. A shock shot through her, and she almost jumped up again, but he held her tightly, and she couldn't.

"Don't be scared, Joy. I'll never hurt you."

"You promised to beat me every day after we're married," she reminded him, striving for a jocular tone.

His chuckle was deep and rich and curled through Joy like smoke. She began to relax slightly.

"I didn't mean that, and you know it. Besides, you said if I did, you'd shoot me. That scared me, and I'd never dare beat you with a threat like that hanging over my head."

"A likely story."

"It's true. You had me shaking in my boots."

That was so patent a stretcher that Joy laughed. Elijah hugged her, and she slipped an arm around his neck.

He nuzzled her neck, and a delicious sensation of warmth swept through her. She dropped her head back and sighed deeply. It felt so good to be cradled in Elijah's strong arms. Joy hadn't ever expected any man to love her and to want to take care of her. That the man to do so was Elijah Perry was as surprising to her as it was delightful.

As if to prove to her that she wasn't dreaming, Elijah murmured, "I love you, Joy."

She kissed his forehead. "I love you, too, Elijah."

"I don't know how it happened. Life's funny that way, I reckon."

"I reckon."

"Hell—I mean shoot—I didn't even like you when we first met."

"I didn't like you either."

"But that was a long time ago."

"A very long time ago."

"Before I got shot."

"Before I realized how wrong I'd been all those years."

"You weren't wrong, darling. It was your mother who was wrong."

Again Joy recalled the conversation she'd carried on with her mother in the cottonwood tree. She drew away slightly from Elijah, who drew her back again. She smiled, deciding she could think as well in this position as any other. "I—I wonder if my mother meant to be cruel."

"Maybe not. It doesn't make much difference. The result was the same. She whupped you into submission."

She sighed again. "You're right, of course. And she was cruel, whether she meant to be or not. She was cruel to my poor father, too."

"Yeah. That's too bad. Of course, your dad could have stood up to her and didn't. It took more backbone than he had, I guess."

"I guess." She gasped when she felt Elijah's hand on her breast, unbound tonight since she was in her nightgown. His hand felt good there, and her nipples began to pebble. She wondered what this would lead to, and decided she was interested in finding out.

"I won't do anything you don't want me to do, Joy." Elijah's voice had gone gravelly. "But I've been dreaming about this for a long time now."

"You have?" Her own voice quavered with apprehension and happiness.

"I have. A long, long time."

"Mercy sakes."

Neither of them spoke for a while after that. As the storm crashed and raged outside Mac's snug little store, Elijah proceeded to give Joy her very first lesson in the art of lovemaking.

He started slowly. Joy appreciated his restraint because having a man's hands touching such intimate places on her body took some getting used to. Her mother's voice remained blessedly silent, however, and Elijah was so skilled at what he was doing that she adjusted quickly. His voice, low and rumbling, shocked her.

"You have beautiful breasts, Joy. I've been wanting to do this forever."

What he was doing that he'd wanted to do for so long was squeeze her breasts, teasing her nipples until she thought she might scream with the sheer pleasure of it.

"I—" She had to clear her throat. "I didn't know people talked at times like this."

He laughed again, low in his throat. The seductive sound shot through her this time, and lodged in several indelicate places. Merciful heavens, so this was what being loved by a man felt like. Joy was almost glad she'd never known before, or she'd have had an even harder time of it than she'd had already.

She sat on Elijah's lap, lost in sensation, her insides thundering and crashing much as the storm was doing outside. When Elijah pulled back slightly, took his hands from her breasts, and cupped her head, she blinked, confused. Good Lord, he wasn't going to stop now, was he? Joy opened her mouth to protest, but discovered her vocal cords wouldn't work.

Elijah stared deeply into her eyes. His own appeared much too serious for Joy's comfort. She hoped he wasn't going to withdraw his offer of marriage. Not now, when she was so deeply in love with him. Not now, when she was on the verge of discovering new and miraculous things with him.

"Joy," he said, and his voice was no more than a tender croak. "I don't want to hurt you. I'll never hurt you if I can help it. What I want to do from now on in my life is protect and cherish you."

If that wasn't the sweetest thing anyone had ever said to her, Joy didn't know what was. She tried to speak again, and again she discovered she couldn't. In fact, her tonsils didn't seem to want to do anything but make soft little purring sounds. She kissed his wonderful lips to let him know she loved him and appreciated his kind words.

He kissed her back and kept kissing her until he drew back once more, breathing hard.

"Don't distract me, Joy. I have something serious to talk to you about."

This didn't sound good. She squinted at him, not wanting to be diverted by serious things at the moment.

"I want to make love to you," Elijah declared, sounding shaky. "But I don't want to frighten you or worry you."

Joy was so touched, she nearly cried. Since she figured Elijah might not survive if she burst into tears, she swallowed them and made a valiant effort to get her voice to work. "I love you, Elijah." She considered that a good start. "And I want to make love to you, too." Of course, she didn't know how, but she figured Elijah would take care of the particulars. She saw him swallow.

"I talked to Mac after you went to bed, Joy. He said the circuit rider should be here any day now. I don't want you to think I'm only taking advantage of you. I'm going to marry you whether you want to marry me or not."

She smiled. "I want to marry you, Elijah. And I want to help you run your hotel here in Rio Hondo."

He swallowed again. "You do? I mean, you mean that? You don't want to go back to Boston? Really?"

"Auburn." Joy heaved a sigh, half-amused and half-exasperated that he insisted on keeping up his teasing even now. "Yes, Elijah. I really mean that. I was stifled in Auburn. I learned how to live here. With you. I'm not about to give that up. Not even for civilization and restaurants and decent linen."

He continued to stare at her for several moments. Joy held her breath and wished he'd get on with it. She didn't want to lose the mood. Not that there was much chance of that.

Suddenly he grabbed her close to his chest and buried

his face in her hair. Joy was glad she hadn't braided it
for bed yet. She felt wild and free with her hair down
and her corset off.

"Thank God," he murmured. "Thank God." He
sounded very sincere.

Then he kissed her again, and Joy could feel a change
in his approach. There was nothing tentative about this
kiss, nothing soft and sweet. This kiss was hard and deep
and she could tell he meant it.

Thank the good Lord for small mercies. She kissed
him back with all the love in her heart.

"We can't very well make love in this chair," he said
after a moment.

"No?"

"No." He picked her up and carried her to the bed. Joy
was delighted. "We need a bed."

"How fortunate there's one handy."

His laugh came again, deep, rumbling, and so sweet
that Joy wanted to curl up and die in it. With a gentleness
that seemed foreign in him, he set her on the bed. Before
she knew what she was about, he'd unburdened her of
her nightgown. She opened her eyes wide, shocked that
she should be sitting on the bed, buck naked, with Elijah
Perry staring at her with the avid expression of a starving
man eyeing a steak. She felt herself flush, and tried to
cross her arms over her breasts.

He caught her hands before she succeeded. "No, Joy.
Let me look at you. You're beautiful. You're a perfect,
gorgeous woman. Don't hide yourself. Not from me. I
love you. I'm going to be your husband any day now."

She gulped and nodded.

His smile showed her his perfect understanding of her
discomfiture. "All right, I'll stop pestering you. But I'm
warning you to prepare yourself, because I'm going to

join you right now." With that, he began unbuttoning his shirt.

"Mercy," she whispered as he revealed himself. He truly was a magnificent example of the male animal. His arms were corded with muscle, and his chest was magnificent, even with the scar from that dreadful bullet hole. And if his belly wasn't as firm as it might be, and if his hair was silvering and receding, to Joy he was the most perfect man in the universe. Her heart filled with such a potent combination of love and longing as she watched him disrobe that she feared she might faint.

Then he pushed his trousers down, baring the lower portion of his anatomy, and Joy's mouth dropped open and her eyes opened wide. *Good heavens!*

She'd nursed Elijah Perry for weeks, and she'd seen his naked body before. Although profoundly unnerved as she'd done it, she'd bandaged his thigh and even seen his . . . thing as she'd tended him. She'd never seen it in this condition, though.

Elijah read her thoughts. "Don't be afraid, Joy. I won't hurt you."

"But . . . but . . . it's so big."

He laughed again. Joy wasn't sure she appreciated a laugh at the moment. Naturally, this was nothing to him. Merely one more sexual experience. But to her, it was new and . . . and—her eyes were drawn once more to his erect sex—astonishing.

Before she could leap from the bed and run screaming from the room, Elijah plopped down next to her and put his arms around her. "It's all right, Joy. Men and women have been doing this from the beginning of time."

She turned to stare at him. What he said was true, she reckoned. But *she* hadn't done this before, and she was scared spitless.

"Here, darling, let me show you how good it can be."

He took her hand and gently guided it to his sex. Merciful heavens, did people really do that? Good people, that is? It was hard and silky and hot, and very, very different from anything she'd ever touched before. Fascinated, Joy felt it tentatively. Elijah groaned, and she let go as if she'd been handling a live coal.

"There's nothing wrong with the act of love, Joy," Elijah said as if he'd read her mind. "This is how babies are made. This is how the human race is perpetuated. This is what we have to do in order to get enough kids in the family to keep the business going."

His words were so unexpected that Joy actually forgot her fear and laughed. "I see. So that's your motivation, is it?"

He laughed, too. "Not entirely. Here, I'll take over now."

Thank God. Joy didn't say so aloud, but she was vastly relieved.

With exquisite care, Elijah pressed her back onto the bed. Then his hands began an inventory of her body that had Joy squirming and breathless in seconds. Sensations danced over her skin. Everywhere Elijah's hands touched her, she felt hot. She, whose life had been cold and lonely and barren, who had believed God meant her only to suffer, discovered that He had created a magnificent way for a man and a woman to come together and create new life.

God created this, she realized with a jolt. *Could anything God created be evil? Of course not.* It was people who made a mess of God's creations, as her mother had done with her. It was people who twisted the good and rendered it bad. She and Elijah loved and honored each other and, what was more, they were going to be married as soon as the preacher showed up. This wasn't bad; it

342

was as close to heaven as Joy expected she'd ever get on earth.

And, with that realization, the very last of her anxiety dissipated like so much steam. Which was a good thing, since Elijah's hand had traveled to her most intimate place, and had begun to probe gently.

"Elijah!"

He kissed her deeply as his fingers rubbed and dipped. She gasped into his mouth and felt him smile.

"Does that feel good, Joy? I want you to feel good."

Did it feel good? He didn't honestly expect an answer to that, did he? He couldn't possibly. Her hips had begun to arch as he gently rubbed the erect nub of sensation located between her legs.

"That's the way," Elijah whispered. "This is how it's done, Joy. It's supposed to feel good to both of us."

So that was what that was for. Joy had often wondered, during moments of agony when she'd been sure she was evil and wicked and headed straight to the devil for feeling things she'd been taught were depraved.

Good heavens, she was wet down there! Was she supposed to be wet? Her eyes opened and she scanned Elijah's face.

As if he understood, he whispered, "That's the way, Joy. Your body is getting ready for mine. This is exactly what's supposed to happen."

Thank the Lord. She'd been worried there for a moment. Grateful to him for his understanding, she relaxed again and decided to give up worrying and enjoy herself. Heaven alone knew that Elijah Perry, of all people, would want her to.

A groan escaped her as Elijah's magic fingers continued to rub and probe her secrets. Pressure built up in her body, pressure that was half pleasure and half frustration. Without knowing exactly what she was straining for, Joy

343

strained, her body going alternately tense and slack.

Elijah murmured soft, sweet words of love in her ear. She expected he was watching her, but didn't bother to look. Too many things were happening too quickly for her to take notice of any one of them.

She felt as though her were driving her to some precipice, and she had to get there or die. As sensations built in her body, she strained to achieve whatever it was. And then it happened. Out of the blue, Elijah's steady, gentle teasing sent her over the edge, and Joy gasped as her body stiffened and then convulsed with her climax.

"Beautiful," Elijah murmured. "Wonderful. Gorgeous."

Joy heard the words, but couldn't comprehend their meaning. So caught up was she in sensation that she could make sense of nothing but the fantastic sense of release and completion Elijah had created in her.

Her brain was mush. She panted like a racehorse that had just won the Belmont Stakes. Her mouth dry as cotton, she still managed to whisper, "Mercy sakes."

Elijah's chuckle was music to her ears. "So, you think you're going to like this part of the married state, do you?"

She cracked one eye open and found him. It wasn't difficult, since he leaned over her and was inspecting her face as if he feared for her health. "Oh, yes. Oh, yes indeed."

He grinned the wickedest grin she'd ever seen, and she realized she absolutely adored his wicked grins. In fact, she adored everything about this marvelous, baffling gambling man. Soon to be her very own marvelous, baffling hotel keeper and husband. With a burst of energy she didn't know she possessed, Joy threw her arms around him and kissed him with all the ardor in her soul.

Elijah seemed delighted. He pressed her back against

the sheets once more and positioned himself over her. She figured it was his turn now, and braced herself. Her mother had taught her absolutely nothing about the marriage bed except that, if any man was ever foolish enough to marry her, Joy should keep her mouth shut, her eyes squeezed tight, and do her duty without complaint.

Duty be hanged. Joy was so eager to feel Elijah in her that she didn't hesitate a second. As he very gently probed her damp secret with his sex, she arched her hips and captured him. With a gasp of surprise, Elijah plunged in.

It didn't hurt nearly as much as Joy had been led to expect. She felt rather as if she'd been skewered by an extremely large cucumber, but overall, the sensation was new and interesting rather than frightening or painful.

Then Elijah, after taking a moment to recover, began moving in her, and Joy realized how very wrong her mother had been. She should have expected it. Her mother had been wrong about everything else; why not this?

Her second climax came as almost more of a surprise than her first one. This one was sweeter, though, because, with a wild cry, Elijah toppled over the precipice with her.

Joy had never been happier in her life than she was when Elijah collapsed at her side, drew her into his arms, and dropped little kisses over her face. He was panting like a racehorse, too, and Joy loved him ever so much.

"I've never been happier in my life, Joy," he said, echoing her sentiments.

She couldn't stand it any longer. She cried.

Chapter Twenty

"Well, how was I to know they were tears of joy, Joy? You've never been joyful before." Elijah wasn't really grumpy; he just figured he'd better act like himself instead of a lovesick schoolboy or Joy wouldn't know him anymore.

She laughed at him. Elijah could scarcely believe his eyes and ears. Joy Hardesty, the woman he loved in spite of herself and himself and everything he knew about life, had the brass balls to *laugh* at him. He'd never been this happy, and it kind of scared him, although he knew his fear was only a leftover manifestation of the cynicism he'd honed so diligently over the years. He was through with cynicism now, though. Joy deserved more from him than pessimism. So did he, for that matter. He propped his head on his hands and leaned back against Joy's pillows, delighted with the show she was putting on for him.

"Don't you say another word about my crying, Elijah

Perry," she said as she put one long, slender, lovely leg and then the other into her drawers and pulled them up.

Elijah sighed when she tied the tapes. He was ready for another go-around on the sheets, although he knew she needed to recover from their first tangle. Lordy, he was glad she'd taken to sex. He'd been a little worried there. He ought to have known better. Joy was a constant surprise to him. And a joy. She was his very own pride and joy.

"You cried, too," she reminded him.

"Those weren't tears. Something got into my eyes."

"Ha! I don't believe a word of it."

All right, so he'd cried a little. Even a man had a right to cry every now and then, didn't he? And besides, he couldn't help it. All the emotions he'd kept tamped down for so many years had just erupted all of a sudden. It wasn't his fault.

"I thought it was sweet," Joy went on to say as she slipped a lacy camisole over her head.

"Skip the corset, all right, sweetheart?"

She eyed him dubiously. "During the daytime?"

She sounded shocked, and it tickled Elijah. "Sure. You don't see men running around with corsets on, do you?"

"Well, of course not. Men don't have—" She didn't finished, but blushed instead.

If she got any cuter, Elijah wasn't sure he could stand it. "Men do too have breasts."

She primmed her lips. "Not like women's, they don't."

"Thank God for that. But leave the corset off anyway. Please? For me?" He whined a little on the last two words, hoping she'd either feel guilty or amused and humor him.

She laughed again, and he was pleased. "Oh, all right. But if I shock the neighbors, it's not my fault."

"I'll take full responsibility for any shocking of the neighbors you do, love. Promise."

She pulled her dress on over her head and began to button the bodice in a businesslike manner. Elijah sighed. He liked Joy in her underwear. It was lacy and had pink things on it, and it suited her.

"Not that there are any neighbors out here in this desolate place," she muttered as she buttoned the last button and turned to pick up her hairbrush.

Elijah had another bright idea. "Why don't you leave your hair down, Joy? You have beautiful hair, but no one can see it when you braid it up and tack it to your head."

She peered at him over her shoulder. "I do *not* tack it to my head. Ugh." She shuddered. "And I won't wear it down, either, because Rio Hondo is too hot and dusty for that. I'd die of heatstroke."

Another sigh leaked from Elijah's lips. He was disappointed. He loved Joy's hair. It was shiny and pretty and had all sorts of interesting highlights to it.

"However," she continued, and he brightened, "I may fix it into one long braid and let it hang down my back. That won't be too uncomfortable. Will you settle for that?"

"Sounds good to me. Then I can pull it if you get out of hand."

"Ha. I'd like to see you try."

So would he.

They both started when they heard Mac's voice outside Joy's door. She whirled around, hairbrush in hand, and stared with horror at Elijah. He knew she'd be mortified if Mac discovered that the two of them had shared her bed all night. Elijah, on the other hand, figured Mac already knew. Mac always knew.

"Joy, m'dear, a visitor has come to meet ye."

She blinked at Elijah, who shrugged.

"A visitor? My goodness, who could it be, Mac?"

"Susan Blackworth craves an audience, lass. Ye've heard folks talk about Mrs. Blackworth, I'm sure."

"Oh. Oh, yes, certainly. Let me just . . . finish brushing my hair, and I'll be right out."

"Take your time, lass. Susan and I have a lot of catching up to do. As soon as you're ready, come to the house. We're takin' tea in the parlor."

Elijah relaxed. The old fox *did* know. Elijah would stake anything on it. Mac hadn't even knocked at the door. *Oh, yes.* He knew, all right. "I guess I'd better get up, too, then."

"Shhhh! Hush up, Elijah!"

He rolled his eyes. "It doesn't matter, Joy. Mac already knows, and if he's right about the preacher, we may be married by nightfall. Let's go out and meet this dragon of a female everyone always talks about."

She'd already braided her hair into a thick braid. The sunlight streaming through the window picked out red and gold highlights in it, and it looked beautiful to Elijah. He sighed as he heaved himself out of bed. Testing his muscles, he decided last night's activities hadn't done him any permanent damage. *Good.* He planned to do some similar exercising tonight.

Joy's gasp brought his head up, and he looked at her. She was staring at his erection. He glanced down and grinned. "It's awful what you do to me, Joy. Aren't you ashamed of yourself?"

She seemed to have to drag her gaze from his sex to his face. Her grin was a work of art. Elijah had never seen her look so proud of herself. As well she should. It wasn't every woman who had this effect on him. In fact, she was the only one.

"I'm shocked, Elijah Perry. Shocked."

"Sure you are." With a lunge, he was out of bed and

had captured her in his arms. After kissing her thoroughly and being thoroughly kissed in return, he let her go. He didn't want to, but he knew Joy was right when she protested.

"I have to go out there and meet Mrs. Blackworth, Elijah. Get your clothes on and join us. Maybe Mac knows when Mr. Horgan will be in town."

"Who's Mr. Horgan?"

"The circuit rider."

Elijah eyed her curiously as he drew on his drawers. "How'd you know his name?"

Joy stopped in the middle of tying the end of her braid with a pretty yellow ribbon. She looked at him, puzzled. "I don't remember. I just . . . I guess Mac must have told me."

Hmmm. Elijah would lay wagers that Mac hadn't told her. Not in so many words. Mac was a strange fellow. He knew things and did things and made things happen that Elijah couldn't fathom. He'd never been one to scoff at fate, however, and he took Joy's knowledge of the preacher's name as simply one more manifestation of the enchanted properties of their new home. When Joy opened the door and the room filled with multicolored shimmering dots, he sighed again, and chalked up another one.

"How do you do, Mrs. Blackworth?" Joy held out a hand to the older woman.

"I'm well, thank you. I understand you've been sick. You look a little peaked."

Susan Blackworth, clad all in black, and with her salt-and-pepper hair pulled back into a severe bun, stared at Joy with eyes so dark they reminded her of the onyx stones people in Rio Hondo called Apache tears. Mrs. Blackworth gave Joy an unsettled feeling, as if she knew

351

things that others didn't. She reminded Joy, in fact, of Mac, although Mrs. Blackworth wasn't nearly as jolly as Mac. In fact, it looked to Joy as if Susan's grim presence had even managed to cow the normally exuberant Virginia Gladstone, who sipped tea and watched with big, slightly nervous eyes.

"Aye," Mac said. "Our Joy was nearly called to her maker a while back, but she's getting better every day, Susan."

Mac twinkled at her, and Joy smiled back. "Yes, I am. Thanks to Mac's fine nursing."

"I understand you did some nursing yourself, Miss Hardesty, and that you're soon to marry your patient."

Joy felt her face flush. "Yes. Mr. Perry has done me the honor of asking for my hand." *Whew!* If that wasn't her Auburn upbringing speaking, Joy didn't know what was.

Susan Blackworth's laugh sounded like autumn leaves crackling. "I don't know how much of an honor marriage is, young lady, but I expect you'll discover that for yourself." She sniffed, and added grudgingly, "Although I reckon the Partridges and the O'Fannins have managed to land themselves in happy marriages."

Joy didn't have any idea what to say, so she sipped her tea instead and wished Elijah would hurry up and join them. She looked up eagerly when the front door opened, hoping for Elijah. She was surprised when a woman carrying a baby came inside. Mac rose and went over to her, hands held out, a huge smile on his face.

"Mellie! So ye're fit enough to travel, are ye?"

The woman, young and pretty and as vibrant as any woman Joy had ever seen, hugged Mac hard, baby and all. The baby—Arnold, Joy presumed, if this was Melissa O'Fannin—didn't object. "It's so good to see you, Mac! We miss you." She finally let Mac go and smiled at Susan Blackworth. "Susan. How wonderful to see you here, too."

"How-do, Melissa. Let me hold that child this instant."

With a laugh, Melissa O'Fannin brought baby Arnold over to Susan Blackworth, who took him in her gnarled hands and smiled. Joy watched, astonished, and wondered why the smile didn't crack her leathery cheeks.

"And you must be Miss Hardesty," Melissa went on, holding a hand out to Joy. "Both Mac and Katie have told us ever so much about you, and I've been longing to meet you. There are so few women out here in the territory."

"Yes, indeed." Joy shook Melissa's hand, wondering why she'd been so appalled when Mac had told her she'd been divorced. Obviously, whatever had happened with her first marriage, it wasn't Melissa O'Fannin's fault.

The door opened again, and little Katie bounded in, holding the hand of a tall man with a tanned, rugged face, whose eyes immediately sought out his wife. Melissa looked over at him, their gazes met and locked, and Joy clasped her hands to her bosom, hoping in that second that she and Elijah would establish the kind of bond these two had.

"Miss Tee!"

Joy's attention jerked back to the present, and she caught Katie O'Fannin as she hurled herself against her legs. Laughing, she lifted the little girl up, and silently offered up a prayer that she and Elijah might be blessed with such lovely children as those of the O'Fannins.

"We saw Noah and Grace Partridge heading over here, too, Mac. What did you do? Send up smoke signals?" Cody O'Fannin relegated his hat to the rack beside the door, and came over to shake Joy's hand.

"No need to send up smoke signals, Cody, m'lad. Word gets out, y'know. Word gets out."

Emma Craig

"My goodness," Virginia whispered. She'd risen and come over to meet the O'Fannins. Joy introduced her to Katie, who charmed Virginia every bit as much as she'd charmed Joy. In fact, Virginia took Katie from Joy's arms, so Joy was able to more closely inspect baby Arnold.

"Oh, isn't he a fine boy!"

"Here, child. Hold him. You need the practice." And Susan Blackworth thrust Arnold into Joy's arms.

She was taken back for only a moment before she became engrossed in investigating the baby. What a fine, healthy specimen he was, too.

Mac's front door opened again, and again Joy turned, expecting Elijah. But this time she saw Noah Partridge, the man she'd met when he'd brought Virginia to town. She smiled at him, he nodded back—not much of a smiler, Noah Partridge, Joy decided—and then he stood aside to let his wife, Grace, enter Mac's parlor.

Grace Partridge held the hand of a beautiful little eight-year-old girl who looked as much like her mother as it was possible for a child to look. Her other hand held that of a rugged three-year-old boy, who was the spitting image of his father, except that his face seemed made for smiles. Joy let out a little "Oh," as charmed by the Partridge children as she was by the O'Fannins.

"It's so good to meet you, Miss Hardesty," Grace said as she came to Joy. "I see you've met the latest addition to Rio Hondo." She nodded at Arnold.

"Yes." Joy glanced around at all the children. Grace introduced her to Maddie and Christopher, who curtsied and bowed charmingly before they dashed off to play with the O'Fannin's little girl.

The next time the door opened, it was Elijah. *Thank heaven!* Joy introduced him all around. It occurred to her to wonder why everyone had chosen today, of all days, to visit Mac, but she didn't wonder for long. She was having too good a time chatting with the women. She hadn't had a good hen session—ever. Good Lord, she'd never had a good friend in her life, yet she sensed that these three women—four if Virginia decided to stay in Rio Hondo—were going to be her fast friends for life.

They hadn't been gabbing for a half hour when the front door opened again. Everyone turned to see who had come now, and Joy saw an owlish-looking man in a black frock coat, a black hat held in his hands, standing in the doorway, looking around as if he couldn't believe his eyes.

"It's about time you got here, Joshua. There are two young people here who need to get hitched." Susan Blackworth stood and, in the silence engendered by her tart comment, hobbled to the door, her cane making cracking sounds on the hardwood floor.

"Susan!" The man—Mr. Horgan, Joy presumed from Mrs. Blackworth's comment—blinked at Mrs. Blackworth. "My goodness, what are all these people doing here? Mrs. Partridge. Mrs. O'Fannin." He nodded all around, and received handshakes and greetings from all of Mac's uninvited guests.

"They've come for the wedding, of course," Mrs. Blackworth said tartly. "Why else would we all gather here, waiting for you?"

Before Mr. Horgan could formulate a response, Mrs. Blackworth took him none too gently by the arm and dragged him over to Joy. Elijah had walked over to stand behind her, and he put his hands on her shoulders. She lifted a hand and rested it on one of his, and felt wonderful.

"Miss Hardesty, Mr. Perry, allow me to introduce my brother, Joshua Horgan. He's a preacher, and he can hitch the two of you. I can tell you're in a hurry." Her beady

355

black eyes held humor and no approval. An odd duck, Susan Blackworth.

"You're right," Elijah said, his voice booming into the silence. Joy jumped. "We want to be married as soon as possible, because we have plans. Big plans." He grinned down at Joy and squeezed her shoulders.

"Indeed, we do," she agreed.

"Well, then, let me hang up my hat and coat and fetch my Bible from my saddlebag, and we can take care of it right now. Mac has procured a license, I'm sure."

Joy's happiness fled. "A license?"

Elijah looked startled. "A license?"

Noah Partridge laughed, the sound so unexpected that everyone turned to stare at him. "Don't worry about a license. Mac's a magician. He's got one. Never fear."

A magician. Joy blinked at Mac, who winked back at her. "Sure enough. Noah's right, of course. I have just the thing right here." And, with the grace of a conjurer, Mac whipped a paper from behind his back. "All ye need to do is fill in the blanks."

"Good." Joshua Horgan plopped his hat and coat on the rack and rubbed his hands. "Then let's get started."

"Wait." Grace Partridge stood and held out a hand to her daughter. "Let's gather some flowers first. Every bride needs flowers."

"Good idea," Melissa O'Fannin said. "You and Maddie and Katie gather flowers, and I'll help Miss Hardesty dress."

Dress. Dress? What was she going to dress in? All of Joy's clothes were little more than rags by this time. She'd never been heavy, but during her illness and the rigors of nursing Elijah, she'd lost weight, until most of her gowns hung on her like hand-me-downs on a scarecrow. "Um, I don't think—"

"Don't bother to think, Miss Hardesty," Melissa said

with a laugh. "I'm sure Mac's going to take care of that, too. He finds amazing things in his back room all the time."

"To be sure." Mac winked at Virginia, who smiled conspiratorially.

"Indeed, he's taken care of everything," Virginia said, and she rushed out the door.

Still wondering what was going on, Joy allowed Melissa to lead her to her room. There she took off her day dress, and by the time she was standing in her underthings—and today, of all days, she wore no corset—Virginia was back with a dress.

Joy gasped. "Good heavens, where did that come from?"

"To hear Mac tell it, the freight driver brought it along with yardage from Saint Louis."

It wasn't a real wedding dress. It bore no resemblance whatever to the gowns Joy had seen illustrated in fashion magazines. Nor did it look like any of the gowns she'd seen brides wear back in Auburn. It was perfect for Rio Hondo, though. A simply cut dress in creamy calico with lace at the neck and sleeves, it looked as if it had been made for Joy. When Melissa buttoned up the back and Virginia revealed the veil she'd made, Joy was almost in tears.

"I knew you and Uncle Elijah were going to be married," Virginia said, looking pleased with herself. "So I made this at night, in my room, when no one could see."

"It's beautiful. Thank you so much." Joy kissed Virginia. Then she kissed Melissa. Then she cried a little when she surveyed herself in the mirror. She'd never expected to see herself look so good, and she hoped Elijah would be happy.

He was. He was also as nervous as a typical bridegroom on his wedding day.

Maddie Partridge handed Joy a pretty bouquet put together from all the wildflowers she and her mother and friends had found outside, and Mr. Horgan cleared his throat. As all their newfound friends watched—and the ladies sniffled into their handkerchiefs—Joy Hardesty and Elijah Perry were joined together in holy matrimony. Killer Apricot sat on the piano and watched, looking much happier than cats generally looked.

At the end of the short ceremony, little Katie said, "Perry? We gots a doggie called Perry."

Her daddy swept her up in his arms as everyone laughed. Then Mac went into his kitchen and came out with a confection made of Italian marzipan. "I ordered it from Italy, because I suspected this would happen, y'see."

"I see," said Elijah, eyeing him thoughtfully.

"That's so sweet of you, Mac," said Joy, and embraced him warmly. It didn't occur to her until much later that a spontaneous hug was as foreign to the Joy Hardesty she'd been when she arrived in Rio Hondo as was marzipan candy.

The confection was delicious. It went particularly well with the champagne Mac discovered in his back room.

When Noah Partridge sat down at Mac's piano and began to play like a concert professional, Joy's astonishment was complete. The party lasted all day and into the night. Elijah taught her to dance, and Joy discovered pleasure in one more thing her mother had deplored. Since nothing surprised her much anymore, she wasn't fazed in the slightest by the great delight she took in waltzing with her husband.

Along about nine o'clock that night, the guests departed. They all said it was fortunate that the light from the moon and stars was so bright, because they wouldn't have any trouble getting home. Mac twinkled from his doorway, smoke from his pipe wreathing his head like a halo, and agreed with them.

Elijah gave Joy another lesson in physical love that night. She enjoyed this one even more than the one he'd given her the night before. Along about sunup of the day after their wedding, Joy awoke and, deciding to be bold, attacked her husband in bed. He was delighted.

The Perrys spent their honeymoon in Maryland, where they went to escort Virginia back home. Elijah decided he liked his sister and her husband. He gathered many tips about the hotel business from his Uncle Luke, and by the time they headed back to New Mexico Territory, Joy was over the worst of her morning sickness. Virginia had promised to return to Rio Hondo in time for the baby's birth.

The Pecos Valley Hotel opened for business a year and a half after Joy and Elijah married. Their son, Alexander Micah, was nine months old at the time, and they were expecting their second child. Mac said he'd be delighted to stand godfather for however many children they managed to bring into the world. And he did. All six of them.

Joy never heard from the Reverend Mr. Hezekiah P. Thrash again. She did, however, discover that the people residing in Rio Hondo weren't all debauchees and wastrels. In fact, she was thrilled when the neighboring ranchers and most of the businessmen in town—including the owner of the Pecos Saloon—built a permanent church for Mr. Horgan. She was even more thrilled when Elijah joined her there on Sunday mornings for Mr. Horgan's sermons. He said he figured it was good for the kids. She thought he was probably right.

Elijah wasn't sorry when Mary Ellen Loveless decided to move to San Antonio. He was having more fun as a father and a hotel magnate than he'd ever had as a gambling man.

Mac's wagon yard didn't suffer from the competition. Rather, Mac expanded his grocery business, smoked his pipe, twinkled at the world, and continued helping lost souls find themselves. It was his favorite line of work.

Winter Wonderland

Emma Craig, Leigh Greenwood, Amanda Harte, Linda O. Johnston

Christmas is coming, and the streets are alive with the sounds of the season: "Silver Bells" and sleigh rides, jingle bells and carolers. Choruses of "Here Comes Santa Claus" float over the snow-covered landscape, bringing the joy of the holiday to revelers as they deck the halls and string the lights "Up on the Rooftop." And when the songs of the season touch four charmed couples, melody turns to romance and harmony turns to passion. For these "Merry Gentlemen" and their lovely ladies will learn that with the love they have found, not even a spring thaw will cool their desire or destroy their winter wonderland.

___52339-6 $5.99 US/$6.99 CAN

Dorchester Publishing Co., Inc.
P.O. Box 6640
Wayne, PA 19087-8640

Please add $1.75 for shipping and handling for the first book and $.50 for each book thereafter. NY, NYC, and PA residents, please add appropriate sales tax. No cash, stamps, or C.O.D.s. All orders shipped within 6 weeks via postal service book rate. Canadian orders require $2.00 extra postage and must be paid in U.S. dollars through a U.S. banking facility.

Name_____
Address_____
City_____State_____Zip_____
I have enclosed $_____ in payment for the checked book(s).
Payment <u>must</u> accompany all orders. ❏ Please send a free catalog.
CHECK OUT OUR WEBSITE! www.dorchesterpub.com

A Gentle Magic

EMMA CRAIG

When cattleman Cody O'Fannin hears a high-pitched scream ring out across the harsh New Mexico Territory, he rides straight into the heart of danger, expecting to find a cougar or a Comanche. Instead, he finds a scene far more frightening— a woman in the final stages of childbirth. Alone, the beautiful Melissa Wilmeth clearly needs his assistance, and although he'd rather face a band of thieving outlaws, Cody ignores his quaking insides and helps deliver her baby. When the infant's first wail fills the air, Cody gazes into Melissa's bewitching blue eyes and is spellbound. How else can he explain the sparkles he sees shimmering in the air above her honey-colored hair? Then thoughts of marriage creep into his head, and he doesn't need a crystal ball to realize he hasn't lost his mind or his nerve, but his heart.

___52321-3 $5.50 US/$6.50 CAN

Dorchester Publishing Co., Inc.
P.O. Box 6640
Wayne, PA 19087-8640

Please add $1.75 for shipping and handling for the first book and $.50 for each book thereafter. NY, NYC, and PA residents, please add appropriate sales tax. No cash, stamps, or C.O.D.s. All orders shipped within 6 weeks via postal service book rate. Canadian orders require $2.00 extra postage and must be paid in U.S. dollars through a U.S. banking facility.

Name_____
Address_____
City_____ State_____ Zip_____
I have enclosed $_____ in payment for the checked book(s).
Payment <u>must</u> accompany all orders. ❑ Please send a free catalog.
CHECK OUT OUR WEBSITE! www.dorchesterpub.com

Enchanted Christmas

Emma Craig

Noah Partridge has a cold, cold heart. Honey-haired Grace Richardson has heart to spare. Despite her husband's death, she and her young daughter have hung on to life in the Southwestern desert, as well as to a piece of land just outside the settlement of Rio Hondo. Although she does not live on it, Grace clings to that land like a memory, unwilling to give it up even to Noah Partridge, who is determined to buy it out from under her. But something like magic is at work in this desert land: a magic that makes Noah wonder if it is Grace's land he lusts after, or the sweetness of her body and soul. For he longs to believe that her touch holds the warmth that will melt his icy heart.

___52287-X $5.99 US/$6.99 CAN

THE MAGIC OF Christmas

Emma Craig, Annie Kimberlin, Kathleen Nance, Stobie Piel

"Jack of Hearts" by Emma Craig. With the help of saintly Gentleman Jack Oakes, love warms the hearts of a miner and a laundress.

"The Shepherds and Mr. Weisman" by Annie Kimberlin. A two-thousand-year-old angel must bring together two modern-day soulmates before she can unlock the pearly gates.

"The Yuletide Spirit" by Kathleen Nance. A tall, blonde man fulfills the wish of a beautiful and lonely woman and learns that the spirit of the season is as alive as ever.

"Twelfth Knight" by Stobie Piel. In medieval England, a beautiful thief and a dashing knight have only the twelve days of Christmas to find a secret treasure . . . which just might be buried in each other's arms.

___52283-7 $5.99 US/$6.99 CAN

Dorchester Publishing Co., Inc.
P.O. Box 6640
Wayne, PA 19087-8640

Please add $1.75 for shipping and handling for the first book and $.50 for each book thereafter. NY, NYC, and PA residents, please add appropriate sales tax. No cash, stamps, or C.O.D.s. All orders shipped within 6 weeks via postal service book rate. Canadian orders require $2.00 extra postage and must be paid in U.S. dollars through a U.S. banking facility.

Name_____
Address_____
City_____ State_____ Zip_____
I have enclosed $ _____ in payment for the checked book(s).
Payment <u>must</u> accompany all orders. ❏ Please send a free catalog.

Heartland

Rebecca Brandewyne

After her best friend India dies, leaving eight beautiful children in the care of their drunken wastrel of a father, prim Rachel Wilder knows she has to take the children in. But when notorious Slade Maverick rides onto her small farm, announcing that he is the children's guardian, Rachel is furious. Yet there is something about Slade that makes her tremble at the very thought of his handsome face and sparkling midnight-blue eyes. And when he takes her in his arms in the hayloft and his searing kiss brands her soul, Rachel knows then that the gunfighter Slade Maverick belongs to her, body and soul, just as she belongs to him.

___52327-2 $5.50 US/$6.50 CAN

Dorchester Publishing Co., Inc.
P.O. Box 6640
Wayne, PA 19087-8640

Please add $1.75 for shipping and handling for the first book and $.50 for each book thereafter. NY, NYC, and PA residents, please add appropriate sales tax. No cash, stamps, or C.O.D.s. All orders shipped within 6 weeks via postal service book rate. Canadian orders require $2.00 extra postage and must be paid in U.S. dollars through a U.S. banking facility.

Name_____
Address_____
City_____State_____Zip_____
I have enclosed $_____ in payment for the checked book(s).
Payment <u>must</u> accompany all orders. ❑ Please send a free catalog.
CHECK OUT OUR WEBSITE! www.dorchesterpub.com

A Cry At Midnight

Victoria Chancellor

Suddenly transported to the Old South, twentieth-century beauty Randi Galloway finds herself employed as governess to widower Jackson Durant's only child, Rose. Randi has never met anyone who stirs her soul like the darkly handsome plantation owner with a determined spirit and a mysterious past. But history tells Randi that Rose and Jackson will die in the flood of 1849, and her heart refuses to allow that to happen to the sweet child and her stubborn father; she will not rest until she finds a way to save the little girl she loves and the man she desires.

__52300-0 $5.50 US/$6.50 CAN